On Stranger Tides

Tides

TIM POWERS

ACE BOOKS, NEW YORK

ON STRANGER TIDES

An Ace Book
Published by The Berkley Publishing Group
200 Madison Avenue, New York, New York 10016
The name "Ace" and the "A" logo are trademarks belonging to Charter
Communications, Inc.

Copyright © 1987 by Tim Powers

Book design by Ernie Haim

First Edition: November 1987

Library of Congress Cataloging-in-Publication Data

Powers, Tim, 1952–
    On stranger tides.

    I. Title.
PS3566.09505   1987   813'.54   87-12435
ISBN 0-441-62683-1

Printed in the United States of America

10 9 8 7 6 5 4 3 2 1

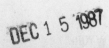

To Jim and Viki Blaylock
most generous and loyal of friends

and to the memories of
Eric Batsford
and
Noel Powers

With thanks to David Carpenter, Bruce Oliver,
Randal Robb, John Swartzel, Phillip Thibo-
deau and Dennis Tupper, for clear answers to
unclear questions.

. . . And unmoor'd souls may drift on stranger tides
Than those men know of, and be overthrown
By winds that would not even stir a hair . . .

—*William Ashbless*

"The Bridegroom's doors are opened wide,
And I am next of kin;
The guests are met, the feast is set:
May'st hear the merry din."

He holds him with his skinny hand,
"There was a ship," quoth he . . .

—*Samuel Taylor Coleridge*

Prologue

Though the evening breeze had chilled his back on the way across, it hadn't yet begun its nightly job of sweeping out from among the island's clustered vines and palm boles the humid air that the day had left behind, and Benjamin Hurwood's face was gleaming with sweat before the black man had led him even a dozen yards into the jungle. Hurwood hefted the machete that he gripped in his left—and only—hand, and peered uneasily into the darkness that seemed to crowd up behind the torchlit vegetation around them and overhead, for the stories he'd heard of cannibals and giant snakes seemed entirely plausible now, and it was difficult, despite recent experiences, to rely for safety on the collection of ox-tails and cloth bags and little statues that dangled from the other man's belt. In this primeval rain forest it didn't help to think of them as *gardes* and *arrets* and *drogues* rather than fetishes, or of his companion as a *bocor* rather than a witch doctor or shaman.

The black man gestured with the torch and looked back at him. "Left now," he said carefully in English, and then added rapidly in one of the debased French dialects of Haiti, "and step carefully—little streams have undercut the path in many places."

"Walk more slowly, then, so I can see where you put your feet," replied Hurwood irritably in his fluent textbook French. He wondered how badly his hitherto perfect accent had suffered from the past month's exposure to so many odd variations of the language.

1

The path became steeper, and soon he had to sheathe his machete in order to have his hand free to grab branches and pull himself along, and for a while his heart was pounding so alarmingly that he thought it would burst, despite the protective *drogue* the black man had given him—then they had got above the level of the surrounding jungle and the sea breeze found them and he called to his companion to stop so that he could catch his breath in the fresh air and enjoy the coolness of it in his sopping white hair and damp shirt.

The breeze clattered and rustled in the palm branches below, and through a gap in the sparser trunks around him he could see water—a moonlight-speckled segment of the Tongue of the Ocean, across which the two of them had sailed from New Providence Island that afternoon. He remembered noticing the prominence they now stood on, and wondering about it, as he'd struggled to keep the sheet trimmed to his bad-tempered guide's satisfaction.

Andros Island it was called on the maps, but the people he'd been associating with lately generally called it Isle de Loas Bossals, which, he'd gathered, meant Island of Untamed (or, perhaps more closely, Evil) Ghosts (or, it sometimes seemed, Gods). Privately he thought of it as Persephone's shore, where he hoped to find, at long last, at least a window into the house of Hades.

He heard a gurgling behind him and turned in time to see his guide recorking one of the bottles. Sharp on the fresh air he could smell the rum. "Damn it," Hurwood snapped, "that's for the ghosts."

The *bocor* shrugged. "Brought too much," he explained. "Too much, too many come."

The one-armed man didn't answer, but wished once again that he knew enough—instead of just *nearly* enough—to do this alone.

"Nigh there now," said the *bocor,* tucking the bottle back into the leather bag slung from his shoulder.

They resumed their steady pace along the damp earth path, but Hurwood sensed a difference now—attention was being paid to them.

The black man sensed it too, and grinned back over his shoulder, exposing gums nearly as white as his teeth. "They smell the rum," he said.

"Are you sure it's not just those poor Indians?"

The man in front answered without looking back. "They still sleep. That's the *loas* you feel watching us."

Though he knew there could be nothing out of the ordinary to see yet, the one-armed man glanced around, and it occurred to him for the first time that this really wasn't so incongruous a setting— these palm trees and this sea breeze probably didn't differ very much from what might be found in the Mediterranean, and this Caribbean island might be very like the island where, thousands of years ago, Odysseus performed almost exactly the same procedure they intended to perform tonight.

It was only after they reached the clearing at the top of the hill that Hurwood realized he'd all along been dreading it. There was nothing overtly sinister about the scene—a cleared patch of flattened dirt with a hut off to one side and, in the middle of the clearing, four poles holding up a small thatched roof over a wooden box—but Hurwood knew that there were two drugged Arawak Indians in the hut, and an oilcloth-lined six-foot trench on the far side of the little shelter.

The black man crossed to the sheltered box—the *trone*, or altar—and very carefully detached a few of the little statues from his belt and set them on it. He bowed, backed away, then straightened and turned to the other man, who had followed him to the center of the clearing. "You know what's next?" the black man asked.

Hurwood knew this was a test. "Sprinkle the rum and flour around the trench," he said, trying to sound confident.

"No," said the *bocor*, "next. Before that." There was definite suspicion in his voice now.

"Oh, I know what you mean," said Hurwood, stalling for time as his mind raced. "I thought *that* went without saying." What on earth did the man mean? Had Odysseus done anything first? No— nothing that got recorded, anyway. But of course Odysseus had lived back when magic was easy . . . and relatively uncorrupted. That must be it—a protective procedure must be necessary now with such a conspicuous action, to keep at bay any monsters that might be drawn to the agitation. "You're referring to the shielding measures."

"Which consist of what?"

When strong magic still worked in the eastern hemisphere,

what guards had been used? Pentagrams and circles. "The marks on the ground."

The black man nodded, mollified. "Yes. The *verver*." He carefully laid the torch on the ground and then fumbled in his pouch and came up with a little bag, from which he dug a pinch of gray ash. "Flour of Guinée, we call this," he explained, then crouched and began sprinkling the stuff on the dirt in a complicated geometrical pattern.

The white man allowed himself to relax a little behind his confident pose. What a lot there was to learn from these people! Primitive they certainly were, but *in touch* with a living power that was just distorted history in more civilized regions.

"Here," said the *bocor*, unslinging his pouch and tossing it. "You can dispose of the flour and rum . . . and there's candy in there, too. The *loas* are partial to a bit of a sweet."

Hurwood took the bag to the shallow trench—his torch-cast shadow stretching ahead of him to the clustered leaves that walled the clearing—and let it thump to the ground. He stooped to get the bottle of rum, uncorked it with his teeth and then straightened and walked slowly around the trench, splashing the aromatic liquor on the dirt. When he'd completed the circuit there was still a cupful left in the bottle, and he drank it before pitching the bottle away. There were also sacks of flour and candy balls in the bag, and he sprinkled these too around the trench, uncomfortably aware that his motions were like those of a sower irrigating and seeding a tract.

A metallic squeaking made him turn toward the hut, and the spectacle advancing toward him across the clearing—it was the *bocor*, straining to push a wheelbarrow in which were tumbled two unconscious dark-skinned bodies—awoke both horror and hope in him. Fleetingly he wished it didn't have to be human blood, that sheep's blood would serve, as it had in Odysseus' day—but he set his jaw and helped the *bocor* lever the bodies out onto the dirt so that their heads were conveniently close to the trench.

The *bocor* had a little paring knife, and held it toward the one-armed man. "You want to?"

Hurwood shook his head. "It's," he said hoarsely, "all yours." He looked away and stared hard at the torch flame while the black man crouched over the bodies, and when, a few moments later, he heard the spatter and gush against the oilskin in the trench, he closed his eyes.

"The words now," said the *bocor*. He began chanting words in a dialect that combined the tongues of France, the Mondongo district of Africa, and the Carib Indians, while the white man, his eyes still closed, began chanting in archaic Hebrew.

The randomly counterpoint chanting grew gradually louder, as if in an attempt to drown out the new noises from the jungle: sounds like whispered giggling and weeping, and cautious rustling in the high branches, and a chitinous scraping like cast-off snakeskins being rubbed together.

Abruptly the two chanted litanies became identical, and the two men were speaking in perfect unison, syllable for syllable—though the white man was still speaking ancient Hebrew and the black man was still speaking his peculiar mix of tongues. Astonished by it even as he participated, Hurwood felt the first tremors of real awe at this impossibly prolonged coincidence. Over the sharp fumes of the spilled rum and the rusty reek of the blood there was suddenly a new smell, the hot-metal smell of magic, though far stronger now than he'd ever encountered it before. . . .

And then all at once they were no longer alone—in fact, the clearing was crowded now with human-shaped forms that were nearly transparent to the torchlight, though the light was dimmed if a number of them overlapped in front of it, and all of these insubstantial things were crowding in toward the blood pit and crying out imploringly in tiny, chittering, birdlike voices. The two men let the chanting stop.

Other things, too, had appeared, though they didn't cross the ash lines the *bocor* had laid around the perimeter of the clearing, but simply peered from between the palm trunks or crouched on branches; Hurwood saw a calf with flaming eye sockets, a head hanging in midair with a ghastly pendulum of naked entrails dangling from its neck, and, in the trees, several little creatures who seemed to be more insect than human; and while the ghosts inside the *verver* lines kept up a ceaseless shrill chatter, the watchers outside were all silent.

The *bocor* was keeping the ghosts away from the trench with wide sweeps of his little knife. "Hurry!" he panted. "Find the one you want!"

Hurwood stepped up to the edge of the trench and scrutinized the filmy creatures.

Under his gaze a few of them became slightly more visible, like webs of egg white in heating water. "Benjamin!" called one of these, its scratchy frail voice rising over the background babble. "Benjamin, it's me, it's Peter! I was groomsman at your wedding, remember? Make him let me sup!"

The *bocor* looked questioningly at the other man.

Hurwood shook his head, and the *bocor*'s knife flashed out and neatly razored the supplicating ghost in half; with a faint cry the thing dissolved like smoke.

"Ben!" screeched up another. "Bless you, son, you've brought refreshments for your father! I knew—"

"No," said Hurwood. His mouth was a straight line as the knife flashed out again and another lost wail flitted away on the breeze.

"Can't hold 'em back forever," panted the *bocor*.

"A little longer," Hurwood snapped. "*Margaret!*"

There was a curdling agitation off to one side, and then a cobwebby form drifted to the front. "Benjamin, how have you come here?"

"Margaret!" His cry was more one of pain than triumph. "Her," he snarled at the *bocor*. "Let her come up."

The *bocor* quit the sweeping motion and began jabbing back all the shadows except the one Hurwood had indicated. The ghost approached the trench, then blurred and shrank and became clearly visible again in a kneeling posture. She reached out toward the blood, then halted and simply touched the flour-and-rum paste on the rim. For a moment she was opaque in the torchlight, and her hand became substantial enough to roll one of the candy balls a few inches. "We shouldn't be here, Benjamin," she said, her voice a bit more resonant now.

"The *blood*, take the *blood*—" the one-armed man shouted, falling to his knees on the other side of the trench.

With no sound at all the ghost's form relaxed into smoke and blew away, though the cold blade hadn't come near her.

"*Margaret!*" the man roared, and dove over the trench into the massed ghosts; they gave way before him like spider webs strung between trees, and his jaw clacked shut against the hard-packed dirt. The ringing in his ears almost prevented him from hearing the chorus of dismayed ghost-voices fading away to silence.

After a few moments Hurwood sat up and squinted around. The torchlight was brighter, now that there were no ghost-forms to filter it.

The *bocor* was staring at him. "I hope it was worth it."

Hurwood didn't answer, just got slowly, wearily to his feet, rubbing his scraped chin and pushing the damp white hair back out of his face. The monsters still stood and crouched and hung just outside the ash lines; evidently none of them had moved, or even blinked, probably, during the whole business.

"Entertained, were you?" shouted Hurwood in English, shaking his lone fist at them. "Dive over the trench again, shall I, just so you won't feel cheated?" His voice was getting tight and shrill, and he was blinking rapidly as he took a step toward the edge of the clearing, pointing at one of the watchers, a huge pig with a cluster of rooster heads sprouting from its neck. "Ah, you there, sir," Hurwood went on in a travesty of hearty friendliness, "*do* favor us with your frankest opinions. Would I have been better advised to do a spot of juggling instead? Or, perhaps, with face paint and a false nose—"

The *bocor* caught his elbow from behind and turned him around and stared at him with wonder and something that was almost pity. "Stop," he said softly. "Most of them can't hear, and I don't think *any* of them understand English. At sunrise they'll go away and we'll leave."

Hurwood pulled free of the other man's grasp, walked back to the center of the clearing and sat down, not far from the trench and the two drained corpses. The hot-metal smell of magic was gone, but the breeze wasn't dispelling the blood-reek very much.

Sunrise wouldn't be for another nine or ten hours; and though he had to stay here until then, it would certainly be impossible to sleep. The prospect of the long wait sickened him.

He remembered the *bocor's* statement: "I hope it was worth it."

He looked up at the stars and sneered a challenge at them. Try to stop me now, he thought, though it may take me years. I know it's true now. It can be done. Yes—even if I'd had to have a *dozen* Indians killed to learn it, a dozen *white* men, a dozen *friends* . . . it would still have been worth it.

BOOK ONE

The seas and the weathers are what is; your vessels adapt to them or sink.

—*Jack Shandy*

BOOK ONE

Chapter One

Gripping one of the taut vertical ropes and leaning far out over the rail, John Chandagnac waited a moment until the swell lifted the huge, creaking structure of the stern and the poop deck on which he stood, and then he flung the biscuit as hard as he could. It looked like quite a long throw at first, but as it dropped by quick degrees toward the water, and kept on falling instead of splashing in, he saw that he hadn't really flung it very far out; but the gull had seen it, and came skimming in above the green water, and at the last moment, as if showing off, snatched it out of the air. The biscuit broke as the gull flapped back up to a comfortable altitude, but he seemed to have got a good beakful.

Chandagnac had another biscuit in his coat pocket, but for a while he just watched the bird glide, absently admiring the way it seemed to need only the slightest hitch and flap now and then to maintain its position just above the *Vociferous Carmichael*'s starboard stern lamp, and he sniffed the elusive land smell that had been in the breeze since dawn. Captain Chaworth had said that they'd see Jamaica's purple and green mountains by early afternoon, then round Morant Point before supper and dock in Kingston before dark; but while the unloading of the *Carmichael*'s cargo would mean the end of the worrying that had visibly slimmed the captain during this last week of the voyage, disembarking would be the beginning of Chandagnac's task.

And do remember too, he told himself coldly as he pulled the biscuit out of his pocket, that both Chaworth and yourself are each at least half to blame for your own problems. He flung the thing harder this time, and the sea gull caught it without having to dip more than a couple of yards.

When he turned back toward the little breakfast table that the captain let the passengers eat at when the morning's shiphandling jobs were routine, he was surprised to see the young woman standing up, her brown eyes alight with interest.

"Did he catch them?" she asked.

"Certainly did," said Chandagnac as he walked back toward the table. He wished now that he had shaved. "Shall I throw him yours too?"

She pushed her chair away and surprised Chandagnac still further by saying, "I'll throw it to him myself . . . if you're sure *he* doesn't object to maggots?"

Chandagnac glanced at the gliding bird. "He hasn't fled, at least."

With only the slightest tremor of hesitation she picked up the inhabited biscuit and strode to the rail. Chandagnac noticed that even her balance was better this morning. She drew back a little when she got to the rail and looked down, for the poop deck was a good dozen feet above the rushing sea. With her left hand she took hold of the rail and pulled at it, as if testing to see if it was loose. "Hate to fall in," she said, a little nervously.

Chandagnac stepped up next to her and gripped her left forearm. "Don't worry," he said. His heart was suddenly beating more strongly, and he was annoyed with himself for the response.

She cocked her arm back and pitched the biscuit, and the white-and-gray bird obligingly dived for it, once again catching it before it hit the water. Her laugh, which Chandagnac heard now for the first time, was bright and cheerful. "I'll wager he follows every Jamaica-bound ship in, knowing the people aboard will be ready to throw the old provisions overboard."

Chandagnac nodded as they returned to the little table. "I'm not on a lavish budget, but I keep thinking about dinner tonight in Kingston. Rare beef, and fresh vegetables, and beer that doesn't smell like hot pitch."

The young woman frowned. "I wish I was permitted meat."

Chandagnac shifted his stool a foot or two to the left so that the tall, taut arch of the spanker sail shaded his face from the morning sun. He wanted to be able to see the expressions on the face of this suddenly interesting person. "I've noticed that you only seem to eat vegetables," he said, idly picking up his napkin.

She nodded. "Nutriments and medicaments—that's what my physician calls them. He says I have an incipient brain fever as a result of the bad airs at a sort of convent I was going to school at in Scotland. He's the expert, so I suppose he's right—though as a matter of fact I felt better, more energetic, before I started following his diet regimen."

Chandagnac had snagged up a loop of thread from his napkin and began working on another. "Your physician?" he asked casually, not wanting to say anything to break her cheery mood and change her back into the clumsy, taciturn fellow passenger she'd been during the past month. "Is he the . . . portly fellow?"

She laughed. "Poor Leo. Say fat. Say corpulent. Yes, that's him. Dr. Leo Friend. An awkward man personally, but my father swears there's no better medical man in the world."

Chandagnac looked up from his napkin work. "Have you been avoiding your . . . medicaments? You seem cheerier today." Her napkin lay on the table, and he picked it up and began picking at it too.

"Well, yes. Last night I just threw the whole plateful out of my cabin window. I hope that poor sea gull didn't sample any—it's nothing but a nasty lot of herbs and weeds Leo grows in a box in his cabin. Then I sneaked across to the galley and had the cook give me some sharp cheese and pickled onions and rum." She smiled sheepishly. "I was desperate for something with some taste to it."

Chandagnac shrugged. "Doesn't sound bad to me." He'd drawn three loops of thread out of each of the napkins, puckering the squares of cloth into bell shapes, and now he slipped three fingers of either hand into the loops and made the napkins stand upright and approach each other with a realistic simulation of walking. Then he had one of them bow while the other curtsied, and the two little cloth figures—one of which he'd somehow made to look subtly feminine—danced around the tabletop in complicated whirls and leaps and pirouettes.

The young woman clapped her hands delightedly, and Chandagnac had the napkins approach her and perform another curtsy and a sweeping Gascon bow before he let them fall from his fingertips.

"Thank you, Miss Hurwood," he said in a master-of-cere-monies voice.

"Thank *you*, Mr. Chandagnac," she said, "and your energetic napkins, too. But don't be formal—call me Beth."

"Very well," said Chandagnac, "and I'm John." Already he was regretting the impulse that had prompted him to draw her out—he had no time, nor any real wish, to get involved with a woman again. He thought of dogs he'd seen in city streets, and called to, just to see if they'd wag their tails and come over, and then too often they had been eager to follow him for hours.

He stood up and gave her a polite smile. "Well," he said, "I'd better be wandering off now. There are a couple of things I've got to be discussing with Captain Chaworth."

Actually, now that he thought of it, he *might* go look for the captain. The *Carmichael* was toiling along smoothly before the wind right now and couldn't be needing too much supervision, and it would be nice to sit down and have one last beery chat with the captain before disembarking. Chandagnac wanted to congratulate Chaworth on the apparent success of his insurance-evasion gam-bit—though unless they were absolutely alone he would have to deliver the congratulations in very veiled terms—and then to warn the man sternly against ever trying such a foolhardy trick again. Chandagnac was, after all, or had been, a successful businessman, and knew the difference between taking carefully calculated risks and letting one's whole career and reputation depend on the toss of a coin. Of course Chandagnac would be careful to deliver the reproof in a bantering tone, so as not to make the old man regret the drunken confidence.

"Oh," said Beth, clearly disappointed that he couldn't stay and talk. "Well, maybe I'll move my chair over by the railing and watch the ocean."

"Here, I'll carry it for you." She stood up, and Chandagnac picked up her chair and walked to the starboard rail, where he set it down on the deck a few yards from one of the post-mounted miniature cannons that he'd heard the sailors call swivel guns. "The shade's only intermittent here," he said doubtfully, "and you'd be catching the full breeze. Are you sure you wouldn't be better off below?"

"Leo would certainly think so," she said, sitting down with a smile of thanks, "but I'd like to continue my experiment of last night, and see what sort of malady it is that one gets from normal food and sunlight and fresh air. Besides, my father's busy with his researches, and he always winds up covering the whole cabin floor with papers and pendulums and tuning forks and I don't know what all. Once he's got it all arranged, there's no way in or out."

Chandagnac hesitated, curious in spite of himself. "Researches? What's he researching?"

"Well . . . I'm not sure. He was involved pretty deeply in mathematics and natural philosophy at one time, but since he retired from his chair at Oxford six years ago . . ."

Chandagnac had seen her father only a few times during the month's voyage—the dignified, one-armed old man had not seemed to desire shipboard sociability, and Chandagnac had not paid much attention to him, but now he snapped his fingers excitedly. "Oxford? *Benjamin* Hurwood?"

"That's right."

"Your father is the—"

"*A sail!*" came a shout from high among the complicated spider webs of the mainmast shrouds. "*Fine ahead port!*"

Beth stood up and the two of them hurried across the deck to the port rail and leaned out and craned their necks to see past the three clusters of standing rigging, which they were viewing end on. Chandagnac thought, it's worse than trying to see the stage from above during a crowded scene in a marionette show. The thought reminded him too clearly of his father, though, and he forced it away and concentrated on squinting ahead.

At last he made out the white fleck on the slowly bobbing horizon, and he pointed it out to Beth Hurwood. They watched it for several minutes, but it didn't seem to be getting any closer, and the sea wind was chillier on this side in spite of the unobstructed sun, so they went back to her chair by the starboard rail.

"Your father's the author of . . . I forget the title. That refutation of Hobbes."

"*The Vindication of Free Will.*" She leaned against the rail and faced astern to let the breeze sweep back her long dark hair. "That's right. Though Hobbes and my father were friends, I understand. Have you read it?"

Again Chandagnac was wishing he'd kept his mouth shut, for

the Hurwood book had been a part of the vast reading program his father had led him through. All that poetry, history, philosophy, art! But a cloddish Roman soldier had shoved a sword through Archimedes, and a bird had dropped a fatal turtle onto the bald head of Aeschylus, mistaking it for a stone useful for breaking turtles open upon.

"Yes. I did think he effectively dismissed Hobbes' idea of a machine-cosmos." Before she could agree or argue, he went on, "But how do pendulums and tuning forks apply?"

Beth frowned. "I don't know. I don't even know what . . . field . . . he's working in now. He's withdrawn terribly during the years since my mother died. I sometimes think he died then too, at least the part of him that . . . I don't know, laughed. He's been more active this last year, though . . . since his disastrous first visit to the West Indies." She shook her head with a puzzled frown. "Odd that losing an arm should vitalize him so."

Chandagnac raised his eyebrows. "What happened?"

"I'm sorry, I thought you'd have heard. The ship he was on was taken by the pirate Blackbeard, and a pistol ball shattered his arm. I'm a little surprised he chose to come back here—though he does have a dozen loaded pistols with him this time, and always carries at least a couple."

Chandagnac grinned inwardly at the idea of the old Oxford don fingering his pistols and waiting to come across a pirate to shoot at.

From out across the blue water rolled a loud, hollow knock, like a large stone dropped onto pavement. Curious, Chandagnac started to cross the poop deck to look again at the approaching vessel, but before he'd taken two steps he was distracted by the abrupt white plume of a splash on the face of the sea, a hundred yards ahead to starboard.

His first thought was that the other vessel was a fishing boat, and that the splash marked the jump of some big fish; then he heard the man at the mast-top shout, more shrilly this time, *"Pirates! A single sloop, the mad fools!"*

Beth was on her feet now. "God in heaven," she said quietly. "Is it true?"

Chandagnac felt light-headed rather than scared, though his heart was pounding. "I don't know," he said, hurrying with her across the deck to the port rail, "but if it is, he's right, they're mad—

a sloop's hardly more than a sailboat, and on the *Carmichael* we've got three masts and eighteen heavy guns."

He had to raise his voice to be heard, for the morning, which had been quiet except for the eternal creak-and-splash-and-slurry, had instantly become clamorous with shouted orders and the slap of bare feet on the lower decks and the buzz of line racing through the block spools; and there was another sound too, distant but far more disquieting—a frenzied metallic clatter and banging underscored by the harsh discord of brass trumpets blown for noise instead of music.

"They *are* pirates," said Beth tensely, clutching the rail next to him. "My father described that noise to me. They'll be dancing, too—they call it 'vaporing'—it's meant to frighten us."

It's effective in that, thought Chandagnac; but to Beth he grinned and said, "It *would* frighten me, if they were in more of a vessel or we in less."

"*Coming over!*" came an authoritative call from one of the lower decks, and below him to his right Chandagnac saw the helmsman and another man pushing the whipstaff hard to starboard, and at the same moment there was a racket of squealing and creaking from overhead as the long horizontal poles of the yards, and the bellied sails they carried, slowly twisted on the axes of the masts, the high ones more widely than the low ones.

All morning the ship had been leaning slightly to starboard; now it straightened to level and then, without pausing there, heeled so far over to port that Chandagnac flung one arm around Beth and the other around a taut length of standing rigging, his hand clutching the limp ratline, and braced his knees against the gunwale as the deck rose behind them and the breakfast table skidded and then tumbled down it to collide with the rail a yard from Beth. The plates and silverware and deformed napkins spun away in the sudden shadow of the hull and splashed directly below where Chandagnac and Beth were clinging.

"Damn me!" grated Chandagnac through clenched teeth as the ship stayed heeled over and he squinted straight down at the choppy sea, "I don't believe the *pirates* can kill us, but our *captain's* certainly having a try!" He had to tilt his head back to look up at the horizon, and it so chilled his stomach to do it that after a few moments he wrenched his gaze back down to the water—but he'd seen the whole vista shifting from right to left, and the pirate vessel, no longer distant, wheeling with the seascape out away from the bow to a position closer and closer to exactly abeam; and though he'd seen it nearly head on, he'd noticed that it was indeed a sloop, a single-masted, gaff-rigged vessel with two shabby, much-patched triangular sails, one tapering back along the boom, the other forward past the bow to the end of the extra-long bowsprit. The gunwales were crowded with ragged figures who did seem to be dancing.

Then the deck was pressing against the soles of his boots and the horizon was falling as the ship righted itself, with the wind and the sun at the starboard quarter now. Keeping his arm around her, Chandagnac hustled Beth toward the companion ladder. "Got to get you out of here!" he shouted.

Her father was clambering up the ladder from the quarter-deck just as they got there, and even in this crisis Chandagnac stared at him, for the old man was wearing a formal vest and long coat and even a powdered wig. He was pulling himself up the ladder by hooking the rungs with the butt of a pistol he gripped in his only hand, and there were at least half a dozen more thrust into the loops of a sash slung over his shoulder. "I'll take her below!" the old man roared, standing up on the poop deck and nudging Beth toward the ladder with his knee. She started down, and the old man was right behind her, peering at her over his shoulder as he followed her. "Carefully!" he shouted. "Carefully, God damn it!"

For one irrational moment Chandagnac wondered if old Hurwood had found time to melt lead and cast some pistol balls in the minute or two since the alarm, for the old man certainly smelled of heated metal . . . but then Hurwood and Beth had disappeared below, and Chandagnac had to skip back across the poop deck to get out of the way of several sailors who were scrambling up the ladder. He retreated to the breakfast table, which stuck out like a little partition from where it was wedged in the railing, and he hoped he was out of everybody's way, wondering all the while what it would feel like when the twelve-pounders were fired, and why the captain was delaying their firing.

Three distinct *booms* shook the deck under his boots. Was that them? he wondered, but when he spun to look out over the rail to port he saw no smoke or splashes.

What he did see was the pirate sloop—which had just swerved east, close-hauled into the steady wind—tack and then continue around so that it was coming up on the *Carmichael* from astern on the port side.

Why in hell, he thought with mounting anxiety, didn't we fire when they were coming straight at us, or when they turned east and showed us their profile? He watched the busy men hurrying past him until he spotted the burly figure of Captain Chaworth on the quarterdeck below, way up by the forecastle ladder, and Chandagnac's stomach felt suddenly hollow when he saw that Chaworth too was surprised by the silence of the guns. Chandagnac edged around the table and hurried to the rail by the ladder to see better what was going on down in the waist.

He saw Chaworth run to the gun deck companionway just as a billow of thick black smoke gushed up from it, and he heard the dismayed shouts of the sailors: "Jesus, one of the guns blew up!" "Three of 'em did, they're all dead below!" "To the boats! The powder'll go next!"

The crack of a pistol shot cut through the rising babble, and Chandagnac saw the man who'd advocated abandoning ship rebound from the capstan barrel and sprawl to the deck, his head smashed gorily open by a pistol ball. Looking away from the corpse, Chandagnac saw that it was the usually good-natured Chaworth who held the smoking pistol.

"You'll go to the boats when I order it!" Chaworth shouted. "No gun blew up, nor's there a fire! Just smoke—"

As if to verify the statement, a dozen violently coughing men came stumbling up the companionway through the smoke, their clothes and faces blackened with something like soot.

"—And it's still just a sloop," the captain went on, "so man the swivels and break out muskets and pistols! Cutlasses hold ready."

A sailor shoved Chandagnac aside to get at one of the swivel guns, and he hurried back to the relative shelter of the jammed table, feeling wildly disoriented. Damn me, he thought bewilderedly as he crouched behind it, is this seagoing warfare? The enemy dancing and blowing horns, men in blackface rushing up from belowdecks like extras in a London stage comedy, the only serious shot fired by our captain to kill one of his own crew?

There were now several sailors standing near him, tensely ready to manipulate the sheets and halliards, and a couple more had sprinted up to the two swivel guns mounted on the poop deck's port rail, one on either side of Chandagnac, and after checking the loads and priming they just waited, watching the pirate sloop and, every few seconds, blowing on the smoldering ends of their slow matches.

Chandagnac crouched to peer between the stanchions rather than over the rail, and he too watched the low, shallow-draft boat gain on the ship. The sloop carried several fairly sizeable cannon, but the capering pirates were ignoring them and hefting pistols, cutlasses and sabers, and grappling hooks.

They must want to capture the *Carmichael* undamaged, Chandagnac thought. If they somehow do, I wonder if they'll ever know how lucky they were that some mephitic catastrophe incapacitated our gunners.

Benjamin Hurwood came struggling back up to the poop deck now, and he absolutely bristled with pistols—there were still six in his sash and one in his hand, and he now had another half-dozen thrust under his belt. Peering over the table edge and seeing the determined look on the one-armed professor's face, Chandagnac had to concede that there was, in this perilous situation, at least, more of dignity than ludicrousness in the man.

The sailor at the aft swivel gun, grasping the ball at the end of the long handle, turned his gun astern and lowered the muzzle to sight along the barrel. He raised his slow match carefully. He was only about five feet from Chandagnac, who was watching him with tense confidence.

Chandagnac tried to picture the gun going off, all the swivel guns going off, muskets and pistols too, lashing lead and scrap shot down into the crowded little pirate boat, two or three volleys perhaps, until a cloud of gunpowder smoke veiled the listing, helpless vessel, on which a few pirates would be glimpsed crawling stunned over the ripped-up corpses of their fellows, as the *Carmichael* came back about onto course and resumed its interrupted journey. Chaworth would have had a bad fright, thinking about his insurance-evasion trick, and would be readier than ever for that beer.

But the gunshot crack came from behind Chandagnac, and the sailor he'd been watching was kicked forward over his gun, and before he tumbled away over the rail Chandagnac had seen the fresh, bloody hole in his back. There was a heavy metallic clank on the deck and then another gunshot, instantly followed by the same clank.

Chandagnac shifted around and peeked over his oak rectangle

in time to see old Hurwood draw a third pistol and fire it directly into the astonished face of one of the two men who'd been handling the spanker sheet. The sailor arced backward to whack the back of his shattered head against the deck, and the other man yiped, ducked, and ran for the ladder. Hurwood dropped the pistol to snatch out another, and the fired one clanked still smoking to the deck. His next shot split the belaying pin the spanker sheet was looped around, and the released line snaked up and down through the bouncing blocks, and then the thirty-foot-tall sail, uncontrolled, bellied and swung its heavy boom to port, tearing through the lines of the standing rigging as though they were rotten yarn; the suddenly unmoored shrouds and ratlines flew upward, the ship shuddered as the mizzen mast leaned to starboard, and from above came the rending crack of overstrained yards giving way.

The man who'd been at the other swivel gun lay face down on the deck, apparently the target of Hurwood's second shot.

Hurwood hadn't noticed Chandagnac behind the table—he drew a fresh pistol, stepped to the head of the ladder and calmly aimed down into the disordered crowd on the quarterdeck.

Without pausing to think, Chandagnac stood up and covered the distance to him in two long strides and drove his shoulder into the small of Hurwood's back just as the old man fired. The shot went harmlessly wide and both men fell down the ladder.

Chandagnac tucked his knees up to somersault in midair and land on his feet, and when he hit the deck he rolled and collided hard with a sailor, bowling the man over. He bounced to his feet and looked back to see how Hurwood had fallen, but in the press of panicking sailors he couldn't see him. Gunfire cracked and boomed irregularly, and the *pyang* of ricochets had people ducking and cringing, but Chandagnac couldn't see who was shooting or being shot at.

Then, preceded by a snapping of cordage overhead, a thick spar came spinning down to crash into the deck, jolting the whole ship and smashing a section of rail near Chandagnac before rebounding away over the side, and just inboard of him a man who'd fallen from aloft hit the deck hard, with a sound like an armful of large books flung down; but it was the next thing landing near him that snapped him out of his horrified daze—a grappling hook came sailing over the rail, its line drawn in as it fell so that its flukes gripped the rail before it could even touch the deck.

A sailor ran forward to yank it free in the moment before weight was put on it, and Chandagnac was right behind him, but a pistol ball from behind punched the sailor off his feet, and Chandagnac tripped over him. Coming up into a crouch against the gunwale, Chandagnac looked around wildly for Hurwood, certain that the one-armed old man had killed the sailor; but when a ball from ahead blew splinters out of the deck in front of his feet and he jerked his head around to see where it had come from, he saw Leo Friend, Beth's fat and foppishly dressed physician, standing on the raised forecastle deck ten yards away and aiming a fresh pistol directly at him.

Chandagnac jackknifed out across the littered deck as the pistol ball tore a hole in the gunwale where he'd been leaning, and he rolled to his feet and ducked and scurried through the crowd all the way across to the starboard rail.

A sailor lay near him curled up on the deck in a shifting puddle of fresh blood, and Chandagnac hastily rolled him over to get at the two primed pistols whose butts he could see sticking up from his belt. The man opened his eyes and tried to speak through splintered teeth, but Chandagnac had for the moment lost all capacity for sympathy. He took the pistols, nodded reassuringly to the dying man, and then turned toward the forecastle.

It took him a few seconds to locate Friend, for the ship was broadside to the wind and rolling and Chandagnac kept having to shuffle to stay upright. Finally he spied the fat man leaning on the waist-facing forecastle rail, dropping a spent pistol and calmly lifting a fresh one out of a box he held in the crook of his left arm.

Chandagnac forced himself to relax. He crouched a little to keep his balance better, and then when the ship paused for a moment at the far point of a roll to port, he raised one of the pistols and took careful aim, squinting over his thumb knuckle at the center of Friend's bulging torso, and squeezed the trigger.

The gun went off, almost spraining his wrist with the recoil, but when the acrid smoke cleared, the fat physician was still standing there, still carefully shooting into the mob of sailors below him.

Chandagnac tossed away the fired pistol and raised the remaining one in both hands and, scarcely aware of what he was doing, walked halfway across the deck toward Friend and from a distance of no more than fifteen feet fired the gun directly up at Friend's stomach.

The fat man, unharmed, turned for a moment to smile contemptuously down at Chandagnac before selecting still another pistol from his box and taking aim at someone else below. Through the smells of burned powder and fear-sweat and fresh-torn wood, Chandagnac caught again a whiff of something like overheated metal.

A moment later Friend put the pistol back into his box unfired, though, for the fight was over. A dozen of the pirates had clambered aboard, and more were swinging over the rail, and the surviving sailors had dropped their weapons.

Chandagnac dropped his pistol and walked slowly backward to the starboard rail, his eyes fixed incredulously on the pirates. They were cheerful, their eyes and yellow teeth flashing in faces that, except for their animation, would have looked like polished mahogany, and a few of them were still singing the song they'd been singing during the pursuit. They were dressed, Chandagnac reflected dazedly, like children who'd been interrupted while ransacking a theater's costume closet; and in spite of their obviously well-used pistols and swords, and the faded scars splashed irregularly across many of the faces and limbs in random patterns of pucker and pinch, they seemed to Chandagnac as innocently savage as predatory birds compared to the coldly methodical viciousness of Hurwood and Friend.

One of the pirates stepped forward and sprang up the companion ladder to the poop deck so lithely that Chandagnac was surprised, when the man turned and tilted back his three-cornered hat, to see the deep lines in his dark cheeks and the quantity of gray in his tangled black hair. He scanned the men below him and grinned, narrowing his eyes and baring a lot of teeth.

"Captives," he said, his harshly good-humored voice undercutting the agitated babble, "I am Philip Davies, the new captain of this ship. Now I want you to gather around the mainmast there and let our lads search you for any . . . *concealed weapons*, eh? Skank, you and 'Tholomew and a couple of others, trot below and fetch up any that're down there. Carefully, mind—there's been blood enough spilt today."

The eight surviving members of the conquered crew shuffled to the center of the deck; Chandagnac joined them, hurrying to the mast and then leaning against its solid bulk and hoping his unsteady gait would be attributed to the rocking of the deck rather than to fear. Looking past the pirate chief, Chandagnac saw the sea

gull, evidently reassured by the cessation of the gunfire, flap down
and perch on one of the stern lanterns. It was difficult to believe
that less than half an hour ago he and Hurwood's daughter had
been idly tossing biscuits to the bird.

"Master Hurwood!" called Davies. After a moment he added,
"I know you weren't killed, Hurwood—where are you?"

"No," came a gasping voice from behind a couple of corpses at
the foot of the poop deck companion ladder. "I'm . . . not killed."
Hurwood sat up, his wig gone and his elegant clothes disordered.
"But I wish . . . I had had a charm . . . against falling."

"You've got Mate Care-For to keep you from hurt," Davies said
unsympathetically. "None of these lads did." He waved at the
scattered corpses and wounded men. "I hope it was a hard fall."

"My daughter's below," said Hurwood, urgency coming into
his voice as his head cleared. "She's guarded, but tell your men
not to—"

"They won't hurt her." The pirate chief squinted around
critically. "It's not too bad a ship you've brought," he said. "I guess
you did pay attention to what we told you. Here, Payne, Rich! Get
some lads aloft and cut away all bad wood and line and canvas, and
get her jury-rigged well enough to get us across the Grand Bahama
Bank."

"Right, Phil," called a couple of the pirates, scrambling to the
shrouds.

Davies climbed back down the ladder to the quarterdeck, and
for several seconds he just stared at the clump of disarmed men by
the mast. He was still smiling. "Four of my men were killed during
our approach and boarding," he remarked softly.

"Jesus," whispered the man next to Chandagnac, closing his
eyes.

"But," Davies went on, "more than half of your own number
have been slain, and I will consider that amends enough."

None of the sailors spoke, but Chandagnac heard several
sharp exhalations, and shufflings of feet. Belatedly he realized that
his death had come very close to being decreed.

"You're free to leave in the ship's boat," Davies continued.
"Hispaniola's east, Cuba north, Jamaica southwest. You'll be given
food, water, charts, sextant and compass. Or," he added cheerfully,
"any of you that fancy it may stay and join us. It's an easier life than
most on the sea, and every man has a share in the profits, and
you're free to retire after every voyage."

No, thank you, thought Chandagnac. Once I finish my . . . errand . . . in Port-au-Prince and get home again, I never want to see another damned ocean in my whole life.

Old Chaworth had for several minutes been slowly looking around at the ship he'd been owner of so recently, and Chandagnac realized that though the captain had reconciled himself to the loss of his cargo, he hadn't until now imagined that he would lose his ship, too. Pirates, after all, were a shallow-water species, always eluding capture by skating over shoals, and seldom venturing out of sight of land. They should have had as little use for a deep-water ship like the *Carmichael* as a highwayman would have for a siege cannon.

The old man was ashen, and it occurred to Chandagnac that until this development Chaworth hadn't quite been ruined; if he hadn't lost the *Carmichael* herself, he could have sold her and perhaps, after paying off the stockholders or co-owners, cleared enough money to reimburse the cargo owners for their losses; the move would no doubt have left him broke, but would at least have kept concealed the secret he'd confided to Chandagnac one drunken evening—that since the price of insurance was now higher than the greatest profit margin he could plausibly try for, he had in desperation charged the cargo owners for insurance . . . and then not bought any.

One of the pirates who'd gone below now stepped up from the after-companionway and, looking back the way he'd come, gestured upward with a pistol. Up the ladder and into the sunlight climbed the cook—who had obviously followed the time-honored custom of facing seagoing disaster by getting drunk as quickly and thoroughly as possible—and the two boys who ran all the errands on the ship, and Beth Hurwood.

Hurwood's daughter was pale, and walked a bit stiffly, but was outwardly calm until she saw her disheveled father. "Papa!" she yelled, running to him. "Did they hurt you?" Without waiting for an answer she whirled on Davies. "Your kind did enough to him last time," she said, her voice an odd mix of anger and pleading. "Meeting Blackbeard cost him his arm! Whatever he's done to you people today was—"

"Was greatly appreciated, Miss," said Davies, grinning at her. "In keeping with the compact he and Thatch—or Blackbeard, if you like—agreed on last year, your daddy's delivered to me this fine ship."

"What are you—" began Beth, but she was interrupted by a shrill oath from Chaworth, who sprang on the nearest pirate, wrenched the saber from the surprised man's hand, and then shoved him away and rushed at Davies, cocking his arm back for a cleaving stroke.

"No!" yelled Chandagnac, started forward, "Chaworth, don't—"

Davies calmly hiked a pistol out of his garish paisley sash, cocked it and fired it into Chaworth's chest; the impact of the fifty-caliber ball stopped the captain's charge and punched him over backward with such force that he was nearly standing on his head for a moment before thumping and rattling down in the absolute limpness of death.

Chandagnac was dizzy, and couldn't take a deep breath. Time seemed to have slowed—no, it was just that each event was suddenly distinct, no longer part of a blended progression. Beth screamed. The burst of smoke from the pistol muzzle churned forward another yard. The sea gull squawked in renewed alarm and flapped upward. The dropped saber spun across the deck and the brass knuckle-guard of it whacked against Chandagnac's ankle. He bent down and picked up the weapon.

Then, without having consciously decided to, he was himself rushing at the pirate chief, and though his legs were pounding and his arm was keeping the heavy blade extended in front of him, in his mind he was deftly rocking the stick and crosspiece and making the Mercutio marionette which dangled from them spring toward the Tybalt marionette in the move his father had always called *coupe-and-flèche*.

Davies, startled and amused, tossed the spent pistol to a companion and, stepping back, drew his rapier and relaxed into the *en garde* crouch.

Taking the final stride, Chandagnac almost thought he could feel the upward yank of the marionette string as he quickly twitched his point over the other man's sword and extended it again in Davies' inside line; and he was so used to the Tybalt puppet's answering lateral parry that he was almost too quick in letting his saber drop under this real, unrehearsed one—but Davies had believed the feint and made the parry, and in the last instant the disengaged saber was pointed at the pirate chief's unguarded flank, and Chandagnac let the momentum of his rush drive it in, and yank the hilt out of his inexpert grip, as he ran past.

The saber clattered to the deck, and then for one long moment all motion did stop. Davies, still standing but twisted around by the thrust, was staring at Chandagnac in astonishment, and Chandagnac, empty-handed and tense with the expectation of a pistol ball at any moment and from any direction, held his breath and stared helplessly into the wounded pirate's eyes.

Finally Davies carefully sheathed his sword and, just as carefully, folded to his knees, and the silence was so absolute that Chandagnac actually heard the patter of blood drops hitting the deck.

"Kill him," said Davies distinctly.

Chandagnac had half turned toward the rail, intending to vault it and try to swim to Hispaniola, when a sarcastic voice said, "For excelling you in swordsmanship, Phil? Faith, that's one way to maintain your supremacy."

This statement was followed by a good deal of muttering among the pirates, and Chandagnac paused hopefully. He glanced back toward Davies and prayed that the man might bleed to death before repeating the order.

But Davies was looking at the pirate who'd spoken, and after a few seconds he smiled wolfishly and pointed at his own gashed side. "Ah, Venner, you think *this* will do? *This* cut?" Davies leaned forward, placed his hands flat on the deck, and strugglingly got one booted foot, and then the other, under him. He looked up at Venner again, still grinning, and then slowly stood up from the crouch. His grin never faltered, though he went pale under his tan and his face was slicked with sweat. "You're . . . new, Venner," Davies said hoarsely. "You should ask Abbott or Gardner how dire a wound must be to slow me down." He inhaled deeply, then swayed and stared down at the deck. His breeches shone darkly with blood down to the calf, where they were tucked into his boot. After a moment he looked up. "Or," he went on, stepping back unsteadily and drawing his rapier again, "would you like to . . . discover for yourself how much this has disabled me?"

Venner was short and stocky, with a ruddy, pockmarked face. Half-smiling, he stared at his captain with the speculative look one gives a card-game opponent whose drunkenness may be a sham, or at least exaggerated. Finally he spread his hands. "Damn me, Phil," he said easily, "you know I didn't mean nothing *challenging*."

Davies nodded and allowed himself to close his eyes for a moment. "Of course not." He thrust his sword away and turned to Chandagnac. "Venner's right, though," he grated, "and I'm glad . . . that nobody killed you . . . if only so I can learn that feint." He permitted himself to lean against the aftercabin bulkhead. "But God's *blood*, man," he burst out loudly, "how in hell is it that you know such a thefty move when you run like a duck and hold a sword the way a cook holds a pot handle?"

Chandagnac tried and failed to think of a good lie, and then hesitantly told the man the truth. "My father ran a marionette show," he faltered, "and I'm . . . for most of my life I was a puppeteer. We . . . performed all over Europe, and when the scripts called for sword fights—we did a lot of Shakespeare—he consulted fencing masters to make it absolutely realistic. So," he shrugged, "I've memorized any number of fencing moves, and performed each of them hundreds of times . . . but only with puppets."

Davies, holding his side, stared at him. "Puppets," he said. "Well, I—goddamn. Puppets." Slowly he let himself slide down the bulkhead until he was sitting on the deck. "Where the devil's Hanson?"

"Here, Phil." One of the pirates hurried over to him, opening a small clasp knife. "You're gonna have to be lying down," he said.

Davies obediently lay back, but propped himself up on his elbows to look at Chandagnac while Hanson, who evidently served as the pirates' surgeon, began cutting away the blood-sopped shirttail. "Well!" Davies said. "Venner has suggested that I was too . . . harsh, in ordering you killed, and we—*ow*, damn your soul, Hanson, be careful!" He closed his eyes for a moment, then took a deep breath and resumed. "And we do business on the understanding that all orders are open to discussion, except when we're in serious action. Nevertheless you did stab me, so I can't just . . . let you leave in the boat." He looked around at his companions. "I propose giving him the choice."

There were satisfied nods and shouts of agreement.

Davies looked up at Chandagnac. "Join us, wholly adopt our goals as your own, or be killed right now where you stand."

Chandagnac turned to Beth Hurwood, but she was whispering to her father, who didn't even seem to be aware of her. Looking past the two of them he saw the broad figure of Leo Friend, who was scowling—possibly disappointed that Chandagnac was still alive. Chandagnac had never felt more friendless and unprotected. Suddenly, and terribly, he missed his father.

He turned back to Davies. "I'll join you."

Davies nodded thoughtfully. "That is the standard decision," he said. "I wasn't entirely sure it'd be yours."

Hanson stood up and stared dubiously at the bandage he'd belted to his chief. "That's all I can do for you, Phil," he said. "Get milord Hurwood to make sure it stops bleeding and don't mortify."

Chandagnac glanced at Hanson in surprise. Surely, he thought, you mean Leo Friend. Philosophy doesn't knit up wounds.

Hearing his name, Hurwood came out of his reverie and blinked around. "Where's Thatch?" he asked, too loudly. "He was supposed to be here."

"He's runnin' late this year," Davies said, not even bothering to try to twist his head around and face Hurwood. "Right now he's up in Charles Town getting the supplies you wanted. We'll meet him in Florida. Now come here and do something to make sure I don't die of this perforation."

Beth started to say something, but Hurwood waved her to silence. "He let *you* have the pointer?" he said, obviously not pleased.

Davies grimaced. "The mummied dog head? Sure. And it sure enough did start hissing and spinning around in its bucket of rum yesterday, and then at noon or so settled, staring hard southeast, and shifting only when we'd shift course, so we headed where it was looking." He shrugged as well as he could. "It led us to you, right enough, but it's sure a nasty-looking bit of trash. Had a time keeping the rats from chewing it up."

"Damn that lunatic Thatch," Hurwood exploded, "for letting common brigands carry sophisticated apparatus! If rats have *touched* that pointer, then they'll devour you entire, Davies, I promise you. You careless fool, how often do you think two-headed dogs are born? Send a man back to your vessel for it immediately."

Davies smiled and lay back on the deck. "*Wellll,*" he said, "no. You can have the other half of your filthy pair back as soon as I've stepped ashore at New Providence Island, as healthy as I was an hour ago. If I don't recover totally between now and then, my lads will burn the goddamn thing. Am I right?"

"You said it, Phil!" shouted one of the pirates, and the others were all nodding happily.

Hurwood glared around, but crossed to where Davies was lying and knelt beside him. He looked at the bandage and lifted it and peered underneath. "Hell, you might very well recover even without my help," he said, "but just for the sake of my pointer set I'll make it certain." He began digging in the deep pockets of his knee-length coat.

Chandagnac looked to his left and behind him. Chaworth's body, clearly dead, shifted loosely back and forth in the sun as the ship rolled, and one outflung hand rocked back and forth, palm up and then palm down, in an oddly philosophical gesture. It comes and goes, the movement seemed to indicate; good and bad, life and death, joy and horror, and nothing should come as a surprise.

Chandagnac found it embarrassingly inappropriate, as if the dead man had been left with his pants down, and he wished somebody would move the hand to a more fitting position. He looked away.

Never having seen a wound worked on by a physician, which it seemed Hurwood was, Chandagnac stepped forward to watch; and for one bewildering moment he thought Hurwood was going to begin by tidying up Davies' appearance, for what he pulled out of his pocket looked like a small whisk broom.

"This ox-tail," said Hurwood in what must have been his auditorium-addressing voice, "has been treated to become a focus of the attention of the being you call Mate Care-For. If he was a grander thing he could pay attention to all of us at once, but as it is he can only thoroughly look after a couple of people at a time. In this recent scuffle he preserved myself and Mr. Friend, and since the danger to us is passed, I'll let you occupy his attention." He tucked the bristly object down the front of Davies' lime green shirt. "Let's see . . ." Again he went fumbling through his pockets, "and here," he said, producing a little cloth bag of something, "is a *drogue* that makes the bowels behave properly. Again, you are in more danger in that regard than I am, at the moment—though I'll want it back." He took Davies' hat off and set it on the deck, laid the little bag on top of the pirate's head and then replaced the hat. "That's that," he said, standing up. "Let's waste no more time. Get the ones who are leaving into the boat, and then let's go."

The *Carmichael*'s new owners swung the ship's boat out on the davit cranes and lowered it with a careless splash to the water on the starboard side, and they flung a net of shrouds and ratlines after it for the people to climb down on. At the next swell the boat was slammed up against the hull of the ship and took on a lot of water, but Davies tiredly called out some orders and the ship shifted ponderously around until the wind was on the starboard quarter and the rolling abated.

Davies got to his feet, wincing irritably. "All off that's getting off," he growled.

Wistfully Chandagnac watched the *Carmichael*'s original crew shambling toward the starboard rail, several of them supporting wounded companions. Beth Hurwood, a black hood pulled over her coppery ringlets, started forward, then turned and called, "Father! Join me in the boat."

Hurwood looked up, and produced a laugh like the last clatter of unoiled machinery. "Wouldn't they be glad of my company! Half of these slain owe their present state to my pistol collection and my hand. No, my dear, I stay aboard this ship—and so do you."

His statement had rocked her, but she turned and started toward the rail.

"Stop her," snapped Hurwood impatiently.

Davies nodded, and several grinning pirates stepped in front of her.

Hurwood permitted himself another laugh, but it turned into a retching cough. "Let's *go*," he croaked. Chandagnac happened to glance at Leo Friend, and he was almost glad that he'd been forced to stay aboard, for the physician was blinking rapidly, and his prominent lips were wet, and his eyes were on Beth Hurwood.

"Right," said Davies. "Here, you clods, get these corpses over the side—mind you don't pitch 'em into the boat—and then let's be off." He looked upward. "How is it, Rich?"

"Can't jibe," came a shout from aloft, "with the spanker carried away. But this wind and sea are good enough to tack her in, I think, if we get all the lads up on the footropes."

"Good. Elliot, you take a couple of men and pilot the sloop back home."

"Right, Phil."

Beth Hurwood turned her gaze from her father to Leo Friend, who smiled and stepped forward—Chandagnac noticed for the first time that the fat physician's finery included a ludicrous pair of

red-heeled shoes with "windmill wing" ties—and proffered an arm
like an ornate, overstuffed bolster, but Beth crossed to Chandagnac
and stood beside him, not speaking. Her lips were pressed together
as firmly as before, but Chandagnac glimpsed the shine of tears in
her eyes a moment before she impatiently blotted them on her cuff.

"Shall I take you below?" Chandagnac asked quietly.

She shook her head. "I couldn't bear it."

Davies glanced at the two of them. "You've got no duties yet,"
he told Chandagnac. "Take her up forward somewhere out of the
way. You might get her some rum while you're at it."

"I hardly think—," Chandagnac began stiffly, but Elizabeth
interrupted.

"For God's sake, yes," she said.

Davies grinned at Chandagnac and waved them forward.

A few minutes later they were on the forecastle deck by the
starboard anchor, shielded from the wind by the taut mainsail
behind them. Chandagnac had gone to the galley and filled two
ceramic cups with rum, and he handed one to her.

Line began buzzing through the blocks again and the spars
creaked as the sails, trimmed and full once more, were turned to
best catch the steady east wind; the ship came around in a slow arc
to the north, and then to the northeast, and Chandagnac watched
the crowded lifeboat recede and finally disappear behind the high
stern. The sloop, still on the port side, was pacing the *Vociferous
Carmichael*. From where he now leaned against the rail sipping
warm rum, Chandagnac could see the mast and sails of the smaller
vessel, and as their speed picked up and the sloop edged away from
the ship to give it room he was able to see its long, low hull too. He
shook his head slightly, still incredulous.

"Well, we could both be worse off," he remarked quietly to
Beth, trying to convince himself as much as her. "I'm apparently
forgiven for my attack on their chief, and you're protected from
these creatures by . . . your father's position among them." Below
him to his left, one of the pirates was walking up and down the
waist, whistling and sprinkling sand from a bucket onto the many
splashes and puddles of blood on the deck. Chandagnac looked
away and went on. "And when we *do* manage to get out of this
situation, all the sailors in the boat can testify that you and I stayed
unwillingly." He was proud of the steadiness of his voice, and he

gulped some more rum to still the post-crisis trembling he could feel beginning in his hands and legs.

"My God," Beth said dazedly, "all I can hope for is that he *dies* out here. He can't ever go back. They wouldn't even put him in a madhouse—they'd *hang* him."

Chandagnac nodded, reflecting that even hanging was less than what her father deserved.

"I should have seen his madness coming on," she said. "I *did* know he'd become . . . eccentric, taking up researches that . . . seemed a little crazy . . . but I never dreamt he'd go wild, like a rabid dog, and start *killing* people."

Chandagnac thought of a sailor he'd seen killed at the swivel gun, and the one Hurwood had shot in the face a moment later. "It wasn't done in any kind of . . . frenzy, Miss Hurwood," he said shortly. "It was cold—methodical—like a cook squashing ants on a kitchen counter, one by one, and then wiping his hands and turning to the next job. And the fat boy was at the other end of the ship, matching him shot for shot."

"Friend, yes," she said. "There's always been something hateful about him. No doubt he led my poor father into this scheme, whatever it is. But my father *is* insane. Listen, just before we left England last month, he stayed out all night, and came back all muddy and hatless in the morning, clutching a smelly little wooden box. He wouldn't say what it was—when I asked him, he just stared at me as if he'd never seen me before—but he hasn't been without it since. It's in his cabin now, and I swear he whispers to it late at night. And my God, you read his book! He used to be brilliant! What explanation besides lunacy could explain the author of *The Vindication of Free Will* babbling all that nonsense about ox-tails and two-headed dogs?"

Chandagnac heard the note of strain and doubt under her carefully controlled diction. "I can't argue with that," he conceded gently.

She finished her rum. "Maybe I will go below. Oh, uh, John, could you help me get food?"

Chandagnac stared at her. "Right now? Sure, I guess so. What did you—"

"No, I mean at mealtimes. It might be even harder now to avoid the diet Friend has prescribed for me, and now more than ever I want to stay alert."

Chandagnac smiled, but he was thinking again about the consequences of throwing scraps to stray dogs. "I'll do what I can. But God knows what these devils eat. Friend's herbs might be preferable."

"You haven't tried them." She started toward the ladder, but paused and looked back. "That was very brave, John, challenging that pirate the way you did."

"It wasn't a challenge, it was just . . . some kind of reflex." He found that he was getting irritable. "I'd got to like old Chaworth. He reminded me of . . . another old man. Neither one of them had any goddamn sense. And I guess I don't either, or I'd be in the boat right now." He bolted the remainder of his rum. "Well, see you later."

He looked ahead, past the bowsprit at the blue horizon, and when he looked back she had left. He relaxed a little and watched the new crew at work. They were scrambling around up in the rigging, agile as spiders, and casually cursing each other in English, French, Italian and a couple of languages Chandagnac had never heard, and though their grammar was atrocious he had to concede that, in terms of obscenity, blasphemy and elaborate insult, the pirates got the most out of every language he was able to understand.

He was smiling, and he had time to wonder why before he realized that this multilingual, good-naturedly fearsome badinage was just like what he used to hear in the taverns of Amsterdam and Marseille and Brighton and Venice; in his memory they all blended into one archetypal seaport tavern in which his father and he were eternally sitting at a table by the fire, drinking the local specialty and exchanging news with other travelers. It had sometimes seemed to the young Chandagnac that the marionettes were a party of wooden aristocracy traveling with two flesh-and-blood servants; and now, seven years after quitting that life, he reflected that the puppets hadn't been bad masters. The pay had been irregular, for the great days of European puppet theaters had ended in 1690, the year of Chandagnac's birth, when Germany lifted the clergy's ten-year ban on plays using living actors, but the money had still occasionally been lavish, and then the hot dinners and warm beds were made all the pleasanter by memories of the previous months of frosty rooms and missed meals.

The pirate with the bucket of sand had apparently finished his job, but as he was stumping aft past the mainmast his heel skidded. He glared around as though daring anyone to laugh, and then he dumped all the rest of his sand on the slippery patch and strode away.

Chandagnac wondered if the blood he'd slipped on had been Chaworth's. And he remembered the night in Nantes when his father had pulled a knife on a gang of rough men who'd waited outside one wine shop for Chandagnac *père et fils* and then had cornered the pair and demanded all their money. Old François Chandagnac had had a lot of money on him on that night, and he was in his mid-sixties and doubtful of his future, and so instead of handing over the cash as he'd done the couple of times he'd been robbed before, he unpocketed the knife he carved marionette faces and hands with, and brandished it at the thieves.

Chandagnac leaned back against one of the unfired starboard-side swivel guns now and, cautiously, basked in the realization that the sun was warm on his back, and that he was slightly drunk, and that he wasn't in pain anywhere.

The knife had been knocked out of his father's hand with the first, contemptuous kick, and then there had simply been fists, teeth, knees and boots in the darkness, and when the gang walked away, laughing and crowing as they counted the money in the unexpectedly fat purse, they must certainly have supposed they were leaving two corpses in the alley behind them.

In the years since, Chandagnac had sometimes wished they'd been right in that supposition, for neither his father nor he had ever really recovered.

The two of them had eventually managed to get back to their room. His father had lost his front teeth and eventually lost his left eye, and had suffered fractures in several ribs and possibly his skull. Young John Chandagnac had lost most of the use of his right hand because of a heavy man's boot-heel, and for a month he walked with a cane, and it was a full year before his urine was quite free of blood. The bad hand, though he eventually regained nearly full use of it, provided a good excuse to quit that nomadic career, and through thinly disguised pleading he managed to secure travel money and lodging with a relative in England, and before his twenty-second birthday he had got a position as a bookkeeper with an English textile firm.

His father, in ever-worsening health, had single-handedly run the marionette show for another two years before dying in Brussels in the winter of 1714. He never even learned about the money that had become his, the money that could so dramatically have prolonged and brightened his life . . . the money that had been cleverly stolen from him by his own younger brother, Sebastian.

Chandagnac looked over his right shoulder, squinting at the eastern horizon until he thought he saw a faintly darker line that might have been Hispaniola. I was to have arrived there in about a week, he thought angrily, after establishing my credit with the bank in Jamaica. How long will it take now? Don't die, Uncle Sebastian. Don't die before I get there.

Chapter Two

Even in the twilight, with cooking fires beginning to dot the darkening beach, the harbor's mottling of shoals was clearly visible, and the boats rounding the distant corner of Hog Island could be seen to change course frequently as they kept to the darker blue water on their way in from the open sea to the New Providence settlement. Most of the settlement's boats were already moored for the night, out in the harbor or along the decrepit wharf or, in the cases of a number of the smaller craft, dragged right up onto the white sand, and the island's population was beginning to concern itself with dinner. At this hour the settlement's stench contended most strongly with the clean sea breeze, for added to its usual melange of tar-smoke, sulfur, old food and the countless informal latrines was the often startling olfactory spectrum of inexpert cooking: the smell of feathers burnt off chickens by men too impatient to pluck them, of odd stews into which the enthusiastic hand of the amateur had flung quantities of hijacked mint and cilantro and Chinese mustard to conceal the taste of dubious meats, and of weird and sometimes explosive experiments in the art of punch-making.

Benjamin Hurwood had taken his daughter and Leo Friend off the *Carmichael* four hours earlier, shortly after the ship was laboriously tugged, tacked and block-and-tackled into the harbor, and long before the pirates had begun the job of careening the vessel. He'd hailed the first boat that had come alongside and demanded that the men in it take them ashore, and he had not only been obeyed, but, it had seemed to Chandagnac, recognized too.

And now the *Carmichael* lay bizarrely on her side, tackles fastened to the mastheads, and relieving tackles strung under the keel and tied to solid moorings on the exposed side, fully half of her hundred-and-ten-foot length out of the water and supported by the sloping white-sand shore of a conveniently deep inlet a hundred yards south of the main cluster of tents; and Chandagnac was plodding up the beach in the company of the pirates, reeling from exhaustion as much as from the novelty of having a motionless surface underfoot, for the pirates had cheerfully assumed that as a new member of the crew he ought to do the work of two men.

"Ah, damn me," remarked the toothless young man who was stumping along next to Chandagnac, "I smell some lively grub." Chandagnac had gathered that this young man's name was Skank.

The ship behind them groaned loudly as her timbers adjusted themselves to the new stresses, and birds—Chandagnac supposed they must be birds—cawed and yelled in the dim jungle.

"Lively's the word," Chandagnac nodded, reflecting that, considering the flames, smells and shouting up ahead, it seemed that the dinner being cooked was not only still alive, but unsubdued.

To Chandagnac's left, visible above the palm fronds, was a rounded rock eminence. "The fort," said his toothless companion, pointing that way.

"Fort?" Chandagnac squinted, and finally noticed walls and a tower, made of the same stone as the hill itself. Even from down on the beach he could see several ragged gaps in the uneven line of the wall. "You people built a fort here?"

"Naw, the Spaniards built it. Or maybe the English. Both of them have took turns claiming this place for years, but there was only one man, a daft old wreck, on the whole island when Jennings came across the place and decided to found his pirate town here. The English think they've got it now—King George has even got a man sailing over here with a pardon for any of us as will quit wickedness and take up, I don't know, farming or something—but that won't last either."

They were in among the cooking fires now, weaving around clusters of people sitting in the sand. Many of these diners had barrels or upright spar sections to lean against, and they all shouted greetings to the new arrivals, waving bottles and charred pieces of meat. Chandagnac nervously eyed the firelit faces, and he was surprised to see that about one in three was female.

"The *Jenny's* moored over there," said Skank, waving unhelpfully. "They'll have got a fire going, and with luck scrounged some stuff to throw in the stewpot."

The ground still felt to Chandagnac as if it were rocking under his boots, and as he stepped over one low ridge of sand he swayed as if to correct his balance on a rolling deck; he managed not to fall, but he did knock a chicken leg out of a woman's hand.

Jesus, he thought in sudden fright. "I'm sorry," he babbled, "I—"

But she just laughed drunkenly, snatched another piece of chicken from an apparently genuine gold platter and mumbled something in a slurred mix of French and Italian; Chandagnac was pretty sure it had been a half-sarcastic sexual invitation, but the slang was too unfamiliar, and the tenses too garbled, for him to be certain.

"Uh," he said hurriedly to Skank as he resumed his lurching pace, "the *Jenny?*"

"That's the sloop we took your *Carmichael* with," said the young pirate. "Yeah," he added, peering ahead as the two of them crested another crowded, littered sand ridge, "they've got a pot of sea water on the fire and they're flinging some junk or other into it."

Skank broke into a plodding run, as did the rest of Davies' men. Chandagnac followed more slowly, peering ahead. There was a fire on the beach, and the cooking pot resting on the blazing planks was almost waist-high. He saw several chickens, headless and gutted but otherwise unprepared, arc out of the darkness and splash in, and then a man lurched up and dumped a bucket of some lumpy fluid into it. Chandagnac suppressed a gag, and then grinned as it occurred to him that he was less afraid of these people than he was of their food.

One stocky old fellow, bald but bearded like a palm tree, leaned over the fire and thrust his tattooed right arm into the stew and stirred it around. "Not hot enough yet," he rumbled. He pulled out a soggy chicken, stepped away from the fire and bit off a wing. Wet feathers made a startling spectacle of his beard, and even over the general conversation Chandagnac could hear bones being crunched. "But it's getting savory," the man decided, tossing the devastated bird back into the pot.

"Let's have a song!" yelled someone. "While we wait."

Cheers followed, but then a lean, grinning figure stepped into the firelight. "Hell with *songs,*" said Philip Davies, staring straight at Chandagnac. "Let's have a puppet show." The amused scorn in his voice made Chandagnac's face heat up.

Davies might have been joking, but the other pirates took up the idea eagerly. " 'At's right," shouted one man, his lone eye nearly popping from his head with excitement, "that lad from the *Carmichael* can work puppets! Christ! He'll do us a show, won't he?" "He'll do it," belched one very drunken man sitting nearby. "He'll do it or I'll . . . kick his arse for him."

All of them seemed to feel that this was the right spirit, and Chandagnac found himself thrust into the open area in front of the fire.

"Wha—but I—" He looked around. The drunken threat didn't seem to have been a joke, and he remembered the casualness of Chaworth's murder.

"You gonna do it or not, boy?" asked Davies. "What's the matter, your shows too *good* for us?"

A wide-eyed black man stared at Chandagnac and then looked around at his fellows. "He called me a *dog,* didn't he?"

"Hold it!" said Chandagnac loudly, raising his hands. "Wait, yes, I'll do it. But I'll need . . . uh . . . a lot of string, a stout needle, a sharp knife and a, say, three-gallon-jug-sized piece of very soft wood."

Several of the pirates who'd sat down leaped to their feet, shouting joyfully.

"Oh," Chandagnac added, "and a couple of bits of cloth'd be useful, and tacks, or small nails. And I see some bottles being passed around back there—how about a drink for the puppeteer?"

A few minutes later he was crouched over his crude tools near the fire, alternately working and taking swigs from a bottle of really very good brandy, and as he quickly whittled limb, torso, pelvis and head pieces out of a split section of palm bole, Chandagnac wondered what sort of show this audience would relish. Shakespeare seemed unlikely. There had been a couple of quick, vulgar dialogues his father would occasionally do in taprooms years ago, when he'd thought young John had gone upstairs to bed, and

Chandagnac suspected that they'd formed part of the old man's professional repertoire back in the lean years before the German ban on live actors. If Chandagnac could remember them, those routines would probably go over well here.

With a deftness he would have claimed not to have anymore, he notched the fronts of the two little wooden heads, producing rough but accurate faces; next he cut small bands of cloth to serve as tacked-on hinges, and then bigger, more complicated shapes to be clothing. It took him no more than one more minute to tack it all together and then cut lengths of string and tack them onto the ears, hands, knees and backs of his two marionettes, with the other ends of each mannikin's strings connected to a cross he'd grip in one hand. Controlling two puppets at once meant he would have to dispense with a separately held stick to control each puppet's knees, but he had learned long ago how to use the stiffly extended first two fingers of each hand instead.

"Very well, here we go," he said finally, trying to seem confident, as his father had always advised when facing a potentially unruly audience, which this certainly was. "Everybody's got to sit down. Could one of you toss me that . . . wrecked barrel there, please? Better than nothing for a set." To his surprise, one of them brought it over and set it down carefully in front of him. Chandagnac eyed the sprung, topless barrel for a moment, then kicked the whole front in, pulled away the broken stave ends and the one remaining hoop and then stood back. He nodded. "Our stage."

Most of the pirates had sat down and had at least stopped shouting, so Chandagnac picked up the control crosses and slid his fingers into the loops. He lifted the marionette whose legs were encased in crude trousers—"Our hero!" he said loudly—and then the one for whom he'd made a dress—"And a woman he encounters!"

His audience seemed to find this promising.

The female puppet was whisked into the open front of the barrel, and the male puppet began sauntering up from a yard away.

Chandagnac was acutely aware that he was standing on a beach on the wrong side of the world, in front of a crowd of drunken murderers. To be performing a *puppet show* under these circumstances seemed as weirdly inappropriate as May Day garlands on a gibbet . . . or, it occurred to him, as dancing and playing musical instruments when getting into position to board a merchant ship and kill more than half of her crew.

From the direction of the other fires now came shambling into the firelight the oldest-looking man Chandagnac had seen since leaving England. His beard and long, ropy hair were the color of old bones, and his face was dark old leather stretched taut over a skull. Chandagnac couldn't guess the man's race, but when several of the pirates greeted the old man as "governor" and made room for him to sit down he guessed that this must be the "daft old wreck" Skank had mentioned, the one who'd been the island's only inhabitant when the pirates found the place.

The male puppet had walked up to the barrel and seemed about to go on past, but the female leaned out of the doorway-like opening and cocked her head. "Evening, sir," said Chandagnac shrilly, feeling like a fool. "Would you care to buy a lady a drink?"

"I beg your pardon?" Chandagnac had the other puppet say in a broad parody of an upper-class English accent. "I'm very hard of—"

"Please speak up, sir," the female puppet interrupted. "I don't hear very well."

"—of hearing."

"You say what, sir? Something you're fearing? I think I know what you're referring to, sir, and you needn't fear it with me. I can guarantee—"

"No, no, hearing, *hearing.*"

"Herring? Hungry, are you? What *about* herring?"

"I say I'm *very hard of it.*"

"Oh! Oh, well, splendid, sir, splendid, *very hard* of it, are you, well, let's get down to business and stop discussing fish, then, shall we—"

"It's a trap!" yelled one of the pirates from the audience. "She'll be leading him straight into the hands of a press gang! That's how the Navy got me!"

"With a woman?" called another pirate incredulously. "*I* just got a *drink*—and I didn't even down half of it before they clocked me in the head and I woke up in the ship's boat."

Davies laughed as he uncorked a fresh bottle. "They got me with candy. I was fifteen, and walking home from the woodcarving shop where I was 'prenticed." He tipped the bottle up and took a long sip.

"They *can't!*" another man spoke up. "It's illegal! Apprentices younger than eighteen is exempt. You should have told the captain, Phil, he'd have put you back ashore with an apology."

"Queen Anne made that law in 1703, but I was pressed four years before that." Davies grinned and tilted the bottle up again, then wiped his moustache and said, "And they didn't make it *retroactive.*" He looked up at Chandagnac. "Yeah, have her lead him to a press gang."

"Uh . . . all right." Chandagnac had seen press gangs in action in several countries, though his age, or citizenship, or possibly an occasional discreet bribe from his father, had kept him from ever becoming their prey.

"Step right this way, sir," the female puppet said alluringly, slinking back inside the barrel. "We can have a drink before proceeding to other matters."

The other puppet's head bobbed idiotically. "I beg your pardon?"

"I say I know this place. We can get a *drink.*"

"Stink? I'll say. My word, no wonder, look at these rough lads, I'm not certain I—" The male puppet followed her inside, and then Chandagnac shook the puppets and rattled the toe of his boot against the back of the barrel. "Ow!" he had a rough voice yell, "Look out! Get him! That's it! Hold him down! And there you go, sir! May I be the first to congratulate you on having took up a life on the high seas."

Chandagnac had some hope of getting his story back into its accustomed channel, but his audience now demanded that he follow his unfortunate protagonist onto a Navy ship, and so he had to tip the barrel over onto its side to serve as the ship, and quickly snip-and-tack the woman's skirt into a pair of trousers so that various male roles could be taken by that puppet.

Prompted by his reminiscent audience, Chandagnac had the poor protagonist puppet—whose upper-class accent had by now disappeared—suffer all sorts of punishments at the hands of the feared and despised officers. He had an ear cut off for replying to an order in tones an officer chose to consider sarcastic, his teeth were knocked in with a belaying pin for some other offense, and then he was "flogged around the fleet," which apparently meant that he was ceremoniously boated to each of a number of ships in order to be flogged aboard each one. Finally the audience permitted him to jump ship at a tropical port and wade ashore. Several members of the audience seemed to lose interest at this point, and began singing, and a couple were fencing with sticks out beyond the circle.

Chandagnac continued despite the distractions, and had the runaway hiding in the jungle to await the arrival of some pirate boat that could use another sailor, but then the very old man leaped to his feet. "The spring!" the old man yelled. "The water that is foul even as it wells from the earth!"

"'At's right, governor," Skank said, "but you're interrupting the show."

"The faces in the spray! *Almas de los perditos!*"

"Pipe down, Sawney!" yelled someone else.

"Ah!" The old man looked around wide-eyed, then winked. *"Vinegar,"* he said then, as portentously as if he was telling them the password to the Heavenly Kingdom, "will drive lice away from your body."

"I am not a dog!" yelled the black man who had helped intimidate Chandagnac into giving this performance. It looked to Chandagnac as though the whole thing was degenerating into chaos.

"That's news Charlie Vane's crew needs more than we do, governor," said Davies. The pirate chief handed the old man the bottle he'd been working on, which was still more than half-full. "Why don't you go tell him?"

Governor Sawney took a long sip and then ambled away, back into the darkness, pausing twice to call out admonitory-sounding bits of Old Testament scripture.

At this point, to Chandagnac's relief, someone yelled that the food was ready. He left the puppets in the barrel and joined the rush to the cooking pot, where he was handed a board with a hot, wet, bloated-looking chicken on it. It smelled fairly good, though, for the bucket he'd seen emptied into the pot earlier had contained a curry that some other crew had found too spicy to be eaten, so he shucked his chicken out of its loosened skin and then impaled the bird on a stick and held it over the flames. Several of the pirates who also were less than enthusiastic about half-boiled chicken did the same, and after they'd all eaten, and chased the still-dubious food with more brandy, someone called out a proposal that the puppeteer should be made the official cook.

The idea drew assenting shouts, and Davies, who'd been among the number who had followed Chandagnac's cooking example, got drunkenly to his feet. "Get up, pup," he said to Chandagnac.

Choosing to regard the term of address as a diminutive of the word *puppeteer,* Chandagnac stood up—though not smiling.

"What's your name, pup?"

"John Chandagnac."

"Shandy-what?"

"Chandagnac." A board in the fire popped loudly, throwing sparks into the sky.

"Hell, boy, life's too short for names like that. Shandy's your name. And plenty of name it is, too, for a cook." He turned to the rest of the pirates, sprawled like battle casualties across the sand. "This here's Jack Shandy," he said, loudly enough to be heard over the perpetual babble. "He's the cook."

Everyone who comprehended it seemed, pleased, and Skank perched one of the unclaimed boiled chickens on a three-cornered hat and made Chandagnac wear it while draining a mug of rum.

After that the evening became, for the new cook, a long foggy blur punctuated by occasional clear impressions: he was splashing in the surf at one point, taking part in some complicated dance, and the music was a drumming that took in as counterpoint the surf roll and the warm wind rattling in the palms and even Chandagnac's own heartbeat; later he had broken free of it and had run ashore and then wandered for a long time between the water and the jungle, skirting the fires and whispering "John Chandagnac" over and over to himself, for with a new name assigned to him he could imagine forgetting the old one, out here in this world of murder and rum and small, vivid islands; and some time after that he saw a gang of naked children who had found his puppets and were making them dance, but weren't touching the wooden figures in any way, only cupping their hands near them, and each tack-head in the jigging puppets was glowing dull red; and then finally he found himself sitting in soft sand that would be even more comfortable to lie down in. He lay back, realized he still had the hat on, fumbled it off, accidentally thrust his hand into the cold chicken's abdomen, jackknifed up to vomit a couple of yards down the slope, then sank back again and slept.

Chapter Three

The summer of 1718 was not a typical one for the outlaw republic on New Providence Island. Traditionally the Caribbean pirates careened their larger vessels in the spring, and when the hulls were cleaned of weed and barnacles, and all rotten planks and cordage were replaced, they stocked the holds with food, water and the best of the winter's loot and then sailed off to the northwest, skating around the Berry Islands and the Biminis and then letting the eternal Gulf Stream assist them as they worked their way up the North American coastline. The governors of the English colonies generally welcomed the pirates, grateful for the prosperity their cut-rate goods brought, and the Caribbean in summer was a steamy breeding ground for malaria and yellow fever and every sort of flux, to say nothing of the hurricanes that chose that season, more often than not, to come slanting up westward from the open Atlantic beyond Barbados, ripping around Cuba and up into the Gulf of Mexico like spinning drill bits across a pane of glass, creating and splitting and even totally obliterating islands in their paths.

But it was July now, and the New Providence harbor was still crowded with sloops and schooners and brigantines, and even a couple of three-masted ships, and cooking fires still smudged the air above the huts and shacks and sailcloth tents along the beach, and the whores and black market wholesale buyers still sauntered among the crews and watched eagerly for incoming craft; for word had it that Woodes Rogers had been appointed governor of the island by King George, and was due to arrive with a Royal Navy escort any day now, bringing the King's Pardon for any pirates that wanted to renounce piracy, and the punishments prescribed by law for any that didn't.

The philosophy commonest among the New Providence residents in the early weeks of July was most frequently summed up in the phrase "Wait and see." A few, such as Philip Davies, were determined to be gone by the time Rogers arrived, and a few others, chiefly Charlie Vane and his crew, had resolved to stay and forcibly resist this incursion from the authorities across the Atlantic; but most of the pirates were inclined to accept the offer of amnesty, and eliminate from their futures the specter of the ceremonial silver oar carried by the executioner when he escorted a condemned pirate to the gibbet and the clergyman and the crowd and the last knot the pirate would ever have dealings with. And after all, if they didn't find life under the new regime an improvement, they could always steal a boat and follow the wind to some other island. Two hundred years ago the Spanish had made a point of stocking all their islands with pigs and cattle, and a man could do a lot worse than to live on some unmonitored shore, subsisting on fruit and fish and meat dried over the buccan fires; the buccaneer way of life had effectively ended a century ago when the Spaniards drove all such harmless beach-gypsies off their islands and onto the sea—and the Spaniards had soon regretted it, for the evicted buccaneers quickly became seagoing predators—but the islands were still there.

Oranges stippled the jungle now like bright gold coins on green satin and crushed velvet, and even the people who'd been raised in England followed the examples of the other races and graced their plain fare with tamarinds, papayas and mangoes; avocados by the hundreds hung fat and darkly green in the trees, often falling and thudding heavily to the sand and startling pirates who weren't accustomed to seeing the things in the season when they were ripe.

Cookery, in fact, had become a bigger part of daily life in the New Providence settlement, both because the imminent arrival of Woodes Rogers meant at least the postponement of piratical ventures, leaving people the time to pay more attention to what they ate, and because the ship's cook of the *Vociferous Carmichael* had not only proven to be competent, but had undertaken to prepare batches big enough to feed several crews in exchange for help in procuring the cooking supplies. In the three weeks since the *Carmichael* had arrived, for example, there had been seven "bouillabaisse endeavors," in which just about everyone, pirates and whores and black marketeers and children, waded out into the harbor at low tide, armed with nets and buckets, and dragged out of the sea enough animals of one sort and another for the cook to make a vast fish stew, and when the stuff was bubbling in the several huge pots over the fire on the beach, pungently aromatic with garlic and onion and saffron, they said incoming ships would smell the stew long before they'd see the island.

And as the month wore on and the days grew to their longest, at dinnertime more and more people had been drifting over to where Davies' crews clustered around the moored sloop *Jenny,* for the *Jenny* and the *Carmichael* were supposed to leave New Providence Island, taking the cook along, on Saturday the twenty-third.

On Friday afternoon the cook was rowing a boat up the harbor from the deep inlet where the *Carmichael* sat; the ship was restored to her normal upright position now, and had been pulled almost all the way back down into the water, and as Jack Shandy watched her recede, his muscled brown arms hauling on the oars and propelling the boat forward, he saw section after section of scaffolding, axed and pried loose from the hull, spin down and splash into the sea.

Before the end of the month, he told himself, I should be able to get to Kingston and get my credit situation established, and then get a boat to Port-au-Prince and pay a visit to the . . . family estate.

Now that he'd seen the colors of these western skies and seas and islands, he didn't feel nearly as disoriented by the drawing he'd seen in the letter his lawyer had found; the wide porches and windows of the Chandagnac house in Port-au-Prince, with the waving palms and giant tree ferns in the background and the parrots sketched flying overhead, now seemed much more attainable, much less like a drawing of imagined dwellings on the moon.

After the death of old François Chandagnac, his father, John's lawyer had located a hitherto unknown Chandagnac cousin in Bayonne, and this cousin had let them have a file of letters from an aunt in Haiti, where John had always vaguely understood he had a grandfather and an uncle. These letters, and then a lot of expensive research in obscure labyrinths of deeds, quitclaims, probate and birth and death records, had finally turned up the information which caused John Chandagnac to terminate his engagement to the daug ιter of a successful coal merchant, resign from his position with the textile firm and book passage aboard the *Vociferous Carmichael* to the far side of the globe: John learned that his grandfather in Haiti had, in his will, left his house, sugarcane plantation and considerable fortune to his eldest son François, John's father, and had then died in 1703; and that François' younger half-brother Sebastian, also a resident of Haiti, had produced forged documents to indicate that François was dead.

On the basis of this fraud, Sebastian had inherited the estate . . . and John Chandagnac's father, not even aware of the inheritance, had gone on giving his marionette performances, in ever-increasing poverty and ill health, until that last lonely night in Brussels in the winter of 1714. His uncle had, in effect, killed his father as well as robbed him.

Jack Shandy squinted now, and pulled harder on the oars as if that might get him into his uncle's presence sooner, as he remembered talking to the landlady of the shabby rooming house in which his father had died. John Chandagnac had gone there as soon as he'd heard of his father's death, and he plied the woman with quantities of syrupy Dutch gin to get her to focus her dim attention on the old puppeteer whose body had been carried down her stairs four days earlier. Finally she had remembered the incident. "*Ah, oui,*" she'd said, smiling and nodding, "*oui. C'etait impossible de savoir ci c'etait le froid ou la faim.*" His father had either frozen to death or starved, and there'd been no one there to notice which death had got him first.

Jack Shandy had no real plan, no particular idea of what he'd *do* when he got to Port-au-Prince—though he had brought his father's death certificate to show to the French authorities in Haiti—but his lawyer had told him that the charges would be virtually impossible to press from another country in another hemisphere, so he was bringing it to where his uncle Sebastian lived. He could only guess at what problems he would run into, difficulties of pressing criminal charges as an alien, hiring a resident attorney, ascertaining precisely which—if any!—*local* laws had been broken . . . he simply knew he had to *confront* his uncle, let the man know that his crime had been uncovered, and had led to the death of the cheated brother. . . .

Shandy hauled on the oars, and watched the long muscles flex in his arms and braced legs, and he allowed himself a grim smile. In addition to extra cannon, powder and shot, sorcerous apparatus—the tools of *vodun,* or voodoo—had been loaded aboard the *Carmichael,* and one magical procedure required the use of a large mirror; another pirate crew had acquired several, and had sold one to Woefully Fat, Davies' chief *bocor,* and Shandy had been given the job of getting the thing aboard. During the operation he had happened to face the mirror squarely—and for a moment he actually hadn't recognized himself, and thought he was looking at one of the pirates beyond the glass.

The weeks of laboring at reconditioning the *Carmichael* had broadened his shoulders, leaned his waist and given him a couple of new scars on his hands, and he realized that he'd have to stop thinking of himself as unshaven and admit he had a beard—sun-bleached in irregular blond streaks, as was his hair, which for convenience he now wore pulled back into a tarred pigtail—but it was the deep cigar-hued tan, acquired during weeks of shirtless work under the tropical sun, that really made him look indistinguishable from the wild men around him.

Yeah, he thought, I'll sneak onto Uncle Sebastian's pirated estate and then when he's walking around, routing poachers from the shrubbery or whatever it is the gentry does around here, I'll rise up all fearsome-looking and menace him with a cutlass.

Then his savage grin turned sheepish, for he remembered the last time he'd talked to Beth Hurwood. She had once again managed to elude Leo Friend, and Shandy and she had gone walking south along the beach in the relaxed hour after dinner when the breeze was cooling and the parrots were fluttering in raucous flocks overhead. Shandy had told her about seeing himself in the mirror, and how he'd thought for a moment that he was seeing one of the members of Davies' crew; "One of the *other* members, I guess I should say," he had added, with perhaps just a touch of adolescent pride in his voice.

Beth had laughed indulgently and taken his hand. "You're not a member, John," she said. "Could you have killed those sailors, or shot old Captain Chaworth?"

Sobered, and hoping his tan would conceal the sudden reddening of his face, he had muttered, "No."

They had walked without speaking for a while then, and Beth didn't take her hand from his until they reached the careened *Carmichael* and had to turn around.

Pulling a little harder on the left oar to slant the boat toward shore, he looked over his right shoulder and saw Skank and the others waiting for him beside the stack of Carrara marble slabs, which was at least visibly lower now than it had been that morning. Behind them the white beach, dazzling in the afternoon glare, sloped up to the tawdry litter of tents and shacks, and beyond that to the jungle. A woman in a tattered purple dress was trudging along the top of the sand slope.

Venner waded out when Shandy had got the boat into the shallows, and Shandy climbed over the gunwale and helped him drag it up onto the sand.

"I could row the next few lots over if yer gettin' tired, Jack," said Venner, his smile as constant as the sunburn across his broad shoulders. Behind him stood Mr. Bird, the black man who frequently thought someone had called him a dog.

"Naw, 'at's all right, Venner," Shandy said, crouching to get a grip on the topmost marble slab. He hoisted it up, stumped stiff-legged and grimacing to the boat, and then slid the stone over the gunwale and onto the rear thwart, and from there to the floor. "At the *Carmichael* they're lowering me a stout net, and I just loop it around each block and then wave 'em to lift." He walked back to the stack as Skank edged past him, carrying another one of the blocks.

"Good," said Venner, taking the other side of the next block Shandy crouched over. "Take it easy and don't lose no sweat nor blood is my way."

Shandy squinted thoughtfully at Venner as the two of them shambled toward the boat. Venner never seemed to do quite his share of any hard work, but the man *had* prevented Shandy from being killed on that day when Davies took the *Carmichael*, and his avoid-all-strain philosophy tempted Shandy to confide his escape plan to him. Venner must regard the upcoming enterprise as at least a regrettable strain, and if Shandy was going to hide ashore until the *Jenny* and the *Carmichael* had left, and then re-emerge and wait for the arrival of the new governor from England, a partner who knew the island and its customs would be valuable indeed.

Mr. Bird had picked up one of the blocks and was shambling along behind them, peering around suspiciously. Shandy was about to ask Venner to meet him after this job was finished, to discuss some pragmatic applications of his philosophy, but he heard a scuffing from up the slope and turned to see who was approaching.

It was the woman in the purple dress, and when he and Venner had disposed of their block, Shandy shaded his eyes to look at her.

"Howdy, Jack," she said, and Shandy realized it was Jim Bonny's wife.

"Hello, Ann," he said. It annoyed him to realize that, even though she was a big, chunky teenager with crooked teeth, his chest felt suddenly chilly inside, and his heart was thudding like a hammer into soft dirt. Though in Beth Hurwood's company he was a little ashamed of his beard and tarred hair and deep-bitten tan, when Bonny's wife was around he was furtively proud of them.

"Still *ballasting* that thing?" she said, nodding past him at the *Carmichael*. She had learned the term while watching him work one afternoon a few days ago.

"Yeah," he said, walking up out of the water and trying not to stare at her breasts, clearly visible under her carelessly buttoned blouse. He forced himself to keep his mind on his job. "At least this is the last of it, the moveable ballast. The *Carmichael* was awfully crank—heeled something terrible coming over sharply in a strong wind. Almost spilled us all right over the side when she came around to face the *Jenny* that day." He recalled the breakfast table tumbling across the poop deck, and the napkins spinning away into the sea directly below where he and Beth had clung to the rail and each other—and then he realized that his gaze had drifted back to Ann's bosom. He turned to the stack and took hold of another slab.

"Sounds like an awful lot of work," Ann said. "Do you have to do quite so much of it?"

He shrugged. "The seas and the weathers are what is; your vessels adapt to them or sink." He lifted the slab, turned his back on her and shuffled toward the boat, where Mr. Bird and Skank were lowering one in. Venner was sitting on the beach, making a show of worriedly scrutinizing the bottom of his foot.

Shandy's pulse and breathing were loud in his head, so he didn't hear Ann splashing along right behind him; Skank and Mr. Bird strode back ashore, and when Shandy straightened up from laying down his block, and turned around, he found himself being kissed.

Ann's arms were around him and her mouth was open, and against his bare chest he could feel her nipples right through the fabric of her blouse; like most people on the island she smelled of sweat and liquor, but in her case it was with such a female tang that Shandy forgot his resolutions about her and forgot Beth and his father and his uncle, and just brought his arms up and pulled her closer. The girl, together with the hot sun on his back and the warm water around his ankles, seemed for a moment to moor him to the island like some tree, animated only by biological promptings and reflexes and not even minimally self-aware.

Then he recollected himself and lowered his arms; she stepped back, grinning at him.

"What," Shandy began to croak, "what," he went on more strongly, "was *that* for?"

She laughed. "For? For luck, man."

"Heads up, Jack," said Skank quietly.

Jim Bonny was floundering down the slope, his round face red under a dark cloth, and his boots kicking up plumes of white sand. "Shandy you son of a bitch!" he was squalling. "You goddamn sneaking son of a bitch!"

Though apprehensive, Shandy faced him. "What do you want, Jim?" he called evenly.

Bonny halted in front of his wife with his boots just short of the water, and for a moment he seemed about to hit her. Then he hesitated, and his gaze fell away from hers, and he scowled across at Shandy. He fumbled a clasp knife out of his pocket—Shandy stepped back, snatching at his own—but when Bonny had unfolded his blade he pressed the point into the tip of his own left forefinger and flicked the blade outward, throwing a couple of drops of blood toward Shandy, and at the same time he began chanting a nonsensical multi-language rhyme.

Shandy noticed that the sun was suddenly hotter—shockingly hotter—and then Skank had leaped onto Jim Bonny's back from behind and knocked him forward onto his knees in the water, and then hopped off and planted a bare foot between the shoulders of Bonny's coat and shoved him onto his face in the shallows.

Bonny was floundering and splashing and cursing, but the sudden sweat was cooling on Shandy's face and shoulders, and

Skank waded in and kicked Bonny in the arm. "You ain't forgettin' any of the *rules* now, are you, Jim?" Skank asked. "No *vodun* offenses among us unless it's a declared *duel,* isn't that the way?" Bonny had been struggling to push himself up out of the water, but Skank kicked him again, harder, and he collapsed with a sputtering cry of protest.

Shandy glanced at Ann, and was a little surprised to see that she seemed concerned. Mr. Bird was watching with evident disapproval.

"You're no *bocor,*" Skank went on, "and there's pickney infants on the island that could set your head blazing like a torch and laugh at any lame *drogue* you could make to stop 'em with, but Shandy's new and don't know nothin' about all that. You think Davies'll be pleased if I tell him about this?"

Bonny had scuttled away, and now floundered to his feet. "But—but he was kissin' my—"

Skank threateningly took a step forward. "Think he will?"

Bonny retreated, splashing. "Don't tell him," he muttered.

"Get out of here," Skank told him. "Ann—you too."

Without meeting Shandy's eye, Ann followed her sopping husband back up the slope.

Shandy turned to Skank. "Thanks . . . for whatever."

"Ah, you'll learn." Skank looked toward the rowboat. "It's sitting low," he said. "One more block ought to make this load."

Shandy walked up to the rough wooden sled the marble blocks sat on—and then noticed Venner, who had not even stood up during the entire altercation. The man was smiling as amiably as ever, but all at once Shandy decided not to confide the escape plan to him.

Chapter Four

Because the *Carmichael* was to leave next morning, the talk around the fires that night was a fantastic fabric of speculations, warnings and impossible stories. Jack Shandy, insulated from the anxiety felt by the rest of Davies' crew, nevertheless listened with great interest to stories of ships crewed by zombies and glimpsed only at midnight by doomed men, of various magical precautions that would be necessary in Florida, so far from the protection of Mate Care-For and the rest of the *vodun loas,* of the Spaniards they might encounter in the Gulf of Mexico, and what tactics to use against them; old legends were retold, and Shandy heard the story of the pirate Pierre le Grand, who with a tiny boat and a handful of men took a galleon of the Spanish plate fleet fifty years earlier, and he heard a spirited version of the four-hour sea battle between the English *Charlotte Bailey* and the Spanish *Nuestra Señora de Lagrimas,* which ended with the sinking of both ships, and then for a while the pirates tried to outdo each other with stories about the suck-you-byes, female demons that weirdly and erotically occupied the last hours of men marooned on barren islands.

And the *Carmichael* was supposed to rendezvous with Black-beard's *Queen Ann's Revenge* in Florida, and so there was lots of gossip about that most colorful pirate chief, and speculations about why he was returning to that uncivilized shore where, a year or two ago, he had gone far inland in search of some sort of sorcerous power-focus and had come limping out days later, unsuccessful, sick, and infested with the ghosts that now plagued him as fleas would a dog.

Shandy had cooked up his best dinner yet, and, full and slightly drunk, was very much enjoying the evening . . . until he noticed the other members of the crew, the ones that weren't bravely drinking and laughing around the fire. Several had shuffled off to the sailcloth tents, and once when the wind slacked Shandy thought he heard quiet sobbing from that direction, and he saw Skank sitting in the dimness under a palm tree, carefully sharpening a dagger, an expression of intent concentration—almost of sadness—on his young face.

Shandy stood up and walked down to the shore. Just visible across the harbor's half mile of dark water was the silhouette of Hog Island against the stars, and nearer at hand he could see bare masts swaying gently to the breeze and the low swells. He heard the chuff of boots approaching from behind him, and when he turned back toward the fires he saw the lean figure of Philip Davies striding toward him, a bottle of wine in each hand. Behind him the settlement musicians had begun tuning up their random instruments.

"Here y'are," said Davies drunkenly. "Who deserves the best of the wine, if not the cook?" He held out one of the bottles, which for lack of a corkscrew had simply been broken off at the neck.

"Thank you, captain," said Shandy, taking the bottle and eyeing the jagged neck mistrustfully.

"Chateau Latour, 1702," Davies said, tilting up his own bottle for a swig.

Shandy sniffed his and then raised it and poured some into his mouth. It was the driest, smoothest Bordeaux he'd ever tasted—and his father and he had had some fine ones at times—but he kept any pleasure from showing in his face. "Huh," he said carelessly. "Wish I'd found some of this when I was scouting up ingredients for the stew."

"For the stew." Half of Davies' face was lit by the firelight, and Shandy saw it crinkle in a sour grin. "I was a youngster in Bristol, and one Christmas evening when I was just leaving the woodworking shop where I was 'prenticed, some street boys broke our window to snatch some stuff. What they didn't take they knocked over, and there was this . . ." He paused for a sip of the wine.

"There was this set of little carved choirboys, none of 'em bigger than your thumb, all painted nice, and I saw one of 'em fall out onto the snow, and one of the boys caught it with his toe as he ran off, and it ricocheted away down the street. And I remember thinking that whatever became of that little wooden fellow, he'd never again sit in that little slot he fell out of." Davies turned toward the harbor and breathed deeply of the sea breeze. "I know what you're planning," he said to Shandy over his shoulder. "You've heard about how Woodes Rogers is due here any day with the King's Pardon, so you're planning to slip away up the beach tonight, around out of sight of the settlement, and hide till the *Carmichael* leaves—no, don't interrupt, I'll let you talk in a moment—and then you'll walk back here and resume your cooking and lay about in the sun and the rum until Rogers arrives. Right?"

After a long pause, Shandy laughed softly and had another sip of the excellent wine. "It did seem feasible," he admitted.

Davies nodded and turned to face him. "Sure it did," he said, "but you're still thinking in terms of that shop window you fell out of, see? You won't *ever* get back to where you were." He had a slug from his bottle and then sighed and ran a hand through his tangled black hair.

"*First,*" Davies said, "it's a capital offense to jump ship in the middle of an enterprise, and so if you came wandering back into the settlement tomorrow after the *Carmichael* was gone, you'd be killed—regretfully, since you're a likeable lad and you can cook, but the rules are the rules. Remember Vanringham?"

Shandy nodded. Vanringham had been a cheerful boy of not more than eighteen, who'd been convicted of having hidden below when the brigantine he was in was fired on by a Royal Navy vessel. When the pirate ship had limped its way back to New Providence, its captain, a burly old veteran named Burgess, had let Vanringham believe that the prescribed penalty would be waived in consideration of his youth . . . and then that night after dinner Burgess walked up behind Vanringham and, with tears glinting in his eyes, for he liked the boy, put a pistol ball through Vanringham's head.

"*Second,*" Davies went on, "you *cut* me, after having surrendered. True, it was because I'd just killed your friend when I suppose I could have stopped him less lethally—but then he'd surrendered, too. In any case, you owe your life to the fact that I didn't care to have my showdown with Venner right then. But when I let you take the choice, it *wasn't* a choice between death on the one hand and three weeks of free food and drink on a tropical island on the other. You owe me hard service for that cut, and I'm not letting you out of the bargain you made."

The musicians, having found some basis for cooperation, began to play *Greensleeves,* and the melancholy old melody was at once so familiar and so out of place here—the tune rolling away down the lonely beach, bizarrely mocked by the cries of alarmed tropical birds—that it made all Old World things, and gods, and philosophies, seem distant and tenuous.

"And third," Davies said, the hard edge gone from his voice, "it may be that all those kings and merchants on the far side of the Atlantic are about to see the end of their involvement with these new lands. To them, Europe and Asia are still the chessboard that matters; they can't see this new world except in terms of two purposes: as a source of quick, careless profit, and as a dumping ground for criminals. It may be a . . . surprising crop, that springs up from such ploughing and sowing, and Rogers may find when he arrives that none of us need, nor could even benefit from, a pardon issued by a man who rules a cold little island on the other side of the world."

The sea breeze, a bit chilly now, whispered among the palms on Hog Island and made the pirates' fires flicker and jump.

Davies' words had upset Shandy, and not least because they seemed to take the righteousness out of the purpose he'd crossed the ocean for—suddenly his uncle's action seemed as impersonally pragmatic as the devouring of the baby sea turtles by the hungry sea gulls, and his own mission as ill-considered as an attempt to teach the gulls compassion. He opened his mouth to object, but was pre-empted by a call from the crowd around the fires behind him.

"Phil!" someone was yelling. "Cap'n Davies! Some of the boys is askin' questions too hard for me to answer!"

Davies dropped his bottle into the sand. "That's Venner," he said thoughtfully. "How did that move go? Over the blade and fake a poke inside, then when he parries across you duck under—but not all the way around—and hit him in the flank?"

Shandy shut his eyes and pictured it. "Right. And then run past him on his outside."

"Got it." Raising his voice, Davies said, "With you in a moment, Venner."

As the two men trudged back toward the fires, Davies pulled a pistol out of his belt. "If Venner plays me square I can handle him," he said quietly. "But if he doesn't, I want you to hang back with this and make sure no—" He stopped talking suddenly and gave a weary laugh. "Never mind. I forgot I was talking to the little wooden choirboy." He put the pistol away and lengthened his stride.

Shandy followed, angry with himself—partly for feeling bad at staying out of a squabble between pirates—like a child feeling bad about refusing a foolish dare!—but partly, too, at the same time, for staying out of it.

His petticoat breeches whirling out around his knees at each ponderous step, Leo Friend reached the bottom of the sandstone track that led down from the ruined fort, and, sweating profusely in the confinement of his fantastically ribboned doublet, struck out across the sand toward the fires where Davies' crew was. Beth Hurwood strode along next to him, sobbing with fury and trying to disentangle the mummified dog paw that Friend had shoved into her hair—"This'll protect you in case we get separated!" he'd snarled impatiently—just before dragging her out of her windowless room and unceremoniously propelling her ahead of him down the track.

Though she was having no difficulty in keeping up with the laboring young man, he turned around to face her every few steps, both to wheeze, "Hurry, can't you?" and to peer furtively down the neckline of her dress.

Damn all these delays, Friend thought, and damn the sort of fools we have to consort with in order to get to the focus in Florida! Why did it have to be ignorant, bickering brigands that found it? Though of course if a more savvy sort had found it, Hurwood and I wouldn't be able to manipulate them this way . . . and I gather this Blackbeard fellow is very nearly too clever for us anyway. He's hanging back now, letting us commit ourselves to this Florida trip before joining us; he *could* have got those protective Indian medicinal herbs just by *purchasing* them, for God's sake, but instead he has to blockade the entire city of Charles Town, capture nine ships and a whole crowd of hostages including a member of the Governor's Council, and then ask for the crate of medicinal herbs as ransom. I wish I knew, thought Friend, whether the man is just showing off, just keeping his crew in battle trim, or whether he's using all that spectacle to conceal some furtive *other* purpose. But what plans could the man have that would involve the all-too-civilized and law-and-orderly Carolina coast?

He glanced again at Beth Hurwood, who had finally pulled the dog paw free of her hair, and as she flung it away he whispered a quick phrase and caressed the air, and her dress flew up—but she forced it back down before he'd seen anything more than her knees. Oh, just wait, girl, he thought, his mouth going dry and his heart thumping even faster—soon enough you'll be so hungry for me you won't be able to take a deep breath.

Friend came blundering into the fireside crowd just as Davies entered it from the beach side. The pirate chief was grinning confidently, and Friend rolled his eyes in exasperation. Oh, spare us the brave show, captain, thought the fat physician; you're in no danger from anyone here . . . unless you really annoy *me* with your gallant *posturing*.

"Ah, here's our captain!" cried one of the pirates, a stocky red-haired man with a broad, freckled, smiling face; and though some of the men in the crowd were frowning angrily, Friend watched this smiling man, for he sensed that it was he who posed the threat. "Phil," the man said earnestly, "some of the lads here were wonderin' exactly what action we've worked so hard outfitting the *Carmichael* for, and how much profit we stand to take from it compared to what sorts of perils there be waitin'. I tried to answer 'em in general, but they want *specific* answers."

Davies laughed. "I'd have thought they'd all know better than to go to *you* for *specifics*, Venner," he said easily—though to Friend the apprehension behind the unconcerned pose was obvious.

Friend saw the new recruit—Elizabeth's friend, what was his name? Shandy, that was it—scuffling his way through the crowd behind Davies, and for a moment the physician considered engineering things so that the interfering puppeteer would be killed . . . or, better, maimed, rendered simple-minded by a blow to the head . . . but he regretfully decided that it would be difficult enough to restrain a crowd this big and wild from mutiny, without trying to get them to swat his personal fly at the same time.

He returned his attention to Venner, whose face, despite the smile, shone with sweat in the firelight. "That's what I told 'em, cap'n," he said, and for a moment the falsity of his smile must have been obvious to everyone present, "but several have said they plain won't sail if we be goin' to that damned place on the Florida coast where Thatch got infested by ghosts."

Davies shrugged. "Any of 'em who be not satisfied with my promise to make 'em rich, or who doubt my word on that, can see me privately to settle it. And any that want to desert in mid-endeavor know the prescribed penalties. Do you fit into any of those groups, Venner?"

Friend, peering in from the periphery, whispered and held up his hand.

Venner tried to reply, but produced only a choked grunt.

Should I have him provoke his own death, Friend wondered, or save him? Better let him live—there *is* real fear and anger in this crowd, and I don't want it stirred to a blaze. He whispered and gestured again, and Venner suddenly hunched forward and vomited onto the sand. The people near him drew away, and coarse laughter broke the tension.

Playing to the audience, Davies said, "I don't call that a responsive answer."

Friend's fat fingers danced in the air, and Venner straightened and said, loudly but haltingly, "No . . . Phil. I . . . trust you. I . . . *what's happening here? These aren't my* . . . I was just drunk, and wanted to . . . stir up a bit of trouble. All these lads . . . know you've got their best . . . *damn me!* . . . interests at heart."

Davies raised his eyebrows in surprise, then frowned suspiciously and peered around among the crowd; but Venner's words had been convincing enough for one pirate, who clumped up and punched the would-be mutineer in the face.

"Treacherous pig," the pirate muttered as Venner sat down in the sand, blood spilling from his nose. The man turned to Davies. "Your word sooner'n his, anytime, cap'n."

Davies smiled. "Try not to forget, Tom," he said mildly.

Out at the edge of the crowd, Friend smiled too—all this was so much easier here than it had been back in the eastern hemisphere—and then he turned to Elizabeth Hurwood. "We can return to the fort now," he told her.

She stared at him. "That's all? You ran down here, so fast I thought your heart was going to burst, just to see that man throw up and get hit?"

"I wanted to make sure that was all that did happen," said Friend impatiently. "Now come on."

"No," she said. "As long as we're here, I'll say hello to John."

Friend turned on her furiously, then caught himself. He smirked and raised his eyebrows. "The keel-scraper and brigand chef? I believe he's here," he said, simpering, "unless what I smell is a wet dog."

"Go back to the fort," she said wearily.

"So you c-can . . . have *c-c-congress* with him, I suppose?" sputtered Friend, his voice shrill with scorn. He wished he could refer to sexual matters without stuttering. "B-banish that thought, my d-d-d—Elizabeth. Your father commanded me not to let you out of my sight." He nodded virtuously.

"Do as you please then, you damned wretch," she said softly, and with a flash of uncharacteristic and unwelcome insight Friend realized she wasn't using *damned* as a mere adjective of emphasis. "I'm going to go and speak to him. Follow or not."

"I'll watch you from here," said Friend, and he raised his voice as she walked away from him: "Fear not I'd follow! I'd not subject my nostrils to proximity to the fellow!"

The confrontation by the fire being over and more or less settled, some of the pirates and prostitutes nearby looked toward Friend for further amusement—and evidently found some, for there were whisperings and guffaws and giggling behind jewel-studded hands.

Friend scowled and raised his hand, but already he could feel the strain in his mind, so he lowered his hand and made do with just saying, "Vermin!" and striding away to stand on a slight rise, his arms crossed dramatically, and staring at Hurwood's daughter. She had found the Shandy fellow, and they'd moved a dozen yards away to talk.

Despise me, he thought, all of you—you've only got about a week left to do it in.

For the first time in years, Friend thought about the old

man who had started him on the . . . he paused to savor the
phrase . . . the road to godhood. How old had Friend been?
About eight years old—but already he had learned Latin and
Greek, and had read Newton's *Principia* and Paracelsus' *De Sagis
Earumque Operibus* . . . and already, he now recalled, envy of his
intellect and his sturdy physique had begun to cause small-minded
people to dislike and fear him. Even his father, sensing and
resenting a greatness he could never hope to comprehend, had
abused him, tried to make him take up pointless physical exercises
and reduce his daily allotment of the sweets that provided him with
the blood sugar his body required; only his mother had truly
recognized his genius, and had seen to it that he didn't have to go
to school with other children. Yes, he'd been about eight when he'd
seen the ragged old man leaning in the back window of the pastry
shop.

The old fellow was obviously simple-minded, and drawn to the
window by the smell of fresh-cooked fruit pies, but he was
gesturing in an odd way, his hands making digging motions in
front of him as if they were encountering resistance in the empty
air; and for the first time in his life Friend's nose was irritated by
that smell that was like overheated metal.

Already graceful and sure-footed despite what everyone
thought about his bulk, Friend had silently climbed onto a box
behind the old man to be able to see in through the window—and
what he saw set his young heart thumping. A fresh pie was moving
jerkily through the air toward the window, and its hesitations and
jigglings corresponded exactly to the old man's gestures. The shop
girl was on her hands and knees in the far corner, too busy being
violently ill to notice the airborne pie, and every few seconds the
old man would let the pie pause while he gigglingly made other
gestures that, at a distance, disarranged the girl's clothing.

Tremendously excited, Friend had climbed down from the
box and hidden, and then a few minutes later followed the old man
as he gleefully pranced away with the stolen pie. The boy followed
the old man all that day, watching as he procured lunch and beer
and caused pretty girls' skirts to fly up over their heads, all simply
by gesturing and muttering, and little Leo Friend's breathing was
fast and shallow as it became clear that none of the people the old
man robbed or manhandled realized that the grinning, winking old

vagabond was responsible. That night the old man broke the lock of an unoccupied house and retired, yawning cavernously, within.

Friend was out in front of the house next morning, walking back and forth carrying the biggest, grandest cake he'd been able to buy with the money from his father's rent-box. It was a sight to arouse lust in any lover of sweets, and the boy had been careful to refrost it to conceal all evidence of the tampering he'd done.

After an hour and a half of plodding back and forth, his chubby arms aching cruelly with the torture of holding up the heavy cake, little Friend finally saw the old man emerge, yawning again but dressed now in a gaudy velvet coat with taffeta lining. Friend held the cake a bit higher as he walked past this time, and he exulted when, simultaneously, abruptly induced cramps knotted his stomach and the cake floated up out of his hands.

The cramp doubled the boy up and had him rolling on the pavement, but he forced himself to open his eyes against the pain and watch the levitating cake; it was rising straight up into the air, and then it shifted a bit and descended on the far side of the house. The giggling old man went back inside, and Friend's cramp relaxed. The boy struggled to his feet, hobbled up to the front door, and, silently, went in.

He heard the old man noisily gobbling the cake in another room, and Friend waited in the dusty entry hall until the chomping stopped and the whimpering began. He walked boldly into the next room then, and saw the old man rolling on the floor between indistinct, sheet-covered pieces of furniture. "I've got the medicine hidden," the boy piped up. "Tell me how you do your magic and I'll let you have it."

He had to repeat this a few times, more loudly, but eventually the old man had understood. Haltingly, and with much use of expressive gestures when his wretched vocabulary failed him, the old man had explained to the boy the basis for the exchange that was sorcery, as simple a concept, but as unevident, as the usefulness of a purchase and block and tackle to dramatically increase a pulling force. The boy grasped the notion quickly, but insisted that the old man actually teach him to move things at a distance before he'd fetch the antidote; and after young Friend had successfully impelled a couch against the ceiling hard enough to crack the plaster, the old man had begged him to end his pain.

Friend had laughingly obliged, and then scampered home, leaving the devastated corpse to be found by the house's tenants whenever they might return.

As he grew older, though, and studied the records of the ancient magics—all so tantalizingly consistent, from culture to culture!—he came to the bitter realization that the really splendid, godlike sorceries had, gradually over the millennia, become impossible. It was as if magic had once been a spring at which a sorceror could fill the vessel of himself to the vessel's capacity, but was now just damp dirt from which only a few drops could be wrung, and even that with difficulty . . . or as if there were invisible stepping-stones in the sky, but the sky had expanded and pulled them far apart, so that, though ancient magicians had been able to step up them with just a little stretching, it now took almost a lifetime's strength just to leap from one stone to the next.

But he worked with what remained, and by the time he was fifteen he was able to take anything he wanted, and he could make people do virtually anything, against their wills . . . and then he tried to give his mother, who alone had always had faith in him, access to this secret world he'd found. He could never remember exactly what had happened then . . . but he knew that his father had hit him, and that he had fled his parents' house and had not ever returned.

His sorcerous skills enabled him to live comfortably for the next five years as a student. The best of food, clothing and lodging were his for the reaching—though a profound mistrust of sex had kept him from doing anything more about that subject than to have disturbing, unremembered, sheet-fouling dreams—and so one day he was alarmed, as a man might be alarmed to realize that his usual daily dose of laudanum is no longer enough to sustain him, to realize that he wanted—needed—more than this.

For after all, it was not what he was able to take that made magic wonderful, but the *taking*, the violation of another person's will, the holding of the better hand, the perception of his own will staining the landscape in all directions; and so it was disquieting to realize that his violation of other people was not complete, that there were spots in the picture that resisted his will the way waxed areas on a lithographer's stone resist ink—he couldn't reach their minds. He could force people to do his bidding, but he couldn't force them to *want* to. And as long as there was the slightest tremor of protest or outrage in the minds of the people he used, then his domination of them, his absorption of them, was not absolute.

He needed it to be absolute . . . but until he met Benjamin Hurwood he'd thought it couldn't be done.

Chapter Five

"Why do you call him that?" Beth Hurwood asked irritably.

"What, *hunsi kanzo?*" said Shandy. "It's his title. I don't know, it seems too familiar to call him Thatch, and too theatrical to call him Blackbeard."

"His title? What does it mean?"

"It means he's a . . . an initiate. That he's been through the ordeal by fire."

"Initiated into what?" She seemed upset that Shandy should know all this.

Shandy started to speak, then shrugged. "All this magic stuff. Even living up there in the old fort, you must have noticed that magic is as much in use here as . . . as fire is back in England."

"I've observed that these people are superstitious, of course. I suppose all uneducated communities—" She froze, then stared at him. "Good Lord, John—*you* don't believe any of it, do you?"

Shandy frowned, and looked past the flickering fire to the jungle. "I won't insult you by being less than frank. This is a new world, and these pirates live much more intimately with it than the Europeans in Kingston and Cartagena and Port-au-Prince, who try to transplant as much of the Old World as they can. If you believe what's in the Old Testament you believe some weird things . . . and you shouldn't be too quick to dictate what is and isn't possible."

Mr. Bird flung his food away and leaped to his feet, glaring around at no one in particular. "I am not a dog!" he shouted angrily, his gold earrings flashing in the firelight. "You son of a bitch!"

Beth looked over at him in alarm, but Shandy smiled and muttered to her, "Nothing to worry about—it's a rare night that he doesn't do this at least once. Whatever it is he's angry about has nothing to do with New Providence Island or 1718."

"God damn you!" shouted Mr. Bird. "I am not a *dog!* I am not a *dog!* I am not a *dog!*"

"I guess someone called him a dog once," Shandy said quietly, "and when he has a few drinks he remembers it."

"Evidently," agreed Beth bleakly. "But John, do you mean to tell me you . . . I don't know . . . carry charms so you'll be protected by this Mate Care-For?"

"No," said Shandy, "but I remember firing a pistol at your physician's stomach when *he* was carrying such a charm, that day Davies took the *Carmichael.*

"And listen, during the first week we were here, I caught a chicken and cooked it and ate it, and next day I came down with a bad fever. Old Governor Sawney was wandering by, jabbering and swatting invisible flies the way he does, and he saw me sweating and moaning in my tent, and right away he asked me if I'd eaten a chicken with words written on its beak. Well, I *had* noticed markings on its beak, and I admitted it. 'I thought so,' says the governor. 'That's the chicken I magicked Rouncivel's fever into. Never eat 'em if there's writing on their beaks—you'll get whatever it was someone wanted to get rid of.' And then he got another chicken, and did his tricks, and I was recovered next morning."

"Oh, John," Beth said, "don't tell me you think his tricks *cured* you!"

Shandy shrugged, a little irritably. "I wouldn't eat that chicken." He decided not even to try to tell her about the man he'd seen down the beach one night. The man's pockets had all been torn open, and he didn't speak because his jaw was bound up in a cloth that was knotted over his head. As he had walked past Shandy, Shandy had noticed that his coat was sewn shut rather than buttoned. There was no point in telling her about it, or what he'd later learned about people who were dressed that way.

She dismissed the subject with an impatient wave. "John," she said urgently, "Friend won't let me stay long—can *you* tell me where it is we're sailing for, tomorrow morning?"

Shandy blinked at her. "*You're* not going, are you?"

"Yes. My father—"

"But are you *certain*? I'd have thought that, with Woodes Rogers due here any day, the obvious thing for your father to do would be—"

"Yes, John, I'm certain. I saw my father today, the first time I've seen him in a week or so, and of course he was carrying that little wooden box that smells so bad, and he told me I'm going along. He went on and on about how thoroughly I'd be protected from any injuries or ailments—but he wouldn't say a word about where we're going, or why."

"Jesus." Shandy took a deep breath and then let it out. "Well, Davies hasn't said either, but the rumor is that we're headed for a place on the Florida west coast, a place where the *huns*—uh, where Blackbeard accidentally let a number of ghosts attach themselves to him." He smiled nervously at her. "Something like lamprey eels, I gather; or leeches. And," he added, hoping he was concealing the apprehension he felt, "we'll rendezvous there with Blackbeard himself."

"God help us," she said softly.

And Mate Care-For too, thought Shandy.

With a lot of impressive swishing and spraying of sand and audible grunts of effort, Friend came waddling and arm-swinging over to them. "That's . . . enough, Elizabeth," he panted. "Dinner awaits us . . . at the fort." He mopped his forehead with a lacy handkerchief.

Beth Hurwood looked toward the pirates' cooking pots so longingly that Shandy asked, "Dinner?"

"Herbs and greens and black bread," she sighed.

"Plain but wholesome," pronounced Friend. "We have to keep her healthy." He too glanced toward the pots, briefly feigned gagging, then took Beth's arm and led her away.

A couple of the people nearby laughed and told Shandy that such things were to be expected, that girls always chose men with good looks over ones that had nothing but honest hearts.

Shandy laughed too, if a little forcedly, and said he thought it was more Friend's unfailing cheer and life-of-the-party attitude that did it. He turned down an offer of more stew but accepted another beheaded bottle of Latour, and he plodded away from the fires south along the beach toward the *Carmichael*.

The ship's bow was still up in the narrow inlet, supported by a stout wooden framework and a last couple of cables moored to trees, and the stern sat very low out in the harbor; but in spite of her present awkward posture she seemed much more like his ship now than she had during the month he'd been a passenger on her. He knew her intimately now—he'd been up scrambling like an ape in the high spars when they rerigged her, he'd swung an axe when they chopped down the forecastle structure and most of the railing, he'd sweated with saw and drill when they opened new ports for more cannon, and, for more hours than he could yet bear to remember, he'd sat in a sling halfway between the gunwale above and the sand or water below, and, foot by foot, chiseled charred seaweed and barnacles off her hull and dug out the teredo worms, and hammered into the wood little brass *drogues,* carved and chanted over by Davies' *bocor* to be powerful antiworm charms.

And, he thought now as he approached her, tomorrow we tow her the rest of the way into the water, tighten the shrouds, and sail away. And my life as a pirate will commence.

He noticed that there was someone sitting in the sand under the high arch of the bow, and after a moment of peering he saw by the moonlight that it was the mad old man the pirates always addressed as "governor"—possibly because of uncertainty about his name, which Shandy had variously heard rendered as Sawney, Gonsey and 'Pon-sea. The scene before Shandy—the old man sitting under ship's bow—reminded him of something that eluded him . . . but, oddly, he knew it was some picture or story that, by the comparison, lent a sad dignity to old Sawney. It startled Shandy to see the old lunatic, even by analogy, as something more than a sorcerously clever but half-witted clown.

Then he remembered what the scene reminded him of: the age-crippled Jason, sitting under the hull of the beached and abandoned *Argo.*

"Who's that?" the old man quavered when he heard Shandy's boots in the sand.

"Jack Shandy, governor. Just wanted one last look at her in this position."

"Did you bring me a drink?"

"Uh, yes." Shandy paused, took several deep gulps, and then handed the half-full bottle to the old man.

"You sail tomorrow?"

"Right," said Shandy, surprised that the old man knew it and had remembered it.

"To join the *hunsi kanzo* and his puppy."

Shandy squinted at the old man and wondered if he really was in one of his lucid periods after all. "His puppy?"

"Bonnett. I seen you playing at the poopets, you know about makin' the little fellows jump when you got the strings on 'em."

"Oh. Yeah." Shandy had heard of the new pirate Stede Bonnett, who'd recently, inexplicably, left behind a prosperous Barbados plantation in order to "go on the account," but he hadn't heard that the man had any connection with Blackbeard; of course old Sawney was hardly a reliable source.

"North, ye be goin', I hear," the governor went on. He paused to gulp some wine. "To *Florida.*" He pronounced it with a strong Spanish accent. "Beautiful name, but fever country. I know the area. I've killed quite a few Carib Indians around there, and took a nasty arrow wound from 'em once. You want to watch out for 'em— they're the meanest. Cannibals. They keep pens of women and children from other tribes . . . the way we'd keep pens of cattle."

Shandy didn't believe this, but to be polite he whistled and shook his head. "Damnation," he said. "I'll steer clear of 'em."

"See you do . . . until you get to that damned geyser, anyway. After that, if you know how to handle it, you got nothing to worry about."

"That's what I want," agreed Shandy. "Nothing to worry about."

The governor chuckled and replied in Spanish, but though Shandy was learning the crude Spanish of the mongrel pirates, the governor's dialect foiled him. It seemed at once too archaic and too pure. The old man finished, though, with an obscene suggestion, in all-too-fluent English, of what capabilities Blackbeard hoped to acquire by this trip.

Shandy laughed weakly, bade the old man farewell, and walked back the way he had come. After a couple of dozen paces he crested a sand dune, and he stopped and looked back at the ship. She was slightly heeled toward him, and he could see most of the quarterdeck and an end-on edge of the poop deck out over the water to his left. He tried to determine where Chaworth had died, and where he had stabbed Davies, and where he and Beth had stood when they'd tossed maggotty biscuits to that sea gull. He noticed that the section of rail they'd leaned on was cut away now, and it bothered him a little that he couldn't remember whether or not that was a section he'd cut down himself.

He tried to imagine what other sorts of events might eventually take place on that deck, and after a moment he was startled to realize that he instinctively imagined himself as being present during them. But that's wrong, he told himself with a nervous smile. Beth and I will be jumping ship at the first opportunity. This ship will go on without me, in spite of all the sweat of mine—and blood, sometimes, when a chisel would slip—that's soaked into her wood. I've got an uncle who needs hanging.

He turned back toward the fires and started walking again, and it occurred to him that he wasn't far from the spot where he'd seen the man with the torn pockets and the bound-up jaw; and the memory of it made him walk a little faster, not because the man had looked threatening, but because of what Davies had said when Shandy told him about it.

Davies had spat and shaken his head in annoyance. "That'll be Duplessis, from Thatch's last stop here. Thatch never takes time to do the little things right anymore. Duplessis was a *bocor,* and he bought a lot of *loas,* and that creates a debt even death can't free you from. I guess Thatch buried him without all the proper restraints."

Shandy had stared. "Buried him?"

Davies grinned at him, and in a contemptuously faked upper-class accent quoted the punch line of the old joke: "Had to—dead, you know." Resuming his normal tone, he went on, "At least Thatch didn't bury him with his boots on. Ghosts like to wander onto the boats, and if they're shod, you can't sleep for them clumping about all night."

When Shandy got back to the fires, most of the pirates had either wandered off to the huts or had settled down with bottles for serious, laconic, all-night drinking; Shandy decided that he had drunk enough to be able to sleep, and he started for the planks-and-sailcloth lean-to he'd built for himself up under the trees. He walked up the sand slope, but halted when, from ahead, a voice as deep as an organ at the bottom of a mine shaft called quietly to him to stop. Shandy peered, trying to see by the shifting, dappled moonlight under the palm trees, and finally made out a giant black figure seated cross-legged in an outlined and carefully cleared circle in the sand.

"Don't enter the circle," the figure said to him without looking around, and Shandy belatedly recognized Woefully Fat, Davies' *bocor*. The man was supposed to be deaf, so Shandy just nodded—realizing as he did that it was of even less use than speaking, since the man was looking away—and shuffled back a step or two.

Woefully Fat didn't look around. He was digging at the air with the wooden knife he always carried, and he seemed to be having trouble moving it through the air. "*Raasclaat*," he swore softly, then rumbled, "Ah cain't quite get the faastie bastards to behave. Been reasonin' with 'em all naht." The *bocor* had been raised in Virginia, and, being deaf, had never lost that accent.

"Uh . . . ," Shandy said uncertainly, looking around and trying to remember the nearest alternate route up the slope, for Woefully Fat had this way blocked, "uh, why don't I . . ."

The *bocor*'s arm came up suddenly, pointing the wooden knife at the sky.

Shandy automatically looked up, and between the shaggy blacknesses of two palms he saw a brief shooting star, like a line of luminous chalk on a distant slate. Thirty seconds later the wind stopped . . . then resumed, a little more strongly.

Woefully Fat lowered his arm and stood up—lithely, in spite of his awesome bulk. He turned and gave Shandy an unreassuring smile and stood aside. "Go ahead," he said. " 'Tain't nothin' now but a line drawed in the sand."

". . . Thanks." Shandy edged past the giant, skipped quickly over the circle and walked on.

He heard Woefully Fat striding away toward the beach; the huge *bocor* chuckled and, in his low but eerily carrying voice, said, "*C'etait impossible de savoir ci c'etait le froid ou la faim.*" Then, chuckling again, he receded out of Shandy's hearing.

Shandy paused, and for several minutes stared after the man restlessly, as if he might follow; then he glanced uneasily up at the stars, and picked his way silently to his lean-to, glad that he'd set it up under a particularly thick ceiling of greenery.

Chapter Six

Davies might not have slept—when dawn was still just a dim blue glow behind the palms on Hog Island he flung someone's old cape over the dusty white coals of one of last night's fires, and as the garment ballooned up, began smoldering and then erupted in flame, he strode around shouting, pulling the hair and beards of sleepers and kicking support poles out from under makeshift tents. The groaning pirates struggled up and shambled to the fire, many of them dragging pieces of their soon to be abandoned tents and shacks to throw onto the revived flames, and Davies gave them time to heat a pot of rum-and-ale, and swallow enough of the pungent restorative to ready them for work, before he got them trooping down the beach to where the *Carmichael* sat.

For an hour they strung up and hauled on—then took down and rearranged—various complicated webs of blocks and line, and swore terrible oaths, and fell into the water, and wept with rage . . . but when the sun was up the ship was in the water, and Davies was striding back and forth on the poop deck, calling directions to the sail-handlers and the men on the sloop *Jenny,* which was towing the ship. For another hour the *Carmichael* slowly zigzagged along the deepest channels of the harbor, working under minimum sail and frequently stopping altogether while Davies and Hodge, who was captaining the *Jenny,* shouted at each other, and the early rising members of the crews of other vessels stood on the beach and called rude suggestions across the brightening water;

but eventually the ship was in the north mouth of the harbor, and then past it and into the deeper water that edged the Northeast Providence Channel, and Davies ordered all canvas spread, even the studdingsails that flanked the mainsails, and all three of the triangular jibs along the bowsprit. The tow cable was released, and both vessels picked up speed; their sails bright in the morning sun, they slanted away to the northwest.

Davies had claimed that the principles of sailing were better learned on a boat than on a ship, so Shandy was helping to crew the *Jenny.* After having become so familiar with the *Carmichael,* the *Jenny* with her single mast and fore-and-aft sails seemed like little more than a turtle boat to him; but she did carry fourteen small cannon and twelve swivel guns, and when they had crowded on sail after releasing the tow cable, he could feel through the soles of his bare feet that she was potentially a much faster vessel.

The *Carmichael* took the lead, though, and Shandy, who'd been told to stand idle and stay out of everybody's way until they were comfortably out at sea, crouched on the hardly table-sized forecastle deck and watched the ship surge along majestically a couple of hundred yards ahead, and he wondered what spot Beth had found to stay out of the way in, now that the ship had been so ruthlessly streamlined.

"Here y'go, Jack," said Skank, handing Shandy a wooden cup full of rum before lurching back to help trim the jib sheet. "Any more and I pitch over the side."

"Thanks," said Shandy, accepting it cautiously and wondering if these people were ever completely sober. He looked back over the port quarter and watched the jagged green and purple pile that was New Providence Island recede away behind them on the crystal blue face of the sea. It occurred to him that in some ways he would miss the place.

Skank ambled back up to the forecastle and leaned on one of the swivel gun posts. "Yeah," he said, as if agreeing to something Shandy had said, "we may never go back there again. Next year it'll be harder to sell our take, 'cause there won't be the usual agreed-on place for the rich island merchants to send their buyers to."

Shandy sipped the rum. "Rich merchants deal with pirates?"

"Well, sure—how do you think they got rich? And stay it? Of course they generally didn't come over in *person*—they'd send their foremen and trusted fellows like that to arrange the buys.

Sometimes for big money deals we'd even deliver the stuff; lots of moonless nights I've hauled a heavy-loaded boat with muffled oars into some nowhere cove in Jamaica or Haiti or Barbados. The whole thing makes sense for everybody, of course; we can sell goods to 'em tremendous cheap, since we didn't pay for 'em atall."

Not for quite everybody, Shandy thought. "These merchants you sell to—do they know the stuff's stolen?"

"Oh, sure, Jack, how could they not? In fact, some can even afford to bribe the Royal Navy shore patrols to be lookin' somewhere else when we ferry it in. And Thatch himself set up most of our contacts with the really rich ones: Bonnet on Barbados—of course he's turned pirate himself now, I can't quite understand that—and Lapin and Shander-knack on Haiti, and—"

"*Who* on Haiti?" Shandy took hold of a taut shroud to steady himself, and he had to consciously keep from dropping the cup.

"Lapin—that means rabbit, they say, kind of fits the man, actually—and Shander-knack or however Frenchies pronounce it really." Skank frowned drunkenly. "Your real name is something like that, ain't it?"

"A little like it." Shandy took a deep breath and let it out. "Does this . . . Shander-knack character have a lot of dealings with y— with us?"

"Oh, aye, he's a *speculator*. Thatch does love comin' across a *speculator*. That sort is always just about to get rich, you know, but somehow if you come back in a year they're still just about to. When they have money they can't wait to give it to us, and when they don't have it they want credit—and with rich citizens Thatch is happy to give it to 'em."

"Must be a hard sort of debt to *enforce*, though," Shandy mused.

Skank gave him a pitying smile, pushed away from the swivel gun post and ambled back aft.

Shandy stayed on the forecastle, and a smile slowly deepened the lines in his dark face, and his eyes narrowed in anticipation of the day when he'd be able to use this new bit of information against his uncle. He was glad the pirates were only going to an uninhabited section of the Florida coast, and not aiming at some fray, for it would be unthinkable for him to be killed before dealing with his father's brother.

As soon as they had got north of the Bahama shoals and were

into the deep blue water of the Providence Channel, Shandy was summoned aft by Hodge, the *Jenny*'s lean, grinning skipper, and told that he would now begin to earn his keep . . . and for the next five hours Shandy was kept exhaustingly busy. He learned to hoist the peak of the gaff-spar until a few wrinkles were visible in the mainsail, running parallel to the spar, and not just so that the sail was smooth, as looked to him to be more correct; he had already grasped the baffling fact that sheets and shrouds were ropes, not sails, but now he learned some of the tricks of using the sheets to oppose the sails most profitably against the wind, and, the *Jenny* being so much more nimble than the *Carmichael* that Hodge decided to let the new recruit get a taste of maneuvering tactics, he learned the principles of tacking into the wind, and when to let a shift in the headwind be a cue to tack; he learned to glance up at the wooden hoops that held the mainsail to the mast, and to know by their trembling when the boat should bear slightly away from the wind for maximum speed.

As if to help out with Shandy's education, the cauliflower bump of a cumulo-nimbus cloud appeared on the eastern horizon, and though it must have been many miles away, Hodge got everyone busy preparing for a storm, "taking in the laundry," as Hodge referred to reefing the sails, and getting a white-haired old *bocor* up on deck to whistle a Dahomey wind-quelling tune, and restringing some of the shrouds so that loose sheets or likely-to-break spars wouldn't foul them.

The squall crawled blackly across the cobalt blue of the sky and was on them within an hour of its first sighting—Shandy, who'd never had occasion to pay particular attention to the weather, was awed by its speed—and even just under the minimum working canvas the boat heeled when the wind buffeted her.

Hard-driving rain followed a minute later, giving the waves a steamy, blurred look and making a gray silhouette of the *Carmichael*. Hodge ordered all shrouds loosened against the inevitable shrinking, and Shandy was surprised that the skipper didn't seem at all dismayed by the storm.

"This anything serious?" he called nervously to Hodge.

"This?" replied Hodge, shouting against the drumming of the rain on the deck. "Nah. Just enough to dry your clothes. Now if the *rain* had come first, we might be in some trouble."

Shandy nodded and went back up to the forecastle. The rain

wasn't uncomfortably cold, and, as Hodge had pointed out, it would be pleasant to have the salt washed out of his clothes so that tomorrow they would—for once—dry out completely. The first fury of the downpour had abated, and the *Carmichael* was again clearly visible ahead. Chandagnac knew that in a few hours he'd be crawling below, still in his sopping wet clothes, to find a corner to sleep in, and he hoped Beth Hurwood was finding more comfortable accommodations aboard the ship. He leaned back and let his aching muscles relax for the next task Hodge would set for him.

The next day's leisure moments were spent in gunnery practice, and Shandy, always good at things demanding dexterity, was soon an expert at the tricky craft of aiming a swivel gun and touching a slow match to the vent without either jiggling the long barrel out of line or scorching out an eye when the powder charge went off. When he'd rapidly blown to splinters six in a row of the empty crates that the men aboard the *Carmichael* were dropping overboard for targets, Hodge had Shandy switch from pupil to instructor, and by dusk every man on the boat was at least a somewhat better marksman than he had been that morning.

On the third day they did more maneuvering practice, and in the afternoon Shandy was allowed to take the tiller and give the commands, and in a period of twenty minutes he piloted the sloop in a long but complete circle around the *Carmichael*. Emergency drills followed, and when they were practicing battle tactics Davies helpfully fired a couple of the *Carmichael*'s cannons into the water near them to make it seem more realistic.

Shandy was proud of the way he could scramble around on the decks and in the rigging now, and of the fact that—though many of the pirates protested against these energetic activities—he was only pleasantly tired when the lowering, ambering sun began to bounce needles of gold glare off the waves ahead; but his pleasure in his seamanship evaporated when Davies, yelling across the water, told them that too much time had been lost last night when they had laid to, and that tonight they would keep sailing straight through to dawn.

Shandy was assigned the midnight-to-four watch, and the first thing he learned when he crawled up onto the deck was that night sailing was wet and cold. The dew was heavy, and made even the rough deck planks slick, and every length of rigging he grabbed on the way aft spilled chilly water down his sleeve. Hodge was sitting behind the bittacle-pillar, his humorous, angular face weirdly lit from below by the red-glassed bittacle lamp that let him watch the compass without being dazzled; to Shandy's relief, the jobs the skipper gave him were easy and infrequent: periodically take a lantern and check certain recalcitrant sections of the rigging, keep watch ahead against the long chance that another vessel might be somewhere nearby on the vast face of the sea tonight, and make sure the lamp on the bow stayed lit and kept casting the dim glow that prevented the *Carmichael's* night helmsman from either crowding the sloop or bearing too far off.

The *Carmichael* was a flapping, creaking tower of darkness on the starboard side, but sometimes Shandy stood by the port rail and stared out across the miles of moonlit ocean, sleepily wondering if he didn't see heads and upraised, beckoning arms in the farther middle distance, and faintly hear choirs singing an eternal two-toned song as old as the tides.

At four Hodge gave him a cup of rum warmed over the bittacle lamp, told him who to rouse and send up for a replacement, and then sent him below to sleep for as long as he could.

It was at about noon of the next day, Tuesday the twenty-sixth of June, just as the two vessels encountered the north-flowing Gulf Stream between the Bimini Islands and Florida, that the Royal Navy man-of-war found them.

When it was first sighted, a white fleck on the southern horizon, it had seemed to be a merchant ship of about the *Carmichael's* size, and several of the pirates half-heartedly proposed taking it instead of going to Florida; then a few minutes later the man in the bow with the telescope shouted, excitedly, the news that it was a British Navy vessel.

In the first few minutes after this discovery there was tension but no panic, for the *Carmichael* had been altered for maximum speed and the *Jenny* could easily tack back to the Bimini shoals, where the water in many areas was twelve feet deep or less—the *Jenny* only drew eight feet of water, and could skate safely over shoals the man-of-war wouldn't dare approach.

But the *Carmichael* surged steadily along on her southwest course, her sails bright and unshifting in the tropical sunlight, and Hodge didn't call to have the *Jenny* come about.

"Why do we wait, cap'n?" queried one bare-chested, white-bearded giant. "We might not be able to lose 'em if they get too close."

Shandy was crouched on the starboard rail beside the horizontal bar—which was called, for some reason, the cathead—that supported the hoisted anchor, and he looked expectantly at Hodge. Shandy thought he saw a new pallor under the man's tan, but the captain swore foully and shook his head. "We'd lose a day, at least, outrunning them and sneaking around back onto course, and with Saturday's rain and that damn layover Sunday night we'll already have to work her thefty to get to the rendezvous in Florida by Lammas Eve. No, lads, this is one time the Navy can run. But hell, the *Carmichael* is at least as well armed as yonder man-o'-war, and we're no fishing boat ourselves, and we've still got Mate Care-For and Legba and Bosu up our sleeves."

The burly old man stared at Hodge in disbelief; then as if explaining something to a child, he pointed at the no longer distant sails and said distinctly, "Henry—it's the bleeding *Royal Navy.*"

Hodge turned on him angrily. "And we're in *action,* Isaac, and I'm the captain here today, and Davies' quartermaster besides. God's blood, man, do you think *I* like these orders? The *hunsi kanzo* will have us all for zombies if we back off now—but in going on all we risk is death."

To Shandy's uneasy surprise the crew found this logic unfortunate but unassailable, and they set hastily about preparing for combat. The lighter sails were reefed and a couple of men were sent aloft with buckets of alum solution to splash onto the sails to keep them from burning, the shrouds were replaced with lengths of chain, the cannons were trundled forward so that their muzzles poked out of the ports, the *bocor* went to the bow and began chanting and flinging shards of carefully broken mirror toward the British ship, and Shandy was ordered to fill all available buckets with sea water and soak a spare sail and then clump all of it around the powder kegs.

During the last three weeks Shandy had been taking some satisfaction in how well he'd behaved when the *Carmichael* was originally taken, but now, watching his own hands tremble while dragging another bucket of sea water up over the high gunwale, he realized that his relative coolness on that day had been a result of shock, and, even more than that, of ignorance: for he had hardly grasped the fact that he was truly in trouble before he was out of it. This time, though, the trouble was approaching with torturing slowness, and this time he knew in advance exactly how a man died of a gunshot wound in the head, or a saber chop in the abdomen.

This time he was so terrified that he felt drunk—all colors were too vivid, all sounds too loud, he felt suspended halfway between weeping and vomiting, and he had to keep thinking about not wetting his pants.

When he'd got the powder kegs surrounded with full buckets and draped over with wet canvas, he hurried back up to the deck, where he was grabbed, handed a smoldering match-cord, and hustled to the starboard bow swivel gun. "Don't shoot till Hodge says, Jack," snapped the man who'd shoved him at the gun, "and then make it count."

Looking out ahead over the pitted muzzle of his gun, Shandy saw that all three vessels were slanting east, into the wind, the *Carmichael* and the *Jenny* more sharply than the man-of-war— which was in three-quarter profile to him now, the beige-and-black checkerboard pattern of her gunports visible along her port side.

I *can't* fire on a Royal Navy vessel, he thought. But if I refuse to shoot, these men will kill me . . . as a matter of fact, if I don't do a good job here, the Royal Navy may very well kill me, along with everyone else on the *Jenny*. My God, there simply *isn't* an acceptable course of action for me.

A white plume of smoke jetted from the Navy ship's side, and a moment later the cannon's hollow drumbeat rolled across the half mile of blue water that separated the vessels, and a moment after that a towering splash bloomed on the sea face to Shandy's left, stood for an instant, and then fell back like an upflung shovelful of diamonds.

"That's past us," called the tension-shrill voice of Hodge. "She's in range—fire!"

And, as many soldiers have been surprised to discover, the intensive, exhaustingly repetitive training he had received made obeying the order automatic; he had aimed, touched the match-end to the vent, and stepped back to the next gun before he'd even made up his mind whether or not to obey the order. Well you're in it now, he thought despairingly as he aimed the second gun; you may as well work hard for the side you've cast your lot with.

As he touched the match-cord to the second gun's vent, the

sloop's seven starboard cannons all went off at more or less the same instant, and the boat, which he hadn't realized until now was heeled over to starboard, was kicked almost back up to level by the recoil.

Then the *Vociferous Carmichael,* moving awesomely fast for the bulk of her, swept into the smoke-veiled gap between the man-of-war and the *Jenny,* close enough so that Shandy could clearly recognize the men in her rigging and hear Davies shout, *"Fire!"* an instant before the *Carmichael's* starboard guns went off with a sound like close thunder, rendering the man-of-war's sails quite invisible for a moment behind a churning mountain range of white smoke.

The *Jenny* was maintaining her sharp turn to windward, following the *Carmichael,* and when the cannon smoke was left behind, Shandy was horrified to see the man-of-war, apparently unhurt, pacing the *Jenny* only a hundred yards away; but when Skank had grabbed him again and flung him onto another swivel gun, and he automatically sighted along the barrel at the bigger vessel, he realized that the man-of-war was not undamaged after all—the safety net over her waist was bouncing and angular with fallen spars, and the checkerboard pattern of the gunports was marred by a half-dozen fresh, ragged holes—and he realized too that the *Jenny* was moving faster than the Navy ship and would in a minute or so be safely out in front of her. Almost certainly against orders, Davies had driven through and punched the man-of-war to buy the *Jenny* time to get away.

"Hit a forward gun port!" Skank yelled, and Shandy obediently aimed at one of the gleaming cannon muzzles poking out of the Navy ship's bow and touched his match-cord to the vent. His gun went off with a jolting boom, and squinting through the acrid smoke he was pleased to see dust and splinters fly from the port he'd been aiming at.

"Good!" snarled Skank. "Now hit 'em—"

Smoke erupted from the remaining guns in the man-of-war's flank but the roar of the cannon fire was lost in the sudden hammering crash that swept the *Jenny,* and Shandy was slammed violently away from his gun and flung tumbling into the mass of men behind him. Deafened and stunned, he wound up sprawled across a motionless body, trying to get air into his lungs without choking on all the blood and pieces of tooth in his mouth. Over the ringing in his ears he was aware of shouts of rage and panic, and of a new, sluggish shifting of the deck under him.

Hodge was shouting orders, and Shandy finally rolled over and sat up, coughing and spitting. Fearfully he looked down at his body, and he was profoundly grateful to see all limbs present, unpunctured and apparently unbroken—especially after he looked around at the vessel. Dead and injured men were scattered everywhere, and the luffing sails were torn and spattered with blood, and the weather-darkened wood of mast and gunwales was ploughed up in many places to show the bright, fresh wood underneath. It looked, thought Shandy dazedly, as if God had leaned down from heaven and swiped a sharp-tined rake across the boat a few times.

"Tiller hard to starboard, God damn it," Hodge was yelling. The captain cuffed away some of the blood that was coursing down his forehead. "And somebody grab the mainsail sheet!"

A man by the tiller tried spasmodically to obey, but fell helplessly to his knees, blood frothing from a ragged hole in his chest; Skank had desperately clambered over a pile of his ripped-up companions to the sheet . . . but it was too late. The *Jenny*, uncontrolled in the moments after the gust of scrap metal and chain shot had lashed into her, had drifted around to the point where her bow pointed directly into the wind, and for at least the next several minutes she would sit dead in the water. Shandy had heard this predicament described as "being in irons," and it occurred to him that in this case the term could hardly be more appropriate.

The tall, graceful edifice of the man-of-war, slanted enough against the wind to maintain headway, now crowded across the sloop's starboard bow, and as the high hull ground up against the *Jenny*'s forecastle, snapping the shroud chains and even breaking the catted anchor, grappling hooks clattered and thudded down onto the smaller vessel's deck, and a harsh voice shouted, "There's a pistol trained on every one of you bastards, so drop all weapons, and when we throw down the rope ladder come up one at a time and *slow*."

Chapter Seven

Though broken spars swung in the safety net overhead, the man-of-war's deck was intimidatingly clean and neat, the halliards spiral-coiled in perfect circles instead of just lying where they fell, as the *Jenny's* generally had been, and Shandy tried to keep his head tilted back so as not to drip blood onto the pale, sanded oak. His nose had been bleeding energetically ever since the Navy ship's blast, and the whole left side of his head was beginning to ache, and he decided that the blast must have struck the swivel gun he'd been standing behind, slamming the breech end of it against his head.

Along with the ten other relatively unhurt members of the sloop's crew, he stood now in the ship's waist near the spoked barrel of the capstan, trying not to hear the screams and groans of the badly hurt pirates who had been left sprawled on the *Jenny's* deck.

The Navy sailors who stood by the rails and kept pistols pointed at the captives all wore tight gray jackets, striped breeches and leather caps, and their plain, utilitarian garb made the gaudy, tar-stained finery of the pirates look ridiculous. Glancing nervously at the Navy men, Shandy noticed something in their expressions besides contempt and anger, and he wasn't reassured when he finally identified it: the morbid fascination of looking at men who, though breathing well enough at the moment, would soon be having their breath stopped forever in the bight of a noose.

Though the *Carmichael* was already just a distant tower of segmented white far off to the south, the Navy captain had lowered one of the ship's boats, and now, from his vantage point up on the poop deck, the captain peered through his telescope and laughed. "By God, Hendricks was right—one of 'em did fall overboard, and we've got him." He turned and looked down at his prisoners with a hard grin. "It seems," he called, "that one of your fellows just couldn't bear to leave you behind."

After a moment of bafflement, Shandy decided it might very well be Beth, taking the chance of being missed in the water for the sake of getting away from the pirates and her insane father. He hoped that was the case, for then both of them would at last have come out the end of this savage interlude, and Davies and Blackbeard and Hurwood and Friend could go to Florida or to Hell, for all the two of them need care.

The thought reminded him that it was high time he stopped staring around, stupidly tonguing the gap where one of his molars had recently been, and told the Navy captain who he was, and how he had come to be aboard the sloop.

He took a deep breath, forced his eyes to focus, and then, holding his arms out placatingly, he stepped away from the huddled, silent pirates—and was promptly nearly killed, for one of the guards fired a pistol at him.

Shandy heard the bang of the shot but *felt* the concussion in the air as the ball whipped past his ear, and he fell to his knees, still holding up his hands. "Jesus!" he screeched, "don't shoot, I'm not doing anything!"

The captain's attention had been effectively drawn, and he shouted angrily at Shandy, "Damn you, get back among your fellows!"

"They're not my fellows, captain," called Shandy, cautiously standing up and trying to appear calm. "My name is . . . is John Chandagnac, and I was a paying passenger aboard the *Vociferous Carmichael* before it was taken by Philip Davies and his men. During that . . . encounter, I wounded Davies, and so instead of being allowed to leave on the boat with the crew, I was forced on pain of death to enlist among my captors. Also forced to remain was another passenger, Elizabeth Hurwood, whom I suspect is the person who jumped overboard from the *Carmichael* just now." Glancing back at his recent companions, Shandy saw not only contempt but real hatred, and he added quickly, "I realize it will take time to verify my story, but I do request that you confine me somewhere separate from the rest of these men . . . just to make sure I survive to be a witness at the trial of Philip Davies."

The captain had moved forward to the poop deck rail and was squinting down at him. "Davies?" He scanned the prisoners around the capstan and then glanced toward the *Jenny's* mast, visible above the forecastle. "Is he with you? Injured?"

"No," Shandy told him. "He's on the *Carmichael.*" He nodded toward the departing ship.

"Ah," said the captain thoughtfully. "His trial won't be soon then." He blinked and looked again down at Shandy. "A forced man from the *Carmichael,* are you? You'll be pleased—or maybe not—to know that we can check your story right now. It was only this recentest Friday that we left Kingston, and the *Carmichael* was taken, as I recall, about a month ago, so our current shipping reports will cover it." He turned to a midshipman standing nearby. "Fetch the reports volume, will you, Mr. Nourse?"

"Aye aye, captain." The young officer hurried down the companion ladder and disappeared below.

"For a forced man, you handled that gun pretty thefty," said Skank, behind Shandy. "Turncoat son of a bitch." Shandy heard him spit.

The blood rushed to Shandy's face as he remembered the day Skank had roughed up Jim Bonny to save Shandy from a—real or imaginary—magical attack, and he wanted to face Skank now and plead with him to remember the circumstances of his recruitment three and a half weeks ago . . . but after a moment he just said quietly to the nearest armed sailor, "Can I take another step forward?"

"Aye," the sailor said. "Slow."

Shandy did, listening to the pirates behind him moodily arguing about whether he was a treacherous coward or just a pragmatic one. Looking out over the starboard quarter he could see the returning ship's boat, and he squinted against the glitter of sunlight on the wet oars, trying to see if it was indeed Beth Hurwood huddled in the stern.

The captain raised his telescope again and scrutinized the boat. "It's no one named Elizabeth," he said drily.

Damn me, Shandy thought, then she's still with them. Why in hell *didn't* she think of jumping overboard? Well, it's not my business any longer—it's for people like this fellow, or some other

Navy captain, to go and rescue her. I'm for Haiti. And perhaps Friend and her father mean her no harm.

He grinned bleakly at the willful naïveté of that thought; and then he allowed himself to remember, gingerly and one at a time, the stories he'd heard about Blackbeard—the time the man decided that his crew would benefit from spending some time in "a hell of our own," and so had everyone go below deck, where he gleefully lit a number of pots of brimstone, and at pistol point prevented anyone from leaving before half the crew was unconscious and in real danger of suffocation, and even then Blackbeard himself had been the last to emerge into the fresh air . . . though it was regarded as just another of his barbaric whims at the time, the ritualistic nature of the event was noted later, and one drunkenly indiscreet *bocor* had hinted that it had been a necessary renewal of Blackbeard's *hunsi kanzo* status, and not entirely successful because none of the crew had actually died of it; and Shandy recalled his rumored dealings with the genuinely dreaded *loa* known as Baron Samedi, whose domain is the graveyard and whose secret *drogue* is low-smoldering fire, which was why Blackbeard always braided lit slow matches into his hair and massive beard before going into any risky encounter; and he had heard of the superficially insane but sorcerously explainable uses to which the legendary pirate put any unfortunate woman that he could get linked to himself in wedlock . . . and Shandy thought of Beth's futile courage, and the innately cheerful nature she'd only been able to indulge for half an hour on the *Carmichael's* poop deck three and a half weeks ago.

Midshipman Nourse reappeared from below with a bound journal or log and clambered up the companion ladder to where the captain stood.

"Thank you," said the captain, taking the volume from him and tucking the telescope under his arm. He leafed through the pages for a couple of minutes and then looked down at Shandy with somewhat less sternness in his craggy face. "They do mention a John Chandagnac who was forced to join." He flipped to another page. "You boarded the *Carmichael* when and where?"

"On the morning of the third of June, at the Batsford Company Dock in Bristol."

"And . . . let's see . . . what ship sailed with you through the St. George Channel?"

"The *Mershon*. They turned north past Mizen Head, bound for Galway and the Aran Islands."

For a moment the captain lowered the book and stared at Shandy in reappraisal. "Hm . . ." He turned to the page he'd been reading before. "Yes, and the *Carmichael* survivors mention the attack by Chandagnac upon Davies . . . quite a brave thing that seems to have been. . . ."

"Hah," said Skank scornfully. "Took him by surprise. Davies wasn't even looking."

"Thank you, young man," the captain said to Skank with a frosty smile. "You've effectively confirmed this man's claim. Mr. Chandagnac, you may step away from those brigands and come up here."

Shandy sighed and relaxed, and realized that he'd been tense for weeks without being aware of it, living among people for whom savage violence was a casual thing. He crossed to the companion ladder and climbed up to the higher deck. The officers standing there made room, staring at him curiously.

"Here," said the captain, handing him the telescope. "See if you can identify our swimmer."

Shandy glanced down at the boat that was rocking closer on the blue water, and he didn't even have to look through the glass. "It's Davies," he said quietly.

The captain turned to the young midshipman again. "Keep those men where they are, Mr. Nourse," he said, pointing to the dispirited rabble around the capstan, "but have Davies brought to me in the great cabin. Mr. Chandagnac, I'll want you present, too, to witness Davies' statement."

Oh God, thought Shandy. "Very well, captain."

The captain started toward the ladder, then paused. "It will be a few minutes before the prisoner is brought aboard, Mr. Chandagnac. The purser could give you some clothes from the slop chest, if you'd like to get out of that . . . costume."

"Thank you, captain, I'd like that." Standing among all these officers, with their sober blue uniforms and brass buttons and epaulettes, Chandagnac had begun to feel like a clown in his red breeches and gold-worked belt—though such dress hadn't been at all inappropriate on New Providence Island.

Behind and below him he heard Skank's disgusted snicker.

• • •

A little later, feeling much more civilized in a blue-checked shirt, canvas breeches, gray woolen stockings and a pair of shoes, Shandy sat at one end of a long table in the great cabin and stared out the stern window—it was too big to be called a port or scuttle— the bull's-eye leaded glass pane of which had been propped open to let the breeze into the cabin. For the first time, he wondered what he'd do *after* prosecuting his uncle. Go back to England and get another position as an accountant? He shook his head doubtfully. England seemed chilly and far away.

Then, and the thought soothed a guilt-cramp that had been troubling his mind ever since the swimmer had been identified as Davies, Shandy knew what he would do: he'd work hard to get his uncle arrested, convicted and imprisoned as soon as possible, and then he'd use the—surely considerable—amount of money that would justly accrue to him to rescue Beth Hurwood. He ought to be able to hire a boat, a Caribbean-tempered captain and a tough, bounty-hungry crew. . . .

He heard boots clumping beyond the bulkhead, and then the door opened and two officers led Philip Davies into the cabin. The pirate chief's arms were bound behind his back and the left side of his sea-wet shirt was glisteningly blotted with blood from the shoulder to the waist, and his face, half-hidden by tangled wet hair, was paler and more drawn than usual—but he grinned as he maneuvered himself into a chair, and when he noticed Shandy he winked at him. "Restored to the shop window, eh?"

"That's right," Shandy said evenly.

"No chips? Paint still bright?"

Shandy didn't answer. The two officers sat down on either side of Davies.

The door opened again and the captain and Midshipman Nourse walked in. Nourse had pen, inkwell and paper, and sat down beside Shandy, while the captain ponderously sat down across the table from Davies. Each Navy man wore, evidently as part of the uniform, a sword and pistol.

"Let the record show, Mr. Nourse," said the captain, "that on Tuesday the twenty-sixth of June, 1718, we pulled from the sea the pirate captain Philip Davies, who had fallen overboard from the hijacked ship *Vociferous Carmichael* as a result of having been shot in the back by one of his confederates."

"Just the shoulder," Davies remarked to Shandy. "I think it was that fat boy, Friend."

"Why would Friend shoot you?" asked Shandy in surprise.

"The *Jenny*," said Davies, some strain beginning to rasp his voice, "was escorting the *Carmichael* only to . . . draw fire . . . occupy any hostiles so that the *Carmichael* would be able to carry on unimpeded. Hodge knew that. But I thought that if the *Carmichael* came around again and belted these Navy bastards one more time, we could *all* get away. Friend was mad as hell even when I cut in the first time to give the *Jenny* a few extra moments to run, and I guess he disagreed . . . strongly . . . with the idea of going back *again*. It's true I'd have been disobeying orders . . . and so just when I started to speak the command, I was shot right off the port ratlines." He started to laugh, but winced and had to make do with a jerky grin. "And I had Mate Care-For holding my hand! I expect . . . the ball would have split my spine, else." Sweat slicked his pain-lined face.

Shandy shook his head unhappily.

"Such is honor among thieves," said the captain. "Philip Davies, you will be conveyed to Kingston to stand trial for a considerable number of offenses, perhaps the most recent of which is the murder of Arthur Chaworth, the rightful captain of the *Vociferous Carmichael*." The captain cleared his throat. "Do you wish to make any statement?"

Davies was hunched forward, and he looked up at the captain with a skull-like grin. "Wilson, isn't it?" he said hoarsely. "*Sam* Wilson, right? I recognize you. What, now? A *statement*? Like for in court?" He squinted speculatively at the captain. "No, thank you, Sam. But tell me . . ." He seemed to brace himself, then spoke quickly, "Is it by any chance true what Panda Beecher once told me about you?"

Captain Wilson's mouth pinched whitely shut, he glanced rapidly at the other officers in the room, and then in almost a single motion he got to his feet, drew his pistol, cocked it and raised it. Shandy had leaped to his feet in the same instant and lunged across the table to knock the gun out of line just as the captain pulled the trigger.

The loud bang set Shandy's abused ears ringing, but he heard the captain shout, "God damn you, Chandagnac, I could have you arrested for that! Nourse, give me your pistol!"

Shandy darted a glance at Davies, who seemed tense but not uncheerful, then at Nourse. The young midshipman was shaking his head in horror.

"It's *murder* if you just *shoot* him, Captain," Nourse protested shrilly. "He has to stand trial! If we—"

Captain Wilson swore furiously and, as Nourse and Shandy both shouted at him to stop, he leaned across the table, snatched the pistol from the belt of one of Davies' guards, then stepped back out of everyone's reach and raised the pistol—

—Davies was smiling derisively at him—

—And, dizzy with fear even as he did it, Shandy reached down, drew Nourse's pistol and fired it at the captain.

The two explosions were almost simultaneous, but while Captain Wilson's shot missed Davies and tore a hole in the arm of the officer at Davies' right, Shandy's shot punched straight through Captain Wilson's throat and sent the man's spouting body rebounding from the far bulkhead to tumble noisily to the deck.

The ringing in Shandy's ears seemed to be outside him, the sound of a second stretched out twanging taut. He turned his head, with difficulty in the tension-thickened air, and saw raw astonishment on the faces of the other four men in the room. By far the most astonished was Davies.

"Leaping Jesus, boy," he cried, consternation having replaced his cheer, "do you know what you've done?"

"Saved your life—I guess," gasped Shandy. He didn't seem to be able to take a deep breath. "How do we get out of here?"

The arm-shot officer had pushed his chair back and was trying to reach his pistol with his good hand. Shandy stepped forward and almost absent-mindedly struck him just above the ear with the gun he'd used to kill the captain; and as the man slumped sideways, half off of his chair, Shandy dropped his own spent pistol and quickly took the unfired one from the man's belt, and then with his other hand drew his sword, too. Straightening as the man rolled off the chair and thudded and clopped to the deck, Shandy crossed to the door and with two free fingers of his sword-gripping hand he slid the bolt into the locked position.

"You two," Shandy said to Nourse and the officer whose pistol Captain Wilson had taken, "lay your swords on the table and stand by the stern bulkhead. Davies, get up and turn around."

Davies did, though the effort narrowed his eyes and bared his teeth. Keeping the pistol aimed at the two officers, Shandy worked the saber's point in under one loop of Davies' bindings, and thrust. Davies staggered, but the sawing edge cut the rope, and Davies shook free of it just as someone began pounding on the door.

"Is all well, Captain?" someone outside shouted. "Who's been shot?"

Shandy looked at Nourse over the pistol's muzzle. "Tell 'em . . . tell 'em Davies knocked the captain unconscious, and then was slain by your officers," he said softly. "Tell him to fetch the ship's surgeon."

Nourse repeated the message loudly, the quaver in his voice lending a nice touch of sincerity.

Davies held up a hand. "And the captured pirates," he whispered, "should be moved away—forward, up by the fore-castle."

Nourse relayed this order too, and the man outside acknowledged it and hurried away.

"Now," Shandy repeated desperately, "how do we get *out* of here?" He glanced out the window at the sea, tempted simply to vault out and swim. The poor old *Jenny* seemed hopelessly far away.

Some color had come back to Davies' lean face, and he was grinning again. "Why the surgeon?"

Shandy shrugged. "Wouldn't it have sounded implausible otherwise?"

"Might have, at that." He ran his good hand through his damp gray hair. "Well! Unless the Navy's changed since my day, the powder magazine is two or three decks directly below us." He turned to Nourse. "Is that right?"

"I'll answer no such questions," said Nourse, trembling.

Davies picked up one of the swords from the table, walked over to Nourse and gave him a light poke in the belly with the point of it. "You'll take me there or I'll work you ill. I'm Davies," he reminded him.

Nourse had clearly heard stories about him, for the stiffness slumped out of his shoulders and he muttered, "Very well . . . if you give me your word you'll not harm me, or the ship."

Davies stared at him. "You have my solemn word," he said

softly. Then he turned to Shandy. "Through that door's the captain's bunk. Get blankets and wrap up old Wilson in 'em, along with that sword you've got and the other two and any primed pistols you can find. Then you and this laddie," he nodded toward the officer who was still conscious, "will carry the bundle forward to where the *Jenny*'s boys are. Say it's my corpse. Everybody got that? Good. Now when the powder magazine goes up—and it should really *go*, I've been saving a couple of potent fire-sprite rhymes, and I won't lack for blood to draw their attention— when it explodes I'll appear from the forward hatch, with weapons, Mate Care-For willing, and you'll flip open the captain's blankets for a weapon or three more, and we'll fight our way to the sloop and cut out. And if I *don't* appear right after the explosion, *don't* hang around waiting for me."

Nourse was gaping at Davies. "You—" he sputtered, "you gave me your *word!*"

Davies laughed. "You see what it's worth. But listen, you'll lead me to the magazine or I'll cut off your ears and make you eat them. I've done that before to people who be troublesome."

Nourse looked away, and again Shandy got the impression that the midshipman was remembering some awful story about Davies. How can it be, Shandy wondered in horror, that I'm on this monster's side?

A couple of minutes later they decided they were all ready to go—Shandy and the unhappy officer had the dead captain and the swords and a set of fancy dueling pistols rolled up in a portable position that would allow Shandy to keep his pistol both concealed by a flap of fabric and aimed at the officer, and Davies had struggled into the unconscious officer's bloody-sleeved jacket— when someone knocked on the cabin door.

Shandy jumped in surprise and nearly dropped his pistol.

"It's the surgeon," hissed Davies tensely. He crossed the cabin and leaned on the bulkhead beyond the door's hinges, then beckoned to Nourse with his sword point. "Let him in."

Nourse was trembling even more than Shandy, and he rolled his eyes miserably as he unbolted the door and drew it open. "We carried the captain to his bunk," he stammered as the surgeon bustled in.

As neatly as if it were a dance move they'd been practicing,

Davies stepped out and punched the old surgeon in the head with the knuckle-guard of his sword, and Nourse caught the man as he fell.

"Great," said Davies with satisfaction. "Off we go."

Chapter Eight

No more than a minute later Shandy and the trembling officer were dragging the blanket-wrapped corpse and swords across the deck. The long bundle had proved to be too heavy and awkward to carry—especially if Shandy was to keep his concealed pistol aimed at the officer, who had the feet-end of the burden—and so they'd had to simply *drag* it in this awkward, crouching, torturingly slow way.

Shandy was sweating heavily, and not just because of the hot tropical sun that beat down on his head and glared on the white deck—he was as acutely aware of each armed sailor as he would have been of a scorpion clinging to his clothing, and he tried to keep his mind on the task of lugging the unwieldy bundle to the forecastle, and not imagine what would happen when the powder magazine exploded, or when the sailors caught on and opened fire on them, or when it occurred to the white-lipped officer at the other end of the blanket that when pandemonium erupted he'd be caught squarely in the crossfire.

As they scuffed and shambled along, passing the midships hatch cover now, both men panting through open mouths, the officer's eyes never left Shandy's concealed right hand, and Shandy knew that if his cramping grip of the sweat-slick weapon should slip, his corpse-carrying partner would instantly be sprinting away, shouting the alarm.

The disarmed captives up on the forecastle watched them

approach. They had heard that this was the corpse of Philip Davies being dragged over to them, and they were bitterly glad that Shandy was being made to bring it. "Come just a bit closer, Shandy, you boasie raasclaat!" shouted one man. "It'll be worth missing my hanging to get my hands on your neck." "This is how you thank Davies for letting you live?" put in another. "There'll be zombies sent after you, don't doubt it."

Some of the Navy sailors, mostly younger ones, snickered at this bit of superstition.

A long, scuffling minute later—just as they were hobbling past the forward hatch cover—Shandy actually *saw* his unwilling companion finally work out what would happen in the next couple of minutes.

"I won't hesitate," Shandy gasped, but the officer had suddenly dropped the captain's feet and was running back the way they'd come.

"It's a trick!" he was yelling. "Davies is below rigging a fuse to the magazine!"

Shandy breathed a sigh of what was almost relief, for at least the tight, silent suspense was over. Quickly but carefully he crouched, flipped the blanket open and rolled Captain Wilson's body flop-thudding onto the deck, kicked the weapons back onto the cloth, bundled it all up like a sack . . . then paused for an instant, looking around.

Only one of the surrounding Navy men had grasped the situation and was leveling a pistol at him. Shandy fired at him without aiming—missing, but spoiling the man's aim so that the ball splintered the rail behind Shandy—and then, waving the bundle of weapons around his head, he ran headlong for the forecastle.

Gunfire banged and cracked, and he heard pistol balls buzz past and felt one whack against his whirling bundle. Just short of the raised forecastle deck he flung the bundle up at the astonished pirates, and let the momentum of the contortion carry him into a leap sideways toward the companion ladder.

Sounding like quick strokes of a hammer, two pistol balls punched the bulkhead he'd been in front of.

One foot touched a ladder rung and then he was up on the forecastle, wrenching open the dueling-pistols case. "Onto the *Jenny!*" he gasped, snatching the two pistols out of the velvet-lined case and turning back toward the waist.

But before he could decide who to shoot at he was flung to his knees as the whole ship lurched violently forward and a *basso profundo* thunderclap shook the air all the way up to the mast-tops and the entire stern of the ship swelled incredibly upward and outward, dissolving into a towering cloud of dust and smoke and spinning timbers. The boiling sea was shadowed for dozens of yards to port and starboard by the sudden, churning cloud, and pockmarked by the splashes of things falling into it, and the prolonged thunder rolled away across the waves.

Then masts started coming down, first with a snapping of lines, which, though loud as pistol shots, could scarcely be heard over the continuing roar of the explosion, then with a ponderous rushing through the smoky air, finally culminating in the twangy yielding of the safety nets and the bone-jarring crash as the timbers hit the deck.

The deck Shandy crouched on wasn't level anymore—it was tilted down toward the stern, and even as he noticed it, the tilt became more pronounced. He scrabbled around, dropping both pistols, and on his hands and knees crawled up the slanting forecastle deck to the port rail and grabbed one of the stanchions.

He looked aft, which was down. The stern half of the ship was probably under water, but the torn and crumpled sails, and beyond them the thick smoke, made it impossible to be sure. Captain Wilson's corpse had apparently rolled away while he wasn't looking, but he saw one of the unfired dueling pistols cartwheel into oblivion. All around him he could hear air hissing up out of the hull, and bits of wood and metal still clattering down out of the black sky.

Someone was shaking his arm, and when he looked up he saw that it was Davies, his Navy jacket hacked to tatters, straddling the rail and shouting at him. Shandy couldn't make out the words, but it was clear that Davies wanted him to follow him, so Shandy scrambled up onto the rail.

In the choppy water below rocked the *Jenny*, freed of all but one of the lines mooring her to the stricken man-of-war, and even as he noticed it he saw one of the pirates chop the last line through with a saber and then jump from the ship's up-tilted bow to the water thirty feet below.

"Go!" yelled Davies, giving Shandy a hard slap between the shoulders and then leaping from the rail after him.

• • •

The first few minutes aboard the *Jenny* were a scrambling nightmare—a dozen men, half of them wounded, struggled to hoist sails, half of them torn by shot, in a desperate effort to get headway and tack clear before the man-of-war sank, creating a turbulence powerful enough to founder bigger vessels than the *Jenny.*

At last, when the Navy ship had sunk to her middle, and her vast, dripping bow was raised entirely out of the water, and her two boats, crowded with sailors, had rowed thirty yards to the south, the *Jenny*'s mainsail stopped luffing and flumped out taut. A few moments later the sloop began moving through the water and Davies ordered the tiller eased. They were a hundred yards southeast and picking up speed when the man-of-war's bow, spurting smoke as the explosion-fouled air in her was forced out, disappeared and was replaced by a white commotion of boiling and splashing.

"Hold her steady as she is . . . while we inventory," called Davies wearily, leaning by the stern. He was pale under his tan, and didn't seem to have the strength to push away from the rail.

Skank secured the jib sheet around a belaying pin and then leaned on the gunwale to catch his breath. "How . . . in *hell* . . . did we get out of that?"

Davies laughed weakly and waved at Shandy, who was crouched on the stern rail and shivering, more from shock than because of his wet clothes. "Our boy Shandy got the captain's confidence with his song-and-dance about being a forced man— and then, first chance he got, Shandy shot him."

In the stunned silence that followed this pronouncement, Shandy turned away, looking back at the tangled litter visible on the distant blue-green wave faces whenever the swell raised the *Jenny*'s stern.

Skank, his weariness forgotten, scrambled over the corpses and fouled rigging to the stern. "*Really?*" he asked, his voice hoarse with awe. "All that I'm-not-one-of-these talk you gave him was just *play-acting?*"

Shandy sighed, and when he shrugged he could feel that the tension had cramped its way back into his muscles. This is my life now, he thought. The men in those lifeboats know who I am. I couldn't be more committed. He turned around and grinned at

Skank. "That's right," he said. "And I had to make it convincing enough to fool you lads too, so you'd react naturally."

Skank was frowning in bewilderment. "But you *couldn't* have been pretending . . . I was right next to you. . . ."

"I told you I was involved with the theater for years, didn't I?" asked Shandy with affected lightness. "Anyway, you saw that Davies was bound when he was brought aboard, didn't you? Who do you think cut him loose, the captain? And who threw the swords to you?"

"Damn," Skank muttered, shaking his head. "You're good."

Davies was squinting at Shandy, and he laughed softly. "Yes," he said, "You're a good actor, Jack." Davies blinked and swayed, paler than before, then shook his head sharply. "Did Hodge's old *bocor* survive?"

After a moment's search, the *bocor*'s eviscerated body was found draped from the deck edge down into the hold. "No, Phil," came a hoarse call from a narrowed throat.

"Well, find where he hid his restorative snackies and bring 'em to me up by the bow." He turned to Shandy and said, more quietly, "Dried liver and black sausage and raisins, mostly. *Bocors* always gorge on such trash after doing heavy magic, and I did one hell of a piece of it today. Them fire-sprites were ready and hungry."

"So I saw. Why liver and sausage and raisins?"

"Don't know. They claim it keeps their gums red, but all old *bocors* have white gums anyway." Davies took a deep breath, then slapped him on the back. "There's rum forward—I need some to wake up Mate Care-For so he'll get busy on my shoulder wound, and I'll bet you won't turn down a gulp or two."

"No," Shandy said fervently.

"Did Hodge come through?" Davies asked a man near him.

"No, Phil. He caught a ball in the belly as we were going over the rail, and he jumped but he never bobbed up again."

"All right, I'll take it. Bear to southwest," Davies called to the disheartened crew. "All of you that are too hurt to work, mend sails and splice line. We're going to have to sail thefty, night and day, to get to the Florida rendezvous in time."

"Aw hell, Phil," complained one lean old fellow, "we're too shot up. Nobody could blame us if we just went back to N'Providence."

Davies gave him a wolfish grin. "When did any of us worry about what we'd be blamed for? The *Carmichael* is my ship, and I want her back; and I think Ed Thatch is soon to be King of the West Indies, and I want to be sitting high when the smoke clears. It's too bad some of you are old enough to remember the peaceful buccaneer days, because those days are long gone—the summer's over and empire season is here, and in a few more years it probably won't be possible anywhere in the Caribbean to just sit in the sun and cook scavenged Spanish livestock over the buccan fires. It's a new world, right enough, a world for the taking, and we're the ones who know how to live in it without having to pretend it's a district of England or France or Spain. All that could hold us back is laziness."

"Well, Phil," the man said, a bit baffled by this speech, "laziness is what I do best."

Davies dismissed him with a wave. "Then obey orders—stick with me and you'll eat and drink your fill, or be dead and not care." He pulled Shandy along toward the nodding bow, and when they got there he fumbled under a pile of canvas, and, with a glad cry, produced a bottle. He pulled out the cork with his teeth and handed the bottle to Shandy.

Shandy took several deep gulps of the sun-warmed liquor; it seemed to consist of vapor as much as liquid, and when he inhaled after handing the bottle back, it was like taking another sip.

"Now tell me," said Davies after swigging quite a bit of it himself, "why *did* you shoot Wilson?"

Shandy spread his hands. "He was going to kill you. Like that midshipman said, it would have been murder."

Davies peered intently at him. "Really? That was the entire reason?"

Shandy nodded. "Yes, God help me."

"And when you got your new clothes, and said you were a forced man and no real pirate . . . was that sincere?"

Shandy sighed hopelessly. "Yes."

Davies shook his head in wonder and took another sip of the warm rum.

"Uh," said Shandy, "who's . . . was it Peachy Bander?"

"Hm?"

"Could I have a bit more of that? Thanks." Shandy took several gulps and handed the bottle back. "Percher Bandy?" he said, a bit dizzily. "You know, the one who told you something about Captain Wilson, and was it true?"

"Oh!" Davies laughed. "Panda Beecher! He was—still is,

maybe—a spice wholesaler, and he always got Navy captains to carry his goods in the holds of Navy ships; it's illegal as hell, but a lot of merchants do it—they can pay the captain enough to make it worth his while, but still come out lots better than if they had commercial captains do it, what with either their extra insurance charges or the twelve-and-a-half percent of the cargo charge for an official Navy escort to keep pirates away. I was in the Navy myself for twenty-four years, and I know of many a Navy captain who's made extra cash by dealing with Panda and his sort, even though being caught at it would mean a nasty court-martial for the captain. I learned the captain's name from one of the men in the boat, so I pretended to remember him. It seemed not too long a shot to hope that Wilson had had such dealings, and would believe I knew of 'em. Then too, back in the nineties, Panda ran a couple of whorehouses that particularly catered to Royal Navy officers, and I've heard that the . . . stresses of Caribbean service led some of the young officers to prefer oddities—boys, you know, and whips, and Oriental variations—and there was the possibility that Wilson might have been one such."

Shandy nodded owlishly. "And you phrased your question so that it could seem to refer to either business."

"Exactly. And one barb or the other did, sure enough, seem to strike home, didn't it? We'll never know now which one it was." Skank shuffled up, handed Davies a foul-smelling canvas bag and then hurried away aft, wiping his hands on the rail. Davies pulled out an end of black sausage and took an unenthusiastic bite. "You see," he went on, chewing, "after the damned Utrecht Treaty left the privateers jobless, and ruined sailoring as a legal livelihood, and I turned pirate, I promised myself I'd never hang. I've *seen* too many hangings, over the years. So," he reached for the bottle and gulped quite a bit more, "I was thankful to have thought of that Panda Beecher question . . . in the same way that a man marooned on a barren reef is thankful to be left with a pistol."

Shandy frowned at the intricacy of this; then his eyebrows went up in comprehension. "It was suicide!" he exclaimed, too drunk to be tactful. "You *wanted* him to kill you when you said that."

"Preferred it, let's say. To a trial and eventual noose. Yes." He shook his head again, clearly still astounded by Shandy's action. "Just because it would have been murder?"

Shandy waved back at the other men in the boat. "Any of them would have done the same."

"With assured safety on the other hand?" Davies laughed. "Not ever. Not one. You remember Lot?"

"I beg your pardon?"

"Lot—the fellow with the wife who was made out of salt."

"Oh, that Lot." Shandy nodded. "Sure."

"'Member when Yahweh came over to his house?"

Shandy scowled in concentration. "No."

"Well, Yahweh told him he was going to stomp the town, because everybody was such bastards. So Lot says hold on, if I can find ten decent lads will you let the town alone? Yahweh huffs and puffs a bit, but finally allows as how yeah, if there's ten good men he won't kick the place to bits. Then Lot, being crafty, see, says, well, how about if there was three? Yahweh gets up and walks around, thinking about it, and then says, all right, I'll go three. So Lot says, how about one. Yahweh's all confused by this point, having had his heart set on wrecking the town, but at last he says all *right*, one decent man, even. And then of course Lot couldn't find even one, and Yahweh got to torch the town anyway." Davies waved at the other men in the boat, a gesture that managed to take in the *Carmichael*, too, and New Providence Island, and perhaps the whole Caribbean. "*Don't*, Jack, *ever* make the mistake of thinking he'd find one among these."

BOOK TWO

Cut off from the land that bore us,
Betrayed by the land we find,
Where the brightest have gone before us,
And the dullest are most behind—
Stand, stand to your glasses, steady!
'T is all we have left to prize:
One cup to the dead already—
Hurrah for the next that dies!

—*Bartholomew Dowling*

Chapter Nine

The evening breeze was strong and from the sea; the three ships moored offshore were nudged parallel, and the fires on the beach threw sparks away from the setting sun toward the black Florida cypress swamps. In the raised hut the pirates had built on a sandy rise just inland of the fires, Beth Hurwood peered out at the sky and the sea, and filled her lungs with the cool sea air, and prayed that the breeze would hold until dawn. She didn't want to spend a third night locked into the stifling "mosquito shelter" her father had forced the pirates to build—a canvas-walled box just big enough to lie down in.

She had never thought she would look back fondly on her two and a half years in the convent in Scotland, but now she mourned the day her father took her out of the place. The pale sisters in their robes and hoods had virtually never spoken, the rooms were stark old stone, the only food ever served was an oily gray porridge with lumps of dispirited vegetable stuff in it, and there was not a book in the place, not even a Bible—in fact, she'd never learned what Order the sisters belonged to, nor even what sort of faith; there had been no pictures, statues or crucifixes, and they might have been Moslems for all she knew—but at least they had left her alone, and she was free to stroll through the garden and feed the birds, or stand on the catwalk at the top of the wall and watch the road across the fields of heather, hoping to see strangers. Once in a while she would see someone, a farmer driving a cart, or a hunter with dogs, but though she waved to them they always hurried away—almost as if they were afraid of the place. Nevertheless she'd felt closer to those distant, hurrying figures than to the more profoundly remote sisters. Everyone in her life, after all, was a stranger to her.

Her mother had died when Beth was thirteen, and that was when her father became a stranger. He quit his position at Oxford, put his daughter in the care of relatives, and then left—engaged in "independent study," he had once said. And she was fifteen when he met Leo Friend.

The *swish* of boots approaching through the sand made her look down, and she was relieved to see that it was at least not Friend. Blinking against the afterimage of the sun, she didn't recognize the figure until he climbed the steps and ducked in under the low thatched roof; then she almost smiled, for it was just old Stede Bonnett. He had arrived only yesterday in his ship the *Revenge,* but though he was a pirate captain, and was said to be a partner of Blackbeard's, he seemed to have been well brought up, and had none of the mocking, sardonic cheer of a man like Philip Davies, nor the cold, driven savagery of her father. Beth wondered what could have led him into piracy.

"I'm sorry," he muttered, actually doffing his hat to her. "I didn't—realize—"

"It's all right, Mr. Bonnett." She waved at the log that served as a bench. "Do sit down."

"Thank you," he said, lowering himself onto it. A long-necked bird flapped up out of the marshes and gave a squawk that made Bonnett jump. He peered after the bird suspiciously.

"You . . . don't seem happy, Mr. Bonnett," Beth ventured.

He looked at her then, and seemed for the first time really to see her. He licked his lips and smiled hesitantly, but a moment later his worried scowl had returned and his gaze had moved away from her. "Happy? Hah—I defy anyone, after that spectacle at Charles Town—before Thatch demanded the ransom, they thought we meant to take the town—I turned a glass on the place—women and children running weeping through the streets—Jesus—and for what? A chest of black medicinal tobacco, and so that *he* could go look at the Ocracoke Inlet. And I find myself saying things, doing things . . . even my dreams aren't my own anymore. . . ."

The breeze shifted slightly, blowing Beth's long hair across her face, and belatedly she smelled the brandy on Bonnett's breath. An idea struck her, but out of fear of disappointment she forced down her sudden surge of hope.

She bit her lower lip. She'd have to be careful. . . .

"Where do you come from?" she asked.

For a long time he was silent, and she wondered if he hadn't heard her, or didn't intend to answer. I've *got* to get away from here, she thought; I have to believe that in some normal place, far from Friend and my father, my sanity won't seem such a fragile, flawed, imperiled thing.

"Barbados," he said quietly. "I . . . owned . . . a sugarcane plantation."

"Ah. You didn't prosper at it?"

"I was doing fine," he said hoarsely. "I'm a retired Army major, I had slaves and stables, the plantation was thriving. . . . I was a gentleman."

Beth resisted the impulse to ask him why he had turned to piracy, if all that was true. Instead she just asked him, "Would you like to go back?"

Again he looked at her. "Yes. But I can't. I'd be hanged."

"Take the King's Pardon."

"I—" He stuck a finger in his mouth and gnawed at the nail. "Thatch would never let me."

Beth's heart was pounding. "We could sneak away tonight, you and I. They're all distracted by this thing they've got to do up the river." Looking up the shore to her right, she wondered why they called that expanse of marsh a river.

Bonnett smiled nervously and licked his lips again, and once more she smelled the brandy. "You and I," he began, reaching out a pudgy hand.

"Right," she said, stepping back away from him. "Escape. Tonight. When the *hunsi kanzo* is busy up the river."

The reference to Blackbeard sobered Bonnett, and he scowled and resumed chewing his fingernail.

Not wanting to let him see the desperate hope in her eyes, Beth Hurwood looked away from him, back toward the marsh. Perhaps, she thought, they call it a river because it's so *nearly* one. All the local moisture does tend to move westward, though as slowly in most places as brandy working its way through a fruitcake, and the shallow evening fogs certainly follow the course of it and would soon drench an exposed person almost as thoroughly as if he'd been swimming.

She closed her eyes. Calling this swamp a river seemed typical of the way this dreadful New World worked—everything was still raw and unformed out here on the world's western edge, and bore only the most remote resemblances to the settled and solidified eastern hemisphere. And though now she heard Bonnett shift on the log, and quickly turned to face him, it fleetingly occurred to her that the undeveloped nature of these lands might have a lot to do with why her father had come, and why he had taken her with him.

Bonnett was leaning forward, and in the early twilight she could see the frown of tenuous determination on his pudgy old face. "I'll do it," he said almost in a whisper. "I think I must. I think going up the river tonight would be the end of me . . . though no doubt my body would still walk and speak and carry out Thatch's orders."

"Are there enough men aboard your ship right now to sail it?" she asked, standing up so quickly that the hut rocked on its wooden stilts.

Bonnett squinted up at her. "The *Revenge*? We can't take her. Do you imagine no one would see or hear us raise anchor and set the sails and move out? No, we'll provision a boat and put in it whatever we can find to improvise a mast and sail, and row away down the coast with muffled oars, and then just take our chances on the open sea. God's far more merciful than Thatch." He gasped suddenly and grabbed her wrist. "Christ! Wait a minute! Is this a trap? Did Thatch send you here—to *test* me? I forgot your father's his *partner*. . . ."

"No," said Beth tensely. "It's not a trap. I've got to get away from here. Now let's go get that boat."

Bonnett released her wrist, though he didn't look entirely convinced. "But . . . you've been with them for nearly a month, as I hear it. Why have you waited until now to escape? I'm sure it would have been far easier at New Providence."

She sighed. "It *never* would have been *easy*. But—" Another bird flapped past overhead, making both of them jump. Beth laughed weakly. "Well, for one thing, until we arrived here I didn't think my father actively meant me any harm, but now . . . well, he *doesn't* mean me any harm, but . . . the day before yesterday, when we were disembarking, I cut myself, and my father was frantic with worry that it might mortify and give me a fever. He told Leo Friend that the protective Caribbean magics," she spoke the words with distaste, "are sluggish here, and they'd have to watch me closely for any sign of illness. But his concern was . . . impersonal—it wasn't the concern of a father for a threatened daughter, but more like, I don't know, a captain's concern for the seaworthiness of a vessel his life depends on."

Bonnett hadn't really been listening—he patted the curls of his wig in place and licked his moustache, then stood up and walked over to where she stood—the hut swayed dangerously—and leaned beside her. Grotesquely, his face was puckered into a trembling but insinuating smile. " 'For one thing,' you said." His voice was huskier now. "Is there another?"

Beth wasn't looking at him, and she smiled sadly. "Yes; foolish, but I think so. I didn't figure it out until Tuesday, when the Navy killed him—he was aboard that boat, the *Jenny,* and Friend says none of them could have survived that broadside—but I don't think I really wanted to get away, without . . . well, you never met him. A man who was also a passenger on the *Carmichael.*"

Bonnett pursed his lips and stepped away, letting his paunch relax again. "I needn't take you, you know," he snapped.

Beth blinked in surprise and turned to look at him. "What? Of course you need to. If you don't, what's to stop me from raising the alarm before you're well away?" Abruptly she remembered that this was, despite the good manners, a pirate, and she added hastily, "At any rate, your case will certainly look better to the authorities if you've not only repented but rescued a captive of Blackbeard's as well."

"Something in that, I suppose," Bonnett muttered grudgingly. "Very well, now, listen. We'll go, right now, by separate routes, to the shore, where one of the *Revenge*'s boats is dragged up on the sand—you'll see me by it—and you'll get in quick and crouch low, out of sight. There's old canvas in there, hide under it. The tide's high again, so it shouldn't be difficult for me to wrestle the boat into the water. Then I'll row us out to the *Revenge,* load as much stuff into the boat as I can without raising the suspicions of that treacherous crew, and then just row away south along the coastline. Can you navigate by the stars?"

"No," said Beth. "Why, can't you?"

"Oh, surely," said Bonnett hastily. "I was just, uh, thinking of when I might be asleep. Anyway, if we just bear south we'll be in the trade lanes before too long. And then," he went on, stepping to the ladder, "if I can get far enough away from him before he learns that I've fled, maybe he won't be able to call me back."

This didn't reassure Beth, but she followed him down the ladder to the sand and walked off, away from him. She hoped to skirt around the three fires and make her way to the shore without being seen by the ever-vigilant Leo Friend.

Slowly and thoughtfully, with lines of genuine sorrow almost ennobling his pouchy face, Stede Bonnett plodded straight down the sandy slope toward the fires, his boots making sounds like slow crickets as the leather soles rasped against the saw grass.

Talking about escape with Hurwood's daughter—and then letting himself be aroused by her, even, foolishly, thinking she might respond in kind!—had brought back with far too painful a degree of clarity the life he'd been deprived of three months before. But of course even if he succeeded in escaping Blackbeard and taking the pardon, he could hardly return to Barbados and his wife. There was some consolation in that.

Perhaps in some other country, with another name, he could start over again—he was only fifty-eight, after all; with reasonable care he was a good decade short of needing to take up religion. There would still be many young women for him to focus his attention on.

For a moment a smile puckered his face, and his hands caressed an imaginary form, and he felt the old confidence, the old sureness of himself—the wife he married four years ago had taken it away from him, had made a cowed little man of what had once been a stern officer, and it wasn't until he met the girls at Ramona's that it was restored—but then, of course, he remembered how he had left the last of those girls, and he was dropped right back into the horror he'd been living in for three months. His wrinkled old hands fell back limply to his sides.

Out on the redly glittering face of the sea, looking in end-on silhouette like the upright black skeleton of some leviathan, Blackbeard's *Queen Anne's Revenge* stood motionless at anchor. Bonnett instantly looked away from it, not sure Blackbeard couldn't track his thoughts back along the line of his gaze.

This escape *has* to work, Bonnett thought as he plodded down

the ever-marshier slope. Thank God the king has offered total
amnesty! None of this was my fault, but no jury would ever believe
that. What jurist could understand the way a *hunsi kanzo* can use
your blood to unhinge your mind from your body? *I* didn't outfit
the *Revenge* . . . I'm not even sure it was me that killed that last
girl at Ramona's, though I'll admit it was my hand that swung the
chair leg—over and over and over again, so that, though I can't
remember it, my shoulder ached for days. And even if it *was* me, I
was drugged . . . and who do you suppose picked that precise girl
for me, with just those features, and who told her to use those
words and that tone?

A terrible thought struck him, and he stopped walking, slid a
yard or so and almost fell over. Why assume, as he had been doing,
that Blackbeard had first noticed him at Ramona's, and had only
then decided that a moneyed, landed military man would be a
useful partner? What if—and despite all the trouble he was in
Bonnett's face now burned with humiliation—what if Blackbeard
had wanted him *before,* and had set the whole supposedly spontane-
ous thing up? What if that first girl had only been *pretending* to have
sprained her ankle, and in fact been chosen just because she was
the skinniest, so that he would be able to lift her and take her inside
to her bed? She, and the other girls too, had refused to take any
payment from him in his subsequent visits, insisting that his
unprecedented virility was ample reward and had in fact become
an indispensable remedy for all classes of malaise, vapors and
depression; but what if *Blackbeard* had been paying them? And
paying dearly, no doubt, for in addition to their plain services he
was buying a considerable amount of . . . *acting.*

Again he glanced out across the water at Blackbeard's lightless
ship, this time with hatred. That's how it must have been, he
thought; he wanted to rope me in, and he researched me to find
the quickest, easiest lever with which to pry me out of my place in
the ordered world. If I hadn't been married to that castrating
woman, he'd have had to find some other lever. . . . I wonder
what *that* might have been . . . my pride, perhaps, he could
have maneuvered me into an illegal but unavoidable-with-honor
duel . . . or my honesty, put me in the position of having to
beggar myself by repaying some dire debt undertaken by my
wife. . . .

But of course I made it easy for him. All he had to do was pay

Ramona's whores to give me back what my wife had taken from me, and then eventually to drug me and send a girl in who was a perfect duplicate, in looks and derisive manner, of my wife. . . .

And then afterward, when my laboring heart had purged my bloodstream of the drug, and I was staring down at the dead girl's face, which no longer bore a resemblance to anyone, that evil giant strode into the room, a grin on him like a stratum of exposed granite in a mountainside, and he offered me the choice.

Some choice.

Chapter Ten

To Beth Hurwood's right lay the vast swamp that penetrated, they said, far inland—a region where land and water blurred into each other, seldom distinct, where snakes swam in the pools and fish crawled along the banks, where the very arrangement of channels and islands would, like a diabolically animate maze, change, rendering maps no more useful for navigating than sketches of clouds would be, where still air became stagnant like still water, and so miasmally thick that insects too large to do more than crawl anywhere else could fly here. Even as she glanced at that dark quarter of the landscape, far off in the marsh there appeared one of the randomly floating spheres of phosphorescence that the pirates called spirit balls; it lifted above the wispy surface of the fog and bounced slowly among the cypress branches and the dangling masses of Spanish moss, and then, just as slowly, fell back into the fog-river, and the glow became nebulous and then died out.

She looked in the other direction then toward the steel-gray sea, below which the sun had sunk half an hour before in so vast and molten a blaze that the high, wispy cirrus clouds still glowed pink; and being on higher ground and undazzled by the fires, she saw the sail a moment before the pirates did.

First a shout came faintly across the water from one of the three moored ships, and then one of the men down by the fires pointed and yelled, "A sail!"

The pirates all leaped up and sprinted for the boats, instinc-

tively preferring to be on the water rather than on the land if there
was to be trouble. Beth wavered uncertainly. If the sail—a single
one, and disappointingly small—was a Royal Navy craft, she
certainly didn't want to be aboard any ship that succeeded in
fleeing them; but if she hid and stayed behind, would the Navy
craft stop and send someone to check for stragglers ashore?

Someone giggled very close by, and she jumped and smoth-
ered a scream.

Leo Friend stepped out from behind a cluster of swamp maple
trees. "Going for a walk, my d-d-d—Elizabeth?" His eyes, she
noticed, seemed to show too much white around the irises, and a
smile came and went on his face as quickly and randomly as
something that should have been secured in a wind.

"Uh, yes," she said, wondering desperately how to be rid of
him. "What sail is that, do you suppose?"

"It doesn't matter," Friend said. His voice was shriller than
usual tonight. "Royal Navy, rival pirates—it's too late for anyone to
stop us." The smile poked his pudgy lips out and then disappeared
again. "And t-t-tomorrow w-w-we'll—to-m-morrow we s-s-sail from
h-h . . . damn it . . . here." He pulled a lace handkerchief from
his sleeve and mopped his forehead. "In the meantime I'll walk
with you."

"I'm going down toward the fires to see what's going on," she
told him, knowing that since shooting Davies the fat physician had
been reluctant, even with his various protective fetishes, to mingle
with the pirates.

"Your buccaneer s-sweetheart's *dead*, Elizabeth," Friend
snapped, his sparky cheer abruptly gone, "and I think it shows at
least a lack of imagination to choose his suc-suc-suc-*successor* from
out of the same stew."

Beth ignored him and began picking her way down the slope.
To her alarm, she heard Friend following. How on earth, she
wondered frantically, can I get away from him and keep the
appointment with Bonnett?

A man out on the anchored *Carmichael* shouted something
Beth couldn't hear, but the message was repeated by the men on
the beach. "It's the bleedin' *Jenny!*" came a wondering shout. "The
Jenny got free of that man-o'-war!"

With no clear transition point the pirates' panicky rout became
a riot of celebration. Bells began ringing on the *Vociferous Car-*

michael and Bonnett's *Revenge*—though not on Blackbeard's ship—
and muskets were fired into the darkening sky, and the various
ships' musicians hastily snatched up their instruments and began
clamoring.

Glad now that it wasn't a Royal Navy vessel, Beth Hurwood
quickened her pace, while Friend, seeing that the vessel was not
one that offered her a chance of escape, sulkily slacked off his own
pace.

Having a much shallower draft than the three ships, the *Jenny*
was able to tack in very close to shore before dropping her
anchor—the rattling of the chain lost in the general pandemonium—and a few of the men aboard her didn't wait for boats but
took running dives off the bow, daringly trusting the speed and
angle of their dives to carry them into water that wouldn't be over
their chins in depth. A few could actually swim, and took this
opportunity to show off their exotic skill by paddling around in
circles, splashing and blowing like dolphins, before heading in to
shore with theatrically nonchalant strokes.

One of them, though, just dove in and made his way to shore
in a swift, unpretentious crawl, and he was the first to stand up in
the shallows and wade in through the surge and ebb to the sand.

"Saints be praised!" cried one of the men waiting ashore. "The
cook survived!"

"Whip us up one of your dinners, Shandy," called another,
"before the captains start inland!"

A few more sailors had made their way ashore by this time,
and the ships' boats were being dragged down the sand to the surf
to facilitate the more formal disembarking, and Jack Shandy was
able to avoid the worst of the welcoming press. He glanced around,
clearly trying to keep from ruining his night vision by looking
directly into the fires, and then his dark, bearded face split in a
smile when he saw the slim figure of Beth Hurwood just now
striding into the central clearing.

She hurried across the sand to him even as he broke into an
unsteady run toward her, and when they met it seemed to her only
natural to throw her arms around his neck.

"Everybody told me you were all killed—in that last broadside," she gasped.

"A lot of us were," he said. "Listen, I've been talking to Davies
a lot during these last five days, and—"

"No, you listen. Stede Bonnett and I are going to steal a boat and escape tonight, and I'm sure there'll be room for you too. The *Jenny*'s arrival will postpone it a little, I imagine, but it should at the same time provide a fine diversion. Now here's what you do— linger by the shore for a while until Bonnett can choose a boat, and then watch for me. I'll—"

"*Shandy!*" came a yell from the fireside crowd. "Jack! Where in hell are you?"

"Damn," said Shandy. "I'll be back." He strode away from her toward the crowd.

"Here he is!" shouted Davies. "May I present, gentlemen, my new quartermaster!" The applause that followed this announcement was sporadic, but Davies went on. "I know—you all think it's cookery and puppets he does best, and so did I, but it develops his real values are brassier; courage and deceit and a quick, steady hand with a pistol. You want to know *how* we got away from that man-o'-war?"

The pirates loudly indicated that they wanted to know. On the outskirts of the crowd, Beth Hurwood took several slow steps backward, her face expressionless. Shandy looked back at her over his shoulder, clearly wanting to return and say something to her, but a dozen hands, and even an encouraging boot or two, were propelling him toward Davies and the flattened clearing between the fires. The lean old pirate chief grinned at him; though Davies had cursed the absence of a *bocor* during the past five days, he had, himself, taken the dead *bocor*'s kit and managed to "slap Mate Care-For awake" and to some extent keep that personage's attention on the sloop, and now the wounded men were recovering unfevered and Davies' shoulder seemed to be restored.

"After I was shot off the *Carmichael*," said Davies loudly, "a circumstance I'll take up with certain parties presently, I was picked out of the water by the Navy boys and taken aboard their ship. I found the *Jenny* crippled and captured, and all her surviving lads under armed guard—*except* for our boy Shandy, who'd told the captain, 'Oh dear me, sir, *I'm* not one of these dirty pirates, I was *forced* to join them, and I'll be delighted to testify at their trials."

Several of the *Jenny*'s crew had attained the shore and joined the crowd, and now they hollered their delighted agreement. "That's just what he said, Phil!" "Innocent as a bloody sheep, that captain thought Jacky was!"

"*But*," Davies went on, "he tipped me a wink when no one was looking, so I waited to see what he was up to. And what Jack did was convince the captain that I should be questioned privately, down in the great cabin, and no sooner had the three of us and a couple of officers got in there and shut the door than Jack snatched a pistol and shot the captain's head clean off his body!"

The applause this time was tumultuous, and Shandy was forcibly picked up and marched around the fires on the shoulders of a number of pirates. Beth took another backward step and then turned and ran toward the dark shoreline, as Davies, behind her, went on with relish to describe the way Shandy had engineered the utter destruction of the British man-of-war.

She found Bonnett standing just to the dry side of the high-water line, staring out at the darkening sea, his hands locked behind his back and the tilt of his three-cornered hat indicating that he was staring into the sky.

"Let's go, quickly," Beth panted. "I'm afraid I've confided our intentions to one who'll betray us, but perhaps if we leave instantly that won't matter. And the arrival of the *Jenny* can surely be used to our profit—you can pretend that the supplies you take from your ship are to replenish those of the ravaged *Jenny*, can't you? So for God's sake, let's *go*, every second—"

She halted then, for Bonnett had turned around to look at her, and his face bore an uncharacteristically sardonic smile. "Ah!" he said gently. "Escape, is it? Furtive flight? That explains his extreme tension and anxiety . . . very conspicuous states of mind, if one has learned to smell such things." He shrugged, and gave her a smile not devoid of sympathy. "I'm sorry. Neither of the two pieces you propose removing from the board is dispensable right now."

Beth gasped, then whirled and ran back in despair toward the fires, her most basic assumptions about the world shaken for the first time; for she knew beyond hope of rationalization that, though the voice had been Bonnett's and had come out of his mouth, it had been someone else speaking to her through them.

Shandy swore under his breath, for he'd lost sight of Beth, and he'd hoped to be able to give her his account of Davies' rescue before she heard the flamboyant version the *Jenny*'s crew had come to agree on.

He was about to demand that the pirates put him down when

he caught a whiff of the by now not unfamiliar smell of overheated metal. He tensed, trying to remember some of the things Davies had taught him during the past five days. He exhaled totally and hummed one of the simpler parrying-tunes, and he shifted around on his unsteady perch, trying to face all corners of the compass.

He found that his nose burned most uncomfortably when he was facing the farthest fire, and after a moment's peering he noticed the stocky, red-haired figure of Venner standing there. Shandy braced himself, then raised his left hand, curling the fingers into the uncomfortable position Davies had shown him, but as soon as Venner realized Shandy had noticed him he looked away, and the smell was gone instantly.

Shandy whistlingly sucked air into his heaving lungs. Well now, he thought as the pirates wearied of their sport and let him hop down to the packed sand, *that's* worth knowing. I guess Venner doesn't agree that I'm the best man for the quartermaster job.

The cheering and howling had abated in the clumps of the crowd nearest to the shore, and after a few seconds the stillness spread to the rest of the crowd; an inattentive pirate or two shouted, and one drunken old man worked his way to the end of a long fit of laughter, and Mr. Bird reminded everyone one more time that he was not a dog, but after that the silence on shore was absolute.

And from the dark sea came the *kalunk . . . clunk . . . kalunk . . . clunk* of oars knocking in oarlocks.

Shandy blinked around in uneasy puzzlement. "What's up?" he whispered to a man near him. "A boat's coming in—what's so terrible?"

The man's right hand darted to his forehead, but he hesitated and then just scratched his scalp. Shandy guessed his first impulse had been to make the sign of the cross. "It's Thatch," the man said quietly.

". . . Oh." Shandy stared out at the boat that was now halfway between the shore and the lightless bulk of the *Queen Anne's Revenge*. There were two figures in the boat, one of whom, the bigger one, seemed at this distance to be wearing a tiara of fireflies.

More profoundly than ever, Shandy wished that Captain Wilson had not tried to kill Davies. He recalled all the stories he'd heard about this man in the approaching boat, and it occurred to him that Thatch—Blackbeard—the dreaded *hunsi kanzo*—was the most successful of the buccaneers who had tried to adapt to this new, western world. Blackbeard seemed as much and as inseparably a part of this world as the Gulf Stream.

Shandy glanced at Davies, who was squinting more than the fire glare called for, and though the set of his jaw made his cheeks even more lined and hollow than usual, Shandy caught a hint of how Davies must have looked as a young man—willful, and determined to conceal any misgivings once a course had been considered and decided on.

Boots grated on the sand nearby, and looking around Shandy saw old one-armed Benjamin Hurwood standing near him and staring out at the boat. Shandy thought Hurwood too was concealing what he felt, but, unlike Davies, Beth's father seemed to be tense with eagerness and impatience. Remembering some things Davies had told him about Hurwood, Shandy was pretty sure he knew why—and though he knew Hurwood was a murderer, he knew too that if he himself were ever to be in Hurwood's situation, and refrain from taking the course Hurwood was taking, it would be because of fear rather than virtue.

The boat crested an incoming breaker, and as the wave crashed to churning foam the boat rushed in until its keel jarred against the sand in the swirling shallows, and Blackbeard vaulted over the gunwale and splashed ponderously up to shore. His boatman—who, Shandy noticed with a shudder, had his jaw bound up—just sat in the boat, neither attempting to beach the thing nor to get out to deeper water before the next wave broke.

Blackbeard strode up the sand slope toward the fires, and paused for a moment where it leveled out, a big, jagged silhouette against the purple sky; his three-cornered hat seemed too tapering and long at the corners, and with the points of red light bobbing around his head he looked to Shandy like some three-horned demon newly climbed up from Hell.

Then he approached the fires, and the luminous red dots around his head were revealed to be the lit ends of match-cords woven into his shaggy mane and beard. He was a tall man, taller than Davies, and as solidly massive as a wind-etched rock outcrop.

"And here we are one year later, Mr. Hurwood," Blackbeard said. "You've brought us a fine ship, as you promised, and I've brought the herb you say we need—and here we are on Lammas Eve, in spite of your fears I'd be late." He spoke English with a slight accent, and Shandy couldn't decide whether it indicated a non-English origin or just a lack of interest and aptitude in speaking. "May we both get what we're seeking."

Behind the huge pirate Shandy saw Leo Friend, still panting from having hurried to the fires, grin furtively; and for the first time Shandy wondered if the fat young physician might have ambitions of his own in all this.

Blackbeard clumped in to the center of the cleared space, and Shandy noticed that his craggy face gleamed with sweat—perhaps because of his heavy black coat, the voluminous folds of which hung all the way down to his shins. "Phil?" said Blackbeard.

"Here, sir," said Davies, stepping forward.

"Feel recovered enough to come along?"

"Try me."

"Oh, aye, I'll do that. These are trying times." Blackbeard grinned, a rictus that exposed most of his teeth. "You *were* disobeying the orders."

Davies grinned back. "Unlike what you'd have done, of course."

"Hah." The giant looked around at the crowd, which was more or less separated into three groups—the three ships' crews. "Who else is—" He paused abruptly and stared at his own wide-cuffed sleeve, all expression leaving his dark face. The men nearby drew back, muttering cantrips, though Hurwood and Friend leaned forward and stared.

Shandy stared too, though not eagerly, and thought for a moment he saw the cuff twitch, and a faint puff of smoke curl out; then, very clearly, he saw a line of blood run down Blackbeard's two middle fingers and begin to drip off and fall to the sand. The pirate's long coat seemed to shiver, as though rats were running around underneath.

"Rum," the giant said in a voice both tense and quiet.

One of the men from the *Carmichael*'s crew hurried forward with a jug, but Davies caught his collar and yanked him back. "Not just raw rum," Davies snapped. He took the jug, called for a cup, and after filling the cup he hurriedly uncorked his powder flask and shook a couple of handfuls of gunpowder into the drink. "Jack," he said. "A light, quick."

Shandy sprinted to the nearest fire and snatched up a stick with a flaming end, then hurried back to Davies, who was now holding the cup out away from himself, and he touched the blazing end of the stick to the cup's rim.

Instantly it was flaming and bubbling, and Davies took it to Blackbeard. Shandy thought he saw something like a little featherless bird clinging to Blackbeard's hand, but he was distracted by the sight of the huge pirate tilting his head all the way back and then simply inverting the fiery cup over his open mouth.

For a moment it seemed that his entire head had caught fire; then as quick as it had appeared the blaze was out, leaving just the dim corona of lit match-cords, and a puff of churning, redly luminous smoke hung over his head—and as soon as Shandy noticed its resemblance to a rage-contorted face, it was gone.

"Who's going with us?" Blackbeard asked harshly.

"Me and my quartermaster here, Jack Shandy," said Davies briskly, "and Bonnett and Hurwood, of course, and probably Hurwood's apprentice, Leo Friend, he's that fat boy there . . . and Hurwood's daughter."

People were looking at Shandy, though Blackbeard wasn't yet, so Shandy didn't let his astonishment show—but he was angry that Davies hadn't told him Beth would be coming along into the swamp, for Davies *had* described to him the journey they were going to make tonight through the perilous marshes, and, evidently even more perilous, the "magical balancing point" they sought, way back in the nearly impenetrable fastnesses of primeval ooze and loathesomely adapted creatures, and he couldn't imagine bringing Beth Hurwood along.

"Your quartermaster," Blackbeard rumbled, absently crushing the cup. "What became of Hodge?"

"He was killed when we escaped from the Navy man-of-war," Davies said. "Shandy accomplished that escape."

"Caught some news of that," Blackbeard said thoughtfully. "Shandy—step forward."

Shandy did, and the huge pirate-king turned his gaze on him, and Shandy felt buffeted by the sheer impact of the man's undivided attention. For a moment Blackbeard just stared down into his eyes, and Shandy felt his face heating up, for he could almost feel the closets and cupboards of his mind being opened and their contents being appraised.

"I see there was more aboard the *Vociferous Carmichael* than we knew," the giant said quietly, almost with suspicion. Then, more

loudly, he said, "Welcome to the world, Shandy—I can see that
Davies picked the right man."

"Thank you, sir," Shandy found himself saying. "Though
don't . . . I mean, it wasn't all quite . . ."

"It never is. Prove yourself tonight when we reach the
Fountain . . . and though we travel with Baron Samedi and
Maître Carrefour, stand on your own feet." He turned away then,
and Shandy, feeling as if he'd just stepped out of glaring sunlight
into shade, heaved a sigh and let his constricted psyche spring back
out to its normal extent.

Incoming waves had first half filled Blackbeard's boat but then
nudged it up into the shallows, and several sailors had begun to
unload a large box from the craft, awkwardly because of their
reluctance to get near the stiffly motionless boatman. The pirate-
king spat in disgust and strode away to oversee the work.

Shandy turned around and almost bumped into the imposing
belly of Davies' *bocor*, Woefully Fat. A night for giants, Shandy
thought as he tried to peer around the bulky sorceror. "Excuse
me," he said before remembering that the *bocor* was supposed to be
deaf, "have you seen Phil? Uh, Captain Davies? Oh hell, that's
right, you can't hear, can you? So why am I . . ." The intensity of
the *bocor*'s stare made him stop jabbering. Why can't these people
give these looks to somebody else, Shandy thought with a shiver, or
each other?

Unlike Blackbeard, who had seemed vaguely suspicious of
Shandy, Woefully Fat stared down at him with evident doubt—
almost with disappointment, as though Shandy were a bottle of
expensive wine that someone might have left out too long in direct
sunlight.

Shandy gave the sorceror a nervously polite smile, then backed
away and hurried around him. Davies, he saw now, was standing on
the edge of the sand slope a few yards away, and Shandy plodded
over there.

Davies saw him, grinned, and then nodded down toward
Blackbeard. "A powerful man, eh?"

"God knows," Shandy agreed, not smiling. "Listen, Phil," he
went on quietly, "you never told me Beth Hurwood was coming
along into the swamps with us."

Davies raised his eyebrows. "Didn't I? Perhaps not—probably
because it's none of your concern."

Shandy thought the older man was speaking a little defensively, and that alarmed him even more. "What do they mean to *do* with her?"

Davies sighed and shook his head. "Frankly, Jack, I'm not certain—though I do know they're anxious to keep her from all harm. Some higher magic, I gather."

"Having to do with Hurwood's dead wife."

"Oh, certainly that," Davies agreed. "As I told you on the *Jenny*, the hope of getting her back is all that keeps the old boy moving."

Shandy shook his head worriedly. "But if the Caribee *loas* are weak here, as you told me, how on earth do they expect to keep her safe out in that swamp? And who is this Maître Carrefour?"

"Hm? Oh, that's our old friend Mate Care-For. Thatch just pronounces it right. It means master of the crossroads. Master of different possibilities, in other words—of chance. But yes, he and Samedi and the rest of the spirit boys have grown weaker for us as we've moved so far north of the places they're anchored to. No doubt there are *loas* here too, but they'll be Indian ones—less than no help to us. Aye, we're pretty much on our own here. Like Thatch said, we've got to stand on our own feet. But of course after we get to this magical focus, or fountain, or whatever it is, if Hurwood can come through on his promise to show us how to use it—and not get infested, as Thatch did when he found the place—why then we'll probably be able to just *fly* out."

Shandy frowned angrily. "Damn it—I can't see why Blackbeard even came here in the first place. I guess he knew somehow that there was some big magic deep in this jungle, but what made him go to so much trouble to get *at* it? Especially since he doesn't even seem to have been handy enough at magic to keep himself out of trouble."

Davies started to speak, then chuckled and shook his head. "You've been in the western hemisphere how long now, Jack?"

"You know how long."

"So I do. A month, call it. Well, I first saw these islands when I was sixteen, the year after the press gang grabbed me in a Bristol street and informed me I was a sailor in His Majesty's Navy. No, let me talk. You can talk after. Anyway, I was a sailor on the frigate *Swan*, and in May of 1692—I was eighteen by then—the *Swan* was in Port Royal, which was Jamaica's main seaport in those days, and we had her up on the careening ground a hundred yards west of the walls of Fort Carlyle." Davies sighed. "I guess ten years earlier Port Royal had been a real hellhole—it was Henry Morgan's home base—but when I was there it was just a nice, lively town. Well, on the second day of June, while my mates were working in the sun scraping barnacles off the *Swan*'s hull, I was down the beach a ways reporting a shipping error at the King's warehouses, and when I had finished that I ducked in next door, at Littleton's tavern. And I'll tell you what, Jack, just as I left the place, full of beer and Littleton's excellent stew—beef and turtle, it was, as I recall— Thames Street jumped under my feet, and a sound like cannons or thunder came rolling out from the mainland. I turned back toward the tavern just in time to see the whole front wall of the place split into quarters like you'd cut a pie, and then the brick street broke up into . . . strips, like . . . and slid right down into the sea, with the whole town following right behind."

Shandy was listening avidly, having for the moment forgotten their original topic.

"I think I was under water for three minutes," Davies went on, "being battered by bricks and dirt, and just about being disjointed by the water itself, which couldn't make up its mind which way it wanted to fall. Finally I got to the surface and grabbed hold of somebody's roof beam, which was bobbing around like a toothpick on the choppiest, craziest sea you ever heard of. Eventually I was picked up by the *Swan* herself, which was one of the damn few vessels that hadn't been wrecked—maybe because she was already tipped over when the earthquake struck. She was crisscrossing the new patch of ocean which had, until about noon, been Port Royal, and we pulled lots of others out of that white sea—it was all bubbling and seething, you know? Like a huge pot of wild beer— but I later heard that two thousand died there."

"Jesus," said Shandy respectfully. Then, "Uh, but how does this relate to—"

"Oh, right, sorry—I'm getting carried away by my memories. Well sir, three blocks inland, on Broad Street, on that same terrible June second, an old magician from England—sort of like Hurwood, I guess—was trying out a heavy piece of resurrection magic. I don't think he was very skilled at it, but he had with him that day a sixteen-year-old boy who'd grown up among the free blacks in the Jamaica mountains, a boy who, though white, had been deeply educated in *vodun* and had, just the year before, been consecrated to the most fearsome of the *loas*, the Lord of Cemeteries, Baron Samedi, whose secret *drogue* is low-smoldering fire. It was reincarnation magic they were playing with, trying to learn how to put old souls into new bodies, and that requires fresh human blood, and they'd grabbed some poor devil to provide it. The old English magician had tried this stuff before, and, I don't know, maybe he'd managed on his best day to bring a dead bug or two back to life, but today he had this sixteen-year-old boy yoked in double harness with himself, right?"

"Right . . . ?" echoed Shandy.

"Well, it turns out—neither of 'em knew it at the time, though probably a few of the old *bocors* knew it, and certainly the Carib Indians before that—it turns out that big-yield resurrection magic has to be done *at sea*. Something to do with a relationship between blood and sea water, I understand. Well, this white boy turned out to be the most powerful natural magician of his color that anybody'd ever heard of . . . and here he was doing resurrection magic in Port Royal—*on the land*."

Shandy waited a moment. "Uh . . . yeah? So?"

"So the town of Port Royal jumped into the sea, Jack."

"Oh." Shandy looked out at the black ocean. "This . . . this sixteen-year-old boy—"

"—Was named Ed Thatch. He's been trying to perfect the resurrection trick ever since. And *that's* what brought him to this coast two years ago. You asked, remember?"

"Yes." Shandy wasn't feeling at all reassured. "Very well, so what *is* this focus or fountain we're going into the jungle to find?"

Davies blinked at him. "Why, I thought you knew *that*, Jack. It's a hole in the wall between life and death, and anyone standing around is liable to catch the spray from one side or the other. Don't you know any history? It's what Juan Ponce de Leon was looking for—he called it the Fountain of Youth."

Chapter Eleven

When it was fully dark, and Blackbeard, Davies and the rest of them had drunk off the last fortifying cups of rum and begun plodding north along the beach toward the river and the waiting boats, Benjamin Hurwood forced himself to stand up and follow them.

The daydreams that had become increasingly vivid and insistent during the last couple of years had now reached the point where they could almost be called hallucinations, but Hurwood kept his mouth clamped shut and didn't allow his eyes to follow any of the figures and objects he knew were imaginary.

It's 1718, he told himself firmly, and I'm on the shore of the west coast of Florida, with the pirate Edward Thatch and . . . my *daughter* . . . what in hell is her name? *Not* Margaret . . . Elizabeth! That's it. Despite what I'm seeing half the time, I'm *not* at the church in Chelsea . . . I am not forty-three years old, the year isn't 1694 . . . and that is not my bride that I see there, my dear Margaret, my life, or at least my sanity . . . that's our daughter, the . . . the vehicle. . . .

Hurwood squinted against the bright sunlight streaming in through the vestibule window as he handed the flask back to his groomsman. "Thanks, Peter," he grinned. He peeked through the crack between the two doors that were the church's side entrance, but people were still moving uncertainly down the aisles and sidling into the pews, and the minister hadn't appeared yet . . . though there was one frightened-looking altar boy at one of the far kneelers on the altar. "A little time yet," he told his best man. "I'll just take one more peek into the glass."

Peter smiled at the groom's nervousness as Hurwood crossed once again to the mirror he'd propped up on a nearby shelf. "The sin of vanity," Peter muttered.

"Today I believed a touch of vanity can be excused," Hurwood replied, patting his long brown locks into place. Hurwood was a studious, retiring man, but he did take pride in his hair, and, despite the fashion, never wore a wig—he always appeared in society "in his own hair," and despite his years there was no gray in it at all.

"I don't see Margaret yet," Peter remarked, pulling one of the doors open a bit and squinting toward the back of the church. "No doubt she's reconsidered."

Even the suggestion made Hurwood's stomach go cold. "God's blood, Peter, don't even speak such a thought! I'd . . . go mad. I—"

"A joke, merely!" Peter assured him, a hint of concern detectable behind his jovial tone. "Do relax, Ben, of course she'll come. Here, have another pull at the brandy—you're the palest bridegroom I've ever seen."

Hurwood took the proffered flask and drank deeply. "Thanks —but no more. It wouldn't do to be drunk on the altar."

"Shall I put her in the boat?" asked Peter, somehow pulling a curtain across the window so that they stood in darkness except for the light of a lamp Hurwood hadn't noticed. The air was suddenly fresher, but smelled of the sea, and marshes; fleetingly it occurred to Hurwood that they should air out these rooms more frequently—a century of incense smoke and moth-riddled draperies and dry prayer-book bindings produced some unlikely smells.

"I think you're the one that's had too much to drink," snapped Hurwood testily. He could no longer see his hair in the mirror. "Pull back that damned curtain."

"This is no time for visions, Mr. Hurwood," said someone, presumably Peter. "It's time to get into the boats."

Hurwood saw to his alarm that the lamp had somehow started a fire in the side vestibule—no, three fires! "Peter!" he cried. "The church is burning!" He turned to his best man, but instead of the lean, elegant figure of Peter he saw a monstrously fat young man in grotesque clothes. "Who are you?" Hurwood asked, very frightened, for he was now certain that something had happened to his fiancée. "Is Margaret all right?"

"She's *dead*, Mr. Hurwood," said the fat youth impatiently. "That's why you're here, remember?"

"Dead!" Then he must be in church for a funeral, not a wedding—but why was the casket so small, a square wooden box no more than a foot and a half long on any side? And why did it smell so earthy and bad?

Then he snapped out of it, and the memories of this last quarter of a century fell onto him like a landslide, leaving him weak and white-haired.

"Yes, dead," Leo Friend repeated. "And you're going to behave sanely for the next couple of hours even if I've got to control you myself," the fat man added desperately.

"Calm yourself, Leo," said Hurwood, managing to force a bit of detached amusement into his voice. "Yes, by all means get . . . Elizabeth into the boat."

Hurwood strode confidently down the slope toward the river, where the boats were drawn up and the wooden chest from Blackbeard's boat was being pried open—though he lurched a little, because every few seconds he seemed to be walking at a ceremoniously slow pace down the church's center aisle, through alternating patches of shadow and slanting colored light as he passed the high stained-glass windows one by one.

The springy, spidery-looking mangrove roots had been cutlassed away from a hundred-foot section of the river shore, and men were standing knee-deep in the black, torchlight-glittering water and catching oilskin-wrapped bundles tossed from shore and laying them in the boats. There was a flaming torch mounted in the bow of each of the three boats, and Hurwood saw that Davies and the cook were already in one of the boats, Davies holding it steady by gripping a mangrove stump that projected a foot out of the water.

". . . .to have and to hold, from this day forward, until death do you part?" the minister asked, smiling kindly at the earnest couple kneeling before him. Out of the corner of his eye Hurwood saw the altar boy he'd noticed earlier, still at the far kneeler and still looking scared . . . no, more lost than scared.

"I do," said Hurwood.

"How's that again, boss?" asked the pirate who had just taken the last bundle out of the wooden chest and tossed the oilskin-wrapped packet to the men in the water.

"He says he does," snickered the man next to him.

The first pirate winked at his companion. "I thought he looked like the type that did, but I wasn't sure."

"Haw haw."

Hurwood blinked around, then smiled at them. "Most amusing. I'll be sure and bring a couple of mementos back from the Fountain for you gentlemen."

The grins fell off the men's faces. "Meant no disrespect, sir," one of them said sulkily.

"Still, I won't forget." Looking over his shoulder Hurwood saw Leo Friend making his ponderous way down the slope. "We'll go in that one," Hurwood told the cowed pirates, pointing at one of the boats. "Please bring it close, and hold it very steady, for my companion is massive."

The men silently did as they were told, and out of fear of Hurwood they dragged the boat in so close to shore that he was able to step into it without getting his boots wet.

A few people threw rice in spite of Hurwood's stated preference, but he smiled as he stepped up into the carriage beside his bride, for he was far too elated to acknowledge petty annoyances.

He was smiling broadly. "Thank you!" he called to the gaping pirates and Leo Friend. "We'll have you all over for dinner when we return from the continent!"

Shandy leaned out to the side, away from the boat's torch, to see Hurwood better. The old man was still grinning and waving to the shore, to the dumbfoundment of the pirates and Friend—and Beth, who was being led to her father's boat by the apparently sleep-walking Stede Bonnett. I guess she was right after all, Shandy thought, about her father being crazy.

For the last half hour the moon had been alternately hidden and exposed by clouds rushing across its face, and now a warm rain began to fall. The boats were loaded, and the passengers were all more or less settled on the thwarts—Blackbeard and his dubious rower in the first boat, Hurwood, Friend, Elizabeth and Bonnett in the next, and Shandy and Davies in the third. Shandy was surprised to see that Woefully Fat wasn't coming along; did the giant *bocor* know something, perhaps, that the people in the boats didn't?

As the boats pushed away from the shore and the oarlocks began to knock and clank, and steam rose from the torch flames, all the voyagers except Beth Hurwood began humming a low-key counterpoint melody calculated to attract whatever feeble attentions of Baron Samedi and Maître Carrefour might extend to this forsaken northern shore—but after a few minutes the humming dropped off, as if all of them found it incongruous here.

The stream was slow, and it was easy to row up it, and soon even the glow of the three fires on the shore was lost behind them in the black maze. Shandy crouched in the bow of his boat and, as the knobby towers of cypresses loomed out of the darkness, some of them looking like hooded and malformed men, some looking like stones, none of them looking like any kind of tree, he softly called directions back to Davies, who had insisted on rowing in spite of his newly healed shoulder.

Things shifted wetly on the boggy ground as they passed, and there were inexplicable splashings and bubblings, but Shandy saw nothing that looked animate except the pearly oil-smears that slicked the water and seemed to form grasping hands, and warped faces mouthing unreadable words, as the boat keels razored them in half and pushed them away to either side.

Blackbeard's boat was leading the way, and in the nearly silent cathedral of the swamp Shandy thought he could hear intermittent hissing from the pirate-king's strange boatman. The only other sounds from the boats were Friend's muttered directions to Bonnett, who was laboring at their boat's oars, and an occasional soft, fatuous chuckle from Hurwood. Beth huddled in hopeless silence beside her father.

When Shandy consciously noticed the quiet susurration after about an hour of slow progress through the jungly labyrinth, he realized that he'd been aware of the sound for quite a while, but until now hadn't distinguished it from the muted splash and drip of the oars. It sounded to him like hundreds of people, not far ahead, whispering in alarm. At about the same time, he noticed the new smell, which was eclipsing the rich odors of cypress oil and decaying vegetation and black water, and as soon as he became aware of it, he realized he'd been expecting it. He exhaled sharply through his nose, then cleared his throat and spat.

"Aye," muttered Davies, evidently liking it no better, "smells like a cannon that hasn't been let to cool between firings."

Hurwood too seemed to notice it, for he stopped his chortling and snapped, "The herb—put it in the torches now."

Shandy untied the oilskin bundle issued to his boat and, a handful at a time, gently tossed the damp, stringy stuff—the stuff Blackbeard had terrorized Charles Town to obtain—onto the glowing surface of the torch-head. Smoke trickled up fitfully at first, then suddenly in thick billows, and Shandy yanked his head back, huffing and spitting again, this time to get the pungent, almost ammoniac reek out of his head. Why bother, he thought, to qualify it as a *ghost* repellent? This stuff would chase wooden figureheads off the bows of ships.

He was tense but not actively scared—though at the same time he was wryly aware that this was like his relative coolness during the capture of the *Carmichael:* based on ignorance of the danger. But Blackbeard was here once, he told himself, and came out not *too* bad off . . . and of course Blackbeard just blundered in, carelessly, drawn by the Fountain's magical reverberations or whatever it was, like a moth to a candle, while we've got a guide that knows how to handle all this stuff. . . .

His confidence waned a little, though, when he remembered that Hurwood had evidently lost his mind. And why had Blackbeard forbidden them to bring pistols?

The river narrowed, or, more accurately, broke up into dozens of narrow channels, and soon rowing became impossible, and the oars had to be used as barge poles. Blackbeard's boat took the lead, Hurwood's was next, and the boat Shandy was in was last. As the wet vines and wild orchids pressed in ever closer in the orange torchlight, Shandy began to wonder if there wasn't something out there in the marsh, not too far away, pacing them silently in the darkness—something big, though it made no sound as it moved through the moonlight-dappled tangles of bay trees and swamp maples. He tried to force his imagination to relax, though the sound like whispering—louder now—didn't make it easy.

He was kneeling on one of the thwarts, alternately heaving back with his oar against the muddy river bottom and squinting ahead through the noxious smoke to see which channels the other two boats took. Sparks from the torch at the bow had been falling back onto him ever since the boat had cast off, and he'd been absently brushing them away, but now he felt two spots of warmth at his waist, and, glancing down, didn't see any sparks.

He brushed at his shirt, and discovered that his iron belt buckle was uncomfortably hot, as was his sheathed knife. And now that he had noticed those, he was aware too of a warmth on the insteps of his feet—right where his boot buckles were.

"Uh," he began, turning to Davies, but before he could think of what to say, Hurwood called from the boat ahead.

"Iron!" the old man told them. "Apparently the old superstitions—the connection between iron and magic—it'd probably be wise to discard it, as much of it as you can—"

"Keep your weapons," came Blackbeard's bass growl. "I was here before—it doesn't get too hot to bear. And don't ditch your belt buckles if that means your pants are going to fall down."

A scream from the black jungle made Shandy jump, but Davies, leaning on his own oar, laughed quietly and said, "Not a ghost—that was one of those brown-and-white birds that eat the water snails."

"Oh—right."

Shandy pulled in his oar and laid it across the bow. As gingerly as if he were splitting the shell off of a too-hot lobster, he unbuckled his belt, then drew his knife—he could feel the heat of the tang even through the leather wrapping of the grip—and, using the gunwale as a chopping block, sawed off the buckle-end of his belt. It clattered down the hull and splashed into the puddle sloshing back and forth on the floorboards. He slid the hot knife back into its sheath and picked up his oar again.

Davies, who hadn't paused in his own rhythmic poling, grinned mockingly and shook his head. "Your pants better not fall down."

Shandy leaned his full weight against his oar, and wondered if the water was too shallow to float the keel clear and they were poling the boat through mud. "Yours," he gasped, "better not catch fire."

The three boats inched onward through the humid jungle, hazed in the smoke from the torches. As much to relieve his watering eyes from the flame-glare as to watch for some stealthily approaching monster, Shandy kept peering off to the sides; and at

first he was relieved to see that the "whispering" was issuing from
flappy holes in the round pods of a white fungoid growth that was
clustered more and more thickly along the spongy banks—casting
about for an explanation of the phenomenon, he guessed that their
roots were connected to caverns, and that temperature differences
caused air to rush up and be released in this admittedly bizarre
way—but as the boats were pushed farther into the marsh, where
the fungus balls grew bigger, he saw that above the loose-edged,
exhaling holes were bumps and indentations that looked increasingly like noses and eyes.

The sense of a huge and attentive—but silent—entity out in
the darkness became more and more oppressive. Finally Shandy
looked up in fear, and though he could see the moonlight-silvered
interweaving of branches overhead, he knew that a thing was
bending down invisibly above them, a thing that belonged here,
that owned—perhaps largely consisted of—these repellently
fecund swamps and pools and vines and small amphibian lives.

The others obviously felt it too. Friend scrambled heavily to his
feet and then nearly extinguished his boat's torch by dumping a
double fistful of the black herb onto it; the flame guttered low, but
a couple of seconds later flared up again, sending a billowing cloud
of the harsh smoke unfolding upward toward the branches that
roofed the river.

A scream out of the sky shook blossoms from the trees and
raised ripples in the water so tight and steady that for a moment
the boats seemed to be sitting on a pane of extra-ridgy bull's-eye
glass. The sound rang away through the jungle, and then there was
just the cawing of frightened birds, and, after they subsided, just
the whispering of the fungus pods.

Shandy glanced at the nearest cluster of the pods, and he saw
that the fungus lumps were definitely faces now, and from the way
their eyelids twitched he was unhappily sure that soon he'd be
meeting the gaze of eyes when he looked at them.

Behind him Davies was swearing steadily in a weary monotone.

"Don't tell me," Shandy said in a fairly even voice, "that was
one of those brown-and-white birds that eat the goddamned water
snails."

Davies barked one syllable of a laugh, but didn't reply. Shandy
could hear Beth weeping quietly.

"Ah, my dear Margaret," said old Benjamin Hurwood in a

choked but throbbing voice, "may these tears of joy be the only sort you ever shed again! And now indulge, please, a sentimental old Oxford don. On this, our wedding day, I'd like to recite to you a sonnet I've composed." He cleared his throat.

The invisible swamp-presence was still a psychic weight on the foul air, and the insteps of Shandy's feet were getting uncomfortably hot in spite of the thick leather between the boot buckles and his skin.

"Margaret!" Benjamin Hurwood began, *"I require a Dante's muse . . ."*

"We're aground," came Blackbeard's call from ahead. "Stop pushing 'em. From here, we move on foot."

Christ, thought Shandy. "Is he . . . kidding?" he asked, not very hopefully.

Instead of answering, Davies laid his oar in the boat and climbed over the stern and lowered himself into the black water. It proved to be about hip deep.

". . . *Fitly to sing my joy after that day,*" Hurwood crooned on.

Shandy looked ahead. Blackbeard had taken his boat's torch out of its bracket, and he and his disquieting boatman were both already in the water and wading toward the nearest bank. Shadows shifted as they moved, and new clusters of the fungus heads became visible.

"Mr. Hurwood," Leo Friend was hissing, shaking the one-armed man. "Mr. Hurwood! Wake up, damn you!"

"When," Hurwood continued reciting, *"in my life's mid-point, God let me choose . . . to leave the gloomy wood—"*

Shandy could see Beth's shoulders shaking. Bonnett was sitting as stiffly motionless as a mannikin.

Blackbeard and his boatman had climbed up onto the bank, and, ignoring the twitching, whispering white globes at their feet, were hanging on to dangling wild grapevines to keep their footing on the mud and the arching wet roots. "We need him alert," called Blackbeard to Friend. "Slap him—hard. If that doesn't do it I'll come over there and . . . do something to him myself."

Friend smiled nervously, drew back a pudgy hand and then cracked it across Hurwood's simpering face.

Hurwood let go a yell that was almost a sob, then blinked around at the boats, once again aware of his real surroundings.

"Not much farther now," Blackbeard told him patiently, "but we leave the boats here."

Hurwood peered for almost a minute at the water and the mud bank. Finally, he said, "We'll have to carry the girl."

"I'll help carry her," called Shandy.

Friend gave Shandy a venomous glare, but Hurwood didn't even look around. "No," the old man said, "Friend and Bonnett and I can manage."

"Right," said Blackbeard. "The rest of us will be busy chopping us a passage through this jungle."

Shandy sighed and put down his oar. He rocked the boat's torch free of its bracket, handed it and the packet of black herb to Davies, and then climbed out of the boat. At least his boots leaked, and the relatively cool swamp water soothed his hot feet.

Chapter Twelve

For half an hour the odd company splashed, plodded and stumbled through one claustrophobic tangle of vegetation after another; Shandy's knife-wielding arm was shaking with fatigue from chopping vines and tree branches, but he drove doggedly on, climbing up out of pools he blundered into, and forcing himself to breathe the harsh air, and always being terribly careful not to let the torch he carried in his other hand be extinguished, or burn off all its charge of the black herb.

Hurwood, Bonnett and Friend lurched along behind, stopping every few yards to arrange a new way to carry their own torch, Hurwood's boxes, and Beth, and twice Shandy heard a calamitous multiple splash, followed by renewed sobbing from Beth and a burst of almost incomprehensibly shrill cursing from her father.

Shortly after the eight of them had set foot on the first mud bank, the fungus heads had begun sneezing, and a grainy powder like spores or pollen puffed out of the flappy mouths; but the thick, low-hanging torch smoke repelled the dust as if each torch were the source of a powerful wind that only the powder could feel.

"Inhaling that dust," panted Hurwood at one point when several of the things sneezed at once, "is what . . . gave you ghosts, Thatch."

Blackbeard laughed as he chopped a young tree aside with a swipe of his cutlass. "Clouds of ghost eggs, eh?"

Shandy, glancing back for a moment, saw Hurwood's pout of

scholarly dissatisfaction. "Well, roughly," the old man said as he hunched to get his daughter's legs more comfortably arranged on his shoulders.

Shandy turned back to his task. He'd been trying all along to stay away from Blackbeard's boatman, who, blank-faced, was swinging his cutlass so metronomically that he reminded Shandy of one of the water-powered figures in the Tivoli Gardens in Italy, and as a result Shandy found himself working, more often than not, between Davies and Blackbeard.

The sense of a vast, invisible presence was intensifying again, and again Shandy could feel the thing bending down out of the sky over them, glaring with alien outrage at these eight intruders.

Sticking his knife into a tree for a moment, Shandy opened the oilskin bag and dumped a handful of the black stuff onto the torch. After a moment a thick eruption of smoke billowed up and nearly blinded him as he recovered his knife; but this time when the smoke cloud disappeared into the tangled jungle canopy, the forest shook with a low roaring—a boot-shaking rumble that clearly expressed anger, and, just as clearly, emanated from no organic throat.

Blackbeard stepped back, squinting around suspiciously at the greenery that walled them in. "My first time here," he muttered to Davies and Shandy, "I talked to the natives—Creek Indians, mostly. Traded 'em medicine magic for straight talk. They mentioned a thing called *Este Fasta*. Said that meant 'Give Person.' Sounded like some local breed of *loa*. I wonder if that's who our growler was just now."

"But he didn't mess with you on your first visit," said Davies tightly.

"No," Blackbeard agreed, "but that time I didn't have the ghost repellent. He probably figured he didn't need to interfere."

Great, thought Shandy. He glanced at the torchlit web of vegetation in front of them, and was the first by a second or two to notice that the vines and branches were moving—twisting—in the still, stagnant air.

Then Blackbeard noticed it, and even as the plants assumed the crude shape of a giant hand and clawed toward them, the pirate-king dropped his torch and lunged forward and with two strokes of his cutlass, forehand and backhand, he smashed the thing to pieces.

"Come on, devil," Blackbeard raged, a fearsome sight with his teeth and the whites of his mad eyes glittering in the glow of the smoldering match-cords woven into his mane, "wave some more bushes in my face!" Not even waiting for the foreign *loa*'s response, he waded straight into the primeval rain forest, shouting and whirling his cutlass. "Coo yah, you quashie pattu-owl!" he bellowed, reverting almost entirely to what Shandy could now recognize as Jamaican mountain tribe patois. "It take more than one deggeh bungo duppy to scare off a tallowah *hunsi kanzo!*"

Shandy could hardly see Blackbeard now, though he saw the vines jumping and heard the chopping of the cutlass and the clatter and splash of wrecked verdure flying in all directions. Crouched back and gripping his knife, Shandy had a moment to wonder if this maniacal raging was the only way Blackbeard allowed himself to vent fear—and then the giant pirate had burst back out of the jungle, some of his beard-trimming match-cords extinguished but his fury as awesome as before. Blackbeard snatched the oilskin bag from where it stuck out of Shandy's coat pocket, tore it open with his teeth and flung it into the mud.

"Here!" he yelled at the jungle, grabbing Shandy's torch now and slamming its flaming head straight down onto the spilled herb. "I brand you my slave!"

A steamy smoke cloud burst up, stinking of scorched black mud as well as of burning herb, and a scream of inhuman pain and wrath impacted the air from above, stripping leaves from the trees and punching Shandy right off his feet.

As he rolled in the watery muck, struggling to stand up and get air back into his lungs, Shandy dimly saw the silhouette that was Blackbeard tilt back its shaggy head and rid itself of a deafening, grating howl. It was a terrible sound, like the challenge-cry of some gargantuan reptile; Shandy felt more kinship with the wolves that, in his youth, he had occasionally heard crying from vast distances across northern ice-fields.

The trio carrying Beth had halted; Shandy was tensely crouched behind and to one side of Blackbeard, and Davies, expressionless but visibly pale in the light from Hurwood's torch, stood to the other side with his sword drawn and held ready.

A sudden wind blew away the echoes of Blackbeard's howl, and this time the whispering of the fungus heads was the only sound to be heard afterward—any birds in the area were silenced.

Abruptly Shandy realized that the fungus heads had opened their eyes and were talking, in actual languages; the one nearest him was complaining, in French, about how cruel it was that an old woman should be neglected by her children, and one near Davies was using a Scottish dialect to deliver the sort of advice a father would give to a son about to travel to a big city. Shandy stared at it wonderingly when he heard it warn against expressing any opinion on religion or the recent regicide. Regicide? thought Shandy; did someone kill King George during this last month . . . or could this thing be talking about the murder of James the First a century ago?

Blackbeard slowly lowered his head, and glared at a berry-decked bay tree in front of him. A full-armed swing of his cutlass made an aromatic ruin of the tree, and beyond it, instead of more vegetation, was darkness and a cooler breeze and a dim glow, as of a brightly lit city just over the horizon.

Blackbeard swore again and then stepped through the gap, and a moment later so did his boatman. Shandy and Davies exchanged a glance, shrugged, and followed.

The jungle was gone. In front of them a flat and plain stretched away under the unobscured moon, and a couple of hundred yards ahead was the knee-high coping wall of a circular pool that looked wider than the Roman Colosseum. Way out over the center of the pool hung a vast luminosity that might have been fire or spray, and the dimly glowing masses of it rose and fell as slowly as opals in honey. Staring at the shifting lights, Shandy realized with a chill in his belly that he had no idea how far away they were; at one moment they seemed to be colored glass butterflies glowing in the light from Hurwood's torch within easy arm's reach, but at the next moment they were some astronomical phenomenon taking place far beyond the domain of the sun and planets. The pool, too, Shandy noticed now, was optically tricky—he peered and squinted, but finally had to admit that he had not the remotest idea how tall the coping wall was. Far off to the right and left, slender bridges of some kind rose from the wall and arched high and away out of sight toward the center of the pool.

The buckles on Shandy's boots were now very hot. He burned his hand drawing his knife, but managed, crouching first on one foot and then on the other, to hack the buckles off. He straightened again, trying to ignore the way his leather scabbard smoked when he put the knife back and wondering when he'd start to feel the nails that held his boot soles on. Thank God Blackbeard had forbidden pistols.

"I didn't get much farther than right here," said Blackbeard softly. He turned to Davies and grinned. "Go ahead—walk out to the pool's edge."

Davies swallowed, then took a step forward.

"Stop!" called Hurwood from behind them. He and Friend and Bonnett had just blundered through the gap, stumbled, and then managed to put Beth down more or less gently as they fell to the dark sand. Hurwood was the first to sit up. "Apparent directions are no good here. You could walk in a straight line till you die of starvation, and never get any closer to the Fountain. It would, in all probability, seem slowly to *circle* you as you walked."

Blackbeard laughed. "I wasn't going to let him get so far that we couldn't get him back. But you're right, that is how it looked. I walked in toward it for two days before I admitted you can't get there from here, and then it took me three more days to walk back out to where we're standing."

Hurwood stood up, brushing himself off. "Days?" he asked drily.

Blackbeard looked sharply at him. "Well, no, now you mention it. The sun rose but never got much past what you'd call dawn before it decided to go down again. Dawn turned straight into dusk, with no real day between."

Hurwood nodded. "We're not really in Florida now—or not particularly, anyway, not Florida any more than we're in every other place. Have you studied Pythagoras in any depth?"

Davies and Blackbeard both admitted that they had not.

"The contradictions implicit in his philosophy are not contradictions here. I don't know whether the circumstances here are the general or some special case—but here the square root of two is not an irrational number."

"Infinity—*apeiron*—as it exists here, would not have offended Aristotle," added Leo Friend, who, for once, seemed to have forgotten Beth Hurwood.

"Good news for Harry Stottle," said Blackbeard. "But can I get rid of my ghosts here?"

"Yes," said Hurwood. "We've just got to get you to the pool."

Blackbeard waved toward the Fountain. "Lead the way."

"I shall." Hurwood hefted the bundles he'd brought along, then lowered them carefully to the sand.

As Hurwood and Friend crouched to untie the bundles, Shandy sidled over to Beth. "How are you doing?" was all he could think of to say.

"Fine, thank you," she said automatically. Her eyes were unfocused and she was breathing shallowly but very fast.

"Just . . . *hang on*," Shandy whispered, angry at his own helplessness. "As soon as we get back to the beach, I swear, I'll get you out of this. . . ."

Her knees bent and she was falling; he managed to get his arms around her before she hit the sand, and when he saw that she'd fainted, he laid her down gently on her back. Then Friend had shoved him away and was taking her pulse and lifting her eyelids to peer at her pupils.

Shandy stood up and looked over at Hurwood, who was using the torch to light a lantern that had been in one of the bundles. "How can you *do* this to your own daughter?" Shandy asked him hoarsely. "You son of a bitch, I hope your Margaret comes back just long enough to curse you and then collapse in a pile of corruption as foul as your damned soul."

Hurwood glanced up incuriously, then returned to his work. He had got the lantern's wick lit, and now he lowered the hood over it. The hood was metal, but not featureless—random-looking slits had been cut into it, and they cast lines of light out across the dark sand.

Shandy took a step toward the old man, but Blackbeard was suddenly in front of him. "Afterward, sonny," the pirate said. "He and I are working together right now, and if you try to foul my plans you'll find yourself sitting on the ground trying to stuff your guts back into your belly." He turned to Hurwood. "You about ready?"

"Yes." Hurwood stuck the still-flaming torch upright in the sand and then stood up with the lantern. The square wooden box now hung at his belt like a fishing creel. "Is she well?" he asked Friend.

"Fine," said the fat man. "She just fainted."

"Carry her."

Hurwood raised the lantern in his single hand and stared at

the patterns of light-lines it threw onto the sand. After a few seconds of study he nodded and began walking, on a course that led slightly away from the fountain.

Friend managed to stand up with Beth's limp form draped over his shoulders, though the effort darkened his face. He stumped along after Hurwood, the breath whistling in and out of him, and the rest of the group followed, with Bonnett and the odd boatman lurchingly bringing up the rear.

It wasn't a steady walk. Frequently Hurwood paused to peer at the light-lines and fiercely argue mathematical niceties with Friend, and once Shandy heard Friend point out an error in one of "your Black Newton equations." Several times they led the shuffling group in sharp changes of direction, and for a long while they all just marched around and around in the outline of a square; but Shandy had noticed that, no matter what their apparent direction, the moon never shifted from its position above his left shoulder, and he shivered and wasn't tempted to offer any sarcastic comments.

The torch that Hurwood had planted in the sand was as often visible ahead, or off to one side, as behind them, but every time Shandy looked at it it was farther away. The Fountain itself was so difficult to focus on that he couldn't perceive any change in its distance, but he did notice that the two bridgelike structures had moved closer together.

Then he noticed the crowds. At first he thought they were low fog banks or expanses of water, but when he stared hard at the uneven gray lines on the horizon he saw that they were made up of thousands of figures rushing silently back and forth, their arms waving overhead like a field of grass blades stirred by a night wind.

"I should never have believed," said Hurwood softly, pausing in his calculations to look at the distant multitudes, "that death had undone so many."

The *Inferno,* thought Shandy—third canto, if I'm not mistaken. And, at the moment, who cares?

The bridges were very close together now, and the sky was lightening in a direction that might have been east. Hurwood's light-lines were becoming less visible on the sand—which was, in the faint daylight, taking on a rusty hue—and Hurwood and Friend were working faster. The shapes rising and falling above the center of the pool were losing their color and becoming gray, and now looked much more like clouds of water spray than like billows of fire. With the approach of day the total silence seemed even more eerie—there were no bird or insect cries, and neither the unrestful crowds nor the Fountain made any audible sound. The air had cooled since they'd left the jungle, though his feet were warmed by the iron tacks in the soles of his boots, and it was easy to warm his hands by holding them near his smoking knife scabbard.

He had been looking back at the remote dot that was the torch, and so he bumped into Hurwood when the group halted.

There was only one bridge now, and they were right in front of it. It was about six feet wide and paved with broad, flat stones, and stone walls rose at the sides to shoulder height. Though when seen from afar the bridges had seemed to arch steeply up from the pool's edge, from where Shandy now stood it looked almost level, rising only very gradually as it narrowed away with distance and faded among the shifting clouds of the Fountain. In spite of its outlandish location, Shandy thought he'd seen the bridge before.

"After you," said Hurwood to Blackbeard.

The giant pirate, whose belt and boots, Shandy noticed, were smoking and sparking like the match-cords in his mane, stepped onto the bridge—

—and seemed to explode. Fluttering blurs of gray erupted from his mouth, nose and eyes and shot away in all directions, and his clothes leaped and shook on his huge frame like waves in a choppy sea. His hands jigged helplessly in front of him as the gray things blasted out of his sleeves, but in the midst of the ferocious detonations Blackbeard roared and managed to turn around.

"Stay there!" shouted Hurwood. "Don't step off the bridge! It's your ghosts leaving you!"

The exodus was tapering off, but Blackbeard didn't stop jumping. His belt and shoes were on fire, and he grabbed the smoldering hilt of his cutlass, drew the redly glowing blade and touched it to his belt, instantly burning through the leather. He tossed the cutlass out onto the sand and with sizzling fingers snatched his belt buckle loose, drew the pieces of leather free and kicked it all after the sword. He sat down and pulled off his boots, then stood up again and grinned at Hurwood.

"*Now* abandon all iron," he said.

Ye who enter here, thought Shandy.

"You can step down and just wait for Leo and me right here, with the others," said Hurwood. "Your ghosts are gone, and there's still plenty of the black herb—when we recover the two other torches and get them lit too, there'll be no danger of becoming reinfected on the way out of the jungle. Our bargain is completed, and Leo and I will be back here before long to lead you all back to where this region links with the world you know."

Shandy sighed with relief, and he had started to look around for a place to sit, when he noticed that Friend had made no move to put Beth Hurwood down.

"Wh-who," Shandy stammered, "who's going over and who's staying here?"

"Leo and the girl and myself are going over," said Hurwood impatiently, putting his lantern down on the sand. He took off his belt and shoes, and then in a grotesquely unwitting parody of intimacy he knelt in front of Friend and, one-handed, disconnected the ornate belt buckle from the fat man's belt. Friend's mud-caked slippers evidently contained no iron.

"I'm going over, too," pronounced Blackbeard, not stepping down from the bridge. "I didn't fight my way in here two years ago just to pick up a peltful of ghosts." He looked past Hurwood, and a moment later Stede Bonnett and the boatman stepped forward. Bonnett began unbuckling his belt and stepping out of his shoes, but the boatman's clothes were sewn shut and he was barefoot. "They're coming too," Blackbeard said.

Davies' face had become perceptibly more lined and hollowed since leaving the fires by the seashore, but there was some kind of humor in his eyes as he took a step forward and then crouched to shed his boots.

No, Shandy thought almost calmly. It just can't be expected of me. I'm already on the sidewalk outside reality—I'm simply *not* going out farther, into the street. None of these people will ever come back, and I'll have to figure out Hurwood's magic lantern just to find my way back to the goddamned jungle! Why did I ever come along? Why did I ever leave England?

He found he was implicitly confident of a way out . . . and his face reddened when he realized that it was an axiom called up from early childhood—the conviction that if he cried hard enough and long enough, someone would take him home.

What right had these people to put him into such a humiliating situation?

He looked at Beth Hurwood, draped over Friend's shoulders. She was still unconscious, and her face, though heartbreakingly beautiful to him, was drawn and tautened by recent horrors—innocence intolerably abused. Wouldn't it be—couldn't a case be made for it being—kinder to let her die now, unconscious and not yet ruined?

While still in doubt he caught Leo Friend's eye. Friend was smiling at him with confident contempt, and he shifted his pudgy hand on Beth's thigh.

At the same moment, Hurwood began crooning reassuringly, and he got down on his hands and knees. He muttered some vague endearments and then, gently but strongly, he lowered himself flat, face down on the sand. Still murmuring, he began to flop there in a ponderous rhythm.

Leo Friend blushed furiously and snatched his hand off of Beth's leg. "Mr. Hurwood!" he screeched.

Hurwood, not stopping, chuckled indulgently.

"He seems to snap out of these fits before too long," said Blackbeard. "We'll wait this one out and then get moving."

Are you *all* crazy? wondered Shandy. Hurwood was the only chance, and a damn slim one at that, of anyone recrossing this bridge alive, and now he's madder than old Governor Sawney. There is no chance of surviving any further advance, and *I* don't want to take my eternal place among the silent gray legions on this unnatural horizon. Jack Shandy will wait right here, until dark, and when you doomed fools have failed to reappear I'll somehow use Hurwood's lantern to get back to the torch and the jungle and the boats and the shore. I'll no doubt regret this cowardice later, but at least I'll be able to lie in the sun and have a drink while I'm regretting it.

Shandy stepped back, away from the bridge, and sat down. He had meant to avoid meeting anyone's eyes, but as he looked around for Hurwood's lantern, he glanced up and found Davies looking straight at him.

The lean old pirate was grinning at him, evidently pleased.

Shandy grinned back in relief, glad Davies understood . . . and then he realized that Davies thought he had sat down in order to take off his boots.

And suddenly he knew, unhappily, that he couldn't just sit it out. This was stupid, as stupid as his father pulling a woodworking knife on a gang of Nantes alley toughs, or Captain Chaworth rushing with an unfamiliar sword at a pistol-armed pirate chief; but somehow, perhaps like them, he had been robbed of every way out of it. He took off his boots and stood up again.

By the time Friend tore his gaze away from the ludicrously bobbing figure of Benjamin Hurwood, Shandy's boots and knife lay abandoned in the sand and Shandy was standing in front of him.

"What's the matter?" Shandy asked the fat physician. His voice quavered only slightly. "Can't get familiar with a girl unless she's asleep?"

Friend's face got even redder. "D-d-d-don't b-be ab-ab-ab—d-don't—"

"I think he's trying to say, 'Don't be absurd,' Jack," said Davies helpfully.

"Do you?" asked Shandy, his voice still a little wild. "I thought it was, 'Yeah, because that was the only time even my mother didn't gag at the sight of me.'"

Friend began squawking and stuttering in, weirdly, a little-boy voice; then blood burst from his nose and bright red drops tumbled to his silk shirt-front and soaked into the weave in blurrily cross-shaped stains. His knees started to give, and for a moment Shandy thought the physician himself was about to faint, or even die.

Then Friend straightened, took a deep breath, and, without looking at Shandy, shifted his hold on Beth and stepped up onto the bridge.

Hurwood finally rolled over and smiled at the sky for a few moments, then he twitched, glanced around, winced and got to his feet. He walked to the bridge. "Friend and I will lead," was all he said.

Shandy and Davies followed him onto the bridge's paving stones, and then Bonnett and the boatman stepped from the sand onto the bridge surface.

The boatman instantly collapsed in a pile of loose clothing. Shandy looked more closely and saw that clothing was all that lay on the stones—there was no body.

Hurwood noticed the phenomenon and raised an eyebrow. "Your servant was a dead man?"

"Well . . . yes," said Blackbeard.

"Ah." Hurwood shrugged. "To be expected—dust to dust, you know." He turned his back on them and started forward.

Chapter Thirteen

For quite a while they walked without speaking—footsteps were the only sounds, and they were just echoless thuds. As much to distract himself as to satisfy curiosity, Shandy began mentally counting paces; and he had counted more than two thousand when the light began to dim again. He found he had no idea how long the dawn period had lasted.

They seemed now to be passing through alternating patches of light and shade, and for a moment Shandy thought he smelled incense. Hurwood began walking more slowly, and Shandy glanced at him.

They were all walking down the center aisle of a church. Hurwood was somehow dressed in a long formal coat, and his hair was brown and long and carefully curled, but the rest of the people in the procession were still dressed in the mud-caked, ragged, scorched clothes they'd worn through the jungle. Hurwood had one hand on the wooden box that was slung at his side, and his other hand swung back and forth as he walked up the aisle. . . .

He's got his other arm back, thought Shandy with a dreamlike lack of surprise.

Shandy looked ahead, toward the altar. A minister of some sort was smiling as this unsavory crowd approached, but there was an altar boy at a kneeler off to the side who stared at them with far more horror than even their devastated appearance seemed to call for. Nervously, Shandy looked behind himself . . .

. . . And saw just the bridge, and the plain far beyond it, deeply shadowed now in twilight. He turned back toward the church scene, but it was fading. Shandy caught one more whiff of incense, and then the bridge was just the bridge again.

What was *that*? he wondered. A look into Hurwood's mind, his memories? Did Davies and Blackbeard see it too, or was it just me because I happened to glance at him when he was projecting it?

There were smears of blood on the paving stones ahead of them, and when he reached them Shandy noticed that the drops and smudges and handprints seemed to be the tracks of two bleeding people crawling. He paused for a moment to crouch and touch one wide, splash-edged drop—the blood was still wet. For some reason this profoundly upset Shandy, though he had to admit that it was certainly a minor unpleasantness compared to most of the other recent events. There were no figures, walking or crawling, visible ahead of them, but Shandy kept glancing that way, almost fearfully.

The air here had not ever been particularly fresh, but now it was stale—Shandy smelled boiled cabbage and unchanged bed-sheets. He glanced one by one at his companions; and when he looked at Friend a scene came into focus around the fat physician. The fat man was younger, a boy in fact, and though he was keeping up with Shandy and the others he was lying in a bed. Shandy followed the boy's upward gaze, and was startled to see the vague female forms in diaphanous draperies that twisted slowly over-head. There was a naïvely exaggerated eroticism about them, like the crude naked-lady pictures a little boy might draw on a wall . . . but why did they all have gray hair?

The scene dissolved in a burst of whiteness, and again the bridge was visible underfoot, the shoulder-height walls moving past on either side. Shandy's foot skidded on something that felt like a pebble—but he knew it was a tooth, and the knowledge increased his uneasiness.

Then there was deep sand underfoot, and Davies' face was lit by firelight. His face was fuller, his hair darker, and he wore the tattered remains of a Royal Navy officer's jacket. Shandy looked around, and saw that they were walking along the shore of New Providence Island; Hog Island was dimly visible across the starlit harbor to their right, and cooking fires dotted the sand slope to the left—but there were fewer fires, and fewer craft in the harbor, and a couple of big pieces of storm-wrecked ships that Shandy remembered being up on the sand were nowhere to be seen. Shandy couldn't hear the conversation, but Davies was talking to Blackbeard; and though Davies was laughing and shaking his head scornfully, Shandy thought he looked upset—frightened, even. Blackbeard seemed to be making an offer, and wheedling, and Davies didn't seem to be refusing it so much as disparaging it—doubting its genuineness. Finally Blackbeard sighed, stepped back, seemed to brace himself, and gestured at the sand. Shandy smelled hot metal. Then the sand rippled and jumped, as if all the sand crabs were simultaneously struck with apoplexy, and white bones began poking up out of it and rolling and cartwheeling together into a pile; the pile heaved and shifted and shook, then steadied, and Shandy realized it was now a human skeleton in a crouching posture. As Davies stared, his half-smile a rictus of strain now, the skeleton straightened up and faced him. Blackbeard spoke, and the skeleton lowered itself and knelt on one bony knee, and it lowered its skull head. Blackbeard then made a dismissing gesture, at which the skeleton sprang apart and resumed its status as just a scattering of old bones, and Blackbeard continued his soliciting speech. Davies still didn't answer, but his air of amused skepticism was gone.

Then Shandy was once more walking on blood-spattered paving stones.

"Are we getting any closer to the goddamned place?" he asked. As he spoke, he was afraid his voice would betray his mounting fear, but the dead air here muffled his words, and he hardly heard them himself.

They kept walking. A couple of times Shandy thought he heard scuffling sounds, and gasping sobs, ahead of them on the bridge, but it was too dark for him to see clearly.

The air seemed heavy, like syrup so thick that one more grain of sugar would cause the whole works to crystallize; and, though it terrified him to do it, Shandy couldn't prevent himself from turning to look at Blackbeard . . . and he did look, and for a while Shandy stopped being Shandy.

He was a fifteen-year-old boy known to the outlaw mountain blacks as Johnny Con, though since his misuse of some of the spells of the *hungan* he'd been serving, he was no longer a fit assistant for a respectable *vodun* priest, and had no further right—nor even inclination anymore—to call himself an *adjanikon;* Ed Thatch was his real name, his adult name, and in three days he'd be entitled to start using it.

Today would be the first day of his baptism to the *loa* that would be his guide through life, and whose goals he would henceforth share. The black *marrons* who had raised him since childhood had this morning escorted him down from the blue mountains to the house of Jean Petro, a legendary magician who had documentably lived here for more than a hundred years, and was said to have actually made many *loas,* and had to live in a house on stilts because of the way dirt turned rusty and sterile after any long proximity to him; compared to Petro, every other *bocor* in the Caribbean was considered a mere *caplata,* a street-corner turnip-conjuror.

The *marrons* were escaped slaves who, having originally lived in Senegal, and Dahomey, and the nations of the Congo coast, had no difficulty adapting to life in the mountain jungles of Jamaica, and the white colonists were so unnerved by this dangerous and unforgiving population that they paid the blacks a seasonal tribute in exchange for sparing the outlying farms and settlements; but even the *marrons* refused to venture within half a mile of Jean Petro's house, and the boy walked alone down the long path that led to the garden and the livestock pens and, finally, the house on stilts.

A stream ran behind the house, and that's where the old man was—Thatch could see his bare legs, knobby and dark as black-thorn walking sticks, below the raised floor. Thatch was of course barefoot, and he made a "Be silent" gesture at the chickens poking around under the house and then padded across the dusty front yard as noiselessly as the shifting speckles of sunlight. When he had moved around the corner of the house, he could see that old Petro was walking along the stream bank, pausing here and there to lift one squat bottle after another out of the water, peer into the clouded glass, rattle his long fingernails against it, hold the dripping bottle to his ear, and then shake his head and crouch to put it back and fish up another.

Thatch watched while he kept it up, and finally the old *bocor*'s face curdled in a smile when he listened to one bottle, and he rattled his nails on it again; and then he just stood there and took turns tapping the bottle and listening, like a dungeon-confined prisoner whose measured wall-clinking has at long last elicited, however remotely, a response.

"It's our boy, sure enough," he said in a scratchy old-man's voice. "Gede, the *loa* who's the . . . chief foreman, sort of, of the one who wants you."

Thatch realized the old man was aware of him and was talking to him. He stayed where he was, but he called, " 'Wants me'? *I* chose *him*."

The old man chuckled. "Well, anyway, *that* one ain't in the creek here, and we need Gede to call him. Of course even Gede's only here *tokenly*. This is only a part of him, in this jar, his belly button, you might say—just enough to compel him." Petro turned around and hobbled back to the yard where Thatch stood. "The dead become more powerful as time goes by, you see, boy. What was just an unquiet ghost to your grandfather could be a full-fledged *loa* to your grandchildren. And I've learned to *bend* 'em, train 'em in certain directions like you would a vine. Farmer plant a seed in the ground and one day have a tree—I put a ghost in a bottle under running water and one day I have a *loa*." He grinned, revealing a few teeth in white gums, and waved the bottle back toward the stream. "I've grown near a dozen to maturity. They ain't quite the quality of the Rada *loas*, the ones that came with us across the ocean from Guinée, but I can grow 'em to fit what I need."

The chickens in the shade under the house were recovering from Thatch's gesture, and began clucking and fluttering. Petro winked, and they shut up again. "Of course," Petro went on, "the one that wants you—or that you want, if you prefer—old Baron Samedi, he's a different sort of beast." He shook his head and his eyes narrowed in what might have been awe. "Every now and then, no more than twice or three times in my whole life, I think I've accidentally made one that was too much like . . . some thing or other that already existed, was already out there, and the resemblance was too close for 'em to keep on being *separate*. So suddenly I had a thing in a bottle that was too big to fit . . . even just tokenly. My damn house was nearly knocked over when Baron Samedi got too big—bottle went off like a bomb, tossed trees every which way, and the creek didn't refill for an hour. There's still a wide, deep pool there. Nothing'll grow on the bank and every Spring I've got to net dead pollywogs out of it."

Young Thatch stared indignantly at the bottle. "So what you

got in your beer bottle there is just some *servant* of Baron Samedi's?"

"More or less. But Gede's a top-ranking *loa*—he's number-two man here just because the Baron is so much more. And like any other *loa* Gede must be invited, and then entreated, using the rites he demands, to do what we ask. Now, I've got the sheets from the bed a bad man died in, and a black robe for you, and today is Saturday, Gede's sacred day. We'll roast a chicken and a goat for him, and I've got a whole keg of *clairin*—rum—because Gede is lavish in his consumption of it. Today we'll—"

"I didn't come down from the mountains to deal with Baron Samedi's bungo houseboy."

Jean Petro smiled broadly. *"Ohhh!"* He held the bottle out toward the boy. "Well, why don't you tell him that? Just hold the bottle up to the sunlight and peek in through the side until you see him . . . then you can explain your social standards to him."

Thatch had never dealt directly with a *loa*, but he tried to act sure of himself as he contemptuously took the bottle. "Very well, ghostling," he said, holding it up to the sun, "show yourself!" His tone was scornful, but his mouth had gone dry and his heart was thudding hard in his chest.

At first all he could see were blurry flaws in the crudely blown glass, but then he saw movement in there, and focused on it—and for an instant he thought the bottle contained a featherless baby bird, swimming with deformed wings and legs in some cloudy fluid.

Then there was a voice in his head, jabbering shrilly in debased French. Thatch understood only some of it, enough to gather that the speaker was not only demanding chicken and rum, but protesting that it had every right to those things, and to as much candy as it wanted, too, and threatening dire punishments if any of the formalities of its invitation ceremony weren't performed with the greatest pomp and grandeur and respectfulness; and there'd better be no *laughing*. At the same time, Thatch got an impression of great age, and of a power that had grown vast . . . at such great personal expense that only a fragment of the original personality remained, like a chimney still standing in the heart of a furiously burning house. The senile petulance and the terrifying power, Thatch realized, were not contradictory qualities—each was somehow a product of the other.

Then it became aware of him. The tirade halted and he could sense the speaker looking around in some confusion. Thatch imagined a very old king, startled when he had thought he was alone, hastily arranging his robes so that they draped properly, and combing his sparse hair forward to cover his baldness.

At that point Gede evidently called Thatch's words up from memory and paid attention to them, for the voice in the boy's head was suddenly back, and it was roaring now.

"*'Ghostling'?*" Gede raged. "*'Bungo houseboy'?*"

Thatch's head was punched back by something invisible, and suddenly there was blood on his nose and mouth. He reeled a couple of steps backward and tried to fling the bottle away, but it clung to his palm.

"*Thatch is your name, eh?*" The voice ground the inside of the boy's skull like a grating-blade being turned in a coconut.

Thatch's belly imploded visibly—blood sprayed from his nose and he sat down hard. A moment later all of his clothes burst into flame. The boy rolled, blazing, toward the stream, and though along the way he jerked with the impacts of a couple more invisible kicks, he managed to splash into the water. "*I'll tell the Baron,*" said the voice in his head as he floundered, still unable to get rid of the bottle, "*to treat you special.*"

Thatch got his feet under himself and crawled up onto the bank and sat down. His hair was scorched to the scalp and his clothes looked like curtains dug out of the wreckage of a burned-down house and blood was running down his forearm from his bottle-clutching hand, but he didn't tremble as he held the thing up to the sun and grinned into its glass depths. "Do that," he whispered. "You pitiful goddamn pickled herring."

The light dimmed, and suddenly he was dry and upright and walking, and he was Jack Shandy again. The spatters of blood on the bridge's paving stones were less frequent—perhaps the injured crawlers had bandaged their wounds—but when he crouched to touch one smudged patch of wetness, he recoiled in horror. It was actually still warm. Again, louder now, he heard a wheezing gasp from ahead.

He looked up, and all at once he knew why he had thought he'd seen this bridge before. Here were the two bleeding crawlers, almost underfoot now; the white hair of one was matted with gleaming darkness, and the other figure, younger and slimmer, was trying to crawl without touching to the ground his right hand, the fingers of which were bent and blackly swollen. The lights of the city of Nantes were flickering and dim, and Shandy knew that these injured people would not be seen by some helpful wayfarer, but would have to crawl all the way back to their room, and their comfortless beds, and the ever-present marionettes.

Shandy ran ahead and then crouched in the path of his father. One of the old man's eyes was hidden by dirt-caked blood, and Shandy knew that was the eye he would lose. The old man's face was taut with effort, and breath hissed through the fresh gaps in the line of his bared teeth.

"Dad!" Shandy said urgently as his father's ruined face hitched closer. "Dad, you've inherited a lot of money! Your father has died, and left his estate to you! Get in touch with the authorities in Haiti, in Port-au-Prince!"

Old François Chandagnac didn't hear him. Shandy tried twice more to convey his message, then gave up and moved to the other broken crawler, the one that was twenty-one-year-old John Chandagnac.

"John," said Shandy as he crouched in front of his remembered, younger self, "listen. Don't abandon your father! Take him with you. Go to the trouble, you . . . you goddamned wooden choirboy!" He was choking, and tears were running down his older, bearded face as if to match the blood that streaked the younger one. "He *can't* do it alone, but he's not going to admit that to you! Don't leave him, he's all you've got in the world and he loves you and he's going to die alone of cold and starvation, thinking of you, while you're comfortable in England and *not* thinking of him. . . ."

The crawling figure was unaware of him. Shandy, already kneeling, lowered his forehead to the paving stones and sobbed harshly as the image of his younger self crawled right through him, as insubstantial as a shadow.

A hand was shaking his shoulder. He looked up. Davies' haggard face was grinning down at him, not without sympathy. "You can't collapse *now,* Jack," the old pirate said. He nodded past Shandy, ahead. "We're there."

Chapter Fourteen

The bridge was gone, and belatedly Shandy wondered if any of the others had ever seen it. Or had Hurwood, for example, seen the whole thing as a walk up an impossibly long church aisle? Now they were on a muddy slope, facing down, and Shandy could feel icy moisture seeping through the knees of his trousers.

He looked around a little wildly, his earlier panic returning, for something felt very wrong, very disorienting, here—but he could see no excuse for the feeling. The mud slope curled away from them on either side, and, squinting in the dim light, he saw that the edges of it curled back in and met, some distance away; it was a slope-sided pit, and water spouted and splashed way down there at the bottom. The sky was a blanket of eerily fast-roiling clouds lit from above by, presumably, the moon. He glanced around at his seven companions to see if they shared his unease. It was hard to tell. Beth had regained consciousness—Shandy wondered when—but was just blinking dazedly, and Bonnett was as expressionless as an embalmed corpse.

"Onward," said Hurwood, and they all started down.

Though he several times slipped and slid in the mud, Shandy found himself oppressed by the idea of how solid the earth itself was. It gave him a feeling like claustrophobia, in spite of the high, churning clouds.

Then it occurred to him—*seven* companions? There should only have been six! He hung back and identified the laboring figures below him: there was Blackbeard, and Davies, and Bonnett, and Beth and Friend and Hurwood . . . and no one else. That was six. Shandy scrambled after them, and then just to reassure himself he counted the figures . . . and again got seven.

There was a smell, too, like stagnant water and ancient plumbing. A night for terrible smells, he reflected. The thought reminded him of something, and he worked his way over toward Davies. "Speaking of disagreeable smells," Shandy muttered, "I thought you weren't supposed to do resurrection magic on the land."

"Miss the hot-iron smell, do you?" the pirate said quietly. "But no, Jack, they ain't *doing* any of that kind of magic here; they're just getting their souls . . . adapted . . . so they can do it later, somewhere at sea." The slope flattened out now, and they were able to stand up straight without being braced for a fall. "No," Davies went on, "they couldn't do one bit of it here—have you ever *felt* such solid ground? Makes everywhere else feel like . . . just big rafts."

That was it, Shandy realized—that was what had been bothering him. This place gave one no sensation of motion. He'd never thought a place on solid land could seem to be moving, except during earthquakes; before today he'd have laughed at anyone who claimed to be able to *feel* the motion through space of the planet Earth. Now, though, it seemed to him that he had always been fundamentally aware of that motion, albeit as unthinkingly as the way a fish is aware of water.

Copernicus and Galileo and Newton, he thought, would find this place even more disturbing than I do.

They had all reached the level area except Bonnett, who was slowly bumping his way down the slope in a sitting position. "How many of us are there?" Shandy asked Davies.

"Why, uh . . . seven," the pirate answered.

"Count."

Davies did, then swore in alarm. "You and Bonnett and Thatch," he said quickly to himself, "and the three Old Worlders, and me. That's seven. Right, and there's nobody else. Whew, for a moment there it *did* look like eight, didn't it?"

Shandy shook his head unhappily. "Count again, fast, and you'll get eight. Do it slow, naming each one, and you get seven."

Davies counted again, darting a finger at each dim silhouette, once quickly and then once again slowly—and when he was done he spat out a weary obscenity. "Jack," he said, his voice tight with a disgust that Shandy thought concealed terror, "are our eyes bewitched? How can there be a stranger among us who becomes invisible only when we count carefully?"

Shandy didn't even try to answer, for he'd taken a closer look at the Fountain. He had already noticed that the water, though being flung high into the air, was oddly thick, seeming to *slap* more than splash when an upflung mass of it fell, and that it was the source of the dim phosphorescence as well as of the stagnant smell, but now he could see faces in the agitated liquid—hundreds of faces forming one after another as if the Fountain was a mirror spinning in the center of a crowd, and each briefly appearing face was contorted with fear and rage. Though repelled, he took a step closer—and then saw the swaying curtains of palely colored light, like a moving Aurora Borealis, that streamed away upward from the whole expanse of the Fountain and played silently across the face of the clouds far overhead, seeming to be the force that kept them churning.

Hurwood stepped up beside Shandy. The old man was breathing shallowly and quickly. "Don't anyone look around," he said. "Everybody just . . . keep looking wherever you are looking. The thing we need to talk to cannot appear if too much attention is paid to it."

With a chill Shandy realized that the thing Hurwood sought must have been the extra figure that he and Davies had kept coming up with in their counting.

Somebody nearby whispered something, and Shandy expected Hurwood to demand silence, but then the one-armed sorceror was answering in a language Shandy had never heard, and he realized that the whisper had also been in that language, and that the whisperer was not one of their party.

The alien voice spoke again, more firmly but still very softly, and it seemed to Shandy that the speaker was right at his elbow. Shandy was obeying Hurwood and staring straight ahead, but peripherally in the dimness he could see someone beside him. Davies was on his other side . . . was this their mysterious whisperer? Or just Bonnett? Or even Beth? Shandy was strongly tempted to peek.

The voice stopped. "Eyes front," Hurwood reminded every-

one. "Close them if you'd prefer, but no one is to look around."
Then he spoke again, more tensely, in the other language, and
when he finished Leo Friend added a phrase that was obviously a
question.

The soft, unplaceable voice answered, and spoke at some
length, and Shandy wondered how long he could continue staring
straight ahead. The thought of closing his eyes in so horribly
motionless a place as this made his belly go cold, but even holding
still was becoming unbearable.

At last the voice stopped, and all at once Hurwood and Friend
were moving. Shandy risked a squinting glance their way. They
were hurrying toward the shore of the pool around the Fountain,
and when they got there they walked right into the viscous fluid
and crouched in the shallows to dip some of the stuff up in their
hands and eagerly drink it. Then they waded back up onto the
muddy ground, and Hurwood spoke again.

The answer that came a few seconds later was very faint,
perhaps because people had shifted their gazes. The voice spoke
only a few syllables.

Instantly Hurwood and Friend dug into their pockets. Hurwood produced a pocket knife, and Friend finally just yanked a pin
from his powdered wig, and at the same moment each of them
jabbed himself in a finger and shook blood onto the cold mud.

The blood spatters hissed where they fell, and then it looked to
Shandy as if two clawlike hands had burst up out of the mud, but a
moment later the things stopped moving and he realized they were
plants—spindly cactus-looking things, but conspicuous in this
desolate landscape. Shandy now noticed a third plant, farther
down the shore, but it was withered and stiff.

Then Blackbeard strode forward, and, though Hurwood
reached out to stop him, in two long strides the pirate-king was
ankle deep in the pool. He scooped up some of the liquid and
drank it, then walked back out of it, bit his finger and shook off
some blood. Again there was the hissing and the eruption of the
mud, and a moment later another spiny plant had sprung up, a few
yards from Hurwood's and Friend's.

The pair of sorcerors stared at him, an identical surprised and
slightly alarmed expression on their faces, but then Hurwood just
shrugged and muttered, "Nothing to be done."

The one-armed man spoke again, and was again answered by

the faint voice, though now it sounded to Shandy as if it were coming from the other side of the group, beyond Davies.

"Damn," muttered Hurwood when the voice stopped. "It doesn't know that right now."

Shandy saw Friend shrug. "We can wait for a while."

"We'll wait until it knows, and has told me," said Hurwood firmly.

"Who's this *it?*" asked Blackbeard.

"The . . . personality we were questioning," said Hurwood, "though the pronoun 'who' overstates the case." He sighed, apparently at the hopelessness of trying to explain, but then his professorial reflexes seemed to take over. "Newton's laws of mechanics are entirely useful in describing the world we know—for every action there's an equal but opposite reaction, and a uniformly moving object will continue to move uniformly unless acted upon by some force—but if you get *very* particular about *very* small-scale events, if you deal with them in such specific, needlessly obsessive detail as to almost qualify you for a lunatic asylum . . . you find that Newton's mechanical description of reality is only *mostly* correct. In tiny extents of space or time there's an element of indecisiveness, postponement of definition, and you can catch truth as loose as an underdone egg. In our normal world this isn't a big factor because the . . . odds, I guess you'd say . . . are pretty consistent from place to place, and overwhelmingly strong in favor of Newton. But here they're not consistent. They're polarized here, though the overall net values are the same. There is *no* elasticity in this ground, *no* uncertainty, and so there's a lot out here in the air. What we were questioning was a . . . tendency toward personality; the likelihood of an awareness."

Blackbeard snorted. "What language was that, that *likelihoods* speak?"

"The oldest one," said Hurwood imperturbably.

"Is that," Shandy found himself asking, "why the thing is so hard to locate?"

"Yes," said Hurwood, "and don't try. It isn't any *where—where* is as inappropriate to this phenomenon as *who*. If you watch for it you're watching for a *what*, at some particular *where* and *when*—and on that basis you may find many things, but you won't find . . ." He finished the sentence with a vague wave and a fading whistle.

For at least a full minute they all stood there shivering in that cold dark valley, while Hurwood patiently called some unintelligible phrase over and over again. Shandy looked around to see how Beth was enduring, but Hurwood sharply told him to keep his gaze steady.

Finally Blackbeard said, "This delay wasn't part of our bargain."

"Fine," said Hurwood. He sent his strange sentence out once again; and then he added, to Blackbeard, "Go, if you like. Good luck getting back to the jungle."

Blackbeard swore, but stayed where he was. "Your ghost-thing is looking something up for you, hey?"

"No. It will eventually manifest itself again, but it won't be the same personality as before; though at the same time it won't be a different personality either. 'Same' and 'different' are far too specific. And it won't have *learned* what I want to know. It will simply happen to know it this time. Or, if not this time, it will know it some time. It's like waiting for two or twelve to come up in a game of dice."

More time went by, and finally one of Hurwood's patient calls was answered. Beth's father conversed with the unlocated voice for another minute or so, and then Shandy heard him plodding heavily across the mud.

"You can all look anywhere you please now," Hurwood said.

Shandy watched Hurwood, and he wasn't reassured to see the narrowed eyes and the hardened jaw-muscles of the ex–Oxford don.

"Leo," Hurwood said tensely, "hold Elizabeth."

Friend was wheezingly happy to obey. Beth still seemed to be in a stunned daze, though Shandy noticed that she was breathing very rapidly now.

Hurwood reached down and untied the wooden box from his belt; he loosened the wooden lid with his teeth and shook it off. Shandy couldn't see what was inside. Then Hurwood shuffled over to Beth and held it, open end up, under her right hand.

"Cut her hand, Leo," the old man said.

Shandy started forward, but long before he could get there Friend reached down with his hairpin and, his lips wet and his eyes half-closed, drove the pin into Beth Hurwood's thumb.

It brought her out of her daze. She jumped and looked down at her punctured hand, and then looked past it into the box her father was holding, into which the quick drops of her blood were falling—and she shrieked and lunged away, scrambling on all fours up the muddy slope.

Shandy took off after her and caught her a few yards up, and he put his arm around her heaving shoulders and shook her gently. "It's over now, Beth," he gasped. "Your hand's cut but we're alive and I think we're headed back now. The worst is—"

"It's my mother's head!" Beth screamed. *"He's got my mother's head in that box!"*

Shandy couldn't help looking back in horror. Hurwood was sitting down in the mud to slide the wooden lid back onto the box, an expression of almost imbecilic satisfaction lighting up his old face, while Friend just looked hungrily at Beth, his hands still raised in the position they'd been in when he was holding her—but Davies, and even Blackbeard, were staring at the one-armed man with astonishment and loathing.

Hurwood struggled to his feet. "Back," he said. "Back to the sea." He was so tensely cheerful now that he seemed to be having difficulty in speaking.

They all scrambled wearily back up the slope, and when the ground leveled out Shandy put his arm around Beth again and walked with her, though she didn't acknowledge his presence with even a glance.

The bridge was gone. Hurwood led them forward along a rutted dirt road between fields of heather under a rain-threatening sky; mountains rose in the distance, and when Shandy looked back he saw a cluster of old, almost entirely windowless stone buildings behind a wall—a monastery, perhaps, or a convent—and when he peered more closely he saw that a slim, long-haired figure was standing at the wall's top, over the closed gate.

He was unable to elicit any response from the young woman plodding lifelessly along at his side, but, still looking back, he raised his free hand in a wave, and the figure on the wall waved back at him—gratefully, he thought.

Chapter Fifteen

Hurwood and Friend led them back to the plain of dark sand, where they retrieved the still-hot boots and knives, and then the two sorcerors again used the lamp with the slotted hood to find their way back to the burning torch Hurwood had left stuck upright in the sand, and then they were back in the normal world. The black Florida jungle looked comfortingly mundane now to Shandy, and he savored the swamp smells like a man brought back to the aromatic meadows of his youth.

After he had helped Davies and the empty-eyed Bonnett get all the torches lit and push the boats back into deeper water and turn them around, he took Beth's arm and led her over the marshy, shifting ground toward the boat he and Davies had occupied on the way into the swamp. "You ride with us on the way back," he said firmly.

Hurwood heard him and responded passionately, but for a couple of seconds all that came out of his mouth were random, infantile vowel sounds. He became aware of it, closed his eyes in concentration, and then began again. "She—will stay—with—me," he told Shandy.

Hurwood's insistence alarmed Shandy, for he thought he had figured out Hurwood's plan, but now it seemed there was more involved than he'd guessed. "Why?" he asked carefully. "You've no further use for her now."

"Wrong, boy," Hurwood choked. "Just—what're the words?—

cocked it, here. Fire it come Yule—Christmas. Margaret stays with . . . I mean . . . her . . . the girl stays with me in the meantime."

"R-right," put in Friend, his protruding lower lip shiny. "W-w-we'll t-take c-c-c—" He gave up trying to speak, and merely jerked his head back toward the boat Bonnett was already sitting in.

Suddenly it occurred to Shandy what Hurwood's plan might be—and as soon as he thought of it he had to know if he was right. He had no qualms about upsetting Hurwood, and Beth seemed at best minimally aware of her surroundings, so he held his hot knife up near Beth's throat, covering most of the hilt with his hand to keep Hurwood from seeing that it was the blunt side of the blade that was toward her.

The triumphant expression on Hurwood's face was instantly replaced with one of absolute horror. He fell to his knees in one of the oily pools, and then he and Friend both gobbled wordlessly at Shandy.

Shandy, his fears confirmed, grinned at the gibbering pair. "Then it's settled." Walking carefully backward through the spongy bog, keeping his eyes on them and his knife near Beth's throat, he escorted her to the boat where the puzzled Davies waited.

Hurwood turned to Blackbeard and hooted imploringly.

Blackbeard had been watching this torchlit drama with narrowed eyes, and now he slowly shook his head. "Our deal is done," he said. "I won't interfere."

Shandy and the nearly catatonic Beth Hurwood clambered into the boat and Davies pushed away from the mud bank. Shandy sheathed his knife.

Bonnett proved unable to do anything more complicated than row straight ahead, so it was Leo Friend whose ample fundament flexed their boat's center thwart, and whose chubby, uncallused hands gingerly took the oar handles. Hurwood was hunched on the stern thwart, facing him, his face lowered into the palm of his single hand and his shoulders rising and falling as he breathed deeply.

Blackbeard poled his own boat ahead of the other two and then looked back at them, and with the torch right behind his shaggy head he reminded Shandy of a total eclipse of the sun. "I don't suppose," Blackbeard remarked, "that my boatman is going to reappear."

Hurwood lifted his head and, though it took some scowling effort, he was able to reply. "No. No more than . . . your ghosts will. As long as we . . . keep the torches lit . . . and the herb burning, all of them . . . stay here."

"Then I hope I can remember the way out," said Blackbeard.

Friend blinked over his shoulder at the pirate-king in alarm. "What? But you came up the river. All you've got to do is retrace the course you took."

Davies laughed. "You *did* remember to leave a trail of bread crumbs, didn't you, Thatch?"

"Naw," said Blackbeard disgustedly, pulling ahead, "but if we get lost we can just ask directions at the first goddamn *inn* we come to."

Slowly the three boats moved forward, their orangely flickering bow-torches the only points of light in the humid blackness. The white fungus heads along the banks were silent now, except for an intermittent exhalation that flapped their lips. Shandy wondered if they were snoring.

After a few minutes the channel they were following broadened out, and normal rowing became possible, and Shandy, crouched once more on the bow, sat down more comfortably, for he no longer had to be ready to lean out and push off encroaching banks and roots.

Then all at once he was aware of murderous anger, and at first he thought it was his own; he glared back at the boat behind his, but Hurwood just looked exhausted and unhappy, and Friend was whimpering softly with each torturing pull on the oars, and he realized that the rage he was aware of was a different sort from his own. His own was usually sudden and hotly choking and strongly flavored with terror, but this was soured and habitual and mean, and it emanated from a mind far too self-centered ever to entertain terror.

Blackbeard had snatched up his torch and was on his feet. "It's our friend the *Este Fasta* again," he called quietly. "Come back to roar at us again, and wave more bushes in our faces."

The jungle presence seemed to hear him, for Shandy now detected a note of bitter humor in the psychic miasma of rage. He felt the thing think, *bushes.*

Shandy could feel it bending down attentively over the boats—the air was oppressive, and his lungs had to strain to draw breath.

Numbly he fumbled a handful of the herb out of the pouch and tossed it onto the torch flame, and a stinking gout of smoke boiled upward through the thickened air to impact against the vines and moss overhead.

He could feel the thing's sudden agony, but this time there was no scream and retreat. The jungle spirit was sustaining damage but was not going to back off.

The air and water—the whole jungle—began to change.

"Keep . . . moving!" came a choked cry from Hurwood. "Get . . . . out from under!"

"Oh, good luck," rasped Davies bitterly, nevertheless hauling desperately on the oars.

The water was shaking like a jelly now, and the air was steamy and full of wet bits of vegetation that were evidently being shaken out of the trees. The structure of the boat seemed to be changing under Shandy, becoming more flexible, and when he glanced down at the floorboards he saw that they were untrimmed branches, sprouting gleaming green leaves. They were moving, growing as he watched—he could feel them heaving under his boots. There was a clump of wet waterweed on his bared forearm; when he tried to brush it off it clung by one end, and, when he grabbed the free end and pulled, he saw that he was simply pulling more of it out of a hole in his arm, and he could feel the internal tug of it all the way up to his shoulder. He let go instantly, and then saw the tiny green shoots that were poking out painfully from under his fingernails.

He looked back at Davies; the back of the pirate's head was a mass of flowers, and his hat was being pushed askew by new ones opening up as Shandy watched. In Davies' shadow he could see Beth heaving in the grip of the vegetative metamorphosis, but he shuddered and looked beyond her, toward the third boat.

"*Throw him . . . someone,*" howled Hurwood as green stalks began unrolling up out of his throat.

"*Bonnett,*" croaked Friend. His fat hands were now just elbow-lumps in the tree trunks that extended from his shoulders, through the oarlocks, and out sideways into the water. "*Give the thing Bonnett.*"

Blackbeard raised a face that was a huge, unfolding orchid. The stalks of the stamen spasmed and a voice whistled, "*Yes. Bonnett.*"

Davies' bouquet-head nodded.

Shandy felt cold water flowing between his toes and realized that his feet had become roots and had penetrated the boat's hull. He found, though, that he couldn't bring himself to nod. "No," he whispered through a throatful of twisting reeds. "Can't. Did I . . . throw you . . . to the Navy?"

Davies' shoulders slumped. "Damn you," he fluted, "Jack."

Shandy glanced again at the third boat. Leo Friend was a fat wet trunk with branches like spider legs projecting in all directions. A thing like a fungus-overgrown cypress stump seemed to be Stede Bonnett, and Hurwood, no longer able to speak, was now just a thick cluster of ferns that heaved furiously about as if in a high wind.

Davies labored on at the oars, but their boat was coming apart faster than the other two, and had already sunk almost to the gunwales. Shandy thought there was probably still time for Davies to stop rowing, let Hurwood's boat drift up alongside, uproot Bonnett and pitch him into the water. With such a tribute the thing *might* let the rest of them go . . . but Shandy had apparently talked Davies out of that course.

Then Davies hitched himself up, and let go of the oars.

He's going to do it, thought Shandy. It's wrong, Phil, I don't like it, but for God's sake *hurry*.

Davies lifted one booted foot and dragged across its muddy sole the palm frond that had recently been his right hand. The left one joined it, and, while Shandy wondered what the hell the man was doing, the two floppy green hands rolled the mud into a ball.

Goddamn it, Phil, thought Shandy, what good is a *mud ball*?

Shandy's horribly elongated toes had found the river bottom and begun to dig in, and he felt nutrients coursing up his legs. His hands were gone, with not even a seam in the fresh trunks to differentiate what had once been him from what had once been the boat.

Davies put one hand on the twitching gunwale, and instantly the hand took root; but the flowering pirate drew back his other hand, braced himself, and then flung the ball of mud straight up.

And a bomb seemed to go off. The air was compressed in a scream that deafened minds as much as ears, and sent the boats rocking violently away from one another. Then the pressure was gone and the air was suddenly very cold, and Shandy's teeth hurt when he drew a breath. He rolled over—and discovered that he *could* roll over, he was no longer rooted into the fabric of the boat, and the boat was a normal boat again and not a clump of writhing branches; it was even relatively dry inside. Beth was sprawled across the aft thwart—he couldn't tell if she was conscious, but at least she was breathing and had resumed her human shape. Davies was slumped over the oars, his eyes closed, laughing exhaustedly and cradling the hand he'd flung the mud ball with. The hand seemed to be burned. And somehow raindrops were pattering around them all, though the roof of the jungle was as solid as ever.

Shandy's ears were ringing, and he had to shout even to hear himself. "A ball of *mud* killed it?"

"Some of the mud on my boot was from the shore around the Fountain," Davies yelled back, just barely audible to Shandy, "well inside the area that's poison to all dead-but-animate things."

Shandy looked ahead. Blackbeard, apparently willing to get the explanation later, had picked up his oars and was rowing again. "May I presume to suggest," yelled Shandy giddily to Davies, "that we proceed the hell out of here with all due haste."

Davies pushed a stray lock of hair back from his forehead and sat down on the rower's thwart. "My dear fellow consider it done."

There was a sound like dogs barking or pigs grunting around them; with his ears still ringing it took Shandy a minute to realize that it was the fungus heads making the noise. "Vegetable boys noisy tonight!" he called over their racket.

"Drunk, I expect!" returned Davies with a slightly hysterical joviality. "Damned nuisance!"

Beth had pulled herself up and was sitting in the stern. She was staring ahead through half-shut eyes, and might have looked relaxed if it hadn't been for the white knuckles of her gunwale-clutching hands.

Fog began making faint halos around the torches. Some distance ahead of them Blackbeard's boat veered south, and, though Shandy directed Davies through what seemed to be the same channel, they could no longer see his boat; all the glints of reflected orange light seemed to be cast by their own boat's torch, and though they could hear Blackbeard's answering roar when they called, it was distant and they couldn't tell which direction it came from.

After he admitted to himself that they'd lost Blackbeard, Shandy looked back the way they had come. The boat with Hurwood, Friend and Bonnett in it was nowhere to be seen.

"We're on our own," he told Davies. "Do you think you can get us back to the sea?"

Davies paused to stare around at the pools and channels that were identical to all the others they had passed through, partitioned by crowded trees and roots and vines that differed in no perceptible way from any other part of the swamp. "Sure," he said, and spat into the oily water. "I'll steer by the stars."

Shandy looked up. The high roof of moss and branches and tangled vines was as solid as a cathedral ceiling.

For the next hour, during which Shandy called to the other boats but got no reply, and Beth didn't move a muscle, and the fog got steadily thicker, Davies rowed through the twisting channels, watching the slow current and trying to move in the same direction; he was impeded, though, by dead-end channels, still pools, and areas where the current turned back inland. Finally they found a broad channel that seemed to be flowing strongly. Shandy was glad they did, for the torch was burning more dimly all the time.

"This has got to work," Davies gasped as he rowed out into the middle of the current.

Shandy noticed that he winced as he hauled on the oars, and he suddenly remembered that Davies had burned his hand throwing the mud ball at the swamp-*loa*. He was about to insist on a turn at the oars when one of the fungus balls on the shore spoke. "Dead end," it croaked. "Bear left. Narrower, but you get there."

To his surprise, Shandy thought he recognized the voice. "What?" he called quickly to the white, blurry-featured sphere.

It didn't reply, and Davies kept rowing down the broad channel.

"It said this is a dead end," Shandy ventured after a moment.

"In the first place," said Davies, his voice hoarse with exhaustion, "it's stuck in the mud, so I don't see how it can know. And in the second place, why should we assume it wants to give us straight advice? *We* almost took root back there—this lad obviously did. Why should such a one want to give us straight advice? . . . Misery loves company."

Shandy frowned doubtfully at the low-flickering torch. "But

these . . . I don't think these are what we were turning into. We were all turning into normal plants—flowers and bushes and whatnot. And we all seemed to be different from one another. These boys are all alike. . . ."

"Back, Jack," piped up another of the puffy white things. Again Shandy thought he caught a familiar intonation.

"If anything," said Davies stubbornly, "this channel is getting wider."

One of the fungus balls was dangling from a tree over the water, and as they passed it it opened a flap and said, "Bogs and quicksand ahead. Trust me, Jack."

Shandy looked at Davies. "That's . . . my father's voice," he said unsteadily.

"It . . . can't be," snarled Davies, hauling even more strongly on the oars.

Shandy looked away and said, into the darkness ahead, "Left, you say, Dad?"

"Yes," whispered another of the fungi. "But behind you—then with the current, to the sea."

Davies pulled two more strokes, then angrily jammed the oars down into the water. "Very well!" he said, and began working to turn the boat around. "Though I expect we'll wind up as mushroom-heads ourselves, giving wrong directions to the next lot of fools to venture in here."

By the guttering torchlight they found a gap in the mudbank, and Davies reluctantly rowed into it, leaving the wide, steady course behind. The cool white light of a spirit ball or two glowed for a moment in the fog behind them.

The fog was moving downriver thickly now, filtering through the tangled branches and vines like milk dripping into clear water; soon it was solid, and their torch was a diffused, luminous orange stain on the gray-black fabric of the night—but the channel they were in was so narrow that by stretching out his arm Shandy could feel the wet shrubbery on either side.

"It *is* beginning to quick up a bit," Davies admitted grudgingly.

Shandy nodded. The fog had made the night chilly, and when he began to shiver it occurred to him that Elizabeth was clad only in a light cotton shift. He took off his coat and draped it around her.

Then the boat passed through an arch so narrow that Davies had to draw in the oars, and a moment later the craft had surged

out onto the face of a broad expanse of water, and they had left
enough of the fog behind in the rain forest so that, after a few
dozen more downstream oar-strokes, Shandy was able to see the
glow of the three shore fires ahead.

"Hah!" he exclaimed joyfully, slapping Davies on his good
shoulder. "Look at that!"

Davies peered around, then turned back with a grin. "And
look back there," he said, nodding astern.

Shandy shifted around to look back, and saw, back in the fog,
the weak glows of two torches. "The others made it as well," he
observed, not very pleased.

Beth was looking back too. "Is . . . my father in one of those
boats?"

"Yes," Shandy told her, "but I won't let him hurt you."

For several minutes none of them spoke, and the boat began
gradually slanting in toward shore as Davies let his burned hand do
less work. The pirates on the shore finally noticed the approaching
boats and began shouting and blowing horns.

"Did he try to hurt me?" Beth asked.

Shandy looked back at her. "Don't you remember? He . . ."
Belatedly, it occurred to him that there might be a better time to
awaken her recent grisly memories. "Uh . . . he made Friend cut
your hand," he finished lamely.

She glanced at her hand, then didn't speak until they had
drawn in near the fires, and men were wading out to help them
ashore. "I remember you holding a knife to my throat," she said
distantly.

Shandy bared his teeth in anguished impatience. "It was the
dull side, and I never even touched you with it! That was to *test*
him, to see if he still needed you to accomplish this magic, if some
of your blood wasn't all he needed! Damn it, I'm trying to *protect*
you! From *him!*" Several men had splashed up to their boat, and
hands gripped the gunwales and began dragging it in toward
shore.

"Magic," said Beth.

Shandy had to lean forward to hear her over the excited
questions of the pirates. "Like it or not," he said to her loudly, "it's
what we're involved in here."

She swung a leg over the side and jumped into the shallow
water and looked back at him. The rocking bow-torch had almost

expired, but it was bright enough to show the lines of strain in her face. "What you've chosen to become involved in," she said, then turned and began wading up toward the fires.

"You know," Shandy remarked to Davies, "I'm going to get her out of this . . . just for the pleasure of showing her one more thing she's all wrong about."

"Are we glad to see you boys!" one of the jostling pirates exclaimed. They had dragged the boat all the way up onto the sand of the mangrove-shorn notch, and Shandy and Davies got out and stood up, stretching. The shouting began to die down.

"Glad to be out of there," Davies said.

"You must be hungry as hell," another man put in. "Or did you find something to eat in there?"

"Didn't have the leisure." Davies turned to watch the progress of the other two boats. "What time is it? Maybe Jack'd throw together some kind of pre-breakfast for us."

"I don't know, Phil, but it ain't late—no more'n an hour or two after sunset."

Shandy and Davies both turned to stare at him. "But we *left* about an hour after sunset," Shandy said. "And we've been gone at least several hours. . . ."

The pirate was looking at Shandy blankly, and Davies asked, "How long were we gone upriver?"

"Why . . . two days," the man replied in some bewilderment. "Just about precise—dusk to dusk."

"Ah," said Davies, nodding thoughtfully.

"And ashes to ashes," put in Shandy, too tired to bother with making sense. He looked again toward the approaching boats. Idly, for in spite of his deductions all he wanted right now was an authoritative drink and a hammock and twelve hours of sleep, he wondered how he would prevent Hurwood from forcing Beth's soul out of her body so that the ghost of her mother, his wife, could move in.

Chapter Sixteen

In the morning the fog had overflowed its river boundaries and formed a damp, only dimly translucent veil over the land and sea, so chilly that the pirates huddled around the sizzling, popping fires, and it was almost midmorning, when the fog began to break up, before anyone noticed that the *Vociferous Carmichael* was gone; and another half hour of rowing up and down the shore in boats, and shouting and ringing bells, was wasted in confirming the ship's disappearance.

Most of her crew was ashore, and the first supposition was that she had somehow come unmoored and drifted away—then Hurwood came running down the slope from the hut yelling the news that his daughter was gone and he couldn't find Leo Friend.

Shandy was standing on the beach near one of the boats when Hurwood's news was relayed. Davies and Blackbeard stood a hundred feet away, talking in low, urgent tones, but they looked up when this fresh lot of shouting began.

"Not a coincidence," pronounced Blackbeard flatly.

"The fat boy?" protested Davies. "But why?"

"Your quartermaster knows why," Blackbeard said, nodding past Davies at Shandy. "Don't you, Shandy?"

Shandy walked up to them, feeling hollow and colder than the fog. "Yes, sir," he said hoarsely. "I've seen the way he'd look at her sometimes."

"But why take *my ship?*" snarled Davies, whirling angrily to face the still-veiled sea.

"He had to take Beth away," said Shandy. "Her father had plans for her that were . . . incompatible . . . with the plans Friend had for her." He spoke quietly, but he was as tense as a flexed length of steel.

Blackbeard, also staring out to sea, shook his massive head. "I knew he was more than just Hurwood's apprentice—that there was something he was after, all on his own. At the Fountain he finally got what he needed. I should have killed him last night, after we all got back. I think I could have." The giant pirate reached out a hand and squeezed it into a fist, and then drove it into the palm of his other hand.

The sound of the slap was lost in the sudden, jarring crack of a close thunderclap, and the flash of the sky-spanning lightning bolt sent Shandy and Davies reeling back, dazzled.

"I think I could have," Blackbeard repeated thoughtfully.

As the echoes tumbled away along the shoreline and Blackbeard lowered his hands, Shandy half wished he'd thought of dropping some of his own blood on the mud by the Fountain. The thought reminded him of the way Davies had vanquished—perhaps killed—the *loa*-like thing in the jungle. Surreptitiously he lifted his foot and dragged a fingernail down the groove between the sole and the side, and he rolled the resulting bit of muck into a ball and tucked it into his pocket. He didn't know whether it contained any mud actually from the marge of the Fountain, or what sort of enemy he might want to use it against even if it did, but it was clear that anyone with only guns and swords at his disposal was ludicrously ill-equipped for the kind of combat they were engaged in now.

"I've *got* to get my ship back," said Davies, and Shandy realized that when Davies had lost the ship he'd lost his rank, too—without the *Vociferous Carmichael* he was just the skipper of a notably battered but otherwise unimpressive little sloop. Davies looked desperately at Blackbeard. "Will you come along and help? He's more now than he was, and he knew some good tricks even before."

"No," said Blackbeard, his dark face impassive. "By now Woodes Rogers may have arrived in New Providence with the pardon calculated to rob me of my nation." The breeze was from the sea, and it blew back the pirate-king's lion-mane of black hair and beard, and Shandy noticed streaks of gray at the temples and chin. "I meant the *Carmichael*—with you as her captain—to be the flagship of my fleet . . . and I hope you do get her back. But it seems the age of free-for-all piracy is ending . . . just as the merry buccaneer days are passed . . . this is the age of empire." He grinned sidelong at Davies. "Would the Brethren follow me, or take the pardon, given the choice?"

Davies grinned wearily back, and waited for a wave to crash, come swirling and churning almost to their boots, and then slide back, before answering. "They'll take the pardon. To sail with Blackbeard is to leave a pledge with the hangman."

Blackbeard nodded. "But . . . ?"

Davies shrugged. "The problem will still be there—unless King George has the sense to get into another war. The Caribbean is full of men who know no other trade than sailing a fighting ship. Since the peace they're all out of work. Sure, they'll take the pardon—gratefully!—to write off their past crimes . . . but a month or two later every one of 'em will be back on the account."

Blackbeard nodded, and though Shandy and Davies stepped back, he didn't even look down as the next wave boiled up past where he stood and draped a length of kelp across his ankle. Finally he spoke, slowly. "Would they follow a new captain, who had ships and money?"

"Of course—and if this captain truly had no criminal record, he could have his pick of every sailor in the New World, because they wouldn't be violating their pardons by sailing with him. But who have you got in mind? Even Shandy here has got a fair reputation."

"Do you know, Phil, why Juan Ponce de Leon called that place the Fountain of Youth?"

"No." Davies laughed shortly. "If anything, I feel a lot older since being there."

Blackbeard turned to Shandy. "Any guesses, Jack?"

Shandy recalled Hurwood's antics with the head of his dead wife. "Because the place can be used to bring dead people back to life."

Blackbeard nodded. "I was sure you'd figured that out. Yes, old Hurwood plans to raise his wife's ghost from her dried head and plant it in the body of his daughter. Hard luck on the daughter, left with no body." The giant pirate laughed softly. "Hurwood came out to the New World last year—he'd heard that magic was as common as salt out here."

More shouting was going on around the fires behind them, but Blackbeard was caught up in remembering. "A pistol ball smashed his arm all to hell," he said. "We had to chop it right off and tar the stump. Never thought a man his age would survive it. But then only the next day you'd swear he'd forgot about it—all he did was watch me. The ghosts were troubling me pretty bad then, and I was having a rum-and-gunpowder two or three times a day. And even though magic has been dried up in the Old World for thousands of years, he'd tracked down its old footprints and found its bones . . . and studied 'em. He knew what my trouble was and had a pretty good idea of how I'd got infested by all those ghosts. He offered to cure me of 'em—*exorcise* 'em—if I'd show him exactly where it was that I'd picked 'em up. I said fine, let's go, but he said not so fast. We need a ghost repellent, he said, this special medicine weed the Indians grow in Carolina—I was to sail north and get some—and he had to go back to England to get a couple of things: his daughter and his wife's head, it seems. The whole reason he'd begun trying to track down living magic was to get the wife back. But before he went back to England he came to New Providence with us, and lived a few weeks with the *bocors*. One night he sailed off west with one of 'em, and came back next morning all worn out and crazy-looking—but excited. I knew he'd somehow managed to contact the wife. And then he left, promising as the last piece of the deal to bring back a fine ship for me."

Shandy remembered old Chaworth, and the realization that he was now one of the breed that had ruined and killed the kind old man brought a bitterness to his mouth.

"And Hurwood was right, of course," Blackbeard went on quietly. "We do use magic out here, and those of us who aren't above listening to the black *bocors*— especially those of us who live on the sea—know some thefty tricks. I know more, maybe, than anyone . . . and since our trip upriver, I've now got the power to do every one of 'em splendid." He had been facing the sea, but now he turned back to Shandy and Davies. "For years I've heard about this Fountain, and I tracked it down because of a magic I'd heard of in connection with it. A man with the right kind of power can be immortal by means of it, if he takes care to live on the sea. Blood, *fresh* blood, and sea water, and you don't need the head, nor a body for the soul to go into; the sorceror's blood will grow a new one in the sea, in a kind of egg, within hours of dripping into the water . . ."

Davies was frowning thoughtfully. "I see. So you plan to—"

"To sail north, Phil, to some place civilized, where things happen documentably and get recorded official. And I think maybe the famous Blackbeard will be trapped and killed in some sea fight, in such a way that some of his blood will fall into the ocean . . . and then I wouldn't be surprised if some stranger were to appear, who'll happen to know where I've hid all my lucre, and he won't have *any* reputation or previous history or fame to foul him up. I think he'll get a ship in some quiet way—hah! I'll bet Stede Bonnett will help out with that—and then make his way south to New Providence Island. I think he'll want to speak to you, Phil—and I think it'd be a good thing if you'd got the *Carmichael* back."

Davies nodded. "Do you . . . want us to accept this pardon Rogers is bringing?"

"I don't see why not," Blackbeard said.

"Hear that, Jack?" Davies asked Shandy. "Back in the shop window again."

Shandy opened his mouth to answer, then closed it and just shook his head.

"He's too great a sinner, Phil," Blackbeard said, amusement rumbling in his voice.

Benjamin Hurwood covered the last ten yards in a sort of anxious, bounding prance, making the square wooden box tied to his belt jiggle and whirl wildly. "When do we *leave?*" he screamed. "Don't you realize how essential it is that we *hurry?* He may *kill* her, he's certainly got the power now to overcome the protections she has."

Blackbeard ignored Hurwood. "I'm going north," he said, and plodded away back toward the fires.

Davies eyed the pale, trembling Hurwood speculatively. "Can you find 'em?"

"Of *course* I can find them—her, anyway." He slapped the wooden box irreverently. "This thing's a damn lodestone for her now, better than the pointer that led you to the *Carmichael* a month ago."

"We'll leave instantly," said Davies. "As soon as we get the *Jenny* manned. We—" He paused. "The *Carmichael*'s crew," he said. "What's to become of them, the lads we can't carry on the *Jenny?*"

"Who *cares?*" yelled Hurwood. "Let them split up—half with Thatch, half with Bonnett. Damn my *soul,* what I'm going to do to that fat young worm when I find him! Prometheus never suffered as much as Leo Friend will, I promise you—"

"No," said Davies, still thoughtfully, "none of my lads sail north with Thatch . . . I'll load the *Jenny* gunwale-deep with men before I permit that . . ."

Hurwood had been dancing with impatience, and now the raging old man screwed his eyes shut and clenched his fist, and slowly rose up from the sand until he hovered unsupported with his boots dangling fully a yard above the ground. He opened his eyes a squint, hissed angrily and shut his eyes harder—and then was flung like a loose-jointed doll at the sea, and struck with an enormous splash out beyond where the breakers began to swell and roll in.

A number of pirates were on the beach, and several of them had paused in their various labors to gape at this performance, and now were staring wonderingly out at the falling splash spray.

"*Get him,*" Davies rasped at the nearest cluster of them, and the men leaped to the boat, dragged it down to the water and got busy with the oars. To Shandy, Davies muttered, "You want to find the girl, right?"

"Right."

"And I want to find my ship. So let's get Hurwood aboard the *Jenny* before he perfects his flying and flaps away to find them without us."

The sailors had carried and shoved their wide-beamed boat out into the surf. "Don't bring him back," Davies shouted to them. "Take him on to the *Jenny!*"

"Aye aye, Phil," yelled back one of the laboring rowers.

Davies seized Shandy's shoulder. "Back to the camp, Jack," he said. "Send as many of the *Carmichael*'s lads to Bonnett's crew as the *Revenge* can hold—the rest bring down here, and get 'em aboard the *Jenny*. But none of our mates sail on the *Queen Anne's Revenge*, understand?"

"Sure do, Phil," Shandy said. "I'll have 'em down here getting into the boats in three minutes."

"Good. Go."

• • •

Shandy had no sooner run back uphill to the crowd around the smoking charcoal piles than Woefully Fat grabbed him by the upper arm. The *bocor*'s brown eyes glared at him out of the broad black face. "You damn slow, boy," the man said. "I thought you'd fix things upriver. Too late now for it to be any kind of easy—now you got to kill him an' burn him ashore."

"Kill who?" blurted Shandy, forgetting the man was deaf.

"You ain't sailin' on the *Queen Anne's Revenge*," said Woefully Fat.

Belatedly remembering the *bocor*'s deafness, Shandy shook his head and put on an earnestly agreeing expression. He was standing on tiptoe and hoping the giant *bocor* wouldn't lift him any higher. "No sir!" he yelled.

"Di'n't wait five years for you so you could be a puppet o' his, and die just to provide more blood an' make his death scene look more convincin'."

"I ain't going!" said Shandy loudly, exaggerating the movement of his lips. Then he added, "What do you mean, 'five years'?"

Woefully Fat looked around—no one was paying particular attention to them, and he lowered his voice to a whisper that was somehow still a rumble. "When the white men's war ended, an' anybody could see that Thatch had learned too much."

Shandy couldn't tell if this was an answer or something Woefully Fat had been going to say anyway.

"He got away with a lot by calling himself a privateer," the *bocor* went on. "The English let him alone if they think he only be takin' Spanish ships. But he wa'n't interested in any distinctions between *Spanish* or *English* or *Dutch*, just in human lives and blood. He even kilt that old English magician he been studyin' with, an' then tried to bring him back." Woefully Fat laughed. "I help a little, that time, make a turtle eat the blood in the water. Wouldn't have worked for very long anyway, neither of 'em havin' shed blood in Erebus first, but you should have seen that turtle tryin' to write English words on the deck with its claws." He gave Shandy a sharp look. "*You* di'n't shed no blood there, did you?"

"Where?"

"In Erebus, as white people call the place. The place where the Fountain is, where ghosts can't be ghosts, where blood grows plants?"

"No no, not me." Shandy shook his head. "Now let go of me, will you? I've got—"

"No? Good. He have . . . *uses* for you, if'n you did. An' when the war was ended and he was still alive an' gettin' so close an' puttin' together a whole nation, it seem like, of badmen, I saw I had to call a death for him from the Old World. When the one-armed man came last year an' knew about ghosts, I was sure it was my man, 'specially since his wife died the same year I sent my summons—if the bigger *loas* sent him for me they'd maybe have caused her death, as long as the complications of it would drive him out here."

"That's great, really," said Shandy. He made a twisting hop and managed to pull his arm free of the *bocor*'s huge hand. "But right now I've got to see to the crews, all right? Anybody who needs to be killed and burned is just going to have to wait." He turned and ran before Woefully Fat could grab him again.

By threats, and hints that maroonment here was a real possibility, and his own evident consternation, Shandy managed to get a little more than half of the *Carmichael*'s crew accepted by David Herriot, Bonnett's half-bright sailing master, and hustle the remainder down to the boats and onto the water, before the boat that had picked up Hurwood had even reached the *Jenny*.

The fog was definitely breaking up now, and when the boat Shandy was in plunged out of the last veil of mist, he smiled with affection to see the battered old *Jenny* rocking sturdily out there in the bright morning sunlight.

"It'll be nice to get back down south where we belong," he said to Skank, who was crouched in the bow near him.

"Oh, aye," the young pirate agreed, "it's risky tactics to get too far from the attentions of Mate Care-For and that lot."

"Yeah." Shandy hastily patted his pocket to make sure he hadn't lost the ball of mud. "Yeah, there's some unlikely beasts in the world, and it's best to stay near the ones that you've bought drinks for."

In a few minutes they bumped the shot-scarred hull of the *Jenny*, and Shandy reached up, grabbed her gunwale and vaulted over it onto the deck. As he gave some orders about the handling of the tenuously repaired sails and lines, and oversaw the hasty loading of several casks of salt pork and beer he'd managed to commandeer from the camp, he became aware that the planks under his boots were vibrating briefly every couple of seconds, and when he made his way aft to report to Davies that they were ready to go, he saw Hurwood crouched over his grisly box on the narrow poop, and the old man's scratchy breathing exactly corresponded to the deck's vibration.

"Hope he doesn't sneeze," remarked Davies, who had also noticed the phenomenon. "All set?"

"I'd say so, Phil," Shandy answered with a tension-twitchy grin. "Far too many men, nearly no provisions, the rigging all held together with nipper twine, and the navigator a one-armed lunatic taking directions from a severed head in a box."

"Excellent," said Davies, nodding. "Good work. I knew I picked the right man for quartermaster." He looked down at Hurwood. "Which way?" Hurwood pointed south.

"Hoist anchor!" Davies shouted. "And tiller hard to starboard!"

The old sloop came around to face south, and then she sped away so quickly, in spite of being jostlingly overcrowded, that Shandy knew Hurwood must be providing some sort of sorcerous propulsion to aid the tattered sails; and by noon they had ploughed their plunging, wide-waked way down past the tip of the Florida peninsula.

A half hour later things began to happen. Hurwood had been staring into the wooden box since they'd set out, but now he looked up. Shandy, who had been glancing frequently at the old man, noticed the change and walked back to the stern along the railing, balancing himself by reaching out to touch the shrouds every few steps. A few steps from the one-armed magician he paused.

"There are . . . others . . . ," the old man said.

Several of the pirates had climbed up the shrouds to escape the smell and crowding of their companions, perched themselves more or less comfortably in the loops of the ratlines, and were providing entertainment to those below by tossing an ever-lighter rum bottle back and forth among themselves without, so far, dropping it; but now one of them was staring intently to the west. "A sail!" he yelled. "Ow, damn it," he added as the bottle rebounded from his knee and fell into eager hands below. "A sail abeam to starboard and only a mile or two off!"

That's got to be her, thought Shandy, whirling so quickly to look that he had to crouch and grab the rail to keep from tumbling over the side. As soon as he saw the other ship, though, he knew it wasn't the *Carmichael*— this ship had a forecastle structure, and an extra-high poop, and had only two huge sails each on its fore and mainmasts, and even from this distance he could see bright patterns of red and white painted along her side.

"I am not a dog!" yelled Mr. Bird, who had wound up with the rum bottle and was backing away toward the bow with it and glaring around at the rest of the pirates.

Shandy stared at the strange ship. "What is she?" he asked Davies, "and how in hell did she get so close without any of us seeing her?"

"Damned if I know how," Davies growled. "We've been keeping no formal watch, but *one* of those drunken bastards should have noticed before now." He squinted at the ship, which seemed to be pacing them. "It's a Spanish galleon," he said wonderingly. "I didn't know there were any still afloat—they haven't made 'em for at least half a century."

Shandy swore, then smiled tiredly at Davies. "Nothing to do with any of our concerns, obviously."

"Obviously."

"So do we just continue?"

"May as well. Even overloaded, we should be able to outrun that, especially with Hurwood lending his sorcerous push. If—"

"Drowned man!" yelled one of the men up in the shrouds. "To port, twenty yards off."

Shandy looked in that direction and saw sea birds circling over a sodden, floating lump that soon disappeared in the choppy agitation of their wake.

"'Nother one ahead!" the self-appointed lookout yelled. "We may run right over him."

"One of you get a boathook out," commanded Davies, "and snag him."

Another floating corpse was sighted, too far off to starboard to be visible from the deck, but the one that the lookout had seen bobbing ahead was hooked as it slipped past the bow. The sea birds squawked angrily as the floater was lifted out of the sea and dragged aboard.

"Saints preserve us!" exclaimed one of the men who lowered the sopping corpse to the deck. "It's Georgie de Burgo!"

"We're on the fat boy's track, right enough," said Davies flatly, starting forward. "De Burgo was one of the dozen men that were aboard the *Carmichael* when she was moored."

Davies was clearing a way through the crowd on the deck by cuffing men out of his way, and Shandy hurried along behind him before the path could close again. He was wishing he'd got a better look at the corpse he'd seen tumbling away in the wake, and he was torturing himself by trying to remember whether the cloth the thing had been wrapped in was the same color as the cotton shift Beth had been wearing when he'd seen her last.

By the time Davies and Shandy got to the bow the crowd had begun parting for them, and Shandy was able to glimpse de Burgo's corpse while he was still several steps away from it, and it was this moment of preparation that probably saved the contents of his stomach, for Georgie de Burgo's head had been all but cut free of his body by what seemed to have been one stroke of some very sharp and very heavy blade.

Shandy was staring down in queasy fascination at the thing when the lookout yelled again. "And another one to port!"

"Put him back over the side," said Davies tightly, turning back toward the stern.

He and Shandy didn't speak until they had elbowed their way back to the tiller and their eerie navigator. "I think," said Davies then, "we can assume that he's killed all twelve and heaved 'em over the side. I can't imagine how, but that's not the main mystery."

"Right," said Shandy, squinting at the empty blue horizon ahead. "Who's he got crewing for him?"

For a full minute neither of them spoke, then Shandy glanced to starboard at the Spanish galleon. "Uh . . . Phil? Didn't you say we're faster than that Spaniard?"

"Hm? Oh, certainly, on her best day and our worst." Davies too looked to starboard—then froze, staring, for the galleon had moved well ahead of the *Jenny*. "God's teeth," he muttered, "that's not possible."

"No," Shandy agreed. "Neither's the fact that she's leaving no visible wake at all."

Davies stared for a few more seconds, then called for a telescope. One was brought, and for a long minute he peered through it at the receding galleon. "Get the men busy," he said finally, lowering the glass. "At anything, mending line, hoisting and lowering sails, man-overboard drill, even—just keep their attention off that Spaniard."

"Aye aye, Phil," said the mystified Shandy, hurrying forward.

He assigned so many jobs so quickly that one man who had been furtively smoking a pipe—forbidden aboard ship—managed in the confusion to ignite a puddle of Mr. Bird's rum and set half the bow ablaze; greasy hair and tarry clothes sprang into flame and a dozen suddenly burning men, hooting in alarm, went rolling and diving over the rail.

Shandy instantly ordered the helmsman to come about, and within minutes Davies' constant drilling had paid off—the fire was out, and the men in the water were all dragged back aboard before any of them had time to drown. After the excitement had died down and Shandy had had time to catch his breath and gulp some of the surviving rum, he went back to the stern. Hurwood, though he had probably protested when the *Jenny* came around, was staring silently into his wooden box again, and when Shandy looked ahead he saw that the Spaniard was by now just an irregular white fleck on the southern horizon.

"When I said to keep them busy," Davies began, "I didn't mean . . ."

"I know, I know." Shandy scratched at a scorched area of his beard and then leaned back against the taut shroud and looked at Davies. "So why? Just so they wouldn't notice the lack of a wake?"

"Partly that. But more important, I didn't want any of these lads to get a chance to turn a glass on her stern and read her name. She's the *Nuestra Señora de Lagrimas*," he said thoughtfully. "You may not have heard of her, but probably half of these men know her story. She was carrying gold from Veracruz and had the misfortune to meet an English privateer, the *Charlotte Bailey*. A couple of the Englishmen survived to tell about it. Terrible sea battle—lasted four hours—and both ships went to the bottom." He looked over at Shandy and grinned. "This was in 1630."

Shandy blinked. "Nearly a century ago."

"Right. You know anything about raising ghosts?"

"Not really—though the way things've been going I think I'll have it down pat long before I really understand sailing."

"Well, I'm no expert at it myself, but I do know it ain't easy. Even to get a misty, half-wit casting of a dead person takes a lot of sorcerous power." He waved ahead. "And here somebody's raised the entire damned *de Lagrimas*—sails, timber, paint and all, and crew too, to judge by the way she's handling, solid enough to look no different from a real ship, and in bright sunlight at that."

"Leo Friend?"

"I kind of think so. But why?"

Shandy glanced at Hurwood. "I'm afraid we'll probably find out." And I hope, he thought fervently, that he's been too busy—what with murdering pirates and conjuring up ghost ships—to visit his attentions on Beth Hurwood.

Chapter Seventeen

From where she crouched in the corner of the cabin Beth Hurwood could see only disjointed segments of Leo Friend's mincing advance across the deck toward her, for he had shut the door behind himself when he came in, and the only light in the cabin was the quick, regular blue-sky-flash of a bulkhead window that kept appearing and disappearing, evidently in time to the fat man's heartbeat.

She had awakened at dawn to find herself walking down the chilly sand slope toward a boat that rocked in the shallows. When she had seen Leo Friend sitting in it and grinning at her she had tried to stop walking, but couldn't; then she tried to slant her course away from the boat, and couldn't do that either, and was not even able to slow her pace as she waded helplessly out into the icy water and clambered into the boat. She had tried to speak then, but hadn't been able to tense her vocal cords or open her mouth. The boat surged out past the breakers toward where the dim silhouette of the *Vociferous Carmichael* stood; the ride out to the ship had taken only a minute or so, during which time Friend never touched the loosely dragging oars and Beth never managed to move a muscle.

But that had all happened several hours ago, and she had since regained at least enough control over her own actions to crawl into this corner and, when she had heard the pirates screaming and dying, to cover her ears.

Now she watched Friend warily, estimating where on his

blubbery frame she could use her teeth and fingernails to best effect, and trying to tense herself against another episode of magically induced, puppetlike helplessness.

But a moment later she felt herself standing up—painfully, in an awkward, tiptoe posture that she would never have assumed voluntarily; then finally her weight came down on her heels and her arms jerked up and outward, though not for balance, for she was as unable to fall as the mast of a strongly rigged ship.

Friend raised his own arms and she realized that she'd been pulled into this position in order to embrace him. His bulging lower lip was wet and trembling and the window was flashing into and out of existence as fast as the tails side of a spinning coin, and when he stepped into her arms she felt them close around his wobbly-fleshed back, and then his mouth came down hard on hers.

He stank of perfume and sweat and candy, and one of his hands was fumbling inexpertly about her torso, but Beth was for the moment able to keep her eyes and teeth clamped shut. Then his mouth slid off of hers and she heard him passionately whispering some pair of syllables over and over again.

She opened her eyes . . . and blinked in astonishment.

The flickering window, the whole ship's cabin, was gone. The two of them were standing on a knitted rag rug in what appeared to be a shabby English bedroom; the air was close and smelled of boiled cabbage. Beth tried again to pull away from him, and, though she didn't succeed, she did get a glimpse of herself. She was suddenly fat, wearing a long shapeless black dress, and her hair was gray. And then she realized what it was that he was whispering.

"Oh, Mommy, Mommy," he gasped, panting hotly against her throat. "Oh, Mommy Mommy Mommy."

But it wasn't until she realized that he was spasmodically grinding his well-padded pelvis against her that she threw up.

Less than half a minute later Leo Friend was outside on the quarterdeck, pacing back and forth red-faced in the morning sun.

The thing about mistakes, he told himself as he dabbed at the spot on his frilly blouse with a silk handkerchief, is that one must *learn* from them. And that incident just now in the cabin certainly should have taught me something. I simply have to wait—and just a little longer, just until I can get enough peace and quiet to cook up some of the magic I'm now capable of.

And *then,* he thought, looking back at the cabin door which he'd just rebolted from the outside, *then* we'll see who has to fight off whose attentions. He took a deep breath and then let it out, nodding decisively. He looked around the quarterdeck of what he'd made of the *Carmichael,* and after scrutinizing his new crew he decided they were looking a good deal less lively than they had when he'd first conjured them up, several hours ago now. They seemed even paler, and puffier, and they kept cocking their heads as if listening to something, and glancing back north with expressions that even on their dead faces were recognizable as fearful.

"What's the matter?" he snapped at one of the figures working the whipstaff tiller. "You afraid of Blackbeard? Afraid he'll come stick a cutlass into your cold guts? Or Hurwood, come after us for his d-d-d-d—goddamn *offspring*? I've got more power than either of them, don't you worry."

The thing spoken to didn't seem to hear, and just kept turning its pearly gray head around—so far that its neck was beginning to tear—to peek back past the stern. Faintly from its useless throat came hissing that might have been whimpering.

Irritably, for his crew's evident fear had begun to infect him in spite of his confidence and the reassurance that sunny days bring, Friend climbed the companion ladders to the second poop deck— levitation was still too new and uncontrolled a skill—and looked back over the stern rail.

At first he thought the pursuing ship was Blackbeard's *Queen Anne's Revenge,* and his pudgy lips curled in a cruel smile—which disappeared a moment later, though, when he realized that it wasn't any ship he'd ever seen before. This one, he saw, was broader in the beam and was painted red and white around the bow . . . and wasn't the bow advancing awfully steadily? Didn't most ships' bows rise and fall a bit when they were making speed, and fling some spray out to the sides?

He walked to the rail that overlooked the poop and quarter-decks. At least for the moment his ship had stopped shifting its features, and there weren't any masts or decks changing their minds about whether they were there or not from moment to moment. Probably even that window in . . . that cabin . . . was either steadily there or steadily not.

"More speed!" Friend shouted to his necrotic crew. Several gray figures began creeping up the rigging. "Faster!" he shrilled.

"No wonder the damned *Charlotte Bailey* went down, if this is the way you handled her!"

He looked back at the pursuing ship, and wondered if he was just imagining that it was already closer. He was pretty sure it was. Planting his feet firmly on the deck, he roused the new areas of his mind and pointed a sausagelike finger at the strange ship. "Go," he said tightly.

Instantly a wide patch of the sea erupted in steam, curling and boiling up in a white, sharply edged cloud, and Friend giggled delightedly—but the giggling stopped a moment later when the ship came surging out of the cloud, apparently none the worse. Its sails, in fact, still shone the bright bone white of dry canvas.

"Damn," said Friend softly.

It doesn't matter who it is, he thought uneasily. I've got better things to do than deal with it. I could levitate myself and Elizabeth and just fly away . . . but if they pursued us rather than this ship I'd be at a disadvantage, for I'd have to keep using part of my power just to hold us up . . . of course I'm using a good deal of it even now, keeping these damned resurrected sailors moving. . . .

He climbed back down to the next deck, and after shouting some more orders to the silently working gray figures, he glanced down, at the deck planks under his mud-stained but still ornate shoes. I could just rush in there and *take* her, he thought, the hot excitement beginning to choke him again in spite of his anxiety about the pursuing vessel. And this time I could hold her in a total sorcerous vise, so that she couldn't even blink an eye without me specifically letting her . . . or I could even just render her unconscious, and use magic to make her body behave in the ways I want. . . .

He shook his head. No, *that* wouldn't really be any different from the activities he'd been indulging in ever since he learned, in his adolescence, how to sculpt ectoplasmic women in the air over his unrestful bed. At best all he could do right now would be to *rape* Beth Hurwood, and any common *sailor* could commit a rape. Friend wanted—needed—to commit a much more profound violation. He wanted to manipulate her very will, so that not only would she be powerless to prevent herself from coupling with him, she would live for the hope of it. And then if he happened to get her confused with his . . . with someone else . . . she'd be properly *flattered*.

To be able to control people as thoroughly as *that,* though, he would have to have control over vastly more of reality than he had ever had before—over *all* of it, in fact. In order *fully* to define the present, he would have to be able to revise the past—dictate the future—become, in effect, God.

Well, he thought with a nervous smile, why not? Haven't I been getting steadily closer to that all my life?

He crossed to the port rail, leaned out and glanced back again at the mysterious pursuer. The red-and-white painted ship had sped up since he'd last looked, and was slanting over as if to pass the *Carmichael* on the port side, and now he could see another sail, farther back, which the unknown vessel had been concealing. Friend hissed in alarm and squinted at it.

It's too small to be Blackbeard's ship, he thought, or Bonnett's. It must be that damned sloop, the *Jenny.* Hurwood will be aboard, certainly, and the Romeo sea-cook, that Shandy fellow . . . maybe even Davies, still angry about my having shot him. That must be what my lich crew has been looking back at for the last half hour. He glanced over at his ill-preserved helmsmen, but the focus of the dead men's attention had shifted. The lifeless figures weren't looking astern anymore, but off the port quarter instead, at the painted galleon.

"Idiots!" Friend yelled. "The danger's *there!"* He pointed back at the advancing sloop.

His crew of dead men didn't seem to agree.

"That isn't the *Carmichael!"* Davies had exclaimed when the *Nuestra Señora de Lagrimas* slanted to the east on a closer-hauled tack and gave the *Jenny* a clear view of the ship they were pursuing. He kept staring at it through the telescope.

"It has to be," said Shandy.

Hurwood, who hadn't shifted from his crouch since the voyage began, looked up. "It's the ship *she's* on," he said, speaking just loudly enough to be heard over the splash-and-spray and the wind whistling through the harp of the rigging.

Davies shook his head doubtfully. "Poop seems too high, but I guess we'll know soon enough; both of 'em seem to be slowing down. Are we getting every knot of speed out of this?"

Shandy shrugged and gestured down at Hurwood. "Ask

him—but I'd say yes and a risky bit more. After that last speed-up to keep the Spaniard in sight we had to take down all sails, 'cause they were just slowing us down, and the hull strakes flex more and leak worse every time we skate over a big wave."

"Well, it shouldn't take too much longer." Whatever the ship was ahead, they were gaining on it fast, and after a minute or so Davies called "Catch!" and tossed the telescope to Shandy. "What's her name?"

Shandy peered through the telescope. "Uh . . . the *Vochiflerouttes Barimychael?* No . . . no, it's the *Carmichael,* right enough, I see it clear now. . . ."

"Keep the glass on her," said Davies.

". . . Well," said Shandy tiredly after another few moments, "it blurs and shifts. But for a moment there it was the *Charlotte Bailey.*" He sighed and muttered a curse he hadn't known a month ago. "So he raised the crew of the *Charlotte Bailey* to replace the men he murdered, but his new sorcerous strength is so great that he raised the *ship's* ghost too, and it's clinging to the *Carmichael.*"

Davies nodded toward the Spanish galleon. "He even raised the ship that went down with the *Bailey.*"

"God," said Shandy. "I wonder if he knows that."

"I don't think it matters. The *de Lagrimas* seems to want to take up their battle right where they left off a century ago . . . and I don't think we want to permit that."

"No," said Shandy.

"No," agreed Hurwood, who had at last stood up and closed his noisome box. "And to answer your earlier question, no, Friend doesn't know what the Spaniard is, or he wouldn't have wasted energy trying to boil her—she's part of the same magic that's furnished him with a crew, and the only way he can be rid of her is to cancel that magic." He laughed without smiling. "The boy isn't in control of his new strength yet. He reached down to the sea floor for a crew and raised up as well everything and everybody in the vicinity. I'll wager there are fishes aswim below us now that were scattered skeletons yesterday."

"Excuse me," said Shandy quickly, "but can ghost cannon balls damage real ships? The *Lagrimas* seems to be lining up for a broadside."

"I don't know," grated Hurwood. The old man closed his eyes

and took a deep breath, and then half the men aboard the *Jenny* were sent sprawling as the old sloop leaped forward across the shattering waves at a still greater speed. Shandy, braced against the transom and trying to snatch a lungful of the solid, rushing air, considered, and then giddily dismissed, warning Hurwood that the battered old vessel probably couldn't take it.

Smoke bloomed from the Spaniard's starboard flank, and a moment later Shandy rubbed his eyes incredulously, for the *Carmichael* had blurred, seeming simultaneously both to reel and to continue unchecked, seeming to lose spars and sails in a tangled explosion and at the same time maintain her broad spread of canvas untouched.

The drunken pirates aboard the *Jenny* burst out yelling at the sight of this prodigy, and several took it on themselves to try to hoist some sails while others scrambled for the helm. One man was wrenching at the sheaves of the cathead, trying to get the anchor to drop.

Davies grinned at the men who were rushing back toward the helm, and thoughtfully drew a pistol, and Shandy yelled, "There's enough ghosts in this fight without volunteers! Our only *living* opponent is the fat boy—do you want to let him get away with your ship?"

Shandy's words, and, even more effectively, Davies' pistol, halted the rush. The pirates wavered, covering uncertainty by redoubling their shouted oaths and demands and gestures.

Davies fired his pistol into the air, and into the relative silence that followed he yelled, "The Spaniard's a ghost, I admit—but she's distracting the fat boy. He's seen us now—so do we go in and hit him while he's occupied, or wait for him to turn on us at his leisure?"

Miserably, the pirates turned and fought their way back through the hammering headwind to their posts. They had only managed to raise one sail, the little square topsail, and before they could even begin to lower it again it split into a hundred fluttering ribbons, giving the plunging boat a shabbily festive appearance but doing nothing to slow it down.

Almost skipping over the waves now, the *Jenny* crashed into the narrowing gap between the two ships.

"All port guns fire!" Davies roared against the wind. "And then try putting the tiller over to port!"

The *Jenny's* seven portside guns all boomed jarringly, and then after a moment of recoil the sloop heeled sharply with the canvasless jibe to starboard, and Shandy held onto the port rail and blinked against the spray from the waves that were hurtling past just inches below him; and when the port side heaved back up to something closer to its normal position he craned his neck to look back at the *de Lagrimas*.

She was in trouble, sure enough, her stout mainmast broken off at a ragged point about halfway up its length, and most of her rigging was serving now only to connect her to the unwieldy sea-anchor that the mast-top had become—but Shandy swore softly in awe, for the *Jenny* was a much smaller vessel, and her broadside had been leveled at the Spaniard's hull, not up at the masts and rigging . . . and it occurred to him that he was seeing the original conflict between the *Nuestra Señora de Lagrimas* and the *Charlotte Bailey* being re-enacted by the temporarily resurrected principals, who, in some deteriorated sense, still recalled the original sequence of events.

"Keep the tiller over!" commanded Davies, "and let us slow down now," he added to Hurwood. "We'll come around across the *Carmichael's* bow and board her on the starboard side."

The two ships had been slowing even before the *de Lagrimas* lost her mast, and so even overloaded and losing speed the *Jenny* had yards to spare when she came around, still heeling, under the *Carmichael's* bow. Then the *Jenny's* in-turning bow was scraping up splinters along the ship's hull and the sloop rocked and shuddered as it lost its momentum; Davies ordered grappling hooks flung up, and a moment later the pirates were swarming like big, ragged bugs up the ropes. Among the first of them was Shandy, who was finding it ironic that in this second capture of the *Carmichael* by the *Jenny* he should be one of the bearded wild men scrambling up the boarding lines.

When he was halfway up the line, bracing his boot-soles against the hull as he wrenched himself upward, the hull suddenly jumped like a whacked drumskin and he was swung over sideways and slammed hard against it; the impact rang his head against the hull strakes and numbed his right arm, but he managed to keep his left hand clamped onto the rope. Blinking down past his dangling boots, he saw most of the men who'd been on the lines with him splash into the turbulent water between the two vessels.

"The Spaniard just hit her on the other side!" shouted Davies, leaping for one of the slack lines himself. "Now or never!"

Shandy took a deep breath—through his mouth, for his nose was dripping blood—flexed the fingers of his right hand, swung it up to grab the rope, drew his legs up and pushed himself away from the hull and wearily resumed climbing. He was the first to grip the rail and swing a leg over, but, in spite of his concern for Beth Hurwood, when he had wincingly pulled himself up he just crouched there and stared for several seconds.

The Spanish ship was a sky-blotting tangle of shattered spars and fouled rigging, but Shandy's attention was on his immediate surroundings. The ship to whose rail he was clinging was simply not the *Carmichael*—the waist was broader across but shorter fore and aft, there were two poop decks, one behind and even higher than the first, and the cannons were mounted right out on the top deck rather than one deck down—but what drew his unhappy attention were the sailors aboard her.

They moved awkwardly, and their skin was the color of scummy cream of mushroom soup, and their eyes were the milky white that, in fish, was a sign of having been dead too long.

Most of this poorly reanimated crew was rushing to the port bow, where a lot of similarly ruinous mariners were clambering across the shattered rail from the *de Lagrimas*.

Shandy wanted very much to jump back down into the water. He had seen things like these in the most horrible of his childhood dreams, and he wasn't sure he wouldn't drop dead himself if one of these creatures were to turn its dreadfully knowing gaze full on him.

Then he knew they were aware of him, for several of them were moving toward him at an eerie plodding-but-rapid pace, brandishing corroded but very solid-looking cutlasses. Their bare feet, shuffling across the deck, made sounds like someone rolling dead toads down a shingled roof.

His voice shrill with panic, Shandy yelled the beginning phrases of the Hail Mary as he jumped to the deck, wrenched out his saber and stepped into one of the counters against multiple attack that Davies had been making him practice; he feinted as if to charge between two of his attackers, then ducked to the other side, engaging another opponent's blade in a screeching bind that sent Shandy's blade corkscrewing in to chop heavily into the pearly neck. Leaping over the tumbling, nearly beheaded figure, he saw several men shambling toward him—and, on the next deck up, he saw the bedraggled figure of Leo Friend, who was looking both furious and frightened. Friend was staring at something behind and above Shandy, and after he'd done a quick feint-and-slash-and-run and got past his immediate attackers, Shandy risked a quick glance back.

Benjamin Hurwood hung unsupported in midair a dozen feet above the ship's rail and a few yards out from it, and through the white hair that was blowing around his face he was smiling almost affectionately at Friend. "I brought you along," the old man said, and, though he spoke quietly, the clanging, thumping racket of the fighting ghost-crews was muted when he spoke, so that the words carried clearly; "I showed you the way past the impasse you had reached, showed you the place you had failed to discover by yourself." The smile grew wider, beginning to look skull-like. "Did you really think you were superior to me, that you could advance so far that I could not follow you? Hah. I'm glad you revealed your treacherous nature now—eventually you *might* have become powerful enough to do me harm." He closed his eyes.

Other pirates had clambered aboard now, and, after the initial astonishment, were doggedly trading sword-strokes with the cadaverous mariners, quickly catching on that the things had to be dismembered, and fairly thoroughly, to be put out of the fight. The things were quick, too, in a spasmodic, insectlike way, and several of Davies' men were bloodily down in the first few minutes.

Shandy could hear someone banging behind a door below the deck Friend was on, and he guessed it was Beth who was locked in there, but he was finding it more and more difficult to make any headway across the deck. His sword arm was getting tired, and it was all he could do to parry the cutlass chops now—he was just too exhausted to lunge forward and swing his own sword in any effective riposte.

Then one of the lively corpses danced ponderously up to him and whirled a green cutlass at his head—Shandy heaved his saber up and caught the blow on his forte, but the force of it knocked the sword out of his hand. It clattered away, out of reach. The dead thing, too close to run from, drew back its arm for a killing stroke, and Shandy had no choice but to scramble inside its guard and grapple with it.

Its body smelled like unfresh fish and felt like chains and jelly in a wet leather bag, and Shandy actually had to fight to keep himself from fainting at the horror of its proximity. The creature was hissing and thrashing and pounding Shandy's back with the brass guard of its cutlass, but Shandy managed to hobble to the starboard rail and roll the dead sailor over it. The gray hands clung to the lapels of Shandy's jacket, and for several seconds Shandy was bent over the rail staring down into the curdled eyes of the pendulous dead man; then one elbow, and a moment later the other, parted inside the thing's sleeves, and the body plummeted away to splash into the sea, leaving its hands and forearms locked onto Shandy's lapels.

Weaponless now, he stared around wildly for his dropped sword, but even in this panic his attention was caught by what was happening to Leo Friend. The fat young magician had risen from the poop deck up into the air, and flames were licking brightly around him, though his hair and clothing so far remained unscorched. Shandy glanced out beyond the starboard bow at Hurwood and saw flames around him too, though not as much, and he realized he was in the presence of a to-the-death duel between two supremely powerful sorcerors.

"Behind you, Jack!" came a yell from Davies, and Shandy leaped forward, the gray arms on his jacket swinging wildly, an instant before a cutlass blade whistled through the space his head had just been occupying. This put him dangerously close to another of the *Charlotte Bailey*'s crew, who expressionlessly cocked a rubbery arm for a sword swing, but before it could deliver the blow its head sprang tumbling from its shoulders as Davies' blade clunked through its neck.

"Look around you!" Davies snapped, kicking the doubly-dead man's weapon to Shandy. "Didn't I tell you that?"

"Yeah, Phil," Shandy gasped, stooping to pick up the discouragingly heavy cutlass.

None of the *Charlotte Bailey*'s crew were right nearby, and Davies took hold of his own sword with his left hand and then flexed his free right hand; Shandy saw the pirate's eyes narrow as he did it, and he remembered that Davies had apparently burned that hand in the jungle.

"Is your hand—" he began, then yelled, "Look out yourself!" and hopped past Davies to knock away an in-thrusting blade and split the jellyfish face of the figure wielding it. "Is your hand workable?"

"It's got no choice," said Davies tightly, gripping his sword again and looking around the littered deck. "Listen, we've got to make sure Friend loses this fight; try to—"

From behind Shandy came a screeching of overstressed wood, followed by loud cracking and snapping, and looking aft he saw that Friend had stretched his hand down, and though Friend was hovering a dozen yards above the deck and his pudgy hand scarcely extended down past his belt, most of the overdeck and bulkhead had been torn away from the cabin; the ripped up planks and beams hung in midair for a moment, then were dropped carelessly into the waist, and Shandy heard screams through the clattering and thudding, and he knew that some of the men from the *Jenny* had been under the dumped lumber.

Then Friend raised his cupped hand, and up into the sunlight from the now roofless cabin floated Beth Hurwood, struggling against something invisible that held her arms pinned to her sides.

Chapter Eighteen

Oh my God, thought Shandy in sudden panic, he's using her as a diversion; he's probably already raped her, and now he's going to set her on fire or something just to distract Hurwood.

Shandy started toward her across the blood-slippery deck, and he didn't even notice that one of the dead men between himself and the unroofed cabin had focused its attention on him and was now crouched, holding its green cutlass low and ready.

Davies saw it, though. "Goddammit, Jack," he burst out wearily, sprinting forward to get to the necrotic sailor before Shandy did.

Venner, his shirt torn and his red hair made even redder by a long scalp wound, and his habitual ingratiating grin replaced by a snarl of desperate effort, took in the situation at a glance—and he deliberately stepped in Davies' way and drove his burly shoulder into the older man's chest.

Half-winded by the impact, Davies reeled but nevertheless forced himself onward after casting back at Venner one quick glance full of anger and promise.

Shandy had had to duck around a knot of gasping, clanging combat, but now he was running straight toward the ascending figure of Beth Hurwood—and toward the patient, still-unnoticed dead mariner.

Davies had no time for a deceptive attack; he ran the last few steps to the undead sailor and simply swung his sword at the thing's neck.

The blade struck deep, but with his bad hand and lack of breath Davies hadn't been able to put enough force behind the blow to cut the head entirely off, and the dead eyes rolled toward him—and before he could pull his sword free, the thing's corroded cutlass was driven horrifyingly far up into his abdomen.

Suddenly ashen, Davies hitchingly breathed a curse, then tightened his burned hand around the grip of his sword, and with a convulsive heave that was as much a violent shudder of disgust as it was an attacking move, shoved his blade across the gray neck with his last strength, sawing the head free.

The two dead bodies tumbled away across the deck.

Shandy hadn't even noticed the encounter. Near Beth now, he dropped his sword and strained every muscle and tendon in a high jump for her, but his upstretched fingers brushed against an invisible resistance a foot short of her—though for a moment her downward staring eyes met his imploringly, and her lips formed words he couldn't hear.

Then he fell, rebounding painfully from the splintered cabin bulkhead to sprawl breathless on the sun-hot deck and wait, completely exhausted now, for a green blade or two to nail him to the planks.

But suddenly all the lich combatants were paler, translucent against the bright sky. The weight of the dead man's forearms on his chest all but disappeared.

At the same moment Shandy became aware that he was lying on the well-remembered quarterdeck of the *Vociferous Carmichael*, staring at armored planks he remembered having bolted in place himself—and he guessed that Friend was too busy defending himself against Hurwood to maintain the spell that had provided him with a crew.

"I could kill her," Friend said, relaxing his frown of concentration and baring bloody teeth in a smile.

It was Hurwood who wavered now, and Friend pointed his free hand at the older sorceror—and a ball of fire, white-bright even in the cloudless noon, rushed through yielding rigging straight at Hurwood.

The one-armed man parried it with a flailing gesture and it

rebounded down into the *Jenny* where it was greeted with alarmed yells; but Hurwood fell a couple of feet and then caught himself joltingly, and he whimpered and reached out his hand toward his daughter, on the other side of the waist, who was slowly rising toward his adversary. There was no fire at all now flickering around Friend, who, grinning and swollen with triumph, looked like some grotesque, beribboned hot-air balloon.

The young magician inhaled deeply, leaned back and stretched his arms out to either side.

Then in spite of the strong breeze the air was foul with the smell of an empty iron skillet on a fire, and the ship was the squat, multi-decked *Charlotte Bailey* again, and the English and Spanish sailors were not only substantial again but alive-looking—ruddy cheeks, tanned arms, brightly flashing eyes—and Friend was actually glowing in the sky, brightly, like a man-shaped sun. . . .

Leo Friend knew he was close to understanding it all now; he was on the very threshold of godhood—and without any external help, without drawing on anything but his own resources! He could see now that that was how it had to be. You did it for yourself or it didn't happen; and to overpower Benjamin Hurwood he would have to do it, and do it right now.

But to be God—which of course meant to have been God all along—he had to justify every event in his past, define every action in terms that made it consistent with godhood . . . there could no longer be any incidents that were too uncomfortable to remember.

With superhuman rapidity he held up for mental review year after year of remembered behavior—the torturing of pets, the malice toward playmates, the poisoned candy left near schoolyards and workhouses—and he was able to face, and incorporate into divinity, every bit of it, and he could feel himself growing incalculably more powerful as he bloomed closer and closer to the perfect self-satisfaction that would bring omnipotence. . . .

And finally, with Hurwood virtually vanquished, there was only one incident of Friend's life that needed to be sanctified out of plain squalid reality . . . but it was the most harrowing and traumatic experience he'd ever undergone, and even just facing it, even just making himself remember it, was supremely diffi-cult . . . but now, as he hung in midair over his ship, facing his all-but-shattered enemy and watching his all-but-won prize rising up from the broken cabin beneath him, he forced himself to relive it.

He was fifteen years old, standing beside the bookcase in his cluttered, smelly bedroom . . . no, in his elegant panelled bedchamber, aromatic with the jasmine breeze wafting in through the open casements and the breath of fine leather bindings . . . it had *always* been this way, there had *never* been the shabby, polluted room . . . and his mother opened the door and came in. Only for a moment was she a fat, gray-haired old drudge in a black bag dress—then she was a tall, handsome woman in a patterned silk robe that was open down the front . . . Seven years earlier he had discovered magic, and he had pursued it diligently since, and knew a lot now, and he wanted to share the wealth in his mind with the only person who had ever appreciated that mind. . . .

He went to her and kissed her . . .

But it was beginning to get away from him, she was the dumpy old woman again, just come upstairs to put fresh sheets on his bed, and the room was the grubby room again and he was a startled fat boy interrupted in the midst of one of his solitary self-administrations, and he was kissing her dizzily because in his heart-pounding delirium he had misunderstood the reason for her visit. . . . "Oh, Mommy," he was gasping, "you and I can have the world, I know magic, I can do stuff. . . ."

With a huge effort of will he forced her to be the beautiful robed woman, forced the room to expand back out to its regal dimensions . . . and he did it just in time, too, for he knew that his father, his mother's husband, entered the room next, and he really doubted that he could live through that scene again as it had really happened.

Well, he told himself unsteadily, I'm making reality here. In a few minutes that unbearable memory *won't* be what really happened.

Footsteps boomed ponderously on the stairs, ascending. Friend concentrated, and the steps diminished in volume until it might have been a child climbing the stairs. There was a lamp on the landing below, and a huge, bristling shadow darkened the open doorway and began to damage the room . . . but again Friend fought it down to insignificance—now a stooped, thin shadow grew in the doorway, dim, as if the thing casting it wasn't solid.

Now a little man like an upright rat in baggy trousers

shambled into the room, obviously of no danger to anyone, in spite of its squinting and scowling. *"What's—,"* it began in a deafening roar, but Friend concentrated again and its voice came out scratchy and petulant: "What's going on here?" The thing's breath was foul with liquor and tobacco. The father-creature now swaggered ludicrously across the tiled floor to Leo Friend, and in *this* version of reality the blow it leveled at him was a light, trembling slap.

The mother faced the intruder, and just her gaze made the unshaven creature recoil away from the boy. "You ignorant animal," she said softly to it, her low, musical voice echoing from the panelled walls and blending with the random tinkling of the fountains and wind chimes outside. "You thing of grime and sweat and laborer's tools. Beauty and brilliance are beyond your grubby perceptions. Go."

The thing stumbled in confusion back toward the door, its stinks receding, though bits of its ill-fitting black overcoat and leather boots flaked off to mar the floor tiles.

Hurwood fell another foot; he was almost down to the level of the deck now. Sweat plastered his white hair across his forehead and he was breathing in harsh gasps. His eyes were shut—but for a moment one opened, just a slit, and there seemed to be a gleam of guile in it, of almost perfectly concealed triumph.

It jarred Friend, and for a moment his control shook; and in the remembered bedchamber the father began to get bigger and walk away slower. The room was decaying back to its original form, and Friend's mother was babbling, "What'd you hit Leo for, yer always hittin' 'im . . ." and the father started to turn around to face them.

High above the poop deck Leo Friend clenched his glowing fists and used all his willpower; and, slowly, the father was pushed down again, the paneling became at least dimly visible on the walls. . . .

Then Hurwood stopped pretending defeat, and laughed openly, and struck.

And Friend's father, though his back was still turned to him, grew until the doorway lintel was almost too low and narrow for him, and when he turned around he had Hurwood's grinning face, and he opened his huge mouth and assailed Friend's eardrums with the sentence that Friend had tried desperately to trim out of reality: *"What're ye doin' t'yer mother, ye little freak? Look, ye've got 'er sickin' up on the floor!"*

Moaning in abject horror, Leo Friend turned to his mother, but in the moments since he'd last looked at her she'd deteriorated, and she was now a thing like a fat, hairless dog backing away from him on all fours, its belly heaving as it regurgitated its internal organs out onto the dirty floor. . . .

The room had not only devolved back to its original shabbiness, but was becoming even darker, the air staler. Friend tried to escape from it back to the clean sea air and the *Charlotte Bailey*, or even the *Vociferous Carmichael*, but he couldn't find a way out.

"You used it up too fast," said the terrible thing that was his father and Benjamin Hurwood and every other strong grownup who had ever despised him—and then it rushed in, as the room went totally dark, to devour him.

A thunderclap concussed the air and not only deafened Shandy, who had just climbed to his feet, but staggered him too, so that he had to grab a line of rigging to keep from falling, and when he glanced around, choking in the redoubled metallic stench, he saw that the ship had returned to being the familiar old *Carmichael* again and that the resurrected fighters were just dim shadows. The arms on his jacket were gone.

He glanced up. Beth Hurwood hung motionless in midair twenty feet above the poop deck, but Friend was rushing upward into the blue sky, and though he was glowing more brightly than ever now, almost too brightly to stare at, he was thrashing like a man attacked by wasps, and even over the ringing in his ears Shandy could hear him screaming. Finally, far above, there was a flash that left a red blot in front of Shandy's eyes wherever he looked, and the sky was full of fine white ash.

Very gently, Beth Hurwood was lowered back into the cabin, and some of the planks that had been torn away slithered back up and clung across the ragged gaps. The ghosts of the Spanish and English sailors, nearly impossible to see now, drifted this way and that across the deck to the blood puddles around the killed members of *Jenny*'s crew, and though the ghosts momentarily seemed to draw sustenance from the blood, some of the ash that had been Leo Friend swirled silently across the deck and seemed to poison them.

The pile of broken lumber kept shifting even after the animate planks had eeled away to provide bars for Beth's cage, and finally two bloody human figures crawled out from underneath. Shandy started to yell a pleased greeting—then noticed the broken and emptied head of one, and the completely caved-in chest of the other. After that he looked at their eyes and wasn't surprised at the emptiness in them.

Nearer Shandy, the corpse of Mr. Bird sat up, got laboriously to its feet and shambled over to the blocks where the mainsail sheet was controlled; one by one the other corpses joined him there, and when they had all gathered, somehow managing to look expectant in spite of their dead faces, Shandy counted fourteen of them.

"Not Davies," he said thickly, seeing that body standing among them and realizing for the first time that his friend had been killed. "Not Davies."

Hurwood came sailing in over the rail, swerving like a big bird over the heads of Shandy and the rest of the exhausted survivors, and landed on the poop deck near the now partially boarded-over hole. He stared expressionlessly down at Shandy for several seconds, then shook his head. "Sorry," he said to him. "I don't have a big enough crew to be able to spare him. Now get off of my ship."

Shandy looked toward the *Jenny*, whose mast and scorched sail were visible poking up above the starboard rail. The smoke that had been billowing up right after the fireball had fallen into the vessel was just wisps and curls now—evidently the men still aboard her had managed to put out the fire.

The twenty or so living pirates on the *Carmichael*'s deck, many of whom were wounded and bleeding, looked toward Shandy.

He nodded. "Back aboard the *Jenny*," he said, trying to keep out of his voice the choking bitterness he felt. "I'll join you in a moment."

As his men shuffled and limped across the deck to where the *Jenny*'s grappling hooks still clung to the *Carmichael*'s gunwales and rigging, Shandy took a deep breath and, though knowing that it would be useless and quite possibly fatal, walked purposefully across the deck toward the damaged cabin Beth was in.

Hurwood just watched him approach, a faint smile on his face.

Shandy stopped in front of the bolted door, and, feeling ridiculous as well as frightened and determined, knocked on the door. "Beth," he said clearly. "This is Jack Shandy—that is, John Chandagnac." Already the name seemed unnatural to him. "Come with me and I promise to take you directly to the nearest civilized port."

"How," came Beth's voice, surprisingly calm, through the warped door, "can I trust a man who murdered a naval officer in order to save killers from the just consequences of their acts, and later held a knife at my throat to keep me from my own father?"

Shandy brushed a stray lock of salt-stiff hair back from his forehead and squinted up at Hurwood—who smiled at him and shrugged in mock sympathy.

"That Navy captain," Shandy said, striving to keep his voice level, "was about to murder Davies—kill him without a trial. I had no choice. And your father—" He stopped for a moment in despair, then forced himself to go on, ridding himself of the words like a crew flinging cannons and casks overboard from a foundering vessel. "Your father intends to evict your soul from your body so that he can replace it with your mother's."

There was no answer from inside the cabin.

"Please get off my ship now," said Hurwood courteously.

Instead Shandy reached for the door's bolt—and a moment later found himself suspended in midair, rising up and away from the cabin door. His eyes went wide and then clamped shut, and then opened in a tense squint, and his whole body was rigid with uncontrollable vertigo.

When he had passed over the *Carmichael's* gunwale and hung thirty feet above the water in front of the *Jenny's* fire-blackened bow, he was released, and plummeted through the air for one long second before plunging into the cold water.

He thrashed his way to the surface, and wearily swam to the *Jenny,* and brawny arms reached out and pulled him aboard. "It's stinkin' magic, cap'n," Skank said to him when he was safely aboard and leaning against the mast and breathing deeply while a puddle of sea water spread out on the deck around his boots. "Lucky even to get away, we are."

Shandy didn't let show his surprise at being addressed as

captain. After all, Davies was dead and Shandy had been his quartermaster. "Expect you're right," he muttered.

"I'm sure glad you made it, though, Jack," Venner assured him with a broad smile that didn't conceal the chill in his gray eyes.

The last couple of pirates freed the grappling hooks and leaped down into the water and were soon aboard the *Jenny* and demanding rum.

"Yeah, give 'em rum," Shandy said, pushing the stray hair off his forehead again and reflecting that he'd soon have to draw his hair back and add another inch or two to his tarred pigtail. "How bad's the *Jenny* hurt?"

"Well," said Skank judiciously, "she wasn't in great shape even before that fireball. But we ought to be able to get her back to New Providence easy enough—all tack, no jibe."

"New Providence," Shandy said. He looked up and saw the corpse of Mr. Bird climbing the *Carmichael*'s shrouds. The body stepped into the footrope loop that hung just below the yard that supported the main course sail, and with the precision of a clockwork mechanism began unreefing the sail while cooling hands below worked the halliards. The sails filled, the sheets creaked through the blocks, and, slowly at first, the big ship moved away from the *Jenny*.

"New Providence," repeated the new captain of the *Jenny* thoughtfully.

And in the *Carmichael*'s cabin the spell was finally lifted from Beth Hurwood's throat, and she gasped, "I believe you, John! Yes—yes, I'll come with you! Take me away from here, *please!*"

But by then the *Jenny* was a shabby scrap of discolored canvas in the middle distance of the sea's glittering blue face, and, aside from her father's, the only ears her words reached were those of the dead men crewing the *Vociferous Carmichael*.

BOOK THREE

"What's o'clock?"
It wants a quarter to twelve,
And to-morrow's doomsday.

—*T. L. Beddoes*

Chapter Nineteen

Six men climbed out of the boat when it rocked to a halt in the shallows. Stede Bonnett, peering down at them from behind a dogwood tree at the crest of the sandy hill that sheltered his campfire from the chilly onshore wind, grinned with relief when he recognized their leader—it was William Rhett, the same British Army colonel who had captured Bonnett more than a month ago, and was now clearly here to recapture him after his recent escape from the watchhouse that doubled as Charles Town's jail.

Thank God, thought Bonnett; I'm about to be locked up again—if I'm very lucky, in fact, I may be killed here today.

He turned quickly and trudged back down the other side of the hill before any of his companions could come after him and notice the attacking party themselves; and he tried to dampen his excitement, for the black man could sense moods nearly as well as Blackbeard could.

He found the three of them still sitting around the fire, the Indian and the black man on one side, David Herriot on the other.

"Well, David," he said, striving to sound enthusiastic, "the weather is definitely lightening. I imagine you've been looking forward to getting off this damned island and onto another ship, eh?"

Herriot, who had been Bonnett's docile sailing-master from the day the *Revenge* was launched until the day Colonel Rhett captured the ship in the Cape Fear River, just shrugged. His childish elation at their escape from Charles Town had begun to turn to superstitious fear when inexplicably bad weather forced them to take shelter here on Sullivan's Island, and ever since the Indian and the black man joined them he had sunk into a morose lethargy.

The Indian and the black man had simply been standing outside Bonnett's tent one morning a week ago, and though they had offered no introductions they had greeted Bonnett and Herriot by name, and explained that they had come to help them get another ship. Bonnett thought he had seen the Indian aboard the *Queen Anne's Revenge* in May, when Blackbeard had been terrorizing Charles Town to get the ghost-repelling medicinal weed, and the black man's gums were as white as his teeth, the mark of a *bocor*. It was as clear to the simple-minded Herriot as it was to Bonnett that Blackbeard had found them.

For almost a month and a half after that terrible inland voyage to the Fountain of Youth, Bonnett had had no control over his own actions. The *Revenge* accompanied the *Queen Anne's Revenge* north to Virginia, and though it was Bonnett's mouth that called shiphandling orders to his sailors, it was Blackbeard who spoke through it. Like a sleepwalker Bonnett found himself taking the King's Pardon from North Carolina's Governor Eden, and making arrangements to sail south, back home to Barbados, where he would, to whatever extent possible, resume his role as a member of the island's high society of plantation owners. Blackbeard was of course planning to be killed so that he could return in a new body, and he obviously felt that it would be useful to have a wealthy gentleman—or even ex-gentleman—working as his puppet on that rich island.

After he had taken the pardon Bonnett began to regain control of his actions; apparently Blackbeard felt that a return to his previous life was what Bonnett wanted most on earth, and so he didn't particularly bother to force the man's cooperation anymore.

Actually, though, Bonnett dreaded returning to Barbados more than he dreaded death. He had been a respected citizen during his years there—a retired Army major and a wealthy planter—and he could not bear to return as an ex-pirate, one who was still at liberty only because he had chosen to hide under the skirts of the royal amnesty. And any hope he might have had that the citizens of that remote island would be ignorant of his piratical career had been shattered only days after he embarked, for the second ship he took was the *Turbet* . . . a Barbadian ship. Even at the time, he had known that he ought to kill everyone aboard so as to leave no one to testify, but he hadn't had the stomach to give the order . . . and besides, David Herriot would never have stood by while people he had sailed with all his life were murdered.

And the idea of seeing his wife again, *now,* nearly made him faint. The woman had been a vituperative harridan even before he set out—however unwillingly!—on his felonious cruise, and he still frequently woke up sweating, with her scornful cries ringing all too well-remembered in his ears: "Get away from me, you brutal slug! You bitter pig!" Always he had fled the house, his own house, trembling with the desire to commit uxoricide or suicide . . . or both.

But a return to Barbados and her was what the future held . . . unless he could wreck the plans Blackbeard had for him. And so on the fourteenth of September he sent Herriot into town to round up as many members of his original crew as could be found—he wanted no one who had sailed with Blackbeard or Davies—and get them aboard the *Revenge.* The ship was not a prize of piracy—he had paid for every plank and every yard of rigging— and so the harbor authorities had no objection to his taking her out for a cruise. As soon as they were out of the harbor he had his men scrape the name *Revenge* off the ship's transom and paint *Royal James* on instead.

And then Bonnett set about violating his pardon as thoroughly and quickly as he could. Before the sun set on that Wednesday he had taken a ship, and during the next ten days he took eleven more. The plunder was minor—tobacco, pork, pins and needles— but he was demonstrably engaging in piracy. He told the crews of the robbed ships that his name was Captain Thomas, for he didn't want word of his backsliding to get back to Blackbeard until he could get himself safely out of Blackbeard's reach.

To accomplish *that,* he decided to steal Blackbeard's own planned defeat scenario—being entirely under Blackbeard's control, Bonnett had been the only person the pirate-king had dared to discuss his defeat plan with—albeit Bonnett would now employ it for a humbler end; for while Blackbeard planned to use it as a stepping-stone to immortality, Bonnett hoped only for a quick death, or, failing that, a trial and eventual hanging far from Barbados.

He sailed the *Royal James* up the Cape Fear River, ostensibly to careen her for repairs—but he made sure that the captain and crew of the last ship he'd taken saw where his anchorage was before he turned them loose.

The governor's pirate-hunters under Colonel Rhett had obligingly arrived at the river mouth on the evening of the twenty-sixth; and Bonnett made sure that his feigned escape attempt took place at low tide the next morning. Though Herriot had stared in astonishment at the impracticality of his last few orders, Bonnett succeeded in running the ship aground in a position from which any effective fight would be impossible. At the last moment Bonnett had tried to detonate his own powder kegs, which would have scattered the remains of himself and most of his crew across the marshy landscape, but he was stopped before he could ignite it.

Then there had been the voyage back to Charles Town—in shackles. His crew was promptly locked up in the Anabaptist meeting house in the southern corner of town, under the guard of a full company of militia . . . but Bonnett and Herriot were just kept in the watchhouse south of town, on the banks of the Ashley River, with only two guards assigned to them.

One evening two weeks after their arrival there, both of their guards walked back to town for dinner at the same time . . . and the door's lock proved to be so rusty that a hard shove snapped the bolt. Even Bonnett had never really wanted to face the humiliation of a trial and public execution, and so, elated at what seemed to be a stroke of luck, he and Herriot had slipped out and stolen a boat and then rowed east past Johnson's Fort and right on out of the harbor.

The weather had turned foul then, with wind and rain and choppy seas, and they had had to land on Sullivan's Island, just outside and north of the harbor; and, too late, both of them began to wonder uneasily whether their escape really had been just luck.

The weather had not improved. The two fugitives managed to make a tent with their boat's sail, and for two weeks they lived on flounder and turtle cooked over a carefully concealed fire. Bonnett hoped the modest, wind-scattered smoke of it would pass un-noticed against the perpetually gray skies.

Clearly it had not.

Bonnett now tore a fan-shaped frond from one of the ubiquitous palmettos, and threw it onto the fire; it began popping and curling, and he hoped the sounds would cover any noises made by Colonel Rhett and his men as they crept up the seaward side of the hill. "Yes," he went on loudly, "it'll do us both good, David, to get off this island. I'm ready to go out and take more ships—and I've learned from my mistakes! Never again will I leave anyone alive to testify against me!" He hoped Rhett's party was hearing these sentiments. "Rape the women and shoot the men and pitch 'em all over the side for the sharks!"

Herriot was looking even more unhappy, and the *bocor* was staring at Bonnett with lively suspicion.

"What are you doing?" the *bocor* asked. Extra alert because of their distance from the protective Caribbean *loas*, he raised his hand and sifted the breeze through his fingers.

Where are you, Rhett? thought Bonnett desperately, his cheerful expression beginning to falter. Are you in position yet? Guns loaded, primed and aimed?

The Indian stood up and swept the clearing with his gaze. "Yes," he said to the black man, "there are concealed purposes here."

The *bocor*'s fingers were still waving, but the hand was pointing to the seaward slope. "There are . . . others! Nearby!" He turned quickly to the Indian. "Protective magic! Now!"

The Indian's hand darted to the decorated leather bag at his belt—

"*Fire!*" yelled Bonnett.

A dozen nearly simultaneous explosions shook the air as sand was kicked up all over the clearing and the fire threw up a swirl of sparks. Voices were shouting at the top of the slope, but Bonnett couldn't hear what they were saying. Slowly he turned his head and looked around.

The Indian was sitting in the raked-up sand clutching his ripped and bloody thigh, and the *bocor* was gripping his own right wrist and scowling at his torn and nearly fingerless right hand.

David Herriot lay flat on his back, staring intently into the sky; a big hole had been punched into the middle of his face, and blood had already made a dark halo in the sand around his head.

Good-bye, David, thought Bonnett. I'm glad I was able to give you at least this.

Colonel Rhett and his men were sliding and running down this side of the slope, being careful to keep fresh pistols pointed at the men around the fire. It occurred to Bonnett that he himself had not been hit by any of the pistol balls that had been fired into the clearing.

That meant he would live . . . to stand public trial, and then to provide morbid amusement for all the Charles Town citizens—as well as any Indians, and sailors, and trappers that might be in town—with the spectacle of himself twitching and grimacing and publicly losing control of his bladder and bowels while he dangled by the neck for some long minutes at the end of a rope.

He shivered, and wondered if it was too late to provoke Rhett's men into killing him here and now.

It was. Rhett himself had come up behind him and now yanked his arms back and quickly lashed his wrists together with stout twine. "Good day, Major Bonnett," said Rhett coldly.

The fit of shivering had passed, and Bonnett found he was able to relax. He looked up, and he squared his shoulders as befitted a one-time Army Major. Well, I'll die with no credit, he thought, but at least with no outstanding debt either. I've earned the death they'll prepare for me. Not with piracy, for that was never my doing; but now I needn't work to deceive myself any longer about another matter.

"Good day, Colonel Rhett," he said.

"Bind the black and the Indian," Rhett told one of his men, "and then trot them to the boat. Prod them with a knife-point if they won't step along prompt." Then he gave Bonnett a shove. "The same goes for you."

Bonnett strode up the slope toward the gray sky. He was nearly smiling. No, he thought, I needn't pretend to myself any longer that I was drugged when I beat to death that poor whore who did such a convincing imitation of my wife. Now that I'm being called on, for whatever mistaken reasons, to atone for a horrible crime, I can at least be glad they found a man with one to offer.

He thought of Blackbeard. "*Don't* let me escape again, do you understand?" he called to Rhett. "Lock me up in some place I can't be got out of, and keep alert guards over me!"

"Don't worry," said Rhett.

Chapter Twenty

When the faint pink of dawn behind the shoulder of Ocracoke Island became bright enough to resolve the dim blur of the inlet mouth, Blackbeard chuckled softly to see the sails of the two Navy sloops still anchored where they had been at dusk. The giant pirate upended the last bottle of rum, and when it was empty he waved it at Richards. "Here's another one for Miller," he said. "I'll bring it to him." He inhaled deeply, savoring the blend of chilly dawn air and rum fumes, and it seemed to him that the very air was tense—breathing it was like touching a beam of wood flexed to within half a hair of its snapping point.

Though he didn't relish them, he forced himself to chew up and swallow one more mouthful of sugar-and-cocoa balls, and he gagged but got them down. That's got to be enough, he told himself; probably no one in the world ever drank as much rum or ate as much damned candy as I've done this night. I'm sure there's not a drop of my blood that isn't saturated with sugar and alcohol.

"We could still slip east, cap'n," said Richards nervously. "The tide's still high enough for us to clear the shoals in this sloop."

Blackbeard stretched. "And abandon our prize?" he asked, jerking a thumb at the somewhat larger sloop, anchored thirty yards away to starboard, that they had taken yesterday. "Naw. We can deal with these Navy boys."

Richards still frowned worriedly, but didn't venture another objection. Blackbeard grinned as he started aft toward the boat's gun-deck ladder. It looks, he thought, as if shooting Israel Hands served *two* purposes. I've also made the rest of them afraid to argue with me.

His grin became more of a wince—on a tamer face it might have looked like wry sadness—when he remembered that gathering in his tiny cabin two nights ago. Word had just come from Tobias Knight, the collector of Customs, that Virginia's governor Spotswood knew Blackbeard was lingering here and had organized some sort of force to capture him. Israel Hands had instantly begun making plans to abandon this Ocracoke Inlet anchorage.

Blackbeard had leaned forward, keeping his face expressionless in the lamplight, and refilled the several cups on the rough table. "Do you decide what we do, Israel?" he had asked.

"If you fail to, Ed, then yes I do," Hands had replied cheerfully. The two of them had sailed together way back in the privateer days, and then again as pirates under the old buccaneer admiral Ben Hornigold, and Israel Hands dared to be far more familiar with Blackbeard than anyone else did. "Why? Do you want to stay and try to fight from the *Adventure?*" He'd slapped the close bulkhead and low ceiling contemptuously. "She's nothing but a damned sloop, man, scarcely more than a turtle-boat! Let's get back to where we left the *Queen Anne's Revenge* hidden and get out to sea again! To hell with this surf-and-shoal dallying—I want to feel a real deck under my feet again, heaving on a real sea."

And moved by a sudden wave of affection for his loyal old shipmate, Blackbeard had impulsively decided to perform an act of mercy that would never be recognized as such. "I'll see to it," he said, under his breath, "that you do live to sail again, Israel."

Then under the table he drew two pistols, leaned forward and blew out the lamp flame, and crossed the pistols and fired them.

The simultaneous blasts flashed an instant of yellow light up through the cracks and holes in the table, and Israel Hands was flung spinning out of his chair to slam against the bulkhead. When the resulting shouting and scrambling had quieted enough for someone to think of relighting the lamp, Blackbeard saw that his aim had been perfect—one ball had gone harmlessly into the deck, and the other had made an exploded bloody ruin of Israel Hands' knee.

The several men in the cramped cabin, all on their feet now, had stared at Blackbeard with fear and astonishment, but Israel

Hands, crouched against the bulkhead and trying to stop the flow of blood from his ruined leg, looked up at his old companion with hurt betrayal as well as pain in his suddenly gaunt face. "*Why . . . Ed?*" he managed to ask from between clenched teeth.

Unable to tell him the truth, Blackbeard had merely said, gruffly, "Hell—if I didn't shoot one of you now and then you'd forget who I was."

Hands had been taken off the vessel the next morning, feverish and vowing revenge. But, thought Blackbeard now as he climbed down to the low-ceilinged gun deck, at least you'll be alive tomorrow, Israel—you're not here.

"Here's another one," he told Miller, who had already filled a dozen bottles with shot and powder, and, after poking a slow match into the neck of each, laid them carefully in a blanket. "Pretty much ready?"

Miller grinned, further distorting his already scar-crimped face. "Anytime you say, cap'n," he replied happily.

"Fine." With a faint echo of the feeling he'd had for Israel Hands, Blackbeard wished for a moment that he'd cooked up some reason to send all of his crew away, to meet Spotswood's pirate-killers alone. But the more blood that was shed today the better his magic would work, and, sentiment aside, any misfortune for others that prospered him was an acceptable bargain. "No quarter," he said. "More blood-salt than sea-salt in the ocean today, eh?"

"Damn right," agreed Miller, giggling as he funneled powder into the new bottle.

"Damn right," echoed Blackbeard.

"Got match-cords lit over yonder, cap'n," Miller remarked. "Sun coming up, I reckon you'll want to be braidin' 'em on soon."

"No," Blackbeard said thoughtfully, "I don't think I'll wear any today." He turned to the ladder, then paused and, without looking back, waved over his shoulder to Miller and the men hunched over the cannon breeches. "Uh . . . thank you."

On deck again he saw that the day was indeed upon them. The east's faint pink had spread to a sky-spanning gray glow. A line of pelicans flapped past a few yards above the sand, and some stilt-legged birds were dashing busily back and forth on the Ocracoke Island beach a hundred yards off the port bow.

"Here they come, cap'n," said Richards grimly.

The sails of the two Navy sloops were now rigged and full, and the narrow hulls were advancing through the calm silver water, slowly because of its many shoals.

"I wonder if they've got a pilot that knows the inlet," mused Richards.

One of the sloops jarred to a mast-flexing halt; a moment later the other one did too.

"No," said Blackbeard, "they don't." I hope, he thought grimly, that all this hasn't been for nothing. I hope these Navy men aren't incompetent idiots.

He could see the splashes as sailors on the Navy vessels got busy pitching ballast over the side. Hurry, you fools, he thought. The tide's going out. And if I'm not . . . replanted . . . by Christmas, only five weeks distant now, I'll miss her, Hurwood will have done his silly connubial trick and disposed of her.

He wished he had learned sooner—or guessed—that his marriage-magic wouldn't work with ordinary women anymore. Early in his career as a magician he had discovered that there were female aspects to magic as well as male ones, and that no man, alone, could have much access to the female areas. In the past he had always got around that obstacle by getting himself sacramentally linked to a woman and then using that link, which in effect made them equal partners, to complete his otherwise one-sided magical capacity. The ready availability of fresh wives had made him careless of individual ones, and they had all died or gone insane fairly soon after the wedding as he used them up, and the one who would become a widow today was his fourteenth.

She would be sixteen years old now, and had still been pretty when he last saw her, back in May. He had been linking himself to her pretty heavily before that, using the magic-capable areas of her female mind to keep Bonnett under control—for some reason Bonnett had been more vulnerable to the female aspects of magic—and he had finally broken her mind. She was in a madhouse in Virginia now, and when he had visited her there in May to see if she could still be of any use to him, she had screamed and fled from him and then broken a window and tried to kill herself with a long piece of glass. In the ensuing confusion a midwife as well as a priest had been called, for the attendant who caught her had at first thought she was trying to give herself an abortion.

But now Blackbeard was not even remotely of the same

sorcerous status as the average woman. He had drastically changed his status, he had shed blood in Erebus . . . and so he could be profitably wed only to a woman who had also shed blood there.

As far as he knew there was only one woman alive who had done that.

"We could try to slip around them while they're stuck," observed Richards cautiously. "I think if we—" He sighed. "Never-mind. They're off again."

Blackbeard suppressed a grin of satisfaction as he squinted ahead. "They are indeed."

"Christ," Richards said hoarsely, "this is exactly how they caught Bonnett two months ago—cornered him up an inlet on an early morning low tide."

Blackbeard frowned. "You're right," he growled.

Richards glanced up at him, clearly hoping that the pirate-king had finally comprehended the extent of their danger here.

But Blackbeard was just recalling what he had heard about Bonnett's capture. Yes, by the Baron, he thought angrily, aside from the fact that it took place a hundred and fifty miles south of here, it *was* damned similar.

Bonnett stole my defeat scene!

Not only did he disqualify himself for the role I had planned for him, subtly enough for me not to have noticed until it was too late and he'd got himself captured, but he also remembered and appropriated—pirated!—the long-planned defeat scene I intend to enact—re-enact!—today! And the two magicians I sent to fetch him from that island came back without him, and wounded . . . and this last Sunday, at exactly noon, I stopped being psychically aware of him. Apparently he found a loophole through which to escape me—the loop at the end of a hangman's rope.

"Hailing distance in a moment," croaked Richards, his face slick with sweat in spite of the chill that made his breath visible as steam.

"Hailing distance now," said Blackbeard. He squared his massive shoulders and then with slow, measured steps walked up to the bow and braced one booted foot on the bowsprit trunk. He filled his lungs, then shouted at the Navy sloops, *"Damn you for villains, who are you? And from whence came you?"*

There was commotion on the deck of the nearest sloop, and then the British ensign flag mounted fluttering to the top of the mast. "You may see by our colors," came a shouted reply, "we are no pirates!"

Almost formally, as if this were a rhetorical exchange in an old, old litany, Blackbeard called, "Come aboard so that I may see who you are."

"I cannot spare my boat," yelled back the Navy captain, "but I will come aboard of you as soon as I can, with my sloop!"

Blackbeard smiled and seemed to relax. He shouted back, "Damnation seize my soul if I give you quarters, or take any from you."

"We expect none, nor will extend any!"

Blackbeard turned to Richards. "I'd say that's clear," he remarked. "Run up our colors and cut our cable—we're off."

"Aye aye, cap'n," said Richards. "Leaving the prize?" he added, pointing at the captured merchant sloop.

"Sure, I never did care about the prize."

The foremost Navy vessel tacked north, evidently intending to loop around and prevent any flight by Blackbeard to the east, but in a moment Blackbeard's sloop, the *Adventure,* was skating west before the wind across the smooth surface of Pamlico Sound, aiming straight as an arrow between the other Navy sloop and the Ocracoke Island shore, toward the inlet and the open sea beyond. Every man aboard the *Adventure* except for Blackbeard was holding his breath, for the water was hardly more than six feet deep, and the tide was ebbing. Several even dug coins out of their pockets and flung them over the side—the sun hadn't yet cleared the hump of the island, and the coins fell lustreless into the smoke-gray water.

Richards was looking north, at the sloop that had hailed them. He laughed softly. "They're aground again!" he whispered.

Feeling suddenly very tired, Blackbeard drew one of his pistols and said, "Loose sails. We're going to pause to give these boys a broadside."

Richards spun to face him. "*What?* We've *got* it right now, we can get away if we—"

Blackbeard raised the pistol and poked Richards in the mouth with the muzzle. "Loose sails and ready the starboard guns, damn you!"

"*Aye!*" said Richards in a voice that was nearly a sob, turning to relay the order. Most of the men gaped in surprise, but they could see the pistol, and Hands' retirement was still fresh in everyone's memory, and so they obeyed, and the *Adventure* slowed, sails fluttering loosely, and coasted up alongside the Navy sloop.

"Fire starboard guns!" Blackbeard roared, and the *Adventure* rocked as the guns went off, fouling the dawn air with billows of acrid smoke and raising a clamoring scatter of alarmed sea birds.

The smoke drifted away west, toward the inlet, and Blackbeard laughed to see the Navy vessel wallowing helplessly, her rigging blown to tatters and her rail and gunwales a ruin of torn wood.

"Set sail now?" pleaded Richards, eyeing the Ocracoke shore that was drawing slowly closer as the tide ebbed.

Blackbeard was looking at it too. "Yes," he said thoughtfully after a moment, for it was too late.

The wind, fitful at best, had died, and though the pirates crowded on every square yard of canvas like starving fishers spreading nets, the *Adventure* was drifting.

The sloop to the north had got afloat again and the men aboard her had got their oars out and were rowing toward the *Adventure*.

With the gentlest of jars, the *Adventure* went aground.

"Hurry up reloading the starboard guns!" called Blackbeard. "You lads," he added to a gang of pirates who were desperately flinging barrels and lengths of chain over the side, "nevermind that, you can't raise her faster than the tide's dropping her! Look to your pistols and cutlasses."

The remaining Navy sloop was closing steadily. "Hold fire until I say," said Blackbeard.

"Right," said Richards, who had drawn his cutlass and was slowly whirling it at arm's length in a warm-up exercise. Now that there was no hope of avoiding the encounter, most of his anxiety had disappeared. He grinned at Blackbeard. "I hope this is the closest you ever do cut it."

The giant pirate briefly squeezed Richards' shoulder. "Never this close again," he said quietly. "I promise you."

The Navy sloop was only a couple of dozen yards away now, and Blackbeard could even hear, over the knocking of the oars in the ports, grunts of effort from the rowers. He knew that the Navy captain must be considering when to discharge his own guns, and when things were a moment short of being lined up, Blackbeard called, *"Fire."*

Again the *Adventure*'s starboard guns boomed, lashing small-shot like a whistling scythe across the other vessel's deck. Bodies, punched off their feet, spun away like kicked debris in a spray of splinters and blood, and the pirates cheered—but Blackbeard, standing on the *Adventure*'s bowsprit, saw the young officer in charge hurriedly herding all his remaining ambulatory sailors belowdecks.

"Now the grenades!" Blackbeard yelled eagerly as soon as the last of the healthy Navy sailors had disappeared down the hatch.

The pirates happily got busy lighting the fuses protruding from the shot- and powder-filled bottles, and, as soon as a sputtering fire was near a bottle's neck, pitching the thing across the gap onto the Navy vessel's deck. With a staccato series of bangs the bottles exploded, flinging shot in all directions, ravaging the corpses on the deck and finishing off any Navy men who had been too badly hurt to get below.

"They're all dead, except three or four," Blackbeard yelled, drawing his cutlass. "Let's board and cut 'em to pieces!"

Boarding proved easy, for the tide was pulling the Navy sloop toward them, and Blackbeard was able to leap across the gap onto the shot-raked deck; at the same instant the hatch cover was flung back and the officer in charge of the Navy sloop, a lieutenant by his uniform, scrambled up to the deck. Blackbeard bared his teeth in a grin so full of recognition and welcome that the lieutenant actually glanced behind himself to see what old friend the pirate-king had spied.

But behind him was nothing but a crowd of his own men scrambling up the ladder, the eighteen—of the original thirty-five—who could still wield a sword or fire a pistol. The pirates were leaping and clambering aboard right behind their chief, and the lieutenant and his men scarcely had time to draw their rapiers before the yelling pirates were upon them.

For the first few moments the deck was a chaotic riot of howling, clanging, stamping, chopping savagery, punctuated by the occasional bang of a pistol shot, as the pirates used their heavy cutlasses to hatchet through the line of Navy men and then turn back upon them again, and many of the Navy men's rapiers were broken in attempting to parry the sledgehammer blows of weapons that caused nearly as much damage striking flat as they did striking edge on. The deck was soon slippery with the blood that spouted from wrist-stumps, undone bellies and opened throats, and the air that shook with yelling and clanking was foul with the hot iron smell of fresh blood.

But the Navy men had all along been trying simply to evade the ponderous swings of the cutlasses rather than oppose their own fragile blades to them, and, after the first brutal couple of minutes, the panting, sweating pirates worked their ten-pound chunks of steel with less quickness and force, and the light rapier blades were able to dart in around the slow strokes, and puncture throats and eyes and chests. Though damaged less spectacularly, as many pirates were falling now as Navy men.

Blackbeard had wound up fighting by the mast, back to back with one of his men, but when a rapier point spun around the other pirate's descending cutlass and sprang in to transfix his heart, and he tumbled instantly limp to the deck, Blackbeard stepped away from the mast and with his left hand drew his last pistol.

The Navy lieutenant, standing in front of him, drew one of his own.

The two shots were nearly simultaneous, but while Blackbeard's ball missed and went skipping away across the shoals, the lieutenant's ball punched straight into the giant pirate's abdomen.

It rocked him back, but a moment later Blackbeard roared and leaped forward, whirling his cutlass in a chop that broke off the lieutenant's rapier blade an inch from the hilt; Blackbeard raised the cutlass again to split the man's head—but another Navy man stepped up behind the pirate and, with a full over-the-head swing like someone driving a stake, brought the heavy axelike blade of a pike down onto Blackbeard's left shoulder, barely missing his ear. The collarbone snapped audibly and the pirate was slammed down onto one knee. He raised his head and then, incredibly, straightened his massive legs and stood up, swaying back just as the pike came whistling down again, so that it tore open his forehead and cheek instead of crushing his skull.

Blackbeard had dropped the fired pistol, but his good right hand still gripped the cutlass, and he swung it around in a horizontal arc that sent the pike-wielder's head and body tumbling, separately, across the deck.

Another pistol was fired directly into Blackbeard's chest, and as he staggered back, blood spattering onto the deck all around him, two rapiers were driven deep into his back; he whirled so quickly that one of them broke off in him, and his outflung cutlass broke the arm of the man who held the broken sword. Two more shots hammered into him and another blade chugged deeply into his side.

Finally he got his feet solidly under him and straightened to his full height—the Navy men drew back fearfully—and then, straight as a felled tree, he toppled forward, and the wet deck shook when he hit it.

"Jesus Christ," exhaled the lieutenant, sitting down abruptly, his exhaustion-tense hands still locked around the fired pistol and the broken sword.

After a pause, one of the Navy men picked up Blackbeard's cutlass, knelt by the corpse and raised the heavy blade over his head, obviously trying to guess where, under the tumble of tangled black hair, the pirate-king's neck was. A moment later he made up his mind and swung the blade down; it crunched through Blackbeard's spine and into the deck and Blackbeard's severed head rolled over to stare at the sky with a strained but sardonic grin.

When the tide rose again in the early evening, the four battered sloops filed past Beacon Island and out through the Ocracoke Inlet. The surviving pirates were under armed guard aboard the *Adventure,* and Blackbeard's head swung from the Navy sloop's bowsprit. Blood had stopped dripping from the grisly trophy hours ago, and most of it had long since threaded away in the cold salt water to feed tiny fishes, but one clot had remained solid, and clung now to the hull of the sloop just below the water line.

It was, very gently, pulsing.

Chapter Twenty-One

The bang of the pistol shot rolled away across the long harbor of New Providence Island, and though a glint showed on the deck of the *Delicia* as one of the Navy officers aboard her turned a glass on the shore, no one leaped up in fear of being murdered, or anticipation of seeing someone else be, as would have been the case six months ago, and Jack Shandy plodded barefoot across the hot sand to the chicken he'd beheaded with the pistol ball. It was evidently too early in the day for drink to have impaired his aim.

He picked up the head. As he'd feared, the beak had letters inked on it, and he let it drop.

Damn, he thought. So much for grilled chicken. I'm glad old Sawney hasn't started magicking the fever into lobsters yet.

He tucked the pistol into his sash and walked toward the fort. The darker-colored masonry of the new sections of wall gave the whole edifice a pied look, and Shandy thought it was probably the physical improvements, even more than the British flag and the presence of Woodes Rogers, the official governor, that had made mad old Governor Sawney move out of the place.

As he trudged toward the cluster of tents he glanced to his left at the harbor. There were fewer boats these days than there'd been before Rogers' arrival, and it was easy to spot the old *Jenny*. Shandy had abandoned his captaincy when he took the pardon three months ago, and Venner had stepped in and declared himself captain. By that time, though, everybody had taken the pardon, and it was clear to most that the days of piracy were dead, and nobody felt that the issue of who might be captain of one battered old sloop was important enough to dispute, and so Venner's claim had stood. He had careened the vessel, cleaned her up and rerigged her, and it was obvious that he intended to violate his pardon and go back on the account. Shandy had heard that he was furtively recruiting a crew from among the segment of the island's population that missed the bad old days—he hadn't asked Shandy, and Shandy wasn't interested anyway.

The Navy brigantine he'd seen wending its way in among the shoals this morning was moored now, but though supplies were being unloaded and taken ashore, there was none of the festive atmosphere he would have expected—men were standing around in little groups on the beach, talking quietly and shaking their heads, and one of the prostitutes was sobbing theatrically.

"Jack!" someone called. Shandy turned and saw Skank hurrying toward him.

"Mornin', Skank," he said when the young man stopped, panting, in front of him.

"Did you hear the *news?*"

"Probably not," said Shandy. "If I did, I forgot it."

"Blackbeard's dead!"

Shandy smiled reminiscently, as one might at learning that a game remembered from long-ago childhood is still being played by children today. "Ah." He kept walking, and Skank trotted along beside him. "Pretty sure, this news is?" Shandy asked, pausing at the tent that served as a sort of open-air pub.

"Oh, aye, couldn't be surer. It was in North Carolina, a month ago. Half his men were captured, and old Thatch's head was brought right to the governor."

"He died on the water, I daresay," remarked Shandy, accepting the cup of rum he didn't even have to bother specifying anymore.

Skank nodded. "Aye. He was in the Ocracoke Inlet, in a sloop called the *Adventure*. He'd hid the *Queen Anne's Revenge* somewhere, and all his lucre too, they say. They claim he didn't have a single *reale* aboard. That weren't like him, though—probably the Navy men took all the money."

"No—I'll bet—" Shandy paused to take a long sip of the rum. "I'll bet he had hid it all. *Adventure*, eh? An apt name—it was *his* great adventure, I guess."

Skank looked around at the tents and the beach and the half-sunk hulks of abandoned ships that Governor Rogers was already getting people to break up and carry away. "I guess this really isn't a pirate island anymore."

Shandy laughed. "You just now noticed? Two days ago Rogers hanged eight men right over there, remember?—for violating the pardon. And we all just watched, and when it was done we all just wandered away."

"Sure, but—" Skank struggled with the complexity of the idea he was trying to express. "But just knowing old Thatch was out there somewhere . . ."

Shandy shrugged and nodded. "And might come back. Yeah, I know. I can't picture even Woodes Rogers resisting him. Aye, soon now there'll be taxes and wages and laws about where to moor your boat. And you know something? I think magic will stop working here too, like it did back east."

"Goddamn." Skank absently took Shandy's cup, had a deep gulp and then handed it back. "Where'll *you* go, Jack? I'm thinking of signing on with Venner."

"Oh, I'll stay here till I run out of money for rum, and then I suppose I'll move on, get some kind of work. Hell, it's only a matter of time before England declares war on Spain again, and pirating will go back to being legal, and then maybe I'll enlist on a privateer. I don't know, it's a sunny day, and I've got rum—I'll worry about tomorrow's problems tomorrow."

"Huh. You used to be more—" This was Skank's day for abstract concepts. "More . . . jumpy."

"Aye, I did. I remember that." He emptied the cup and handed it back for a refill. "But I believe soon I won't remember it."

Obscurely troubled, Skank nodded and wandered back toward the boats from which the new supplies were being unloaded.

Shandy sat down in the sand and grinned over his sun-warmed rum. More jumpy, he thought. Well, sure, Skank—I had things to be jumpy about. Two things. I wanted to confront my uncle Sebastian and expose to the world—and the law!—what he had done to my father; and, even more than that, I wanted to rescue Beth Hurwood from her father and tell her . . . some conclusions I had come to. But neither of those things turned out to be possible.

Out in the harbor the *Jenny*'s mainsail was jerking, and Shandy focused on it. Someone was apparently trying to raise her gaff-spar to a higher angle. Can't be done, friend, he thought. That old wrought iron gaff-saddle is so shot-bent that you're lucky you can raise the spar as high as you've got it—and frankly she takes the wind better with a few wrinkles up at the throat of the sail anyway. If old Hodge was still alive, or Davies, they'd tell you the same. You'd be better off spending your time replacing some of those overstrained hull-strakes.

Shandy remembered the overhaul he himself had given the *Jenny*, nearly four months ago now, after the old sloop had limped back into the harbor all scorched and sprung and jury-rigged, missing her old captain and half her crew. Woodes Rogers had arrived on New Providence Island only two weeks earlier, but the new governor had already driven out such unrepentant citizens as Charlie Vane, and had made speeches about civic pride, and raised the British flag, and distributed pamphlets from the Society for Promoting Christian Knowledge—and so no one was terribly surprised by the news that Philip Davies was dead and the *Vociferous Carmichael* spirited away. It seemed consistent with the times.

At first Shandy had ignored the old sloop. He had sailed her into the harbor on a Friday afternoon, and that evening, drunk, he made his best yet "bouillabaise endeavor," using up most of the remaining pirated garlic, saffron, tomatoes and olive oil on the island, and it drew praise even from Woodes Rogers himself, who had asked what all the commotion was about on the beach, and, being told, requested some of the seafood stew for himself and his captains; but Shandy tasted only enough of the court bouillon and rouille and seafood to be sure they were cooked correctly, and himself mainly consumed bottle after bottle of Davies' hoarded 1702 Latour bordeaux. He laughed at every joke and joined in the several group songs—none of them, to be sure, rendered quite as heartily as they'd been in the days before Rogers' arrival—but his thoughts were clearly elsewhere, and even Skank noticed and told him to eat and drink and worry about tomorrow's problems tomorrow.

Shandy had eventually wandered away from the fires and the ex-pirates and the nervously observing Navy officers, and had walked down to the shore. He had first set foot on this island only six weeks before, but already it was more of a home than he'd ever had, and he knew its people better than he had known those of any other community. He had made friends here, and seen them die, before the current governor's ships had been even white dots on the eternal blue horizon.

Then he had heard someone scuffing across the sand in the darkness behind him, and he turned, frightened—"Who is it?" he called.

A chunky figure in a ragged dress was silhouetted against the fire. "It's me, Jack," came a girl's low voice in reply. "Ann. Ann Bonny."

He remembered hearing that she was trying to get a divorce from Jim Bonny. "Ann." He hesitated, then slowly walked over to where she stood. He put his hands on her shoulders. "So many of them are dead now, Ann," he said, wondering if he was about to start crying. "Phil . . . and Hodge . . . Mr. Bird . . ."

Ann laughed, but he could hear the tears in her voice. "I am not a dog!" she quoted softly.

"Time passes so much more . . . *quickly,* here," he said, sliding one arm around her shoulders and waving with his other hand at the island's jungly darkness. "I feel as if I've lived here for years. . . ."

They were walking again, down the beach together, away from the fires. "It's a matter of being suited for it, Jack," she said. "This Governor Rogers could live here for fifty years and he still wouldn't belong—he's all wired up with duties and consequences, and punishment for crimes, and so much money for so much cargo on such and such a date at this here port. It's all Old World stuff. But *you,* why, the day I first saw you I said to myself, there's a lad who was born for these islands."

These islands. The words were pregnant with images: flocks of pink flamingoes visible at dawn behind impenetrable barriers of high-arching mangrove roots, piles of pearly conch-shell fragments scattered around the sooty crater of a cooking-fire pit in white sand, and blindingly sun-glittering blue-green sea seen through a haze of rum-drunkenness, scraps of smoke-blackened wadding-cloth tumbling along the beach after a pistol duel like the used pen-wipers of Mars himself. . . .

And he *did* fit in here, or could—there was a part of him that responded to the nearly innocent savagery of it all, the freedom, the abdication of all guilts and capacity for guilt. . . .

She turned to him and kissed him and his free arm went around her waist, and suddenly he wanted her terribly, wanted the loss of identity she could give him; in moments they were lying in the warm sand, and she was hiking her dress up and he was on top of her, panting feverishly—

And a close gunshot deafened him and for an instant lit Ann's straining face, and a moment later a pistol butt slammed down onto the back of his head—it landed on the tarred stump of his chopped-short ponytail, though, and instead of knocking him unconscious the blow only jarred him. He rolled off of Ann on the seaward side and scrambled to his feet.

Ann still lay there on her back; a pockmark in the sand nearby showed where the pistol ball had struck—she wasn't hurt—but she was whining impatiently and hitching up her hips and gnawing on the ragged hem of her dress, and Shandy wanted only to kill whoever had interrupted them and then return to her.

Jim Bonny stood on the other side of her, and he tossed the spent pistol away and raised a hand; Shandy felt the sudden heat in the air around him and flicked his right hand in a quick counter-and-return gesture, then bit his tongue to get blood and spat toward Bonny to give the return more power.

Bonny's hair started to smolder and smoke, but he grabbed a ball of braided fur at his belt, and the heat was dispelled. "Mate Care-For lookin' out for me, you bastard," Bonny whispered. "He and I gonna render you unfit for wife-stealin'."

Too impatient and breathless to be afraid, Shandy snapped his fingers and pointed two of them at Bonny; but Bonny's hand was still on the fur-ball and the attack rebounded, knocking Shandy over and doubling him up with terrible cramps. Bonny took the opportunity to give his wife a kick in the shoulder and to speak a quick rhyme at Shandy.

Blood burst from Shandy's ears and nose, and rationally he knew that he was out-classed here, and should try to flee or yell for help; but he wanted Ann—wanted, in fact, to take her with Jim Bonny's blood hot on his hands. . . .

But with Mate Care-For protecting Bonny there didn't seem to be much he could do. He hunched up onto his knees and whistled a blindness at Bonny, but despite his best parries it too bounced back upon him, and while Shandy was blind Bonny sent a spastic fit at him.

Shandy collapsed, jiggling and hooting helplessly on the sand like the caller at a Saint Vitus' Day dance, and he heard Bonny kick his wife again and then step over her to get at him.

Shandy knew that it was too late now to try to run or call for help—he was going to die, here and now, if he didn't think of something, and—more unbearable than the thought of death—Jim Bonny would be the one who would kneel between Ann's thighs; and at this point she would probably neither notice the difference nor care.

Ignoring the pain of a snagged finger, he shoved his flapping right hand into his trousers pocket; there was still grit in there from the ball of mud he had scraped from his boot on the Florida coast, and he rolled it into a lump between his thumb and forefinger. Then he yanked his hand out and flung the bit of dirt up at the sky.

And then he was in a boat, passing under a bridge strung with colored lanterns, and instead of garlic and wine his mouth tasted of strawberries. He remembered this—this was Paris—he had been, what, nine years old when his father, having made some money, had taken him out for a good dinner and a boat ride down the Seine afterward. The figure beside him turned to him, but this time it was not his father.

It seemed to be an ancient black man, his hair and short beard as white and tightly curled as those of a marble statue.

"Serious *vodun* attacks are generally directed at, and take place in, the memories of the defensive combatant," the black man said in a lilting French dialect, "the memories being the accumulated sum of a person. If I meant you harm, you'd find this remembered scene, the remembered people in it, changing in lethal and frightening ways . . . very like the delirium experienced during a high fever . . . and it would get worse and worse until you either counterattacked or perished." He smiled and held out his hand. "My name is Maître Carrefour."

After a moment's hesitation, Shandy shook the man's hand.

"Luckily for myself," the black man went on, "I am a *loa* whose domain is populated islands. I have many dealings with men, and can anticipate their actions, unlike the natural *loa* you encountered in the Florida rain forest. Your thrown bit of dirt would not kill me—it has lost much of its potency in the week and a half since you brought it out—but it will nevertheless injure me if I stay and refrain from counterattacking. Therefore I am even now withdrawing from the conflict between yourself and Mr. Bonny."

Ashamed, Shandy looked away from him, back the way they had come. Among the pedestrians on the bridge he could see several women; despite the bright lantern light, only their faces were in particular focus, and it occurred to him that that must have been the way women had looked to him at the age of ten. Not anything like the way Ann Bonny had looked to him a minute ago. Which view, he wondered bitterly now, was the narrower?

"Uh . . . thank you," Shandy mumbled. "Why . . . why are you doing this, letting me off? Bonny said you were protecting him."

"Seeing that he comes to no harm. Do you mean him any harm?"

"No—not now, not anymore."

"Then I am not remiss." Something changed silently in the sky. Shandy glanced up and saw that the stars had become less distinct, as if a pane of faintly frosted glass now hung between them and him; Maître Carrefour was apparently letting the illusion dissipate. The old black man chuckled. "You are fortunate, Mr. Chandagnac, that I am one of the Rada *loas* and not one of the younger Petro ones. I have the option of not taking offense."

"I, uh, am glad of that." The taste of strawberries was gone.

"I hope so. You got that tactic, that mud-ball trick, from Philip Davies—and you have wasted it. He gave you something else as well; it would not please me to see you waste that too."

Soft sand was under Shandy's left side and the starry night sky above his right, and he realized he was back on the New Providence beach; and when he heard the *thup* of the upflung bit of mud hitting the sand, he knew that his talk with Maître Carrefour had not taken place in local time.

He was now able to deflect Bonny's magical attacks with a gesture and a whistle; he did so, and struggled tiredly to his feet.

Bonny was still flinging them, and Shandy kept knocking them aside.

"Give it a rest, Jim," he sighed. "You're just buying yourself a month of needing help even to lift a fork. Get a lot of liver and raisins and blood sausage inside you and maybe it won't hit too hard."

Bonny blinked at him in surprise, then clenched his fists and, dark-faced with effort, barked out half a dozen syllables.

Shandy deflected it toward the sea, and a fish leaped out of the water and exploded with a blue flash and a wet pop. Shandy shook his head at Bonny. "Keep it up and your *hair's* gonna turn white too, as well as your gums."

Bonny swayed, took a step toward Shandy and then collapsed limply, face down. Shandy walked around Ann to him and crouched to roll him over so that he wouldn't smother in the sand.

Ann had sat up and half rolled over. "Get over here," she said.

He walked over to her but didn't sit down. "I've got to go, Ann. That . . . wouldn't have been good, what we were about to do. I'm only staying on New Providence Island long enough to get the *Jenny* repaired and provisioned," he said, having decided it only as he was saying it, "and then go take care of some business."

Ann was on her feet in an instant. "Is it *him?*" she demanded, kicking her unconscious husband. "The tale-bearing dog who keeps Governor Rogers' boots damp with lickin' 'em? I've been saving up for a divorce-by-sale, and *you* could buy one for me right *now.*"

"No, Ann, it ain't him—or only partly. I just—"

"You bastard," she shrilled, "you're going after that damned Hurwood bitch again!"

"I'm going to Haiti," he said patiently. "I've got an uncle there who is going to set me up with a proper ocean-going three-masted ship . . . before he hangs."

"Liar!" she yelled. "Goddamn *liar!*"

He walked back up toward the fires, one hand twitching a parry against any malefic spells she might be inserting among the catalog of obscenities she was shouting after him.

I wasn't lying, Ann, he thought. I really *am* going to go to Haiti and ruin my uncle if I possibly can, and use his stolen money to buy a ship. But at the same time you were right. As soon as I get a ship that can take the open seas, I'm going to find, and rescue, and—if there's still any worth in me—*marry* the only woman in whom I can see both a body *and* a face, and with whom I need not resign one or the other of my own.

Chapter Twenty-Two

And so for the next three days he had plied his weary crew with the most lavish dinners he could assemble and the best liquor he could get hold of, in exchange for which he made them slave at the overhauling of the *Jenny;* but even Venner, who complained most often, couldn't claim that their new captain was making them do an unfair amount of work, for Shandy was always the first awake in the morning, the one who made himself lift heavier loads than anyone else was willing to, the one who didn't take rest breaks . . . and then, when evening darkness made further work impossible, Shandy was the one who cooked the bountiful dinner, making works of art out of whatever marinades and slow-simmering stocks he'd left developing when he went to the boat at dawn.

On the morning of Wednesday, the seventeenth of August, the *Jenny* sailed out the southern end of the New Providence harbor. She had taken on powder and shot as well as food and drink, and she carried at least twice as many men as she needed, but the deadline for taking the pardon was still nearly three weeks away, and Shandy was bringing no *bocor* along—he had managed to convey to Woefully Fat a plea to sail with them to Haiti, but the giant sorceror, who had somehow reappeared on the island days before the *Jenny* had arrived, refused—and so Woodes Rogers decided not to imperil his own still-shaky position by attempting to prevent the sloop's departure.

Shandy's crew was nervous about hurricanes, for this was the dangerous month of August, and in every previous year the Caribbean pirates would be well up the American coast by now, but Shandy argued that the southeast trip to Port-au-Prince was actually a little shorter, and far more direct, than the trip to the Florida west coast had been, and that on the way down they could hug the Exumas and the Ragged Islands and the Inaguas, and thus never be more than an hour's close haul from some sheltering shore. And twice during the three-day voyage they did see the ominous iron-gray helmets of distant storm clouds on the southern horizon, but both times the storms moved west to ravage Cuba before the *Jenny* got anywhere near them.

On Saturday morning the *Jenny* tacked in to the Haitian harbor called the Bight of Leograne, in past the fortifications on the jungle slopes at St. Marc and on through the St. Marc Channel to the colonial French village of L'Arcahaye. Shandy rowed the sloop's little boat to shore, and then he used some of Philip Davies' accumulated gold to get his hair cut and buy a coat and a neckerchief to cover his ragged shirt. Looking at least halfway respectable now, he gave a black farmer a couple of coins in exchange for letting him ride along with a wagonload of cassavas and mangoes to the town of Port-au-Prince, eighteen miles farther down the coast.

It was late afternoon by the time they reached town, and the native fishermen were already rowing ashore, dragging their crude longboats up onto the sand beneath the shadowed palms, and hauling away heavy woven-straw baskets and bamboo cages with crabs and rock lobsters moving around like big spiders inside them.

The town of Port-au-Prince proved to be a latticework of narrow streets laid out around a central plaza. The plaza and most of the streets were paved in white stone, though around the shops and warehouses by the waterfront the pavement was nearly hidden beneath hundreds—no, it must have been thousands—of brown, flat-trodden husks. Before stepping out into the crowded square, Shandy picked up one of the husks and smelled it; it was sugarcane, and he realized that this was the source of the gaggingly sweet, half-fermented smell that blended in the afternoon air with the usual rotten fish and smoky cooking odors shared by seaports everywhere. He tossed the thing away, wondering for a moment if it had come from the Chandagnac plantations.

Most of the people bustling through the plaza were black, and
several times as Shandy made his way toward the official-looking
buildings on the far side, he was courteously greeted with, "Bon
jou', blanc." *Good day, white.* He nodded politely each time, and
once, when a young black man muttered to a companion a quick
joke in half-Dahomey patois about Shandy's discreditable shirt
cuffs, he was able to quote back, in the same patois, a *marron*
proverb to the effect that any sort of cuffs, or none at all, were
preferable to iron ones. The young man laughed, but stared
curiously after Shandy, and he realized he would have to watch
himself here. This was civilization, not New Providence Island.

Wary of any kind of law enforcement officers—for it was
possible that the English authorities had told the French about the
John Chandagnac who had assisted in the total destruction of a
Royal Navy man-of-war less than a month ago—Shandy asked a
merchant where he should go to settle questions about deeds and
titles to local property, and he was directed to one of the
government offices right on the plaza.

Yes, he thought as he strode across to the place, first I'll find
out where the old homestead is, and go pay Uncle Sebastian a visit.
No need to let him know right away who I am, though I will
definitely want to do that pretty soon.

The interior of the building looked like any European office—
several white men working at high writing stands, leather-bound
ledgers along one wall—but the tropical breeze swaying the lace
curtains in the tall windows undid the illusion, and the clink of pen-
nib in inkwell, and then the scratch of the nib on paper, seemed as
incongruous here as would the cry of a parrot in Threadneedle
Street.

One of the clerks looked up when Shandy entered. "Yes?"

"Good day," said Shandy, trying for the first time in two
months to speak pure French. "I have a question about the, uh,
Chandagnac estate—"

"Are you another of the employees? There is nothing we here
can do to help you get your back wages."

"No, I'm not an employee." Shandy summoned up his best
Parisian accent. "I have a question about—the title to the house and
land."

"Ah, I see, you are another *creditor*. Well, as I understand it,

everything was sold; but of course you will want to talk to the
executor of the estate."

"Executor?" Shandy's stomach went cold. "Is he—is Sebastian
Chandagnac *dead?*"

"You did not know? I am sorry. Yes, he committed suicide
some time Wednesday night. His—"

"This *last* Wednesday?" Shandy interrupted, fighting to keep
from shouting. "*Three days* ago?"

"Yes. His body was found on Thursday morning by the
housekeeper." The clerk shrugged. "Business reversals, it seems.
They say he had to sell everything, and still left behind many
debts."

Shandy's face felt numb, as if he'd had too much to drink.
"I . . . heard that he was a . . . speculator."

"Exactly, m'sieu'."

"This executor. Where would I find him?"

"At this hour he will probably be having brandy on the terrace
below Vigneron's. He is a small man, somewhat bucktoothed. His
name is Lapin, Georges Lapin."

Shandy found Mr. Lapin at a table overlooking the crowded
harbor, and from the number of saucers in front of him he guessed
he'd been there quite awhile.

The smaller man started violently when he saw him, then
apologized and accepted Shandy's offer to buy him another brandy.

"You are the executor, I understand, of the Chandagnac
estate," began Shandy when he'd pulled out a chair for himself and
sat down. "Uh, two brandies, please," he added to the steward who
had half-suspiciously followed him to Lapin's table.

"You are of Sebastian's family," said Lapin with certainty.

". . . Yes," Shandy admitted.

"There is resemblance—for one instant I thought you were
him." He sighed. "Executor, yes, that is me. Though as it happens
there is nothing to execute—eh?—and all I am doing is pointing
various creditors at one another so that they may fight. Unknown
to any of us his friends, Sebastian had destituted himself." He
picked up his brandy as soon as the steward set it down, and he
drained it at a gulp as if in illustration of Sebastian Chandagnac's
profligacy.

"One more for Mr. Lapin, please," Shandy told the steward.
Turning back to Lapin he asked, "And he's dead? Certainly?"

"I saw the body myself, M'sieur Chandagnac. How odd it is to call someone else that! He had no other surviving family here, you know. Yes, he primed a blunderbuss pistol and then loaded it with all his remaining gold and jewelry." Lapin held out his two hands cupped together. "Not much as a fortune, but as a load of shot it was kingly. And then he raised the gun so that the bell muzzle was a foot away from his face, took one last look, we may suppose, at what remained of his fortune, and then sent that fortune into his brain! Ah, it was poetical, in a way. Though messy in a pragmatic sense, of course—virtually the entirety of his head wound up in the garden below his bedchamber window. Poor Sebastian!—I am certain the local gendarmerie made off with most of the . . . ammunition."

Then Shandy remembered where he'd heard the name Lapin—Skank had said that the big dealers with pirates on Haiti were "Lapin and Shander-knack." And you're right, Skank, Shandy thought now—he does look like a rabbit.

"I suppose I can see why they made it look like suicide," Shandy said ruminatively.

"I beg your pardon," said Lapin—"*Look* like? There was no question—"

"No no," said Shandy hastily, "keep thinking precisely that, I certainly don't mean to tell you anything you don't need to know. *You're* in no danger. I'm sure *you* never had any dealings with," he leaned forward and spoke quietly over the brandies, "pirates."

Lapin's plump face actually turned pale in the evening light. "Pirates?"

Shandy nodded. "An English governor has been sent out to New Providence Island, which is the pirates' home base. Now the pirates are killing off all the respectable merchants they once had dealings with—so as to leave no one to," Shandy winked, "*testify.*" Shandy almost started laughing at the idea of the New Providence pirates being methodical about anything, but he forced himself to maintain a mournful expression.

Lapin swallowed. "*Kill* the merchants?"

"That's right. The pirates are just waiting for each merchant to establish *contact.* As soon as one of their old customers gets in touch with them, or consents to see them if they approach him," Shandy shrugged, "that man is as dead as Sebastian."

"*Mon Dieu!*" Lapin got hastily to his feet, spilling his brandy.

He cast a fearful look at the harbor, as if expecting brigands to rush ashore even now. "It is—later than I had thought. It has been pleasant talking to you, M'sieur Chandagnac, but I am afraid I must bid adieu."

Shandy didn't get up, but raised his glass. "To your very good and continuing health, Monsieur Lapin."

But after Lapin bumbled away, Shandy's momentarily raised spirits fell. His uncle was dead and penniless. There would be no revenge and no ship. He rented a room for the night and then in the morning hitched a ride back out to L'Arcahaye and the waiting *Jenny*.

For the next two weeks he led the *Jenny* on a frantic roundabout tour of the Caribbean, but though he checked at every port registry, even the English ones where he was a wanted man, there was no record of any *Vociferous Carmichael* or even *Charlotte Bailey* having been seen anywhere since the first of August, when, after having magically picked up Shandy and dropped him over the side, Benjamin Hurwood had got his corpse-crew in motion and sailed away.

At the end of the two weeks of fruitless search his crew was on the verge of mutiny and the deadline for taking the King's Pardon was only two days away, so Shandy ordered his men to turn the old sloop toward New Providence Island.

They arrived in the midafternoon of Tuesday, the fifth of September, and when Shandy stepped off the *Jenny* he didn't look back; Venner could captain her from now on, and take her to Hell or the Heavenly Kingdom for all he cared. Once ashore, Shandy had time to go to the fort, officially take the pardon from Governor Rogers, and still be back on the beach in time to cook up a vast dinner. And, in what was to become a tradition through the next three months, he ate nearly none of it himself, contenting himself instead with huge quantities of drink.

Chapter Twenty-Three

Yes, Skank, Shandy thought again now as he watched someone out in the harbor keep on trying to yank the *Jenny*'s gaff-spar higher, yes I *was* more jumpy in those days. I had things to do then; now there's only one task left, and that's . . . forget. He stretched out more comfortably in the sand and swirled the sun-warmed rum in his cup affectionately.

A young Navy ensign hesitantly approached Shandy. "Excuse me . . . you're Jack Shandy?"

Shandy was finishing the cup, and stared owlishly at the young man over the rim. "Right," he said, lowering it finally.

"You're the one—excuse me—that sank the *Whitney,* aren't you?"

"I don't think so. What was the *Whitney?*"

"A man-o'-war that blew up and sank, this last June. They'd captured Philip Davies, and—"

"Oh." Shandy noticed that his cup was empty, and got to his feet. "Right. Until now I never knew her name. Actually, it was Davies that blew her up—I just helped." He put his cup down on the table in front of the liquor tent and nodded at the man who ran it.

"And you shot the captain?" the young ensign went on.

Shandy picked up his refilled cup. "It was a long time ago. I don't remember."

The ensign looked disappointed. "I arrived here on the *Delicia,*

244

with Governor Rogers," he explained. "I, uh . . . guess this was a pretty wild place before, huh? Swordfights, shootings, treasure . . ."

Shandy laughed softly and decided not to burst the boy's romantic bubble. "Oh, aye, all o' that."

Encouraged, the young man pressed on. "And you sailed with Blackbeard himself, I hear, on that mysterious trip to Florida? What was that like?"

Shandy gestured expansively. "Oh . . . hellish, hellish. Treachery, swordfights, men walking the plank, sea battles . . . trackless swamps, terrible fevers, cannibal Carib Indians dogging our tracks . . ." He paused, for the young ensign was blushing and frowning.

"You don't have to make fun of me," the boy snapped.

Shandy blinked, not recalling exactly what he'd been saying. "What do you mean?"

"Just because I'm new out here doesn't mean I don't know *anything*. I knew the Spaniards completely wiped out the Carib Indians two hundred years ago."

"Oh." Shandy scowled in concentration. Where had he heard of Carib Indians? "I didn't know that. Here, lemme buy you some rum, I didn't mean any . . . any . . ."

"I can't drink in uniform," the ensign said, though he seemed mollified.

"I'll have yours then." Shandy drained his cup and put it down on the table again. The man behind the table refilled it and made yet another mark on his credit sheet.

"It does seem that I've missed the great days of piracy," the ensign sighed. "Davies, Bonnett, Blackbeard all dead, Hornigold and Shandy have taken the pardon—though there is one new one. Do you know Ulysse Segundo?"

"No," said Shandy, carefully picking up his cup. "Dressy name."

"Well, sure. He's got a big three-masted ship called the *Ascending Orpheus*, and he's taken dozens of ships in the last couple of months. He's supposed to be the most bloodthirsty of all—people are so scared of him that some have jumped into the sea and drowned themselves when it became clear he was going to take their ship!"

"That's pretty scared," Shandy allowed, nodding.

"There's all sorts of stories about him," the ensign went on eagerly, then halted. "Of course, I don't *believe* most of them. Still, a lot of people seem to. They say he can whistle the wind out of your sails and into his, and that he can navigate and catch you even in the densest fog, and when he captures a ship he not only takes all the gold and jewelry off her, but also the dead bodies of any sailors killed in the capture! Why, he won't even bother with stuff like grain or leather or hardware—he takes only real treasure, though they say he values fresh blood most of all, and has sometimes drained whole crews. One captain who lost his ship to him but lived says there were corpses in the *Orpheus's* rigging, obviously corpses, rotting—but one of them was *talking!*"

Shandy smiled. "What'd it have to say?"

"Well . . . I don't believe *this*, of course . . . but the captain swore this one corpse kept saying, over and over, 'I am not a dog.'—hey, watch it!" he added angrily, for Shandy had dropped his cup, and rum had splashed on the boy's uniform trousers.

"Where was he seen last," Shandy asked quickly, "and when was it?"

The ensign blinked in surprise at this sudden intense interest, so uncharacteristic of the sleepy-eyed, easygoing man who had seemed to have no other goal in life than to be the settlement drunkard. "Why, I don't know, I—"

"*Think!*" Shandy seized the young man by his uniform collar and shook him. "Where and when?"

"Uh—near Jamaica, off Montego Bay—not quite a week ago!"

Shandy flung him away, turned on his heel and sprinted toward the shore. "Skank!" he yelled. "Skank, dammit, where—there you are. Come here!"

The young ex-pirate trotted up to him uncertainly. "What's up, Jack?"

"The *Jenny's* leaving today, this afternoon. Get all the men you can—and provisions—and get aboard her."

"But . . .Jack, Venner's going to wait till January, to link up with Charlie Vane. . . ."

"Damn Venner. Did I ever say I was resigning the captaincy of the *Jenny?*"

"Well, no, Jack, but we all assumed—"

"Damn your assumptions. Round 'em up and get aboard."

Skank's puzzled frown became a smile. "Sure . . . cap'n." He turned and hurried away, his bare feet kicking up sprays of white sand.

Shandy had just run to a beached rowboat and begun to drag it to the water when he remembered where he'd heard of Carib Indians. Crazy old Governor Sawney had mentioned them to him, the night before the *Carmichael* and the *Jenny* sailed to meet Blackbeard in Florida. What had the old man said? Something about having killed his share of them in his day.

Shandy paused to squint speculatively up the slope toward the corner of the settlement where the weird old man had set up a little tent for himself. No, he told himself, resuming his struggle with the heavy boat—Sawney's old, but he's not two hundred.

But Shandy paused again a moment later, for he'd remembered something else. The old man had said something about "when you get to that geyser." The Fountain of Youth *had* been a sort of geyser. And when Shandy gave that first puppet show, and Sawney interrupted it with his ravings, hadn't he said, "faces in the spray . . . *almas de los perditos* . . ."? Faces in the spray, souls of the damned . . .

Had Sawney *been* there at one time?

If so, he *might* be more than two hundred years old. It wouldn't really be surprising. Though it *is* surprising that he's so deteriorated. I wonder, he thought as once again he resumed tugging at the boat, what he did wrong.

Again he stopped. Well, now, if there *is* something, he thought, some effect, that can make a babbling idiot of a sorceror who's powerful enough to get to Erebus and buy a century or two of added lifetime, it's something I damn well better know about—if I want to do something more this time than just be picked up and dropped into the ocean.

Slowly at first, then more quickly as he remembered other puzzling things about old Sawney—his flawless but archaic Spanish, his handiness with magic—Shandy climbed back up the slope to the tents.

"Seen the governor around today?" he asked one lean old ex-pirate. "Sawney, I mean—not Rogers."

Shandy was smiling and had tried to keep his tone casual, but the man had seen the end of his conversation with the young ensign, and he stepped back and raised his hands placatingly as he answered. "Sure, Jack, he's in that tent of his, up toward the inlet. Take it easy, huh?"

Oblivious to the muttering and head-shaking in his wake, Shandy sprinted across the sand, broad-jumped over the cold cooking pit and pounded away toward the inlet where, half a year ago, he'd helped refit the *Carmichael;* and he paused to grin and catch his breath when he saw old Sawney crouched in front of the sailcloth tent he lived in these days, alternately taking swigs from, and peering intently into, a half-full bottle of rum.

The old man was wearing baggy, bright yellow trousers and an embroidered silk jacket, and if he had on any sort of neck-cloth it was concealed under his tangled beard, which was the color of old bleached bones.

Shandy plodded down the slope and sat down near him. "I'd like to talk to you, governor."

"Ah?" Sawney squinted at him. "Not fevered again, are you? Stay away from them chickens."

"No, governor. I want to know . . . about *bocors,* magicians. Especially ones that have been to the . . . the Fountain of Youth."

Sawney had another gulp from, and peek into, his bottle. "Plenty of *bocors* about. I ain't one."

"But you know what I mean by the Fountain of Youth? The . . . geyser?"

The old man's only response was to spin the liquor around in the bottle and sing, in a high, cracked voice,

> *Mas molerá si Dios quisiere—*
> *Cuenta y pasa, que buen viaje faza.*

Shandy did a rough translation of this in his head—*More will flow if God wills—count and let it happen, and the voyage will pass more quickly*—and decided it was no help. "Very well," he said, controlling his impatience, "let's start somewhere else. Do you remember the Carib Indians?"

"Aye, cannibals. We wiped 'em out. Killed 'em all in the Cordoba expedition in '17 amd '18, killed 'em or took 'em to be slaves in Cuba, which meant the same thing. They had all the magic; they kept pens of Arawak Indians, the way you'd keep cattle. To eat, sure—but you know what was more important than that? Hah? The blood, fresh blood. The Caribs kept those Arawaks alive like you'd keep gunpower dry."

"Did they know about the place in the rain forest in Florida? The Fountain in the place where it feels like the ground is . . . too solid?"

"Ah, *Dios* . . . *sí,*" Sawney whispered, darting a glance at the sunlit harbor as if something in the sea might overhear. "It wasn't so dark there, I've heard, before they came . . . damned hole into hell . . ."

Shandy leaned forward a little and spoke quietly. "When did *you* go there?"

"1521," said Sawney clearly. He took an enormous gulp of rum. "I knew by then where it had to be—I could read the signs, in spite of the padres with their holy water and prayers. . . . I went in, and kept the gnat-clouds of ghosts away until I found it; vinegar will drive lice away from your body, but you need the black tobacco weed to drive away ghosts . . . and I shed blood there, by the Fountain . . . sprouted that plant. Did it just in time, too—as soon as I got out of that swamp there was a skirmish with the Indians, and I caught an arrow, and the wound festered . . . I made sure some of my blood got into the sea. Blood and sea water, and I'll live forever, over and over again, while that plant's still there. . . ."

Shandy suddenly remembered the dead, dried shrub he'd seen in Erebus, and he realized that this would probably be the last of Sawney's lifetimes. "How does it happen," he asked gently, "that one powerful enough to plant blood there, and use the blood and sea water magic here to buy many lives, can deteriorate? Can lose the big magics, can become . . . simple?"

Sawney smiled and raised one white eyebrow. "Like me, you mean, eh? Iron."

Though embarrassed that the old man had understood him so clearly, Shandy pressed on. "Iron? What do you mean?"

"You must have smelt it. The magic smell, you know? Like a pan left on a hot fire. Wide-awake iron. And fresh blood smells that way too, and magic needs fresh blood, so obviously there's iron in it. Ever hear the story that the gods came here out of the sky as splashes of red-hot iron? No? Why, the very oldest writers claimed that the souls of stars were in the stuff, because it was the last thing a star exhaled before it started to die."

Shandy was afraid the old man had lost his lucidity again, for obviously there was no iron in blood or stars, but he decided to invest one more question in this tangent. "So how does it diminish magicians?"

"Hm?" Sawney blew across the mouth of the bottle, producing a low hooting. "Oh, it doesn't."

Shandy thumped his fist into the sand. "Damn it, governor, I need to know—"

"It's *cold* iron that messes 'em up—*solid* iron. It's finished, you see, you can't do magic around it because all the magic is finished too, before you even start. You ever make wine?"

Shandy rolled his eyes. "No, but I know about vinegar and lice, thanks. I—"

"You know *vino de Jerez*? Sherry, the English call it. Or port?"

"Sure, governor," said Shandy tiredly, wondering if the old man was going to ask him to fetch him a bottle.

"Well, you know how they're made? You know why some of 'em are so sweet?"

"Uh . . . they're fortified. They mix brandy into the wine and it stops the fermentation, so some sugar can remain in it and not all turn to alcohol."

"Good boy. Yes, the brandy *stops* the fermentation. And so you still have sugar, yes, but for it to change to alcohol now is not possible. And what is this stuff, this brandy, that stops everything so?"

"Well," said Shandy, mystified, "it's distilled wine."

"*Verdad.* A product of fermentation makes more fermentation impossible; do you see?"

Shandy's heart was beating faster, for he thought he almost did see. "Cold iron, solid iron, works on magic the way brandy works on fermentation," he said unsteadily. "Is that what you mean?"

"*Seguro!* A cold iron knife is very good for getting rid of a ghost. Those stories you have heard, I'm sure. With a lot of iron around, solid iron and cold, you still have blood, like the sugar in the sherry, but it cannot be used for magic. *Bocors* carry no iron, and they do magic, and they are very lacking in blood. You've seen their gums? And around the houses of the most powerful ones is a fine rusty red dust of," he leaned closer and whispered, "*iron.*"

Shandy felt goosebumps starting up along his arms. "And in the Old World," he said softly, "magic stopped being an important factor of life at around the same time iron came into general use for tools and weapons."

Sawney nodded and smiled wryly through his wild white beard. "Not a . . . coincidence." He blew across the neck of his bottle again: *hoot.* "And any magically resurrected consciousness is damaged by proximity to *cold* iron. (*Hoot.*) A little at a time. (*Hoot.*) By the time I learned that, it was too late for me. It turns out that ever since I came out of that damned hole in Florida I should have been staying clear of iron—not wear it, not hold it, not even eat something that was cooked in an iron pot! (*Hoot.*) High kings used to have to live that way in the Old World, before magic was quite all gone there. Hell. Salads and raw legumes and such you have to eat if you pursue it."

"No meat?" asked Shandy, who'd thought of something.

"Oh, aye, lots of meat, for magic power but also for plain strength, because sorcerors tend to get so pale and dizzy and weak. But of course it's got to be meat that wasn't killed or cleaned or cooked with anything iron. (*Hoot.*) But you know, I'm not sorry. I've had two hundred extra years of living like a normal man, doing what I please. I'd *really* be crazy if I'd lived the whole time like some damned *bocor*, worrying about every bite I ate and terrified to pound a nail into a board."

"So do you know any way, governor, that I could use cold iron to break a sorceror who's so fresh from the Fountain that he's still got the dust of Erebus in the creases of his boots?"

Sawney stared at him for a long moment and then put the bottle down. "Maybe. Who?"

Shandy decided to be honest with him. "Benjamin Hurwood. Or Ulysse Segundo, as he's apparently calling himself now. He's the—"

"*Yo conozco,* the one with the missing arm. The one who's grooming his daughter's body for his wife's ghost. Poor child—you notice she's fed only greens, and biscuits kept in wood casks? They want her to be conductive magically, but they don't want any strength of will in her, so no meat at all."

Shandy nodded, having realized the significance of Beth Hurwood's odd diet a few moments ago.

"Sure, I'll tell you how to break him. Stab him with a sword."

"Governor," said Shandy in an agony of impatience, "I need something more than that. He—"

"You think *I'm* simple? Haven't you been listening? Link your blood to the cold iron of the sword. Make the atoms of blood and iron line up the way a compass needle lines up to face north. Or vice versa. It's all relative. A working magical force will add energy to it, to its own undoing. Or else the force is undone because the lined up iron system is so energetic, you see? If you don't like the idea of a penny falling to the ground, look at it as the ground rushing up to hit the motionless penny, right? (*Hoot.*)"

"Great, so how do I *do* it?"

"(*Hoot-hoot.*)"

"Governor, how do I get the atoms to line up? How do I link blood and iron?"

Sawney drained the bottle and then put it down and began to sing,

> *Bendita sea el alma,*
> *Y el Señor que nos la manda;*
> *Bendita sea el diá*
> *Y el Señor que nos lo enviá.*

Again Shandy translated mentally: *Blessed be the soul, and the Lord that keeps it in order; blessed be the day, and the Lord that drives it away.*

He tried for at least another minute to get a coherent answer to his question, but the rum had extinguished the brief spark of alertness in the old man's eyes, and eventually he gave up and got to his feet.

"So long, governor."

"Keep well, lad. No chickens."

"Right." Shandy started away, then paused and turned back. "Say . . . what's your name, governor?"

"Juan."

Shandy had heard several versions of the name the governor claimed, but it had always been something like Sawney or 'Pon-sea or Gawnsey—he hadn't heard Juan before. "What's your *full* name, governor?"

The old man cackled and grubbed in the sand for a bit, then looked up at Shandy and said softly but distinctly, "Juan Ponce de Leon."

Shandy simply stood there for several seconds, feeling chilled in spite of the tropical sun that was raising wavering heat mirages over the white sand. At last he nodded, turned, and plodded away, hearing the hooting start up again behind him.

Only after he had crested the rise, and was winding his way through the tangle of tents and huts, did it occur to him that the derelict he'd left hooting into an empty rum bottle really *was,* or had been, at least, governor of this island—as well as of every other island between here and Florida.

He was striding along between the tents, mentally calculating how much of Davies' money he still had after three months of spending it lavishly on rum, and wondering how long a voyage he could afford—of course it wouldn't have to be very long, Christmas was less than two weeks away, and Hurwood had said that he'd consummate the eviction of Beth from her body "come Yule"— when a figure stepped in front of him. He looked up, and recognized Ann Bonny. He remembered that she had started up a romance with another pardoned pirate, Calico Jack Rackam, very shortly after Shandy had sailed for Haiti, and that the two of them had tried, unsuccessfully, to get Ann a divorce-by-sale.

"Hello, Ann," he said, pausing, for he felt he owed her the opportunity to revile him a little.

"Well, well," said Ann, "if it ain't the cook! Crawled out o' the rum cask for once, eh?"

She looked both leaner and older—not surprisingly, for Governor Rogers had chosen to view the time-honored English common law custom of divorce-by-sale as the height of lewdness, and had promised to have her publicly stripped and flogged if she ever raised the subject again, and a couple of monstrously vulgar songs about that imagined punishment had sprung up and become very popular—but she still had the hot aura of sexuality in the way she stood and canted her head.

Shandy smiled cautiously. "That's right."

"And how long do you think it'll be before you crawl right back in?"

"I'm sure it'll be at least two weeks."

"I'm not. I give you . . . half an hour. You're going to die here, Shandy, after a few years of being Governor Sawney's apprentice. Well *I'm* not going to—Jack and I are getting out of here, damned soon. I finally found a man who's not scared of women."

"I'm glad. I've got to admit they often scare me. I hope you and Rackam are happy."

Ann seemed disconcerted, and stepped back. "Huh. So where are *you* going?"

"Somewhere north of Jamaica. A ship's been seen there that I think is the old *Vociferous Carmichael*."

She grinned and seemed to relax, though at the same time she was shaking her head sadly. "My God, it's that girl, still, isn't it? Hurley?"

"Hurwood." He shrugged. "Yeah, it is."

"So will this trip be violating your pardon?"

"I don't know. Will Rackam's involve violating his?"

She smirked. "Just between you and me, Shandy—of course it will. But my Jack's got a girl that don't mind living with an outlaw. Do you?"

"I don't know that either."

She hesitated, then leaned forward and kissed him—very lightly.

"What was that for?" he asked, startled.

Her eyes were very bright. "For? For luck, man."

She turned and walked away, and he strode on toward the shore. Some children were playing with a couple of puppets he'd made once, and as they scrambled out of his way he noticed that they were using strings now to move the little jointed figures. Learn a trade, youngsters, he thought. I don't think your generation will have Mate Care-For to take care of them.

Someone was walking ponderously behind him. He stopped and turned, and then flinched a little to see Woefully Fat staring incuriously down at him. For once remembering that the man was deaf, Shandy just nodded.

"They'll get along without him," the giant *bocor* rumbled. "Every land go through the time when magic work. We heahabouts is nearin' the end o' dat time. Ah'm sailin' with you."

"Oh?" Shandy was surprised, for he'd tried, with no success, to get Davies' *bocor* to come along on the trip to Haiti. "Well great, sure, it certainly seems like a trip we could use a good *bocor* on, and I'm just wasting my time talking, aren't I?" He made do with nodding emphatically.

"You a-goin' to Jamaica."

"Well, no, actually—I mean, we *might*, we're going *near* there—"

"Ah was bo'n in Jamaica, though they ship me to Virginia when Ah was fahv. And now I'm goin' back—to die."

"Uhhh . . ." Shandy was still trying to think of a response to this, and how to express it in gestures, when the *bocor* lumbered past him toward the shore, and Shandy had to sprint to catch up.

There was a gang of arguing men clustered around the boat Shandy had been wrenching at, and when Shandy approached, two of them strode over to him, waving their arms and shouting. One was Skank, and the other was Venner, his face so red at the moment that his freckles were invisible.

"One at a time," said Shandy.

With a furious chop of his hand Venner silenced Skank. "The *Jenny* isn't going anywhere until Vane gets here," he stated.

"She's sailing for Jamaica this afternoon," said Shandy. Though he kept a mild grin on his face, he was peripherally measuring yards and inches and wondering how quickly he could get to Skank's cutlass.

"You're not captain of her anymore," Venner went on raspingly, his face even darker.

"I'm still her captain," Shandy said.

The men standing around shifted and muttered, obviously not sure whose side they wanted to be on. Shandy caught part of a sentence: " . . . damned drunk for a captain . . ."

Then Woefully Fat stepped forward. "*Jenny* goin' t' Jamaica," he said in Old Testament prophet tones. "Leavin' *now*."

The men were startled, for not even Shank had realized that Davies' *bocor* was Shandy's ally in this; and though Shandy never took his eyes off Venner's face he could feel their confidence shift toward himself.

Venner and Shandy stared at each other for several seconds, then Skank drew his cutlass and tossed it to Shandy, who caught it by the grip without looking away from Venner. At last Venner looked down at the blade in Shandy's hand, and Shandy knew Venner had decided he wasn't quite drunk enough to take. Then Venner looked around at the other men, and his mouth became a straight, bitter line as, clearly, he realized that the emotional tide had turned against him when Woefully Fat had spoken.

"Well," growled Venner, "I wish you'd . . . keep us better informed of these things, captain—I—" He paused, then started again, choking out the words as if it hurt his teeth to pass each one. "I certainly . . . didn't mean to crowd you."

Shandy grinned and clapped him on the shoulder. "No problem!"

He turned and surveyed his crew—and carefully didn't let show in his face the disappointment and apprehension that he felt. This crew, he thought, is a testimonial to the effectiveness of Woodes Rogers' tactics—the only ones who'll sign onto a pirating voyage now are the ones who are too stupid, bloodthirsty or lazy to possibly get along in a law-abiding situation. And a pirating voyage it may well have to be, if we can't find the *Carmichael*—these thugs and clods will demand plunder.

Here goes my pardon, likelier than not, he thought. But maybe it's better to be an outlaw with purpose than a citizen without.

"Skank," he said, deciding that that young man was the most reliable of them, "you're quartermaster." He noted, but didn't acknowledge, Venner's quick frown. "Get 'em all aboard and let's be gone before these Navy lads figure out what we intend."

"Aye aye, cap'n."

And twenty minutes later the *Jenny,* with no fanfare, but with some uncertain glances from the officers aboard the H.M.S. *Delicia,* sailed out of the New Providence harbor for the last time.

Chapter Twenty-Four

Patterns of morning sunlight dappled the south-facing balcony of one of the grandest houses on the hill above Spanish Town, and when the breeze-shifted pepper tree branches overhead let the sun shine directly on the elegantly bearded man sitting at the breakfast table, he instinctively shaded his face, for it was important to him to keep himself as unlined and youthful-looking as possible. For one thing, investors seemed to feel that a younger man would know more about current markets and the most recent developments in prices and currency values; and for another, the whole point of attaining wealth was lost if one was obviously an old man when one got it.

Another groan from upstairs made his hand shake so that a splash of tea landed in the saucer instead of in the china cup. Damn, thought the man who called himself Joshua Hicks as he pettishly clanked the teapot down. Can't a man have a peaceful breakfast on his own balcony without all these . . . lamentations? Six more days, he reminded himself, and then I'll have fulfilled my bargain with that damned pirate, and he'll do his tricks and take her away from here and leave me alone.

But even as the thought passed through his mind he recognized it as a vain wish. He'll never leave me alone, he realized, as long as I'm still even a remotely useful tool.

Maybe I should terminate my usefulness, as poor Stede Bonnett had the courage to do when he was in this sort of a situation, with Blackbeard—turn myself in, confess . . . hell, I *met* Bonnett a couple of times when the vagaries of the sugar market brought him on business trips to Port-au-Prince, and he was no hero, no saint. . . .

No, he thought, looking past the polished balcony rail, and past the palm fronds waving in the cool mountain breeze, at the descending terraces of white houses that were the residential area of Spanish Town, and, distantly, just visible along the edge of the blue sea, at the red of the roof-tiles of the surviving, landward end of Port Royal. He reached to the side, lifted the stopper out of a crystal decanter and poured amber cognac, glowing gold in the morning sun, into his tea. No, whatever else he was, Bonnett was a braver man than I am. I could never do what he did—and Ulysse knows it, too, damn him. If I've got to live in a cage, I prefer a luxurious one, with bars which, though stronger than iron, can't be seen or touched.

He drained the fortified tea and got to his feet, making sure he had a calm smile on his face before he turned around to face the sitting room . . . and face the stuffed dog head mounted on the wall like some paltry hunting trophy.

He crossed through the wide sitting room to the hall, but he maintained his smile, for there was a dog head mounted here too. He remembered, with a shudder that made his smile falter, the day in September, shortly after his arrival here, when he'd hung a cloth over every dog head in the house; it had given him a welcome sense of privacy, but within the hour the fearsome black nurse had come in, without knocking of course, and padded all over the house and taken all the cloths off. She hadn't even glanced at him, and of course she couldn't speak with her jaw bound up that way, but the visitation had so upset him that he'd never again tried to blind Ulysse's monitors.

Braced by the brandy, and by the knowledge that the nurse didn't usually arrive until midmorning, Hicks clumped up the stairs and listened outside the door of his guest's room. There was no more moaning, so he pulled back the brass bolt, turned the wooden doorknob and opened the door.

The young woman was asleep, but she woke with a cry when, tiptoeing into the dim room, he accidentally kicked the untouched dinner she'd left on the floor—the wooden bowl turned over in midair and thumped against the wall, scattering the greens all over the carpet. She sat up in bed and squinted at him. "My God . . . John . . . ?"

"No, damn it," said Hicks, "it's me. I heard you moaning, and just wanted to make sure all was well. Who's this John? You've mistaken me for him before."

"Oh." Beth Hurwood slumped back, the hope fading from her eyes. "Yes, all's well."

There were three dog heads in this room, so Hicks drew himself up to his full height and gestured sternly at the scattered leaves and herbs. "Trying to avoid your medicaments again?" he asked. "I won't have that, you know. Ulysse wants you to have them, and what he wants, I enforce!" He just stopped himself from nodding virtuously at the head that was nailed up over the bed.

"My father's a monster," she whispered. "Some day you'll enforce your own immolation."

Hicks forgot the heads and frowned uneasily. In the early days of her captivity he had laughed at Beth's claims that Ulysse Segundo was her father, for she always claimed too that her father had only one arm, while Ulysse very obviously had two; but on the pirate's next visit Hicks had glanced at the man's right hand—it was unarguably living flesh, but it was pink and smooth as a child's, and had no tiniest scar.

"Well," he said now, gruffly, "less than a week from today it will be Christmas. At least then I'll be rid of *you.*"

The young woman flung the bedclothes aside, swung her legs out and tried to stand, but she couldn't lock her knees, and fell back across the bed, panting. "Damn you and my father," she gasped. "Why can't I have *food?*"

"What do you call this stuff you leave around for people to trip over?" Hicks demanded, stooping to pick up a leaf and then waving it furiously in her face.

"Let me see you eat it," she said.

Hicks stared dubiously at the bit of vegetation, then flung it away with a snort, as if to indicate that he didn't have time for childish dares.

"Let's see you lick your fingers," Beth pressed.

"I . . . don't have to prove anything to you," he said.

"What *is* to happen Saturday? You said something once about some 'procedure.'"

Hicks was glad the curtains were drawn across the windows,

for he could feel his face getting red. "You're supposed to be taking your damned medicaments!" he snapped. "You're supposed to be—" Sleepy, he finished mentally; somnambulistic. Not wide awake and asking awkward questions. "Besides, your fa—Captain Segundo, I mean, will almost certainly be here by then, so *I* won't have to do the—what I mean is, you can take it up with *him!*"

He nodded resolutely and turned on his heel to leave, but he spoiled his dignified exit by emitting a shrill squeak and skipping backward, for the black nurse had silently entered the room and was standing right behind him.

Beth Hurwood was laughing and the nurse was just staring in her usual blank, unnerving way, and Hicks fled—wondering, as he edged hastily around the nurse, why the woman's dress was always sewn shut rather than just buttoned, and why, if she was so crazy about sewing things, she didn't repair her ripped-out pockets, and why she always went barefoot.

Also, he thought as he relaxed on the stairs and fished a handkerchief out of his sleeve to mop his forehead with, I wonder why other blacks fear the woman so. Why, the black cook that used to work here took one look at her and jumped through a second-floor window! And so after I discovered that any black would rather be flogged all day than set foot in this house for one second, I had to *hire* servants, white people. And even a lot of *them* have quit.

He went back to his chair on the balcony, but the morning's tranquility was shattered, and he flung the lukewarm tea out of his cup and refilled it with neat cognac. Damn Ulysse and his "help," he thought. I should never have left Haiti and changed my name.

He sipped his brandy and scowled, remembering how convincing Ulysse Segundo had been at first. The man had arrived in Port-au-Prince in the first week of August, and had immediately begun negotiating letters of credit from the most respected European banks. He had made a good impression, socially: he spoke French beautifully, he was cultured, well-dressed, the owner of a fine ship—which, though, he kept at a remote mooring, ostensibly because of a woman aboard who was recovering from a brain fever.

Hicks had been impressed with the man's evident wealth and independence when he was introduced to him, and, a few days later, when Segundo had dinner with him and quietly offered to let him participate in a couple of less than ethical but lucrative-

sounding investments, was impressed too with his intimate knowledge of the international web that was New World economics.
Evidently no deed or grant or purchase or fraud was too ancient or
obscure for Segundo to know of it and make merciless use of it.
Hicks had thought one would have to be able to read minds, or talk
to the dead, to know some of these things.

And then, very late one mid-August evening, Segundo had
come to Hicks' house with bad news. "I'm afraid," he had said as
Hicks blinked sleepily at him and sent an awakened servant for
some brandy, "that you're in danger, my friend."

The man who now called himself Hicks had only been awake
for a minute or so, just since Segundo's midnight pounding on the
door, and at first he thought Segundo meant that robbers or
escaped slaves were approaching his house. "Danger?" he said,
rubbing his eyes. "I have ten trustworthy servants and a dozen
loaded guns—what—"

"I don't mean danger of injury tonight," Segundo had
interrupted, smiling. "I mean danger of legal prosecution soon."

That had awakened him. He took a glass of brandy from his
servant, sipped it, and then stared cautiously at Segundo. "On what
charge?"

"Well," said Segundo with a laugh as he sat down in one of the
dining room chairs, "that's difficult to say. You and I have
a . . . *business associate* in common, and I'm afraid he's been
captured, and is trying to ingratiate himself with the authorities
by implicating everybody he has ever had extra-legal dealings
with . . . smuggling and fencing, mostly, I believe, but he's been
known to do other sorts of favors for certain Caribbean busi-
nessmen, the odd kidnapping or murder or arson. Thank you," he
added as the servant brought him a glass.

Hicks sat down across the table from Segundo. "Who?"

Segundo glanced toward the yawning servant, then leaned
forward. "Shall we call him . . . Ed Thatch?"

Hicks drained his glass, started to ask for a refill, then told the
servant to leave the decanter and get out. "What," he said when the
man had gone, "extra-legal dealings has he told them about?" God
knew Blackbeard had assisted him in a number of such, starting
with the drowning of a too-knowledgeable maiden aunt when he
had begun forging evidence to support his story that his brother
was dead.

"Well now, there's the rub, you see. I don't know. As much as he can remember, we must assume." Hicks groaned and lowered his face into his hands, and Segundo reached across and refilled his glass. "Don't despair," he told him. "Come on, now, look at me—I'm implicated too, at least as direly as you are, and am I downcast? There's a way out of every disaster except your last one."

Hicks had looked up then. "What can we do?"

"That's easy. Leave Haiti. You can take passage on my ship."

"But," Hicks had protested unhappily, "how could I bring along enough money to live comfortably? And they'd be sure to come after me."

Ulysse Segundo had winked. "Not if you were still here. What if a body were found in your bedchamber, in your night-clothes . . . a body of your height and build and color . . . with its face destroyed by a load of shot from a blunderbuss . . . and a suicide note beside it, in your handwriting?"

". . . But . . . who . . ."

"Don't you have some indentured white men working for you? Would one be missed?"

"Well . . . I suppose . . ."

"And as for money, I'll buy you out right now—your house, lands and everything. Foreseeing this eventuality, I have had my solicitor draw up a series of quitclaims, promissory notes and bills of sale, back-dated throughout these last two years, which will seem to indicate that you've lost everything, piece by piece, to a group of creditors—it would take an international army of accountants years to discover that each of the creditors, tracked back through all the silent partnerships and anonymous holdings companies, is me." He smiled brightly. "And that way there will be a motive for your suicide, you see? Financial ruin! For I suppose you do owe various people money, and when they try to collect from your estate, our manufactured story will come out."

And so they had done it. Hicks had signed all the papers; then, after Segundo left, he went to the indentured servants' quarters, woke up a man of the right age and build, and curtly told him to come to the main house. Without explanation he led the man up to his bedchamber and gave him drugged wine, and when the man's mystified eyes had finally closed in unconsciousness, Hicks stripped him and threw his clothes into the fireplace, then dressed the slack body in his own nightshirt. He loaded a blunderbuss pistol with a good double-handful of rings and coins and gold chains, and packed all the rest of his gold and jewelry into three chests. Segundo returned with several ill-looking but powerful sailors before dawn, and the last thing Sebastian Chandagnac did, before abandoning his ancestral home and adopting the name Joshua Hicks, was to fire the gun into the face of the unconscious servant. The recoil sprained his wrist, and he was appalled by the noise and the instant destruction—the shot devastated one entire side of the room, and blew the servant's head, in a million pieces, right through the closed window and out into the garden.

Segundo, though, had been in good spirits, and as they'd ridden away in a four-horse wagon he had claimed to be able to smell the murdered servant's blood on the night breeze. "That's what I'm going after now, you know," he had remarked as he'd cracked the whip over the horses. "I've got just about all the wealth I need—what I've got to get *now* is sea water and blood—positively *insane* quantities of fresh, red blood." His hearty, almost boyish laughter rang away among the coconut palms and breadfruit trees on either side of the shoreward road.

Now, sitting on this balcony in Jamaica, Sebastian Chandagnac grinned unhappily into his brandy. Yes, he thought, I should have waited, and checked for myself. Segundo simply wanted an absolutely captive servant—a well-mannered puppet—to guard that girl upstairs; and, in case Segundo is not back here by Christmas, to . . . how had Segundo put it? . . . "perform the ritual that will make of her an empty vessel ready to be filled." I hope to God he is back before Christmas—not only because I can't bear the thought of performing that ritual he made me memorize, but also because of the dinner party I'm giving here Christmas night; after I've gone to all the itchy trouble of growing a beard just in case someone might otherwise have recognized me as Sebastian Chandagnac, it would be a shame if I had to attend my own introductory party all covered with blood and chicken feathers and smelling of grave dirt.

Chandagnac shook his head sadly, remembering the house and plantation he'd left behind in Port-au-Prince . . . for nothing. He was paid a regular allowance by one of Segundo's banks, but no payment for all that he'd signed over to Segundo had ever been discussed; and only a week ago, in the course of a brief conversation with the postman, he learned that Blackbeard had been killed—not captured—in mid-November: fully three months after the midnight conversation in which Segundo had convinced Chandagnac that Blackbeard had been captured and was implicating everyone he could remember.

He heard the upstairs door close now, and the brass bolt rattle across into the locked position. He hopped to his feet, bolted what was left in his teacup, then grabbed the decanter and ran back into the house, hoping to lock himself into his bedchamber before the dreadful nurse could get downstairs.

Chapter Twenty-Five

Up in the rigging, straddling the headsail yard and leaning against the mast, Jack Shandy lowered his telescope at last, after having stared for nearly a quarter of an hour at the waves, the wispy clouds overhead, and, most intently, at the solid, dark, sharp-edged cloud swelling on the eastern horizon ahead. He reviewed all the weather lore he'd learned from Hodge and Davies and personal experience, and he had to admit, to himself at least, that Venner was right. It *would* be wisest to turn around and try to run the sixty-five miles back to Grand Cayman, jibe through the reef at the Rum Point Channel and then drag the *Jenny* ashore and break out the liquor. And damn soon, too, for the storm was moving faster than the *Jenny* could, and the wind seemed to be falling off.

But today, he thought desperately, is the twenty-third of December. On the day after tomorrow Hurwood is going to do the magic that will evict Beth's soul from her body. I've got to find Ulysse Segundo, as the old fool apparently likes to call himself now, today or tomorrow, or I might as well never have left the New Providence settlement. And if we run back northwest and tuck in to wait out the storm, we'll lose at least the rest of today. But can I take these men out into a storm that may very well kill them all?

Oh hell, he thought, tossing the telescope to one of the pirates below and beginning to climb down, that's the captain's right—my job isn't to avoid risky situations, but to get us through them. And I can't believe Woefully Fat will let himself be prevented from getting onto Jamaican soil . . . even by a hurricane.

He dropped to the deck and grinned confidently at Skank. "We could scoot under that with half of you dead drunk," Shandy said. "We'll continue southeast."

"Jesus Christ, Jack," Skank began hurriedly, but Venner interrupted him.

"*Why?*" Venner demanded. He pointed astern with one big, freckled arm. "Grand Cayman is only a few hours back that way! And even if this wind does die, which it's about to, the goddamn *current*'ll take us there!"

Shandy turned, unhurriedly, to Venner. "I don't *need* to explain, but I will. We wouldn't *get* to Grand Cayman. This storm is going to catch us, and we'd better be bow on when it does." Venner's broad shoulders were hunching with tensed muscles, but Shandy made himself laugh. "And hell, man, the famous Segundo is somewhere ahead, remember? Those turtlers yesterday said they'd seen his ship only that morning! Not only does he have with him the booty from a dozen plundered ships, he's almost certainly in the old *Carmichael,* renamed. That's *our* ship—and it's a full-size, seaworthy vessel, and we'll need it, because little pond-scooters like the *Jenny* here are no good for the long reaches to Madagascar and the Indian Ocean, and that's what these days require. Look what happened to Thatch when he switched to a sloop."

"*And* this Ulysse fellow has got that woman," Venner almost spat, "and don't try to make us believe that ain't your whole reason for wanting to catch him! Well maybe she means more to *you* than your hide does, but she's nothing to *me*. And I ain't risking my hide to get her for you." He faced the rest of the men. "You lads think about that. Why do we have to catch up with this Ulysse or Hurwood *today?* What's wrong with next week?"

Shandy hadn't slept much during the last several days. "It's today because I say it is," he said, a little wildly. "What do you think of that?"

Woefully Fat stepped up beside Shandy, his huge shadow eclipsing Venner. "We goin' to Jamaica," he said.

For several long seconds, while the cloud ahead grew and Grand Cayman became still more distant, Venner stood motionless, his eyes darting back and forth from Shandy and Woefully Fat to the rest of the crew, obviously wondering if he could provoke a mutiny.

Shandy, though he hoped he looked confident, was wondering the same thing. He had been an able enough captain during the month after Hurwood took the *Carmichael,* and he was still looked on with some awe because of the exaggerated part he'd played in the escape from that Navy man-of-war, and it helped to have the support of Davies' old *bocor,* even though his impending death seemed to be all the man could talk about these days; but Shandy could only guess, as Venner was obviously doing too, at how much the men's confidence in him had been eroded by his three months of drunken apathy in the New Providence settlement.

"Shandy knows what he's doin'," grumbled one toothless old wretch.

Skank nodded with a fair show of conviction. "Sure," he said. "We couldn't get back to Grand Cayman before the storm overtook us."

Shandy was very grateful, for he knew Skank wasn't being sincere.

Venner's shoulders slumped, and his grin, which was beginning to look less like lines of cheer than wrinkles in a long-unchanged shirt, was hoisted back onto his face. "Well sure he does," he said hoarsely. "I just . . . wanted to make sure we were all in . . . *agreement.*" He turned and, shoving a couple of men out of his way, lurched away toward the stern as Shandy ordered the removal of the jib and the reefing of the mainsail.

When the sloop was moving forward under minimum working canvas and Shandy paused to squint up at the cloud that now shadowed them, Skank tapped him on the shoulder and, with a jerk of his head, drew him aside.

"What's up?" Shandy asked, tension putting a tightness in his voice.

"Venner ain't near pleased," Skank said quietly. "Watch him. It'll be today, and probably from behind."

"Ah. Well, thanks. I'll keep an eye on him." Shandy started to turn away, but Skank stepped in front of him.

"Did you know," the young pirate went on hurriedly, "I don't think you know—he got Davies killed."

Shandy's impatience was gone. "Tell me," he said. A few heavy drops of rain fell through the still air to thump on the deck and make long dark streaks on the canvas. Rain before wind, Shandy thought, remembering old Hodge's long ago warning. "Loosen the sheets a bit," he called, then turned back to Skank. "Tell me."

"Well," said Skank quickly, peering fearfully at the dark sky as he spoke, "the dead sailor that killed him was going to kill you, a minute before—you was runnin' toward the girl in the air, and you didn't see this dead fellow waitin' for you. So Phil ran up to nail the thing and save you, no trouble—but Venner saw what he was up to, and blocked him—Venner not bein' glad you was made quarter-master."

The rain was falling steadily now, and still there was no wind. "Reef the main a little more," Shandy called uneasily. "No—lower the gaff entirely. We'll meet her with bare spars—and be ready to heave to."

"It threw Davies off his stride," Skank went on, "when Venner bumped him, and it let you get two steps further; but Davies kept running anyway, and by then the only way he could hit the thing wasn't good enough to kill it outright. His second chop cut its head off, but by then it had got its cutlass into him."

Then the wind hit them, and even under bare spars the *Jenny* heeled sharply, losing headway and leaning over so far that men had to grab rails or rigging to keep from tumbling up against the port gunwales. The mast was nearly horizontal.

Close behind the wind came high waves, and Skank scrambled aft to help the helmsman drag the rudder through the strong sea and get the bow pointed more directly into the wind. Slowly, against resistance, the mast came back up.

As the little craft balanced at the top of one foam-streaked wave and then slid down the far side into the trough, the rudder swinging free in the air for a moment and then the long bowsprit stabbing into the next steep gray slope of water ahead, Shandy held his breath, expecting either the bowsprit to break off or the bow and the whole hull to follow it in, and not come up again—but after eight rapid heartbeats the bow did rise, bowsprit intact, throwing off the weight of solid water like a man flinging away a pack of murderous dogs that had almost got him down.

Shandy exhaled. Evidently whoever had built the *Jenny* had known his business. He yelled the order to heave to, and when they had crested the wave the wind was on the starboard bow and enough of the mainsail had been unreefed to keep the *Jenny* falling back onto the same tack and making no headway. In principle they could ride out the storm this way.

Shandy climbed and slid back to the stern and the men laboring at the helm. There were no further orders to give now, and the wind would have torn the words out of his mouth anyway and flung them away unheard, so he just leaned against the transom and tried to guess how long the *Jenny* could continue to take this without breaking up.

The warm wind was still somehow strengthening, and spray flew past in fast clouds like grapeshot, and stung his face and hands; he licked his lips and the salty taste let him know that it was sea-spray and not rain. The waves were as tall and solid-looking as cliffs, and every time the *Jenny* slid down the weather slope of one and crashed into the next, she was jolted and shaken so violently that the mast swung wildly back and forth overhead. The splash spray instantly blew away behind them, and solid water swirled around Shandy's thighs and tugged ever more strongly at him.

He kept squinting against the lash of the wind to make sure they neither faced the wind too directly nor let it come around and hit them broadside, and for several minutes he was amazed at how perfectly the old sloop was riding; then he noticed wisps of steam fluttering away from the joint where the tiller bar was attached to the head of the rudder, and when he peered more closely he saw that the iron pin was glowing a dull red. Woefully Fat was standing braced on the other side of the helm, and Shandy cuffed water out of his eyes and squinted across the deck through narrowed, stinging eyes at the big magician. The *bocor*'s eyes were closed and he was chewing the knuckles of one hand—and even though the rain and sea were scouring the brown hand, Shandy could see red blood springing from where the teeth were working—and he realized that the *Jenny*'s progress was not entirely a result of the helmsman's skill.

Even so, each succeeding wave was taller, and when the little craft laboriously crested the next one, and Shandy blinked around at the sea, it looked to him as if the boat were attached to a vast shiny cloth that was being dragged over the Alps; and the shrieking of the wind was so furious that he had to keep reminding himself that there was no sentient wrath behind it.

They slid down the windward side of the wave and plunged into the next one—the old sloop heaved up, pouring solid water off to both sides—and when the *Jenny* climbed the lee face of it, Shandy could feel her forcibly shift around, and the gaff-saddle, lowered now to head height, glowed orange with the effort of it.

Then they were at the top, and the full force of the wind hit them again, and with a gunshot crack that was audible even over the wind the glowing gaff-saddle broke. The horizontal spar was now just a fire-headed spear laced to a big, fluttering flag—it slammed the deck under the mainsail boom, bounced up on the other side, spun all the way around like a crazy compass needle as the luff side of the sail tore, then flew aft. The boat shook as the spar thudded into the transom.

Shandy had ducked in the second when the thing was so violently tearing around, and now he looked up, fearing that it might have killed the helmsman, or, worse, wrecked the tiller; but the helmsman was still braced against the tiller bar—only after sagging with relief did Shandy notice that the iron-headed spar had struck Woefully Fat squarely in the center of his massive torso, and had nailed him upright to the transom.

"*Christ,*" Shandy cried through spray-numbed lips. Could they survive without the *bocor?*

Shandy was anything but confident, but he pushed away from the rail and grabbed the mainsail boom and pulled himself forward along it, past the tied-down leech-end of the mainsail to the mastward end where the luff side flapped loose. Someone was with him now, on the other side of the swinging boom—it was Skank, his face emaciated with effort, and he had a knife and a length of rope. Together, as the boat skewed down into the trough, the two of them managed to stab several holes through the top edge of what remained of the sail; they held on while the *Jenny* crashed into the streaked face of another wave, and then when the water had swept on past them Shandy strung the rope through the holes. Then as the sloop leaned back, rising to meet the next crest, Shandy threw the end of the rope high toward the port bow—the headwind flung it back around the mast to Skank, who caught it and fell to the port gunwale and managed to flip two loops of it around a belaying pin before the wind hammered them again.

The couple of square yards of raised canvas caught the wind enough to kick the stern back, but Shandy knew it couldn't hold for very long. Several more men had crawled up the deck to help though, and Shandy fell back to the rail and let them take his place—his stomach felt knotted up, either with tension or something rancid at lunch, and he hoped he wouldn't have to do any hard work for a while.

All at once he became aware of a weight on his jacket pulling the back of his collar tighter against his neck, and he glanced down—and then recoiled away from the rail, for clamped tight onto his jacket-front, from God knew where, were what seemed to be two knobby-headed gray eels; it was only when he grabbed one to yank it off that he realized they were two unfresh human arms, severed at the elbows, with the fingers tightly gripping the fabric of his jacket.

One part of his mind was just moaning with the horror of the thing, but after the first frozen moment of shock it occurred to him that this was the same jacket he'd been wearing on the day Hurwood took the *Carmichael* away from Leo Friend—and on that day one of Friend's crew of dead men had hung on to the jacket after being rolled over the rail, and had fallen into the sea only because its arms had parted at the elbows. The clinging arms had seemed to disappear shortly after that, but apparently they'd been ghostily attached to the jacket ever since, like ceiling cobwebs that can be seen only in a certain light.

The intensifying pain in his stomach made him hunch back against the rail, but he forced himself to go on thinking. What then, he asked himself, is the light that makes these grisly things visible? Well, obviously—hostile magic, unencumbered by being performed on land. You'd have known it by the hot iron smell, too, if it weren't for this wind. This pain in your belly is a gift from someone.

Sea water surged over him as the *Jenny* took another wave, and then he straightened up against the powerful preference of his body to fold double—cold sweat on his face made the spray seem even warmer—and he reached out and grabbed the nearest man and dragged him close enough to shout at. *"Where's,"* Shandy roared, *"Venner?"*

The man gaped at the gray forearms swinging from his captain's jacket, but he pointed forward, then down.

Shandy nodded and let go of him and then, one agonized step at a time, hitched himself toward the hatch, bracing against anything he could reach; a sudden gust of wind at the crest of a wave punched him off his feet, and he crawled the last few yards

flat on his belly, the spread-out arms giving him an insectlike look.
With an effort that seemed to pull all his abdominal muscles loose
he lifted the hatch cover and rolled himself in and half climbed,
half tumbled down into the low-ceilinged hold.

It was dark, but he knew where the weapons rack was, and he
let the next roll pitch him against it and he snatched a hilt and
pulled a sword free; it was lighter than a cutlass, but it seemed to be
the right length, and he let his hand settle comfortably around the
grip. There was a dim red glow up in the bow, and he hunched
toward it, his grisly lapel ornaments swinging wildly.

Venner was crouched over a little firepot, whispering and
dropping shreds of stuff onto the glowing coals in it.

Shandy extended the sword and kicked himself into an
agonizing lunge, but the *Jenny* abruptly rocked forward at the crest
of a wave at that moment, and his lunge became a somersault—he
collided heavily with the stocky figure of Venner and the two of
them tumbled into the deep, swirling puddle against the bow
bulkhead. Even over their gasping and the creaking of overstressed
timbers and the howl of the wind, Shandy heard the firepot hiss for
an instant as it was extinguished; and even crumpled nearly
upside-down in cold water in the angle of canted deck and
bulkhead, with Venner's elbow jabbing into his back, he felt the
pain in his belly suddenly unkink and disappear, and the dead
man's arms no longer tugged at his jacket.

The bow slammed into a trough, and for several seconds the
two men were pressed even harder against the bulkhead—Shandy
felt water thrusting in through gaps between the strakes, as if the
sea were spitting at him between wooden teeth, and he felt the still-
hot firepot roll scorchingly across his throat—and then the sloop
tipped sharply back as it began to climb the next slope.

Shandy and Venner and a lot of salty water tumbled aft, and
Shandy tried to keep his sword up and pointed at Venner; twice he
felt the point poke something more yielding than deck timbers,
and he tried to thrust, but sliding prone on the sloshing deck he
could get no traction. Gray light from the open hatch silhouetted
his opponent clearly for a second, but a moment later Venner had
scrambled up the ladder to the deck.

Shandy got to his feet and followed him up, keeping his
sword—which, he now noticed, was a spare rapier of Davies'—
between himself and the light to block any blows from Venner; but

when he reached the deck he saw that Venner had run forward and was now facing him from ten yards away, pointing at Shandy a pistol he'd snatched from someone.

Shandy throttled his instant impulse to dive back down the hatch, for he was the captain, and even in the midst of this storm most of the men were gaping at this confrontation—and a thirty-foot shot on a wet, pitching deck in hard rain would probably miss, and perhaps the rain had got in under the pan-cover to the powder. He did, though, allow himself to stand in profile, facing Venner over his right shoulder. He lifted his sword in a fencer's salute, both for the apparent coolness of the gesture and in the hope that the pistol ball, if well aimed, might strike the blade or the guard.

The rain had not got to the powder. At the same instant that he saw the muzzle flash Shandy felt the hot ball punch across the skin over his solar plexus; he flinched back away from it but didn't fall or drop his sword, and when he had regathered his scattered wits a second or two later he bowed as courteously as he could on the rocking deck—it required grabbing the ratlines with his free hand and planting his feet a little more widely than was customary—and then he advanced toward Venner.

The helmsman, distracted by the drama on the deck, didn't put the bow squarely enough into the next wave, and the *Jenny* took it on her port bow; she heeled ponderously as the solid green water surged over her deck, splashing up explosively at the mast and sweeping at least one man overboard.

Then she lay in the trough, abeam to the waves. More scared by this than by Venner, Shandy scrambled back to the stern, having to drop the saber in order to grab rigging to steady himself. Skank and the other men at the mainsail boom had managed to get several feet of the sail unreefed and threaded with rope, and one man was trying to shinny up the swaying mast with the end of the rope in his teeth, apparently hoping to throw it over the narrow topsail yard so that the men below could use it as a halliard. It was all they could do, and Shandy knew it wouldn't be enough.

Behind him, moving slowly because he didn't want to abandon the cutlass he'd picked up, Venner was picking his way aft.

Shandy glanced at the helmsman, who had the tiller all the way over to port, and he knew he should be there to help the man hold it when the full wind hit them at the crest, but then he saw Woefully Fat.

The big *bocor* had pulled himself away from the transom, and was now standing on the deck and grasping the wooden shaft that impaled him; and even as Shandy watched, Woefully Fat bent it in front of himself—the wind took all sounds, but splinters began to spring up between the two black hands. Shandy assumed the *bocor* was using magic to accomplish it, but Woefully Fat had to shuffle around as the spar was bent farther, and Shandy felt his arms prickle with awe, for he could see the bloody gaff-saddle protruding an inch or so from the broad back, and though the iron still steamed, it wasn't glowing—the *bocor* was breaking the spar with nothing but his own physical strength.

Finally it broke, and the *bocor* fell to his knees. Shandy rushed up to help him, but Woefully Fat one-handedly lifted the gaff-spar and shoved it toward him—an impressive feat in itself, for, even broken off, the thing was a good six feet long, and draped with rigging and the sopping head end of the mainsail.

"*Sea anchor!*" the *bocor* shouted. "*Throw it over the starboard quarter!*"

Shandy understood at once, and took the spar from Woefully Fat—he had to use both hands, and still his teeth ground together at the weight of it—and he turned and heaved it over the starboard rail into the sea.

In that moment they crested the next wave, and the *Jenny* heeled sharply as the wind hit them on the port beam, and then they were sliding down the weather side, the helmsman straining to keep the tiller over. Shandy hastily untied the mainsail halliard and let it play out over the rail to give the sea-anchor line some length.

The *Jenny* hit the trough only slightly straightened out, and again the sea surged entirely over the deck. Shandy clung to the rail underwater, wondering if they had been rolled over, if the *Jenny* was simply going to implode and sink without ever bobbing up again; but then the water became heavy on his hunched shoulders and sluiced away, freeing his head first, then his arms, and when it was still sloshing around his knees he resecured the halliard, for nearly all of the line had been played out.

The spar itself was somewhere behind the last crest, and even as they climbed the next one Shandy could feel the tug of it, could feel the old sloop pulled more straight, and then begin to respond to the sail and the rudder. The bow was coming up into the wind.

Through his fingertips he had been paying very close attention to the feel of the deck, and when he felt a faint scratch nearby he looked up—and then flung himself flat. Venner's cutlass split the rail instead of Shandy's head.

Shandy rolled away while Venner was rocking the heavy blade loose, and when he got up in a crouch Skank took time out from improvising a mainsail to toss him the dropped saber.

The deck was heaving, and rain and spray were in his eyes—he missed the toss, heard the sword clank and slide across wet deck, heard too the creak of the cutlass blade levered free, and Venner's sliding footsteps approaching.

Shandy dove after the saber just as the bow plunged into a wave—he shut his eyes and braced himself against the gunwale as the water crashed over him, then shook his head and blinked around frantically. The light was bad, but he saw the sword rolling in the water, and he went after it in a half-swimming crawl and caught its hilt.

Venner struck as Shandy was trying to stand up, but the deck rocked sharply back just as Venner lunged, and he lost his balance, and though the blow numbed Shandy's shoulder, it was the flat that had hit him, not the edge.

It knocked him back down onto his knees, but Venner had fallen too, and Shandy took a moment to drive his own sword point into the only reachable part of Venner—his knee—before wearily hauling himself to his feet one more time.

Venner was up too.

Shandy realized he might not be able to beat Venner, that this interminable fight might end with that damned cutlass breaking open his head or splitting his abdomen—but he was too exhausted to derive anything more than an oppressive unhappiness from the idea. He leaned back against the transom and flexed his hand on the slippery saber grip.

Venner swung the cutlass at Shandy's head, and Shandy made his numb arm lift the saber to deflect the blow, but he only succeeded in turning the heavier blade, so that once again it was the flat that hit him—squarely on the side of the head this time. His knees gave for a moment as the hot, nauseating pain seemed to ring in his sinuses.

He tried to straighten, but Venner's blade was driving in point-first now—Shandy let himself slump further and then barely managed to jerk his body aside as the blade struck—it scraped his ribs and caught in a loose fold of his jacket, nailing him to the bulkhead and stopping his fall; but he had raised his own sword in a parry that, while late, had put his point more or less in line. As cloppingly as a carelessly worked puppet he got his feet under himself.

His shirt tore as he lunged forward, and then the front of Venner's jacket was punctured to admit two inches—then four, as Shandy caught his balance and remised—of rusty steel.

Suddenly pale, Venner reeled back, off the blade, and the cutlass slipped out of his hand and rang on the deck. The *Jenny* crested the next wave and tilted sharply back for an instant. Everyone except the two combatants grabbed for a handhold or tried to make the tumble a controlled one, but Shandy lunged forward again, in midair as the deck dropped away beneath him, and drove his point into Venner's broad chest with such force that the blade snapped off and both of them sailed through the rainy air toward, and higher than, the port rail. Shandy let go of the broken sword and grabbed the rigging, but Venner and Davies' sword went spinning away over the side. Then the bow fell and the stern rose, tearing Shandy's grip loose and flinging him hard down onto the deck.

Chapter Twenty-Six

He came back to consciousness in slow stages, reluctantly abandoning the dreams that were so much preferable to the cold, aching situation that seemed to be reality—memory dreams, like traveling with his father and the marionettes, and wish dreams, like finding Beth Hurwood and finally telling her the things he wanted to tell her. At first it had seemed that he might be able to choose the situation he would wake up to, just by concentrating on it; but the wet and cold and rocking one became more and more insistent, and when he opened his eyes he was on the *Jenny*'s deck.

He tried to sit up, but sudden nausea pitched him back flat, weak and sweating. He opened his eyes again and saw Skank's concerned face. Shandy started to speak, but his teeth were chattering. He clamped his jaw tight for a moment and then tried again. "What . . . happened?"

"You hit the deck pretty solid after you killed Venner," said Skank.

"Where's Davies?"

Skank frowned in puzzlement. "He's . . . uh, dead, cap'n. When Hurwood took the *Carmichael*. You remember."

It seemed to Shandy he did remember something like that. He tried to sit up again, and again flopped back, shivering. "What happened?"

"Well—you were there, cap'n. And I told you about it today,

277

remember? How one of Hurwood's dead sailors killed him?" Skank looked around unhappily.

"No, I mean what happened just now?"

"You fell on the deck. I just *told* you."

"Ah." Shandy sat up for the third time and made himself stay up. The nausea surged up in him and then abated. "You may have to keep telling me." He struggled to his feet and stood swaying and shuddering, clutching the rail for balance and looking around dizzily. "Uh . . . the storm has . . . stopped," he remarked, proud to be able to demonstrate his awareness of things.

"Yes, cap'n. While you was out cold. We just kept her hove to and rode it out. Your sea-anchor made the difference."

Shandy rubbed his face hard. "My sea-anchor." He decided not to ask. "Good. What's our course?"

"Southeast, more or less."

Shandy beckoned Skank closer, and when the young man had crouched beside him he asked quietly, "Where are we going?"

"Jamaica, you said."

"Ah." He frowned. "What do we hope to find there?"

"Ulysse Segundo," said Skank, looking more worried every second, "and his ship, the *Ascending Orpheus*. You said he's Hurwood, and the *Orpheus* is really the *Carmichael*. We followed reports of him out to the Caymans, where you heard he was heading back toward Jamaica again. Oh, and Woefully Fat wanted to get there, Jamaica, before he died." Skank shook his head sadly.

"Is Woefully Fat dead?"

"Most of us think so. The gaff-spar speared him like a spitted chicken, and after he broke the big piece off and gave it to you he just flopped down. We got him below, for burial when we get to shore, 'cause you don't just pitch a dead *bocor* into the sea if you know what's good for you—but a couple of the men say they can feel a pulse in his wrist, and Lamont says he can't keep his mind on his work because Woefully Fat keeps hummin' real low, though *I* don't hear nothin'."

Shandy tried to concentrate. He remembered some of these things, vaguely, when Skank described them, and he remembered a sense of desperate urgency about them, but he couldn't now remember why that should be. What he most wanted at the moment was an impossibility—a dry place to sleep.

"That storm," he said. "It was very sudden? There was no shelter we could have taken?"

"We might have been able to run back to Grand Cayman," Skank told him. "Venner was for doing that. You said we had to go on."

"Did I . . . say *why?*"

"You said the storm would get us anyway, and we may as well go on after the *Orpheus.* Venner said you wanted to because of that girl. You know, Hurwood's daughter."

"Ah!" He was beginning to see some hints of pattern in his concussion-shuffled memories. "What's the date today?"

"I don't know. It's Friday . . . and, uh, Sunday's Christmas."

"I see," said Shandy tightly. "Keep reminding me of that, will you? And now that the storm is past, get up as much canvas as you can."

The next morning at dawn they spied the *Ascending Orpheus*—and there was no disagreement about what to do, for they'd spent all night bailing water out of the *Jenny,* and in spite of having pulled a tar-smeared sail around under the forward keel, and hammering rice-filled rolls of cloth into the gaps between the strakes, the water was coming in faster every hour, and Shandy doubted that the battered old sloop could hold together long enough to make another landfall. Maximum canvas was crowded on, and the *Jenny* lurched unevenly across the expanse of blue water toward the ship.

Crouched in the sloop's bow, Shandy peered through the telescope, squinting against the blinding glitter of the morning sun on the waves. "She's suffered," he remarked to the haggard, shivering men around him. "There's spars gone and rigging fouled on the foremast . . . but she's still solid. If we do this next hour's work right, there'll be rum and food and dry clothes."

There was a general growl of approval, for most of his men had spent last night laboring over the bilge pumps in the rain, looking forward to the occasional brief break in which to swallow a handful or two of wet biscuit; and the rum cask had come unmoored and broken apart during the storm, filling the hold with the smell of unattainable liquor.

"Did any of our powder stay dry?" Shandy asked.

Skank shrugged. "Maybe."

"Hm. Well, we don't want to wreck the *Orpheus* anyway." He

lowered the telescope. "Assuming our mast doesn't snap off, we ought to be able to cut south and head her off—and then I guess just try to board her."

"That or swim for Jamaica," agreed one ragged, red-eyed young pirate.

"Don't you think he'll try to run when he sees we're after him?" Skank asked.

"Maybe," said Shandy, "though I'll bet we can catch him, even busted up as we are—and anyway, we can't look too formidable." He raised the telescope again. "Well never mind," he said a moment later. "As a matter of fact, he's coming at *us*."

There was a moment of silence. Then, "Lost some men in that storm, I daresay," commented one of the older men grimly. "Be wantin' replacements."

Skank bit his lip and frowned at Shandy. "Last time you tangled with him he picked you up and dropped you into the ocean. You . . . got some reason to think it won't happen that way again?"

Shandy had been pondering that question ever since they had set out from New Providence Island. *Blood,* he remembered Governor Sawney saying, *obviously there's iron in it. Link your blood to the cold iron of the sword. Make the atoms of blood and iron line up the way a compass needle lines up to face north. Or vice versa. It's all relative . . .*

Shandy grinned, a little sickly in spite of his best efforts. "We'd all better hope so. I'll be at the bittacle—have somebody bring me a saber . . . and a hammer and a narrow chisel."

The *Orpheus* had turned and was charging straight downwind, west toward the *Jenny,* the morning sun behind her casting the shadows of her rigging and masts onto the luminous sails. Shandy kept an eye on her as he worked with the hammer and chisel over the grip of the saber Skank had brought him, and when she was still a hundred yards away he straightened and held the sword up by the blade.

He'd cut away the leather wrapping and half of the wood grip, exposing the iron tang that linked the blade to the pommel-weight, and, just where the heel of a swordsman's hand would press, he had chisel-punched a narrow crack into the metal.

Shandy stood up and leaned on the bittacle pillar, looking down through the glass. "If it should . . . go against us here this morning," he said to Skank, who had been staring at him

ncomprehendingly for the last several minutes, "get east of him—
vith the state the *Carmichael*'s in he can no more tack than fly—and
ry for Jamaica."

"It better not go against us."

Shandy smiled, and somehow it made him look even more
ired. "Right." He raised the hammer and brought it down solidly
n the bittacle glass, and then he dropped the hammer and
umbled around among the glass shards; a moment later he lifted
he compass needle out with bloody fingers. "Get the lads ready
vith hooks and lines. With luck we'll be able to start boarding
efore he knows we're trying to be aggressors."

Skank moaned faintly, but nodded and hurried forward.

Shandy carefully inserted the north-pole end of the compass
eedle into the crack he'd cut in the saber tang, then he crouched
nd picked up the hammer again and gave the needle a tap to keep
t in place.

Shandy carefully slid the doctored saber through his belt, and
or a minute after that he just breathed deeply with his eyes shut;
hen when the *Ascending Orpheus* jibed sharply in on the *Jenny*'s port
lank, putting her in shadow, he snatched up a grappling hook,
vhirled it a couple of times in a vertical circle and then let it fly up
oward the big ship's rail; sunlight glittered on the points at the
noment of pause, then the hook dropped onto the rail and
ripped.

Certainly this is the last time the *Jenny* will besiege the
Carmichael, he thought as he began climbing hand over hand up the
ope.

The effort started his nose bleeding and made his head feel as
f it would burst, and when he finally got to the top of the rope and
aused for breath straddling the rail he couldn't remember why he
vas there. Some time seemed to have passed—this was the
Vociferous Carmichael, he was sure . . . but most of the railing was
gone, and the whole forecastle structure, too! Had they still not
eached Jamaica? Where was Captain Chaworth? And that sick girl
vith the fat physician?

His disorientation ebbed a little when he recognized the girl's
ather coming down the ladder from the poop deck—what was his
name? Hurwood, that was it—but then Shandy frowned, for he
ad remembered the man as having only one arm.

He was distracted then by fighting on the quarterdeck, and when he looked closely—it was hard to focus in all this glaring sunlight—he really thought he was losing his mind. Haggard men in ragged but gaudy clothes were climbing aboard all around him and doing desperate battle with impossibly animate corpses whose withered hands shouldn't have been able to clutch a cutlass, and whose milky, sunken eyes shouldn't have been able to direct the strokes. The blood running sluggishly from Shandy's ears and the pounding in his head robbed the scene of nearly all sounds, giving everything the grotesque unreality of a fever dream, and the question of why he had chosen to adorn his jacket with two mummified human forearms seemed relatively unimportant.

He didn't trust his balance, so he climbed very carefully down onto the deck. The man who seemed to be Benjamin Hurwood was coming toward him now, a welcoming smile crinkling his old face. . . .

And then Shandy *was* dreaming, had to be, for he was standing beside his father in the dimness of the scaffolding above a marionette stage, both of them staring into the brightness below and busily working the crosses that controlled the dangling puppets; and it must have been a crowd scene they were doing, for many more crosses were hung in the spring-hooks that kept the idle marionettes below swaying and bobbing slightly. In a moment he had forgotten that it had to be a dream, and was panicking because he didn't know what play they were doing.

He squinted at the little figures below, and instantly recognized them. They were the *Julius Caesar* marionettes. And luckily the third act had begun, there wasn't all that much more to do—they were already in the assassination scene, and the little wooden senators all had their standard right hands replaced by the dagger-clutching ones.

The Caesar puppet was speaking—and Shandy stared, for the face was no longer wood but flesh, and he recognized it. It was his own face. "Hence!" he heard his miniature self say. "Wilt thou lift up Olympus?"

The senator puppets, who were also flesh now, moved in for the kill . . . and then the scene abruptly winked out, leaving Shandy standing on the *Carmichael*'s deck again, squinting against the sun-glare at Hurwood.

A confident smile was fading from the old man's face, but he struck again, and Shandy was kneeling in hot sand on the New Providence beach, staring critically at the four bamboo poles he'd shoved upright in the sand. They had stood well enough until he'd tried to lash others across the tops of them, and now they were all leaning outward like cannons ready to repel an attack from all sides.

"Weaving a basket?" Beth Hurwood asked from behind him.

He hadn't heard her approach, and for a moment he was going to reply irritably, but then he grinned. "It's supposed to be a hut. For me to sleep in."

"It'd be easier if you made a lean-to—here, I'll show you."

It had been a day in July, during the refitting of the *Carmichael;* Beth had shown him how to put together a much stabler structure, and there had been one moment when, standing on tiptoe to loop twine over the peak of one of the leaning poles, she had fallen against him, and for a moment she'd been in his arms, and her brown eyes and coppery hair had made him dizzy with an emotion that included physical attraction only to the extent that an orchestra includes a brass section. It was a memory that often recurred in his dreams.

This time, though, it was going differently. This time she was using a hammer and nails instead of twine, and her eyelids and lips were pulled open as far as they could go and her teeth and the whites of her eyes glared in the tropical sun as she laid his arms out along the bamboo poles and held the first nail to his wrist. . . .

. . . and again he was standing on the *Carmichael's* deck, blinking at Hurwood.

Hurwood now looked definitely uneasy. "What the hell's wrong with your *mind?*" he snarled. "It's like a stripped screw."

Shandy was inclined to agree. He kept trying to remember what he was doing here, and every time he glanced at the nightmare combat going on around him he was astonished and horrified anew. And now, as if to outdo all his previous disorientations, the deck stopped pressing against his boot-soles and he slowly began to rise unsupported into the air.

Instinctively he reached to grab something—and what he grabbed for was not a rail or the rigging, but the hilt of his saber. The protruding compass needle punctured his palm, but the same impulse that had made him grab it made him hang on. He began to sink, and a few seconds later he was again standing on the deck.

He looked around: the fighting was going on as horribly as before, though all sounds were still muffled for him, but none of the combatants were coming anywhere near Hurwood and Shandy—apparently they considered it a private duel.

There was an expression of alarmed wonder on Hurwood's face, and he was saying something too softly for Shandy to hear. Then the old man drew a rapier of his own and ran nimbly at him.

Shandy was still painfully gripping the hilt of his own sword, and now he wrenched it free from his belt just in time to sweep Hurwood's point away with an awkward parry in *prime,* and then he hopped back and more easily knocked aside the old man's next thrust—and then the next. The gray forearms attached to his jacket swung and bumped against each other sickeningly.

Blood from his spiked hand made the saber grip slippery, and every time his blade clanked against Hurwood's the compass needle grated against the bones in his palm, sending an agony like tinfoil on a carious tooth all the way up to his shoulder.

Hurwood barked a harsh syllable of laughter and sprang forward, but Shandy clenched his fist on the saber grip—driving the needle even deeper between the bones of his palm—and caught the incoming blade in a corkscrewing bind that yanked the hilt out of Hurwood's fingers; the pain of the action made Shandy's vision go dark for a moment, but with a last twist he sent Hurwood's sword spinning over the rail, and then he just stared down at the deck and took deep, gasping breaths until his vision cleared.

Hurwood had scrambled back, and now looked off to the side and pointed imperatively at Shandy. Obviously this was no longer a private duel.

One of the decayed mariners lurched obediently across the deck toward them; his clothes were ragged scraps and Shandy could see daylight between the bones of one shin, but the shoulders were broad and one bony wrist was whipping a heavy cutlass through the air as easily as a sailmaker wields a needle.

Shandy was already close to exhaustion, and the needle embedded in his hand was a hot, grating agony. It seemed to him that the jar of a butterfly alighting on the blade of his saber would be more torture than he could bear and stay conscious, but he made himself step back and lift his sword, though the move made the world go gray and drenched him in icy sweat.

The dead man shambled closer—Hurwood smiled at the thing and said, "Kill Shandy."—and the cutlass was whipped back over the bony shoulder for a stroke.

Shandy forced his eyes to focus, forced his ploughed hand to be ready. . . .

But the cutlass lashed out sideways, slamming into Hurwood and flinging him away aft across the deck, and in the instant before the necrotic sailor collapsed in skeletal ruin and, simultaneously, the gray arms evaporated from Shandy's jacket, Shandy's eyes met the gleam in the sailor's sunken eye-sockets and there was exchanged recognition and wry greeting and a farewell between true comrades. Then there was nothing but tumbling old bones and some scraps of gaudy cloth on the deck, but Shandy let go of the torturing saber and dropped to his knees, then forward onto his ravaged hands, and his ears had cleared enough so that he could hear his tears patter on the deck.

"*Phil!*" he wailed. "*Phil! Christ, man, come back!*"

But Davies, and all the dead men, were gone at last, and aside from Hurwood the only men on the sunny deck were men who had climbed up from the *Jenny.*

Hurwood was leaning against the starboard rail, his face white as ashes, clutching the stump where his newly regrown arm had been. There was no blood leaking from it, but evidently it required all the man's sorcerous concentration to keep it that way.

Then Hurwood was moving. He pushed away from the rail and, one ponderously careful step at a time, plodded toward the aft cabin door. Shandy struggled to his feet and shambled after him.

Hurwood gave the door a kick—it opened, and he tottered inside.

Shandy stopped just outside and stared into the dimness. "Beth!" he called. "Are you in there?"

There was no reply except muttering from Hurwood, and Shandy took a deep breath, fumbled his clasp knife out of his pocket with his good hand, and stepped inside.

Hurwood was just straightening up from digging in an open chest against the bulkhead, and in his one hand he was clutching a wooden box Shandy had seen before. He turned and started toward Shandy, and Shandy felt the air thicken, pushing him back. It pushed him back out into the sunlight as Hurwood kept inexorably taking one step after another, and soon it became clear that Hurwood was heading for the ship's boat.

Shandy half opened his knife, laid his forefinger across the groove and then let the blade snap down. Blood spurted from his gashed finger, but the air stopped resisting him. Evidently even unmagnetized iron was enough now to fray Hurwood's spells. He stepped forward and, before Hurwood noticed his sudden freedom to get in close, punched the box out of Hurwood's hand.

The box bounced across the deck. Hurwood, his mouth hanging open from sheer effort, turned and tried to walk; he fell, but then on his knees and one hand he began crawling toward the box.

Hardly able to move any better himself, Shandy lurched ahead of the creeping man and sat down on the hot deck beside the box and, his finger still painfully caught under the clasp-knife blade, fumbled the top of the box off.

"My saber," he croaked to Skank, who was tying a bandage around his own thigh. The weary young pirate paused long enough to kick Shandy's doctored sword clattering across the deck to him.

Without unclamping the knife from his finger, Shandy grasped the injuring saber, squeezing the compass needle deep into his hand again, and then drove the sword's iron point down into the box.

The dried head inside imploded with a sound like old upholstery ripping.

Hurwood stopped, staring, then took a rasping breath and expelled it in a howl that made even the most badly wounded of Shandy's pirates look over in wonder. Then he collapsed, and blood began jetting from the stump of his arm.

With a shudder Shandy dropped the sword again and pulled the knife off his finger. Then he began clumsily using the knife to cut his cursed jacket into strips to use as a tourniquet—for if Beth wasn't aboard, he didn't want Hurwood to bleed to death.

Dizziness, nausea, and occasional moments of blank forgetfulness all helped make Shandy's search of the *Carmichael* a time-consuming one, but the main reason he took so long—looking inside chests that couldn't possibly have contained Beth Hurwood, and checking some cabins twice to see if she'd doubled back on him—was that he dreaded what he'd probably have to do if it became certain she wasn't aboard. The moment came, though, seeming all the bleaker for the postponement, when he had to admit to himself that he'd checked every cubic foot of the vessel. There was more gold and jewelry in the hold than could be unloaded in a day, but no Beth Hurwood.

He climbed listlessly back up to the main deck and blinked around at the battered men who awaited him, until he spotted Skank. "Hurwood regained consciousness yet?" he asked.

"Not last I heard," said Skank. "Listen, though, did you have any luck down there?"

"No." Shandy turned reluctantly toward the cabin where Hurwood had been carried. "Get me a—"

Skank stepped in front of him, backed up by the dozen other men who could still walk; the young pirate's face was as hollowed and hard as a sand-scoured twist of driftwood. "Captain," he rasped, "you said he had his goddamned *loot* aboard, damn you, the stuff from all the ships he—"

"Oh, loot." Shandy nodded. "Yeah, there's that. Plenty of it, just like I said. I think I sprung a gut moving chest of gold ingots around down there. You can all . . . go roll in it. But first, hoist me up a bucket of sea water, will you? And see if you can't find . . . fire, a candle or something . . . somewhere. I'll be in there with him."

A little disconcerted, Skank stepped back. "Uh, sure, cap'n. Sure."

Shandy shook his head unhappily as he limped to the cabin door and went inside. Hurwood lay on the deck planks unconscious, his breath sounding like slow strokes of a saw in dry wood. His shirt was more dark than white, and spatters of blood, nearly dry, blackened the deck around his shoulder, but the bleeding seemed to have been stopped.

Shandy stood over him and wondered who the man really was. The Oxford don, author of *A Vindication of Free Will*? Beth's father? Husband of the unbearably dead Margaret? Ulysse Segundo the pirate? The bones were prominent in the open-mouthed face, and

Shandy tried to imagine what Hurwood had looked like as a young man. He couldn't imagine it.

Shandy knelt down beside him and shook him by his good shoulder. "Mr. Hurwood. Wake up."

The pace of the breathing didn't change, the wrinkled eyelids didn't flutter.

"Mr. Hurwood. It's important. Please wake up."

There was no response.

Shandy knelt there, staring at the devastated old man and trying not to think, until Skank clumped in. New orange light contended weakly with the sunlight from outside.

"Water," Skank said, letting a sloshing bucket clank onto the deck, "and a lamp." After looking around uncertainly he set that too on the deck.

"Fine," Shandy whispered. "Thank you."

Skank left, closing the door, and the lamp's agitated flame became the room's illumination.

Shandy dipped up a handful of cold brine and tossed it across Hurwood's closed eyes. The old man frowned faintly, but that was all. "God damn it," Shandy burst out, almost sobbing, "don't force me!" He grabbed one of Hurwood's ears and twisted it savagely . . . to no effect. In horror as much as rage Shandy stood up, pushing the lamp away with his foot, then lifted the bucket and flung the entire contents onto Hurwood's head. The weight of water turned the old man's face away and plastered the white hair out like a crown, but the breathing continued as steadily as before, without even any choking.

Genuinely sobbing now, Shandy turned away and reached for the lamp . . . and then breathed a prayer of thanks when he heard spitting and groaning behind him.

He crouched beside Hurwood. "Wake up," he said urgently. "You'll never get better advice."

Hurwood's eyes opened. "I'm . . . hurt," he said softly.

"Yes." Shandy brushed the tears out of his eyes to see the old man more clearly. "But you'll probably live. You survived it once. Where's Beth, Elizabeth, your daughter?"

"Oh . . . it's all over, isn't it? All done now." His eyes met Shandy's. "You! You destroyed it . . . Margaret's head . . . I could feel her spirit go out of it. A mere sword!" His voice was gentle, as if he was discussing events in a play they'd both seen. "Not just because it was cold iron . . . ?"

"And linked to my blood. Yes." Shandy tried to match Hurwood's quiet, conversational tone. "Where have you got your daughter hid?"

"Jamaica. In Spanish Town."

"Ah!" Shandy nodded and smiled. "*Where* in Spanish Town?"

"Nice house. She's restrained, of course. A prisoner. But in comfort."

"Whose house?"

"Uh . . . Joshua Hicks." Hurwood seemed childishly proud of being able to remember the name.

Shandy's shoulders drooped with relief.

"Do you have any chocolates?" Hurwood asked politely. "I haven't any."

"Uh, no." Shandy stood up. "We can get you some in Jamaica."

"We're going to Jamaica?"

"You're damn right we are. As soon as we get this old hulk a little more seaworthy. We can afford to relax a little, now that I know where she is. Beth will keep for another day or two while we make some repairs."

"Oh, aye, Hicks will take very good care of her. I've given him the strictest instructions, and given him a nurse to make sure he does everything right."

A nurse? thought Shandy. I can't quite imagine a nurse ordering around a member of the landed gentry. "Well, fine. We'll—"

"In fact, what day is it today?"

"Christmas Eve." Can't you tell by everybody's festive manner? he thought.

"Maybe I should wave to him tomorrow."

Shandy, still smiling with relief, cocked his head. "Wave at who?"

"Hicks. He'll be on a cliff at Portland Point, tomorrow at dawn, with a telescope." Hurwood chuckled. "He doesn't like the idea—he's giving a big dinner party tomorrow night, and he'd far rather be home preparing for it—but he'll be there. He fears me. I told him to watch for this ship and make sure he sees me out on deck, and sees me wave to him."

"We won't be anywhere near Jamaica by tomorrow dawn," said Shandy. "I don't think this ship *could* be."

"Oh." Hurwood closed his eyes. "Then I won't wave to him."

Shandy had been about to leave, but now he paused, staring down at the old man. "Why were you *going* to wave to him? Why will he be out there watching?"

"I want to sleep now."

"Tell me." Shandy's eyes darted to, then away from, the lamp. "Or no chocolates."

Hurwood pursed his lips pettishly, but answered. "If I *don't* sail past and wave, he'll assume I'm not going to arrive in time, and so he'll do the first part of the magic. The part that has to be done on Christmas day. I meant to be in Jamaica today, to save him the trouble of even going out there, but the storm yesterday and you today . . ." Hurwood opened his eyes, though not wide. "I just thought if we *were* going to be near there tomorrow, I'd wave to him and save everybody the trouble. After all, you've made the full procedure impossible by destroying the head." He closed his eyes again.

"What's this . . . *first part* of the magic?" Shandy asked, feeling the first faint webs of anxiety falling over him again.

"The part that can be done on land. The big part, which I would have had to do, has to take place at sea. Tomorrow noon he'll do the first part. He'd rather I did it. He'll be unhappy not to see me sail past."

"He'll do what? God damn it, what *is* this first part?"

Hurwood opened his eyes again and stared wonderingly at Shandy. "Why . . . the dumping of her mind. Elizabeth's mind—her soul. He'll drive it out of her body, with magic. I showed him how. Though," he added with a yawn, "it's a waste of time *now. Now* there's nobody to put in her place."

Sudden pain in his kneecaps let Shandy know he'd fallen to his knees. "Will she come back, then?" he asked, forcing himself not to shout. "Will Beth's soul go back into her body then?"

Hurwood laughed, the light, carefree laughter of a child. "Come *back?* No. When she's gone, she'll be . . . *gone.*"

Shandy restrained himself from hitting or strangling the old man, and he didn't speak until he was sure he could again match Hurwood's casual tone. "Well," he began, but there was a rough edge in his voice, so he started again. "Well, you know what? I'm going to see to it that this ship *does* get to Jamaica by tomorrow dawn. And then you'll wave at your . . . friend, this Hicks, won't you?" He was smiling, but his maimed hands were clenched into fists as tight as stressed knots.

"Very well." Hurwood yawned again. "I'd like to sleep now."

Shandy stood up. "Good idea. We'll be getting up damned early tomorrow."

Peering from the corners of his eyes—he was supposed to look as if he were deep in prayer—the altar boy had to admit that the church really was getting darker. And while he was afraid of the dry, dusty birdlike things that would be free to come out when all the light was gone, he was hoping that total dark would come soon—for after the wedding ceremony the minister would dispense communion, and the altar boy knew he had sinned too direly to take it, and so he wanted to be able to slip away unseen . . . even if that meant becoming one of the cobwebby birdlike creatures himself. He shivered, and wondered unhappily what had become of all the nice things. There had been friends, a wife, scholarship, the respect of colleagues, the respect of himself. . . . Perhaps they had only been a tormenting dream, and there had never really been anything but darkness and cold and the slow in-creeping of imbecility.

He took comfort in the thought.

The wedding couple finally came together in the shadows below the altar and linked arms, slowly, like lengths of seaweed tangled by listless sea-bottom currents. Then they began ascending the steps, and the altar boy realized that the absolute darkness had held off too long.

The bride was just an empty but animate dress; that wasn't so bad—it was always reassuring to find only an absence where it had seemed there might be a presence—but the groom was present and alive: it was impossible to be sure that it was human, for the skinned, bleeding flesh it consisted of might be manlike in form only because of the constriction of the clothes. If it had eyes they were closed, but the altar boy could tell the thing was alive because blood kept running out of it everywhere, and its mouth, albeit silently, was opening wide and clamping shut over and over again.

All at once the altar boy realized that the flayed thing there was himself, but the knowledge carried no horror, because now he knew too that he could move out of himself: all the way, if he was ready to let go of every thing, to non-being.

This, with profound relief, he did.

Chapter Twenty-Seven

When the first hints of the dawn's glow began to dim the brightness of Sirius and the three bright stars in Lepus, Shandy called for the telescope and scanned the faint contrast in dark grays that was the southeast horizon—and then, though after the night-long labor he was too exhausted and hoarse to shout, he bared his teeth in pleasure, for he could see the irregularity that couldn't be anything but Jamaica.

"We're there, Skank," he said quietly to the man beside him as he handed the telescope back. "Ten hours of night sailing and navigating our course by the stars, on one reach because we couldn't tack, and the pre-dawn shows us sitting squarely where we wanted to be! By God, I wish Davies could have seen it."

"Aye," Skank croaked dully.

"Have one of the lads go fetch Hurwood up here. It's nearly time for him to step onstage."

"Aye, cap'n." Skank lurched away into the darkness, leaving Shandy alone on the bow.

Shandy stared out at the dim horizon, trying to spot Jamaica again without the telescope's aid, but after going two nights without sleep, focusing his eyes was a physical effort, and all he could see were illusory transparencies that swirled in different directions every time he moved his eyes. He was desperately looking forward to rescuing Beth, but more because he could then relax and go to sleep somewhere than because of any glory or fulfillment he might derive from accomplishing it.

With the numb objectivity that follows total, all-consuming effort, he wondered if he would be captured in Jamaica . . . and what might ensue if he was. It could be argued that he hadn't violated his pardon, since the only ship he had taken was this one, and Hurwood was certainly not the legal captain. Is stealing stolen property less reprehensible than plain stealing? Well, even if he were captured, and the judgment went against him, he'd free Beth Hurwood first . . . and make her listen to the story her father had to tell, and show her that things were . . . different from the way she thought they were.

He rubbed his aching eyes and, again with no particular feeling, thought of all the things this summer and fall had cost him: his righteous convictions, his legal standing, his skepticism, his youth, his heart . . . and he grinned into the chilly darkness when he realized that, nearly as much as all the dead innocence and friends, he missed the old, battered, slipshod, jury-rigged loyal sloop called the *Jenny*. With no one to man the bilge pumps during yesterday's fighting and recuperation, she had filled and foundered, so that the grappling lines were stretched taut and were making the *Carmichael* list perceptibly to port. Sadly he had ordered her to be cut free, and there had been tears in his eyes as he had watched the mast and the patched sails slowly lean down to the water as the hulk receded away astern . . . and though his hearing was still bad, or perhaps because of it, it had seemed to him that for a few moments he faintly heard a babble of diminishing voices, one still insisting that he was not a dog. . . .

Footsteps scuffed on the deck behind him now, and Skank tapped him on the shoulder. "Uh, cap'n?"

Shandy turned around. "Yes? Where's Hurwood? I don't care if he's ill, he's got to—"

"Cap'n," said Skank, "he's dead."

Shandy felt tears of rage welling up in his eyes. "*Dead?* What? No he's not, the son of a bitch, he can't be, he—"

"Cap'n, he's cold and he ain't breathing—and he don't bleed if you prod him with a knife."

Shandy fell back against the rail and slid down until he was sitting on the deck. "God damn the man," he was whispering shrilly, "God damn him, am I supposed to swim ashore and climb the cliffs and *find* this Hicks person? How in hell am I to—" He lowered his head into his hands, and for several seconds the appalled Skank thought he was weeping; but when Shandy finally raised his head and spoke, his voice was harsh but level.

"Bring him here anyway." Shandy slowly got to his feet, facing Jamaica and flexing his stiff hands. The sky was lightening in the east—the sun would be up terribly soon.

"Uh . . . sure, cap'n." Skank started away, but paused. "Uh . . . *why?*"

"And a couple of stout, yard-long spar sections, and a roll of the strongest, thinnest twine," Shandy went on, still staring at the island, "and a—" He paused, and seemed to gag.

"And a what, captain?" Skank asked softly.

"A sharp sailmaker's needle."

What was the point of leaving Port-au-Prince, Sebastian Chandagnac asked himself fretfully as he tried to find a comfortable position among the rocks and dew-drenched grass, if in this new Joshua Hicks identity I'm still skulking around desolate shores at dawn waiting for signals from pirate ships? He shivered and drew his cloak closer about himself and had another swig from his brandy flask, and was warmed by both the alcohol and the envy of the driver who waited on the carriage several yards behind him.

He scowled around at the horizon, then stiffened, for he could see a light gray fleck out on the sea's dark face. He fumbled the telescope to his eye and squinted through it. Yes, it was a ship, tall and square-rigged. Unable to learn any more about it for now, he lowered the telescope.

That *must* be him, he thought. What other ship would be slanting in past Portland Point at dawn on Christmas? He glanced back at the carriage—and the driver was looking resentful and one of the horses stamped impatiently and blew out a plume of steam—but Chandagnac didn't walk back to them yet, for Ulysse had ordered him to wait until he actually saw him on the deck. "It may be my ship, you see," Segundo had said, with that smile of his which, though cheerful, seemed to expose too many teeth, "but I may not be on it—I may have been detained somewhere, or even killed, so that it wouldn't be until after Christmas that I'd be able to get back here. And the . . . eviction magic has to be done on

Christmas. So you plan on doing it yourself unless you see me wave."

Be aboard, Chandagnac prayed to the man now, be aboard and wave. *I* don't want to get involved in that stuff. It occurred to him that, at the moment, he was happier here on this cold cliff than he would have been at home, for yesterday evening the frightful black nurse had begun making preparations for the magic: burning bugs and snakes in the fireplace—impervious to their frequent stings—then carefully collecting the ash and dusting a couple of spoonfuls of it over the pile of leaves and roots that was to be the captive girl's dinner; tuning and testing at least a dozen little tin whistles; whispering into various dirty old bottles and then instantly corking them, as if to keep the whispered words in; and, worst of all, the thing that had made Chandagnac rush out to keep his cliff-top appointment much earlier than was necessary, she had razored open a vein in her bony wrist and let some of the contents run into a cup, but what had come out was not blood, or any kind of fluid, but a fine black powder. . . .

He shuddered now at the memory of it. Yes, he thought, be aboard, Ulysse, so *you* can be the one who gets to perform your damned sorcery, and I can get everything ready for my big dinner tonight. And you'd better have been right when you assured me that all of your magical trappings will be cleared out of the garden before three o'clock, when the servants will be arriving to set up.

He peered through the telescope again. The sky was brighter and the ship was nearer and he could see that it was indeed the *Ascending Orpheus* . . . looking a bit battered, but coming on strongly enough.

So far so good, he thought with cautious satisfaction. In half an hour I can be rolling east, back toward Spanish Town . . . have lunch and a few drinks at the club, stay away from the house until Ulysse has finished his awful business . . . and then get my wig curled and make sure all my clothes are immaculate. Maybe take a nap. It's essential that I put all this unpleasantness out of my mind so that I can make a good impression on this Edmund Morcilla fellow.

Even in his semi-solitude Chandagnac had heard of Morcilla— the big, bald, smooth-faced rich man who had sailed into Kingston Harbor late in November and was reputed to be investing heavily in all sorts of Caribbean concerns, from sugar to land to slaves. And

Morcilla had last week actually written to Joshua Hicks, proposing a partnership in a land deal. Chandagnac had written back in eager agreement, for he saw Morcilla as a possible means of freedom from Ulysse Segundo; and when Morcilla had replied with a long, friendly letter in which he mentioned his desire to marry some spirited, preferably auburn-haired young lady, Chandagnac was so anxious to ingratiate himself that in his next letter he actually mentioned the young lady "with a slight touch of brain-fever" who was staying at his house. In the same letter he invited Morcilla to his Christmas dinner party, and Chandagnac was so pleased when Morcilla wrote back to accept the invitation that he didn't even let himself worry about Morcilla's postscript, in which the wealthy man expressed a strong interest in meeting the young lady.

A lance of red sunlight in the corner of his left eye snapped him out of his reverie, and when he raised the telescope this time he kept it raised, for the ship was moving past his cliff-perch, showing him her port profile. It did seem to have caught its share of the storm—several spars were broken, and much of the rigging had simply been hacked short and tied off, and somehow one of the lower foremast sails had torn free and become tangled in the standing rigging, and now formed a sort of tent around the crosstree platform—but he could clearly see men on the deck. He scanned these eagerly, bracing the telescope barrel on a ballata tree branch to keep it steady, and in moments he was sure he had spotted Segundo.

The man was standing by the foremast with his back to the shore, but Chandagnac recognized the figure, the clothes, and the white hair—and then Segundo turned around to face the cliff, and Chandagnac laughed with relief, for there was no mistaking that craggy face and that intent stare. While Chandagnac watched, Segundo bent his left knee and lifted his foot up onto one of the rail-stanchion stumps, and, though he kept his right hand in his coat pocket, he waved broadly with his left, nodding reassuringly all the while.

Chandagnac waved the telescope over his head, even though it was unlikely that the gesture would be seen, and he didn't even frown when the cylinder slipped from his cold-numbed fingers and spun away to crash to bits on the rocks below. Whistling cheerfully, he turned away from the sea and strode toward the waiting carriage.

• • •

And Shandy, concealed on the cross-tree platform behind the roped-back forecourse sail, all at once sagged limp in the bindings that moored him to the mast, as the long held off rainbow glitter of unconsciousness finally filled his vision and overwhelmed him. His hands slipped off the blood-slick marionette cross he'd made, and it balanced for a moment on the yardarm, and then slipped off to one side and hung there, making the puppet on the deck below suddenly assume a startling posture: Hurwood's corpse, though still held more or less upright by the twine puppet strings, was now leaning backward at a forty-five degree angle, smiling confidently up into the sky and extending its left leg straight out and well above its head, like a dancer frozen in a particularly energetic moment.

For several seconds the pirates gaped at this prodigy, and then one of them crossed himself, drew his cutlass and chopped through the taut lengths of twine sewn through Hurwood's spine, scalp, limbs and left hand. The suddenly slack twine sprang upward, lashing Shandy across the cheek, and Hurwood's head fell loosely back and the body rattled and thumped onto the deck. With a buzz of twine running over the yardarm, the marionette cross came down and whacked the deck a moment later. The body lay sprawled loose as a broken doll, for rigor mortis had set in, and Shandy had had to do some work with a saw before he'd got busy with his needle and twine.

Roused by the sting of the whipping twine, Shandy blinked around and began trying to stand up and get his weight off the rope that was looped under his arms.

"Fling that overboard," said Skank on the deck below, pointing at Hurwood's abused corpse.

"No!" screamed Shandy, almost losing consciousness again from the effort of it.

The pirates stared up at him.

"Not . . . his body," Shandy grated, still trying to get his feet onto the yardarm, "nor one drop . . . *damn these ropes!* . . . of his blood . . . are to wind up in the sea." His feet under him at last, he straightened up, took several deep breaths, and then looked down. "You understand me? He's to be cremated when you put me ashore."

"Ashore," echoed one old pirate wearily. "You're goin' ashore."

"Of course I am," growled Shandy. He fumbled ineffectually at the knots in the ropes that moored him, hampered by dimming vision and bleeding hands. "Somebody climb up here and help me down. I've got—" He felt unconsciousness crowd him again, but he pushed it back. "I've got a dinner party to go to."

It took the *Carmichael* several hours to get to the southern end of Kingston Harbor, for the ship was unable to tack its bow across the wind, and so had to loop back on its path and jibe all the way around in order to switch the wind from one side of the bow to the other; and since the wind was blowing at them straight southwest from Kingston, they had to do a painstaking series of mile-wide figure-eights to move upwind, and the trip was sixty miles of constant work rather than the nearly straight twenty-five mile run it would have been for an undamaged vessel. Shandy had plenty of time to clip and shave off his gray-shot, salt-stiff beard, dress in some of Hurwood's clothes, and pull a pair of kid leather gloves on over his bandaged hands.

The sun was high when finally he was able to stare across the harbor's forest of masts to the red roofs of the city and, beyond and above them, the purple and green mountains. It occurred to him that he was finally seeing Kingston, and from the deck of the *Carmichael* . . . albeit six months late. He remembered how he and Beth Hurwood had prematurely celebrated the imminent end of the voyage by tossing maggoty biscuits to a hovering sea gull, and how he'd planned to dine ashore that night with Captain Chaworth.

He waved to the helmsman not to go in any closer, and then he turned to Skank. "Have 'em wrap up Hurwood and put him in the boat before you lower it. And then lower it *carefully*. Now I'll need somebody to row me ashore—then you take the *Carmichael* south around Wreck Reef and wait for us there . . . and if we're not back to the ship by midmorning tomorrow, take off—we'll probably have been captured, and with all these Navy craft about, this ship's peril will get worse with every passing hour. You'll be captain, Skank. Run far away, split up the loot, and go live like kings somewhere. I don't know whether this has been a violation of your pardons or not, so go somewhere they never heard of any of us. Get fat and lie in the sun and get drunk every day, because you'll be drinking for me too."

Skank probably wasn't capable of tears, but his narrow eyes were bright as he shook Shandy's hand. "Christ, Jack, you'll make it back. You've been in worse places."

Shandy grinned, lining his face deeply. "Yeah, you're right, quite a few of 'em. Well, have the lads get Hurwood—"

"Leave the body aboard for now," interrupted a rumbling voice from the belowdecks ladder. Both Shandy and Skank recognized the voice, and watched in horrified astonishment as Woefully Fat climbed ponderously up the ladder. The giant black man had draped himself toga-fashion in a section of sail that covered the jagged spar-end protruding from his chest, and he moved more slowly than usual, but otherwise he looked the same as he always had—strong, stern and impassive. "Burn Hurwood's body later on. Ah'll row you ashore now. Ah'm gonna die on Jamaican soil."

Shandy exchanged a lost look with Skank, but then shrugged and nodded. "I, uh, guess I won't need a rower after all. Well—"

"Sure you will, Jack," Skank said. "It seems like Davies' *bocor* is stayin' ashore, an' you can't row back with your hands all cut up."

"That'll be tomorrow. I'll manage." He turned nervously to the *bocor*. Remembering for once that the man was deaf, Shandy made an "after you" gesture toward the rail and the boat that swung from the davit cranes.

Chapter Twenty-Eight

The *Carmichael* jibed around after lowering the boat, and the wind filled her sails and she had disappeared around the southern point before Woefully Fat had taken fifty strokes at the oars. Shandy sat back on the stern thwart and, keeping his eyes off the *bocor*'s weirdly placid face, allowed himself to enjoy the sun and the view and the spicy smells on the breeze. Now that the incriminating ship had retreated, they were just two men in a rowboat—though a look inside Woefully Fat's toga would no doubt surprise even the most worldly harbor-master—and Shandy thought it likely that they would be able to land without arousing any particular interest.

Even when a Royal Navy sloop came angling toward them, her brightwork gleaming and her tall jib-sail intimidatingly white in the noon sun, he thought she might well be leaving the harbor on some errand that had nothing to do with him; it wasn't until the sloop cut in across the rowboat's bow and then loosed all sails and came rocking to a halt in front of it that Shandy began to worry. He caught Woefully Fat's eye and managed to convey to the *bocor* that there was an obstacle ahead.

Woefully Fat looked over his shoulder, nodded, and lifted the oars out of the water. A few seconds later the rowboat collided gently with the Navy vessel.

Flanked by half a dozen sailors with pistols, a young officer stepped to the sloop's rail and stared down at the two men in the rowboat. "Are you John Chandagnac, also known as Jack Shandy, and the witch doctor known as Grievously Fat?" he asked nervously.

"We goin' to Jamaica," interrupted the *bocor* in the middle of the officer's question.

"It's no use talking to him—," Shandy began.

"Well? Are you?" the officer demanded.

"No, dammit," yelled Shandy desperately, "I'm Thomas Hobbes and this is my man Leviathan. We were just—"

"Woe to thee, Babylon warrior," intoned Woefully Fat in his deepest voice, pointing at the officer and opening his alarming eyes wide. "Lion of Judah be troddin' down yo' fig tree and grapevine pickneys!"

"You're under arrest!" shrilled the officer, drawing a pistol of his own. To one of his men he added, "Get down there, make sure they're unarmed, and then bring them aboard as prisoners!"

The sailor stared at the officer. "Aye aye, sir. Why, exactly?"

"*Why?* Did you hear what he threatened to do to my kidneys?"

"That's *pickneys,* it's a slang word for children—," began Shandy, but he stopped when the officer pointed the pistol directly into his face; instead he raised his open hands and smiled broadly. "Good job, man," he whispered to the deaf *bocor*.

The Navy sailors lowered a rope ladder, and Shandy and Woefully Fat climbed up onto the deck of the Navy sloop while a couple of sailors secured a painter to the rowboat to tow it behind. And when the wrists of his captives had been bound in front of them the officer had the two prisoners brought to him in the neat but narrow belowdecks cabin. Woefully Fat had to bend almost double to fit into the chamber. Shandy was uncomfortably reminded of his brief visit aboard the Navy man-of-war that had captured the *Jenny*.

"Prisoners," the officer began, "you were seen to disembark from the pirate vessel the *Ascending Orpheus*. We have received intelligence from the New Providence colony to the effect that John Chandagnac and Grievously Fat left that island on the thirteenth of December, sailing for Jamaica with the intention of making a rendezvous with the pirate Ulysse Segundo. Will you deny that you are these two men?"

"Yes, we deny it," blustered Shandy. "I told you who we are. Where are you taking us?"

"To the Kingston Jail to await arraignment." As if to emphasize his words, the sloop surged forward as the sails were raised again, and a moment later there was a tug aft as the rowboat's painter came taut. "The charges against you are severe," added the officer reprovingly. "I shall be astonished if you do not both hang."

Woefully Fat leaned forward, his massive head seeming to fill the cabin. "Wheah you takin' us," he said intensely, "is the Maritime Law and Records Office."

For a moment Shandy smelled red-hot iron, and smoke rose from behind the giant *bocor.*

As if he hadn't spoken before or heard Woefully Fat's comment, the officer said, "We're taking you to the Maritime Law and Records Office." He added, a little defensively, "That's where the charges originate, after all."

Woefully Fat sat back, evidently satisfied. Shandy could smell the back of the *bocor's* chair burning where the gaff-saddle pressed against it, and he hoped that the dying sorceror had something good in mind. Shandy knew that the Law and Records Office was a bookkeeper's den, not a place to which criminals were ever physically brought.

Shandy and Woefully Fat were locked into the cabin when the officer left, but even through the deck above him and the bulkheads to either side Shandy could hear incredulous protests from the sailors.

The Maritime Law and Records Office proved to be the southernmost of half a dozen government buildings on the west side of the harbor, and it had a dock of its own, to which the Navy sloop made its way. Like most of the waterfront structures, the building was of whitewashed stone, roofed with overlapping red-brick tiles that looked to Shandy as if they'd been moulded over the bases of palm branches. As the officer and several armed sailors led him and Woefully Fat up the walk toward the building, Shandy could see a couple of clerks already peering curiously out through one of the tall, open windows at this incongruous procession. His hands were still bound in front of him, and his eyes were darting around for anything that might be used to cut himself free.

One of the sailors sprinted ahead and held the door open. The officer, who was beginning to look a little unsure of himself, stepped inside first, but it was the sight of Woefully Fat in his sailcloth toga that made the clerks drop their pens and ledger books and leap to their feet with dismayed cries. Taller than any of them and as broad as three, the *bocor* rolled his eyes disapprovingly around the room. Shandy guessed he was looking for a patch of Jamaican soil, as opposed to floorboards.

One of the clerks, prodded forward by his white-haired superior, approached the group. "Wh-what are you doing here?" he quavered. He stared in horror up at Woefully Fat. "What d-do you want?"

The Navy officer started to speak, but Woefully Fat's earth-quake-rumble voice easily overrode him. "Ah'm deaf, Ah cain't hear," the *bocor* announced.

The clerk paled and turned to his superior. "Oh my God, sir, he says he's going to defecate here!"

Chaos erupted on all sides as clerks and bookkeepers knocked over tables and inkstands in their frenzy to get to the doors—several simply leaped out of the windows—but Woefully Fat had seen, through a pair of French doors ahead, a small, enclosed yard with sidewalks, a flagpole, a fountain . . . and grass. He started purposefully toward the doors.

"Uh, stop!" called the Navy officer. Woefully Fat strode on, and the officer drew his pistol. Realizing that nobody was paying any particular attention to him, Shandy shuffled along parallel to the *bocor* but a few feet to the left.

Bang.

The pistol was fired and bloody spray and bits of cloth sprang away from a new hole in the back of Woefully Fat's toga, but the shot didn't even jar the *bocor*. He pushed the French doors open and stepped out onto the sidewalk. Shandy was right behind him.

The officer had dropped his spent pistol and now ran up and grabbed the giant black man, apparently intending to pull him back inside; but he only managed to pull the sailcloth toga free of the huge shoulders.

Several people, including the officer, screamed when they saw the stump of the gaff-spar jutting bloodily from the broad back, but Woefully Fat took another step forward, and one bare foot, and then the other, dented Jamaican soil.

Shandy was following him, and when the *bocor* suddenly toppled backward he instinctively raised his bound hands to break the man's fall.

The jagged iron gaff-saddle ripped the rope around his wrists as the limp body collapsed, and then Woefully Fat lay dead on the sidewalk, his feet still on the grass, a broad smile on his skyward-turned face . . . and Shandy strained at the damaged rope until it broke, and his hands were free.

He skipped out into the enclosed yard. The gunshot had brought people to every surrounding doorway, and quite a number of them were holding swords and pistols. Shandy realized that he was recaptured . . . and then he thought of something.

At a fast walk, hoping to avoid drawing attention, he made his way to the flagpole; then, yawning as if to imply that this was a daily routine, he began climbing the wooden pole, several times gripping the paired flag-hoisting lines with one hand for extra traction. He was halfway to the top before the Navy officer lurched out into the yard and saw him.

"Come down from there!" the man yelled.

"Come up and get me," Shandy called back. He had reached the top now, and was hunched over the brass sphere at the top of the pole, his legs crossed just under it and the British flag draped over his head like a hood.

"Fetch an axe!" yelled the officer, but Shandy had heaved himself backward, hauling on the top of the pole; it swayed back several yards, then stopped, came back up and went past the upright point and bent over the other way; Shandy hung on, and when it swung back in the original direction again he pulled on the pole-top sphere even harder . . . and at the farthest, most straining moment of the bend, the flexed pole snapped. The top six feet, with Shandy at the end, spun rapidly end over end and crashed down onto the tile roof as the rest of the pole whipped its splintered top back over the yard.

Half stunned by the sudden spin and impact, Shandy slid down the roof headforemost, toward the gutter, but he managed to spread his arms and legs and drag to an abrading halt; the flagpole-top and several broken loose tiles rolled past him into the abyss.

Whimpering with vertigo, he began doing a sort of spasmodic reverse backstroke on the slanting tiles, and by the time the bricks and flagpole section clattered and smashed on the sidewalk below, he had got his knees over the roof peak. He slithered around to one side until he could sit up, and then he got to his feet, ran bent-kneed across the cracking tiles to the roof-brushing branches of a tall olive tree, and, with an ease born of many hours scrambling around in the rigging of sailing craft, swung and slapped his way down to the ground. A vegetable wagon was rolling past through the alley he found himself in, and he hopped over its sideboard and lay flat among a bumpy, bristly load of coconuts as the wagon rattled on inland, away from the waterfront.

He clambered out of the wagon when it stopped outside a thatch-roofed market in a main street in Kingston. People stared, but he just gave them a benevolent smile and strode away toward the shops. Hurwood's clothes were torn now, and covered with red brick-dust and strands of coconut bristle, so as he walked he unobtrusively fumbled at the inner lining of his baldric, tore open the loose stitching he'd done that morning, and then worked out a couple of the gold *scudos* he'd sewn into the lining. He glanced at the coins in his gloved palm. That, he thought, should be plenty for a new set of clothes and a good sword.

He halted as a thought struck him, then smirked at himself and walked on, but after a few more steps he stopped again. Oh well, he told himself, why not—it can't hurt, and you can certainly afford it. Yes, you may as well buy a compass, too.

Chapter Twenty-Nine

Somehow the fact of its being Christmas night only emphasized the land's strangeness: the warm odors of punch and roasted turkey and plum pudding just made the dinner guests more aware of the wild spice smells from the inland jungles; the yellow lamplight and stately violin music spilling out from the open windows couldn't stray far from the house before being absorbed by the darkness and the creaking of the tall palm trees in the tropical night breeze; and the guests themselves seemed faintly ill at ease in their European finery. There was a quality of defensiveness in their laughter, and their repartee seemed to strain forlornly for sophistication.

The party was well attended, though. Word had got out that Edmund Morcilla was to be there, and many of Jamaica's moneyed citizens, curious about the wealthy newcomer, had chosen to accept the hospitality of Joshua Hicks, who on his own had little beyond his street address to recommend him.

And their host was clearly overjoyed by the success the evening had been so far. He bustled from one end of the wide ballroom to the other, kissing ladies' hands, making sure cups were filled, and tittering softly at witticisms; and, when he wasn't talking to anyone, glancing around anxiously and smoothing his clothes and well-groomed beard with manicured hands.

By eight o'clock the arriving horses and carriages were actually waiting in line in front of the house, and Sebastian Chandagnac found himself unable to greet each guest personally—though he made it a point to hurry up to the towering figure of Edmund Morcilla and shake his hand—and it happened that one man slipped in unnoticed and crossed unaccosted to the table where the crystal punchbowl stood.

His appearance drew no particular notice, for none of the invited guests could have known that his wig and sword and velvet coat had been purchased only that afternoon with pirates' gold; there was, perhaps, more of a sailor's roll in his walk than would be expected in one so elegantly dressed, and less formality than usual in the way his gloved hand occasionally brushed the hilt of his rapier, but this was after all the New World, and people far from home were often forced to acquire discreditable skills. The servant tending the punchbowl filled a cup and handed it to him without giving him a second glance.

Shandy took the cup of punch and sipped it while he let his gaze traverse the room. He wasn't sure how to proceed, and his only plan so far was to figure out which of these people was Joshua Hicks, get the man alone for a little while and induce him to say where Beth Hurwood was being kept, and then free her, hastily tell her a thing or two, and try to make good his escape from this island.

The hot punch, tart with lemon and cinnamon, reminded Shandy of Christmases in his youth, hurrying with his father through the snowy streets of some European city to the warmth of the inevitable rented room, where his father would prepare at least a token Christmas dinner and drink over the fire that raised sparkling reflections in the glass eyes of the dozens of hanging marionettes. None of these memories—his father, snowy winters, or marionettes—were pleasant subjects for his thoughts, and he forced himself to concentrate on his present surroundings.

Money had certainly been spent on this place—as a sort of informal import and export agent himself, Shandy knew how expensive and difficult it must have been to ship from Europe all these huge, gilt-framed paintings, these crystal chandeliers, this furniture. Nothing in the room was of local manufacture; and, to judge by the smells from the kitchen, even the food was to be as genuinely English as possible. It wasn't terribly enticing to Shandy, who'd grown fond of green turtle, manioc root and salmagundi salad.

One of Hicks's servants now entered the room and, raising his voice to be heard over the waves of conversation, announced, "If you will all please step this way—dinner will be served shortly."

The guests began bolting the last sips of punch and shuffling across the hardwood floor toward the doors that led into the dining room; Shandy kept smiling and let himself be drawn along, but he was worried—if he followed everyone in, it would quickly become apparent that there was no place set for him, and that he hadn't been invited. Where the hell was Hicks? What Shandy needed was a diversion, and he glanced around, hoping to see some especially fat person that he could surreptitiously trip.

Just when he had spotted a likely candidate—a portly old fellow, entirely encased in lace-edged red velvet, who could probably be propelled right into the punchbowl—a diversion took place without his help.

On the far side of the ballroom four men came in through the front door at once, crowding considerably to do it. The first one was neatly bearded and had his back to Shandy most of the time—he seemed to be the host, for he was waving his arms and protesting about something; next to him was a burly giant of a man, watching with evident amusement and puffing on a thin black cigar—he was elegantly dressed but wore no wig, a peculiar omission since his head was completely bald; and behind them, obviously insisting on entering, came two British Naval officers.

"It's for your own safety, and that of your guests," one of the officers said loudly, and the man who Shandy guessed was Hicks finally shrugged and waved the two Navy men inside. Shandy inconspicuously stepped back so as to be behind the fat fellow in red velvet—and, just in case, closer to the window.

The bald giant moved aside to let the two officers get past, and his grin behind the little cigar was so sly and knowing that Shandy stared at him curiously. Abruptly it seemed to Shandy that he'd seen this man before, been in awe of him . . . though the broad, unlined face was certainly not familiar.

He didn't get time to ponder it, though, for the nearest Navy man at once began speaking to the company. "My name is Lieutenant MacKinlay," he said loudly. "We won't prolong our interruption of your dinner longer than to warn you all that the pirate Jack Shandy was briefly apprehended in Kingston today; he escaped, though, and is at large in the island."

There was a stir of interest at this, and even in his sudden fright Shandy noticed that the bald giant raised his bushy eyebrows and took the cigar from his mouth in order to closely scrutinize the diners. The amusement was gone from his face, replaced by a look of watchful caution.

"The reason we feel you should be apprised of this," MacKinlay went on, "is that, after purchasing new clothes, he made several inquiries as to the location of this house. He is described as being well dressed, but wearing white kid leather gloves that show bloodstains at the seams."

The portly old man in front of Shandy hitched ponderously around and pointed at Shandy's gloved hands. He was spitting excitedly and trying to produce words.

Lieutenant MacKinlay hadn't yet noticed the old man's consternation—though people near Shandy were craning their necks curiously—and he continued his speech. "It seems clear to us that Shandy has heard about this dinner, and intends to come here for the purpose of committing some robbery or kidnap. A group of armed Navy men is even now being mustered to come here and apprehend him, and in the meantime my companion and I—"

Hicks had noticed the commotion at the back of the crowd, and he peered alertly in that direction—and then the spitting old man fell to his knees, and Shandy found himself staring straight across the room at Hicks, meeting his gaze.

Both Shandy and Hicks flinched from what seemed the sight of a ghost.

After the first moment of shock, Shandy knew it wasn't his father—the face was too pudgy, and the mouth too pursed—but the eyes, the nose, the cheekbones, the forehead, were all his father's, and just for a moment he marveled that chance could have produced such a resemblance in a stranger; but in the next moment he realized who it must be, and what must have been the real story of the "suicide" of Sebastian Chandagnac.

"My God!" exclaimed a woman near Shandy. "That's him there!"

Several men among the guests frowned and slapped the hilts of their dress swords, but somehow getting room to draw their blades involved moving quickly away from the pirate.

Suddenly and jarringly, the bald man laughed, a deep,

booming mirth like storm surf crashing on rocks, and Shandy recognized him.

Then the two Navy officers had drawn pistols and were shouting for the guests to move aside, and a number of men were reluctantly moving in on Shandy, waving the sort of swords one orders from a tailor, and Sebastian Chandagnac was loudly demanding that the officers shoot the pirate instantly.

Women screamed, men tripped over chairs, and Shandy leaped up onto the table, drawing his saber in midair, and he kicked the punchbowl onto the floor as he sprinted down the table toward the front door; MacKinlay's pistol banged deafeningly, but the ball splintered the wall paneling above Shandy's head, and then he had leaped off the end of the table. MacKinlay's companion was pointing a pistol of his own directly at Shandy's chest, and Shandy, helpless to do anything else, lunged at him, caught the long pistol barrel with his saber blade and got a fast corkscrewing bind on it that sent it flying out of the officer's hand before he could fire.

Men were slipping and cursing on the wet floor behind him, and a couple of swords were noisily dropped, and Shandy leaped to the side, whipped his blade around, and put his point against MacKinlay's chest. Everyone froze. The pistol finished clattering across the floor and clanked against the wall.

"I believe I'll surrender," Shandy said into the sudden silence, "but before I do, I want to tell you who Joshua Hicks is. He's—"

Sebastian Chandagnac had dived for the dropped pistol and now came up with it; sitting, he fired it at Shandy.

The ball exploded the head of Lieutenant MacKinlay—and as the body cartwheeled away and the screaming and crashing resumed, louder, Shandy's uncle scrambled up, drew his own dress sword and ran at him. Shandy parried the blade easily, though his white gloves were gleaming red along the seams, and he rushed in and, one-handed, grabbed his uncle by the throat.

"Beth Hurwood, the girl you're holding," he snarled. "Where is she?"

The bald man Morcilla had stepped forward as if to interfere, but at this he paused.

"Upstairs," wept Sebastian Chandagnac, his eyes closed, "locked room."

Women were sobbing and several men stood nearby with drawn swords, glancing at one another uncertainly. The second

Navy officer had drawn his sword but seemed reluctant to approach while Shandy was apparently holding a hostage.

Shandy's left thumb was on his uncle's larynx, and he knew he could crush it as easily as he could break an egg; but he was sick of deaths, and didn't think he'd derive any sense of fulfillment from watching this scared little man flop around on the floor choking to death on his own throat bones. He switched his grip to the man's collar.

"Who . . . are you?" Sebastian Chandagnac croaked, his eyes wide with horror.

Suddenly Shandy realized that, clean-shaven and with all the new lines of age and weariness in his face, he must look very much like his father had when Sebastian would have seen him last . . . and of course this man didn't know that his nephew John Chandagnac had come to the Caribbean.

Having decided not to kill him, Shandy found that he could not refrain from stirring up the man's guilt. "Look me in the eye," he whispered chokingly.

The old man did, though with much trembling and moaning.

"I'm your *brother,* Sebastian," Shandy said through clenched teeth. "I'm François."

The old man's face was nearly purple. "I heard you had . . . *died. Really* died, I mean."

Shandy grinned ferociously. "I did—but haven't you ever heard of *vodun?*—I've only come back from Hell tonight to fetch *you,* dear brother."

Apparently Sebastian *had* heard of *vodun,* and found Shandy's claim all too plausible; his eyes rolled back in his head and, with as sharp an exhalation as if he'd been punched in the belly, he went limp.

Surprised but not really dismayed, Shandy let the body tumble to the floor.

Then, almost side by side, Shandy and the bald man sprang for the stairs; presumably Edmund Morcilla was pursuing the pirate, but it was hard to be sure they weren't both racing toward some common goal. A few men with swords leaped quickly into their path, and then even more quickly out of it, and a moment later Shandy was bounding up the stairs three at a time, panting and praying that he wouldn't pass out quite yet.

At the top of the stairs was a corridor, and he paused there, his chest heaving, and turned to face the man who called himself Morcilla, who had stopped two steps short of the landing. His eyes were level with Shandy's.

"What . . . do *you* want?" Shandy gasped.

The giant's smile looked cherubic on his smooth face. "The young woman."

There was more shouting and crashing below, and Shandy shook his head impatiently. "No. Forget it. Go back downstairs."

"I've earned her—I've been monitoring this house all day, ready to step in and interfere at the first indication of soul-eviction magic—"

"Which didn't take place because I undid Hurwood's plan," said Shandy. "Get out of here."

The bald man raised his sword. "I'd rather not kill you, Jack, but I promise I will if I have to in order to get her."

Shandy let his shoulders slump defeatedly and let his face relax into lines of exhaustion and despair—and then he flung himself forward, slamming the giant's sword against the wall with his left forearm while his right hand punched his saber into the man's chest. Only the fact that the bald man stood his ground stopped Shandy from pitching head first down the stairs. Shandy caught his balance, raised his right foot and planted it on the man's broad breast next to where the blade transfixed it, and then kicked, bringing himself back upright on the landing and propelling the bald man in a backward tumble down the stairs. Exclamations of horror and surprise erupted above the general clamor below.

Shandy turned and looked down the corridor. One of the doorknobs was wooden, and he reeled to it. It was locked, so he wearily braced himself against the wall it faced, lifted his foot, and with a repetition of the move that had freed his blade from Morcilla's chest, drove his foot at the door. The wooden lock splintered and the door flew inward and Shandy dropped his saber as he fell forward into the room.

He looked up from his hands and knees. There was a lamp lit in the room, but the scene it showed him was far from reassuring: nasty-smelling leaves were all over the floor, someone had hung several severed dog heads on the walls, an obviously long-dead black woman was tumbled carelessly in the corner, and Beth Hurwood was crouched by the window apparently trying to eat the woodwork.

But Beth looked around in alarm, and her eyes were clear and alert. *"John!"* she said hoarsely when she saw who it was. "My God, I'd almost given up praying for you! Bring that sword over here and chop this wooden bolt in half—my teeth aren't making any progress at all."

He got up and hurried over to her, slipping only once on the leaves, and he squinted blearily at the bolt. He raised his sword carefully. "I'm surprised you recognize me," he remarked inanely.

"Of course I do, though you do look thrashed. When did you sleep last?"

". . . I don't remember." He brought the sword down. It cut the bolt, barely. Beth fumbled the pieces out of the brackets and pushed the window open, and the cool night air sluiced away the room's stale smells and brought in the cries of tropical birds out in the jungle.

"There's a roof out here," she said. "At the north end of the house the hill catches up with it enough for us to jump safely. Now listen, John, I—"

"Us?" Shandy interrupted. "No, you're safe now. My uncle—Joshua Hicks—is dead. You're—"

"Don't be silly, of course I'm coming with you. But listen, please! That creature in the corner pitched over dead—dead again, I should say—last night, and so I haven't had to eat any more of those damned plants since then, but I'm terribly weak and I have spells of . . . I don't know, disorientation. I sort of fall asleep with my eyes open. I don't know how long it lasts, but it's tapering off—so if I do it, if I go blank-eyed on you, don't worry, just keep me moving. I'll come out of it."

"Uh . . . very well." Shandy stepped through the window, out onto the roof. "You're sure you want to come with me?"

"Yes." She followed him out, swayed and grabbed his shoulder, then took a deep breath and nodded. "Yes. Let's go."

"Right."

Through the open window behind them he could hear people hesitantly but noisily advancing up the stairs, so he took her elbow and led her as quickly as he dared toward the north end of the roof.

Epilogue

It faded on the crowing of the cock.
Some say that ever 'gainst that season comes
Wherein our Saviour's birth is celebrated,
The bird of dawning singeth all night long;
And then, they say, no spirit can walk abroad;
The nights are wholesome; then no planets strike,
No fairy takes, nor witch hath power to charm,
So hallow'd and so gracious is the time.

—*William Shakespeare*

They walked for hours, avoiding the wider, better-maintained roads because of the bands of mounted, torch-carrying soldiers who were riding back and forth, it seemed, through all of Spanish Town; Shandy led Beth over low stone walls and along narrow footpaths and between rows of sugarcane. Twice dogs barked at them, but both times Shandy was able to silence the alarm by crimping the breeze with a gesture and whistling a certain tune. He wasn't able to deal as easily with the mosquitoes, though, and had to make do with smearing mud on his face and Beth's. He could judge directions and even make a fair guess at the hour by studying the sky whenever their way wasn't roofed with vegetation . . . but he didn't throw away the compass he had bought that afternoon, even though it was an awkward, bulky weight in his coat pocket.

Several times Beth did seem to be sleepwalking, and would

walk straight into trees if he didn't lead her carefully by the hand, and for a while she just slept, and he had to carry her, enviously, in his arms; but she was awake and lucid during most of the walk, and she and Shandy occupied the long miles by conversing in whispers. She told him about her years in the Scottish convent, and he described traveling with his father and the marionettes. She asked him about Ann Bonny in a tone so carefully casual that he could feel his heart thudding in his chest. Drunk with exhaustion and happiness, he let himself answer the question with a long, disjointed monologue that he didn't even bother to listen to—vaguely he knew that it dealt with love and loss and maturity and death and birth and the rest of their lives. Whatever he had said, she didn't seem displeased by it; and even though she wasn't sleepwalking he took her hand.

They kept moving south, and when he judged that it was about three in the morning they came to the sandy end of one of the jungle footpaths they'd been following, stepped out from under an awning of palm fronds, and saw that they were on the beach. Between them and the blackness that was the sea were the faintly starlit blobs of buildings; Shandy thought he recognized the Maritime Law and Records Office, but he couldn't be sure. They walked forward to the beach, and then continued moving south, staying in the shadows of buildings as much as possible and getting across streets and open squares as quickly and quietly as they could. A few lamps glowed in buildings they passed, and a couple of times they could hear drunken voices not too far distant, but nobody hailed them.

They passed several docks and clusters of beached boats . . . but each time Shandy crept closer to look for a stealable boat, there was a stray lantern-gleam or whispering voice nearby; and twice on the night breeze Shandy heard the unmistakable metallic click-and-slide of a sword being loosened in its scabbard, and once he heard a dockside voice whisper a sentence in which the name "Shandy" figured emphatically. Having failed to keep him from entering, the British authorities obviously did not mean to let him get out.

More cautiously than ever, Shandy and Beth walked on southward, passing the last of the stone buildings, then tiptoeing through an area of bamboo shacks and sailcloth tents, and finally, as the stars were fading, they reached a stretch of broad marshes along which the occasional turtle pen or fisherman's shack was the high point of the landscape. The mosquitoes were much worse here, making it necessary for the two fugitives to tie bands of cloth across the lower halves of their faces to avoid inhaling the insects, but Shandy appreciated the loneliness of this stretch of beach, and, no longer having to be perfectly silent, he began taking longer strides.

Just at dawn they found a decrepit pier with a sailboat moored at the end of it, and Shandy stared for several minutes at the half-dozen ragged men huddling around a small brazier—he could see pinpoints of red light in it when the erratic breeze fanned the coals—and then he relaxed and sat back down behind the bush that concealed him and Beth from the shore below.

"Just fishermen," he whispered, mostly to himself, for Beth had drifted off into another of her somnambulistic trances. He had draped his compass-weighted velvet coat around her shoulders hours ago, and he shivered in the dawn sea breeze when he stood up and then laboriously hauled her up to stand swaying and blank-eyed beside him. "Come on," he said, leading her forward and touching his baldric to make sure the weight of all the gold *scudos* was still there. "We're going to buy us a boat."

He knew the two of them would be a strange spectacle with which to confront these fishermen on a chilly winter dawn—an evidently sleep-walking woman in a nightdress and velvet coat escorted from the jungle by a mud-splashed, blood-stained man in formal dress, both their faces smeared with mud—but he was confident that half a dozen of the gold coins would allay all misgivings.

By the time they had slid down the slope and begun shambling through the sand toward the pier, most of the hunched figures had turned to stare at them, though one man, wearing a weathered straw hat and wrapped in a blanket, continued to sit on the end of the pier and face the newly sun-tipped gray waves.

Shandy smiled and held six *scudos* forward in the palm of his gloved hand as he led Beth Hurwood out onto the echoing boards of the pier. . . .

Then his smile faltered and disappeared, for he had noticed the flat, filmed eyes in the gray faces, and the bound-up jaws, and the sewn-shut shirts and the bare feet.

"Oh, damn it," he whispered hopelessly, realizing that neither of them had the strength to run—it was all he could do to continue standing. With no surprise he watched the figure at the end of the pier get to its feet, shed the blanket and toss away the hat so that the dawn sun gleamed on the bald scalp. The man took the cigar out of his mouth and smiled at Shandy.

"Thank you, Jack," he rumbled. "Come, my dear." He beckoned to Beth and she stumbled forward as if pushed from behind. The velvet coat slipped off her shoulders and fell onto the weathered planks of the pier.

Almost at the same moment, Shandy's knees unlocked and he found himself abruptly sitting on the planks. "You're dead," he muttered. "I killed you . . . on the stairs."

Beth took two more quick, balance-catching steps.

The bald man shook his head sadly, as if Shandy was proving to be a disappointing pupil. He puffed on the cigar and waved its glowing head at Shandy. "Come on, Jack, don't you remember the slow matches I used to braid into my hair and beard? Low-smoldering fire, that's the *drogue* that holds Baron Samedi's protective attention. A lit cigar works just as well. Your blade stuck me, sure enough, but the Baron, the good old Lord of the Cemeteries, repaired the damage before I had time to expire."

Beth was swaying halfway between them now, and the sun made her hair gleam like fresh-sheared copper. Shandy scrabbled at the wood and the tail of the coat, trying to find the strength to stand up again.

"But I don't hold grudges," the giant went on, "any more than Davies did, when you cut him. I'm grateful to you for escorting to me my bride—the only woman in the world who has shed blood in Erebus—and I'd like you to be my quartermaster."

Tears dripped from Shandy's squinting eyes onto the weathered planks. "I'll see you in Hell first, Blackbeard."

The giant laughed, though his eyes were now fixed on the slim, approaching figure of Beth Hurwood. "Blackbeard's dead, Jack," he said without looking away from the woman. "You must have heard. It's been *absolutely* verified. I need a new nickname now. Baldy, maybe." He laughed again, and his motionless dead mariners did too, whickering like sick horses through their nostrils.

Shandy had been unthinkingly pulling the velvet coat toward himself, and now he felt a hard lump in it. He slid his hand into the pocket, and by touch recognized the brass-rimmed, glass-topped disk—it was the compass he'd bought. His heart began pounding, and with what he hoped was a convincingly despairing moan, he fell face down onto the pier, over the coat.

The giant reached out a hand toward Beth.

Shandy pulled the compass out of the pocket and then fumbled at it helplessly for a moment—he had nothing to break the glass with!

Blackbeard touched Beth Hurwood, and the air seemed to twang, as if the roof of the sky had been solidly struck.

Shandy opened his mouth and wedged the compass between his jaws, and then he ground them together, tasting abraded brass and feeling at least one molar implode, until he was dizzy and sick and his teeth and jaw muscles were in agony; he lifted his head and saw Blackbeard's hand on Beth's shoulder, and the sight lent him a little more strength. The glass broke under his front teeth, and, spitting glass and blood, he took the device out of his mouth, pried the compass needle loose, then drew his saber and shoved the needle in under the leather wrapping until he felt it grind against the steel of the tang. After that he placed his gloved right hand gently on the grip so that the protruding end of the needle pressed into his palm . . . and he squeezed the grip tightly, driving the needle deep into his hand. With a sudden flash of intuition he raised the sword over his head and yelled, *"Phil!"*

And without having to look around he knew he was no longer alone. With aid he got to his feet, raised his sword with his dripping, pierced hand and shufflingly advanced toward Blackbeard.

But, though the burly figure was starkly silhouetted against the brightening sea and sky, Blackbeard—perhaps against his will—wasn't alone anymore either. As if some kind of cosmic balance had to be maintained, Shandy's cry seemed to have summoned seconds for *both* of them. Shandy wasn't sure how he knew it; a sound? A smell? Yes, that was it—a smell—a faint, disagreeable mix of cologne, chocolate syrup and unwashed linen was disfiguring the clean sea air.

The unmistakable smell of Leo Friend.

Blackbeard's hand slithered up to Beth's shoulder and curled around it. His lips were wet and his eyes couldn't have been opened any wider and his breath was whooshing in and out through his open mouth. The cigar clung precariously to his lower lip. Shandy realized, even as he started forward, that the disembodied Leo

Friend was somehow inhabiting the same space as Blackbeard, and, at least at the moment, was in control.

Shandy grabbed Beth's other shoulder and spun her aside, and then with the back of his hand he slapped the cigar out of the big man's slack mouth, and when it hissed as it hit the water below the pier he drove his sword with all his remaining strength into the giant's belly.

The big man's eyes stayed wide open, but now they were staring straight into Shandy's and it was only Blackbeard looking out of them. The mouth opened in a bloody but confident smile.

Blackbeard took a step forward. Nearly fainting with the pain, Shandy leaned on the saber and tried to stand his ground, but though the blade was forced another couple of inches into Blackbeard's body, the needle was grating in his wrist-bones and he had to step back. The scuffing of his boots sounded loud on the planks of the pier.

The giant, still grinning bloodily, took another step, and again Shandy braced himself against the torment in his hand, and this time he felt the blade punch out through the man's back—but Blackbeard had reached the brazier now and reached down, picked up one of the glowing, ash-dusted coals as daintily as if it were a candy on a proffered tray, and squeezed it in his huge left fist.

All over the harbor, for miles up and down the shore, sea birds flapped up into the air, clamoring in alarm.

Smoke spurted from between Blackbeard's fingers and blew away, and Shandy could hear the flesh sizzling. "Low-smoldering fire," the giant grated. Blackbeard stepped lithely back, so that as Shandy kept his grip on the saber hilt the blade slid out of him, and with his right hand he drew his own rapier. For a moment he paused, staring at the quick drops of blood falling from Shandy's hand. "Ah, Jack," Blackbeard said softly. "Someone taught you the blood and iron trick? You've clenched your fist over a compass needle? That won't work against Baron Samedi—he's more than a *loa* and he's not bound by their rules. He was showing the Carib Indians why night is to be feared centuries before Jean Petro was born. Drop the sword."

Shandy was sure he had lost, but he could feel Philip Davies at his back, and when he spoke he half thought Davies was prompting him. "My men and I," said Shandy hoarsely but distinctly, "are sailing to New Providence, to surrender to Woodes Rogers." He bared his teeth in a smile. "I'm giving you the choice. Join us, wholly adopt our goals as your own, or be killed right now where you stand."

Blackbeard looked startled, then laughed—

—And suddenly Shandy lurched back on the carpentry shop bench, staring at the marionette he held in his right hand. It was one of the expensive yard-high Sicilian marionettes, and he had to hold it steady until the glue that held its head on had dried, but a long splinter was sticking out from the back of the mannikin and stabbing him painfully in the palm. The thing was heavy, too. His arm was trembling with the weight and agony of the thing. But if he let it go it would be ruined.

Its brightly painted eyes were on him, and then its mouth opened. "Drop me," it said. "Open your hand and drop me."

The little wooden man was speaking with Shandy's own voice! Didn't that mean that it must be all right to do as it said? Shandy wanted to, but he remembered how proud his father had been when they'd got this one. He couldn't just drop it, no matter how much it hurt to hold it up.

"Drop me," the marionette repeated.

Well, why not, he thought as the sting of the splinter became more intense. What if it *is* my life I'm holding? It hurts, and none of these things lasts forever anyway.

Then he remembered something an ancient black man had said to him once in a boat on the Seine: "You got that tactic, that mud-ball trick, from Philip Davies—and you have wasted it. He gave you something else as well; it would not please me to see you waste that too."

The black man was gone, but a soft, reassuring hand gripped his shoulder, and he decided he could hold up the torturing mannikin for a while longer.

He opened his eyes, and found himself staring into Beth Hurwood's face.

Beth had been understandably slow to realize that she had drifted out of her delirium and was again wide awake—on a pier at dawn, dressed in her nightgown and surrounded by standing dead men. John Chandagnac was in front of her, holding a sword in a hand from which blood dripped energetically, facing a big bald man with a smoking fist and a terrible cut in his belly.

It had been the sharp chill in the air, and the clean smell of the sea, that finally convinced her that this strange scene was not another dream. There was tension and dire challenge in the air, and she hastily called on her memory for some of the recent speech here: *Ah, Jack. Someone taught you the blood and iron trick? You've clenched your fist over a compass needle? That won't work against Baron Samedi. . . . Drop the sword.*

Her eyes had darted to Shandy's sword hand, and she'd winced to see the blood pooling in the curve of the saber's knuckle-guard and running down his forearm . . . but at the same time she'd grasped the fact that the iron needle shredding his palm was his only hope . . . and that this bald man was trying to make him drop it.

Shandy's eyes were shut and the sword was wobbling in his hand—obviously he was ready to let go of it—but Beth was already moving forward. She took his shoulder firmly with one hand, and with the other she steadied the sword—by gripping the razor-edged blade tightly. Her own hot blood ran down the cold steel, followed the tang through the bell guard, and mingled with Shandy's. His eyes opened and met hers.

When the two bloods mixed the bald man was pushed back, but she knew he was only hampered, not beaten.

And then she heard a voice in her head, and at first she didn't want to listen because of its cynically humorous tone . . . it was the voice of that pirate, that Philip Davies! . . . but he was explaining something she needed to know, something about the areas of magic that were accessible only to women, and could be used by men only under certain specific conditions. . . .

"Do you, John, take me, Elizabeth, to be your lawful wedded wife, to have and to hold from this day forward . . . uh, forsaking all others . . . for richer, for poorer, in sickness and in health, I think that's all of it, till death do us part?" Her nightgown was flapping around her ankles in the chilly sea breeze and she was shivering like a wet cat. Her slashed hand trembled as it gripped the saber blade.

Blackbeard was pushed back another step. He had drawn his rapier and he swung it around him in great whistling arcs as if to clear the air of resistance. "No," he choked, "you are for me! You can't—"

"I do," said Shandy. "And do you, Elizabeth, take me, J-John, to be your lawful wedded husband, to have and to hold from this day forward,"—he grinned—"forsaking all others, for richer, for poorer, in sickness and in health, till death do us part?"

Blackbeard howled with rage.

"I do," said Beth.

She now let go of the blade and hugged her slashed hand to herself, but Shandy felt himself waking up, felt alertness pouring into him and expanding his field of vision and making his saber feel lighter, springier. The surrounding dead men moved in, and then were pushed back by some force that withered them.

Shandy couldn't tell if it was his father or Davies who prompted him, but he found himself rushing at Blackbeard, and though his legs were pounding and his arm was keeping the blade extended in front of him, he could almost feel hands far above him deftly rocking the stick and crosspiece and making the willing marionette which was himself spring toward the bald man in a *coupé-and-fleche*.

Startled, Blackbeard crouched behind his own extended sword.

Taking the final stride, Shandy almost thought he could feel the upward yank of the string as he quickly flipped his point over the other man's sword and extended it again in Blackbeard's inside line; the big man parried across, but Shandy's point wasn't there anymore—it had ducked under the parry back to the low outside line, and Shandy used the momentum of his run to punch the blade into, and right through, Blackbeard's side.

Heat exploded in Shandy's hand and he almost pitched right off the end of the pier; but Blackbeard was still standing, and he forced himself not to flinch back or let go of the blood-slick saber hilt, for he could feel strength pulsing through the connection he was a link of—the magnetic iron in his hand, the mingled blood of himself and Beth, and the cold iron of the sword—and then just for a moment his point of view expanded outward: he could look across the pier at himself through Beth's eyes, and, horrifyingly, *feel* Blackbeard's entrails with the blade of the saber. . . .

. . . And then things began dying around him. With a sense that wasn't quite hearing he caught the cries of evicted beings fleeing from the sunlight into the sea and into the jungle . . . spurious personalities, constructed by sorcery out of inert elements, sprang back into oblivion like yanked-on slipknots. . . . Shandy felt, but didn't respond to, wheedlingly seductive things pleading for shelter within his mind . . . and one unseen but towering being, as black and cold as the death of all light, forced to relinquish its broken vehicle, made an icy promise to Shandy before stalking away toward the night that was receding to the west. . . .

And when Blackbeard toppled forward onto the boards of the pier, pulling the sword finally out of Shandy's numb hand, Shandy stared down at the corpse in wonder, for it was riddled with sword cuts and the exploded-looking wounds pistol balls make, and the left shoulder had been cleft nearly all the way through, as if by a solid blow from a pike blade.

Woefully Fat's summons seemed to have worked—Shandy had indeed proven to be the death that came out of the Old World for Blackbeard.

After a while he looked up. The dead men were gone. Beth stood with her arms at her sides, and blood was dripping metronomically from her left hand. The sun was up, and it occurred to Shandy that he'd have to hurry if he was going to get Beth and himself bandaged, set up and ignite a pyre for Blackbeard, and then somehow with his ruined hands work this sailboat out to where the *Carmichael* waited, before Skank catted the anchor and sailed away.

And even then his problems wouldn't be over. Beth would probably stop having these blank-out spells in time, but would his devastated crew mutiny when he ordered them to sail back to New Providence? And could Woodes Rogers be convinced that none of the past two weeks' actions had constituted a violation of the King's Pardon?

He noticed that the compass needle still stuck out from his blood-sopping right glove. Thoughtfully, without even wincing, he worked the needle back and forth in his numbed flesh and finally pulled it out and stared at it. He smiled, tossed it off the end of the pier into the dawn-sparkling sea . . . and, squinting into the sun, he laughed softly and with complete contentment, for he was married to Beth Hurwood. Obviously his luck was strong, and he was confident that he could bail and jury-rig their way through these difficulties. He'd weathered far, far worse.

Still smiling, he began tearing up his lace-cuffed silk shirt for bandages.